BREATHE

BREATHE

A Novel of Colorado

LISA T. BERGREN

BOOK 1 of THE HOMEWARD TRILOGY

David C Cook®

transforming lives together

BREATHE
Published by David C. Cook
4050 Lee Vance View
Colorado Springs, CO 80918 U.S.A.

David C. Cook Distribution Canada
55 Woodslee Avenue, Paris, Ontario, Canada N3L 3E5

David C. Cook U.K., Kingsway Communications
Eastbourne, East Sussex BN23 6NT, England

The Web site addresses recommended throughout this book are offered as a
resource to you. These Web sites are not intended in any way to be or imply an
endorsement on the part of David C. Cook, nor do we vouch for their content.

This story is a work of fiction. All characters and events are the product of the
author's imagination, although some are based on real-life events and people.

All Scripture quotations are taken from the *Holy Bible, New International
Version*®. *NIV*®. Copyright © 1973, 1978, 1984 by International Bible
Society. Used by permission of Zondervan. All rights reserved.

LCCN 2009924469
ISBN 978-1-4347-6708-0
eISBN 978-1-4347-0029-2

The Team: Don Pape, Traci Depree, Amy Kiechlin,
Jaci Schneider, Sarah Schultz, and Evelin Roncketti
Cover Design: DogEared Design, Kirk DouPonce
Cover Photos: iStockphoto

Printed in the United States of America
First Edition 2009

1 2 3 4 5 6 7 8 9 10

032709

For my friends in Colorado Springs
with love

*"The L*ORD *God formed the man from the dust of the ground
and breathed into his nostrils the breath of life, and the man
became a living being."*

—Genesis 2:7

Chapter ❀ 1

March 1883

Odessa tried to shove back the wave of fear as the slow suffocation began. It was too much, this long ride west. Three days they had been on cursed trains chugging across endless tracks—three days! Hours of dust and dark, choking smoke from the train, the sweet-sour body odor from fellow passengers. She could even smell herself, and the combined force seemed to pour sand in through her nose and down into her lungs, filling them, filling them like two sacks of concrete.

Her father had meant for her to chase the cure; instead, she was merely hastening her own demise.

"Odessa? Dess!" Dominic said, leaning forward in his seat. "Moira, quick. Dampen this handkerchief."

Odessa closed her eyes and concentrated on each breath, her brother's voice, her sister's movement. She willed herself not to panic, not to give in to the black demon that loomed over her. This was worse than before. The creature had moved in and around her, tormenting her as he sat upon her chest.

"Dess, here. You must take your laudanum. Just this once. You've made it this far; we'll be there within hours."

Odessa could feel the cold stares of the people in the seats next to them as she sipped from the blue bottle. She knew she was not the only consumptive patient on this train, but the healthy passengers seemed to consider all of the consumptives a nuisance. She had not the strength to care at this point.

She had to keep herself from coughing.

To begin coughing was to never stop.

But her throat, the mucous, the tickle, the terrible desire to try and take a deep breath, to give it just one attempt, one huge cough to clear the way, to free her from the storm cloud that covered her now, roiling like a summer thunderhead. *Oh God,* she cried silently. *I can't breathe! I can't breathe! Don't let me die!*

Visions of her little brothers filled her mind. Gasping piteously. Blue lips, blue fingernails, eyes rolling back in their heads. Michael, thirteen; Clifford, eleven; Earl, eight; tiny Fred, only three …

"Dess," Dominic said urgently. "*Dess!*"

She could feel herself sliding sideways, her head spinning. She knew it improper, such public loss of control, but she was helpless, giving in to the dark demon that was casting her about, twirling her about like a chicken on a spit.

Dominic picked her up in his arms and laid her gently on the floor between the seats. From far away, she could tell he was placing his coat beneath her head. She could feel the rough woolen fibers at her neck. But how was that possible? Spinning at this rate—

"Stay with us, Odessa St. Clair," he called to her firmly. "We are almost there! Fight it! Fight back! Stay with us!"

It was as if he called to her from the mouth of a long, dark cave. Could he not see the monster? The demon cloud that was spiriting her away? How was she to fight such a thing? Why did they call it the White Death when it was dark, so dark?

The laudanum, the blessed drug, moved through her and began its soothing work. She did not wish to be the latest St. Clair invalid, wasting away of consumption, wasting away the family money, the family's time, the family's attentions. If she was not strong enough to chase the cure, she didn't deserve it at all. She had to find it within her, the hope, the desire, hovering somewhere deep within. Was it even there any longer?

Moira returned to her side and placed a delicate white handkerchief over her nose and mouth, cool and light and smelling faintly of soap—clean, clear soap. It reminded Odessa of her mother, of years ago when she would come to Odessa's sickroom to care for her, to nurse her back to health. She wanted to thank her sister, knowing this collapse was embarrassing her, embarrassing them all, but she could not find the breath to utter one word.

"Nic!" Moira said in alarm. Was she outside, floating away from Odessa? Or was Odessa floating away from them? Out of this train, out of her cave, breaking free?

"Is there a doctor on the train?" Dominic yelled. "*Is there a doctor? Can anyone assist us?*"

"You listen to me," Dominic said lowly and fiercely in her ear, suddenly right beside her. "You are not going to die on this train. You are going to reach the sanatorium and regain your health. You have a life ahead of you, Odessa St. Clair. A life. Not as an invalid. But as a vital, healthy woman. You will know freedom. You will beat this curse on our family. We will be friends into our old age. Do you hear me? *Do you hear me, Odessa?*"

"Is there a doctor aboard this train?" Dominic yelled as he watched Odessa slip into unconsciousness. He looked down the aisle of the rocking, swaying train car, meeting the doleful glances of thirty other passengers. No one moved to help. Moira, his younger sister, wept behind her hand. Odessa grew more lax in his arms. Never had he felt so helpless. What had Father been thinking? He could barely keep himself out of trouble; he was supposed to watch over his sisters, too?

He rose, Odessa in his arms. "Is there anyone who can help us?" he cried.

Halfway down the car, a man rose, hat in hand, and a woman beside him. They hesitantly made their way toward the St. Clairs. Nic studied their faces, then saw the man's collar. A preacher. Nic looked over his shoulder, hoping another was rising, a physician, a nurse, anyone. But no one moved.

"Not the doc you're seeking, man," said the tentative preacher. "But it looks like we're the only ones. Why don't you put your wife—"

"Sister."

"Put your sister down, and we'll pray over her. Heading to the sanatorium, I take it? Best there is in these parts."

"And not far," put in his wife. "We'll be there soon."

Nic studied them a moment longer, then glanced down at Odessa in his arms and Moira on the floor in a heap. "Quit your weeping, Moira," Nic hissed. "And get back on the seat. She's not dead yet." Her tears chafed at him, made him feel more helpless.

Moira only cried harder, but she rose and went back to the bench seat by the window as instructed. Nic gently set Odessa down beside her, head in Moira's lap, then moved aside to let the preacher and his wife gain entrance to the bench seat facing them.

Moira kept crying, her slender shoulders shaking, one hand on her unconscious sister's forehead, the other on the handkerchief dabbing at the corner of her eyes. Her face depicted the same horror Nic felt inside.

He pinched his temples between his third finger and thumb, trying to think his way out of this. *"Use your brain as well as your brawn,"* Father had said to him as they said good-bye in Philadelphia. *"I'm counting on you as a St. Clair."* If he failed in this, failed his father again, here on the border of hope, if he failed his sisters … But try as he might, he could not think of what else to do.

"Nothing to do but pray," said the preacher, staring up at him, waiting, as if reading his thoughts. The preacher's wife stood beside him, silently seeking his permission with her eyes. Odessa was still deathly pale and her breathing now emerged as a tight, wavering whistle.

"No other option, I guess," Nic groused. "Go to it."

The preacher stared at him with eyes of understanding and pity. "It's in God's hands for sure, friend. Let's ask Him to help her make it to the sanatorium. Let's ask Him to restore her to life itself. Will you join us?"

Nic pulled back a little. "No. I mean, you do what you need to. I'll … I'm going to go and ask the conductor how long until we reach the Springs." He turned away and headed down the aisle.

The preacher's wife handed Moira a clean handkerchief and patted her arm. "What's her name?" she asked softly. There was something in her voice that soothed, warmed Moira. Something that reminded Moira of her own mother, dead and gone a year now.

"Odessa," she whispered.

"Your older sister?"

Moira nodded. "By two years." She smiled and stroked Odessa's cheek. How many times, growing up, had Odessa held her, comforted her, nursed her when their mother had been so busy with the boys? "Do you think God will hear us?" she whispered, the woman's face swimming through her tears. "That is, do you think He'll actually save Odessa? I've never seen her ... so poorly."

"I hope so," the woman returned, reaching out to squeeze Moira's hand. "All we can do is ask and hope. Hope."

Moira glanced up to see her brother pacing, waiting to talk to the conductor, clearly not wanting to rejoin them. He had refused to go to church ever since their mother died, claimed he wanted nothing to do with a God who would rob them of so many dear ones.

Nic had gotten into trouble again and again; he'd even gone to jail for brawling. It had horrified her father, infuriated him. Nic claimed Moira's incessant desire to perform, sing, had brought their father so low, but Moira thought Nic's troubles and Odessa's illness were the more likely cause.

Moira looked back down to Odessa, stared at her hard when she realized she wasn't moving, wasn't even taking the tiniest of breaths. "Odessa! *Odessa!*" she screamed. She cast desperate eyes toward her brother, and he came barreling back down the aisle. The preacher and his wife were on their knees beside Odessa, heads bowed, praying. Heart filled with dread, Moira forced herself to look back to her sister, terrified she'd see the same death mask steal over her lovely features as she'd seen on their brothers, their mother.

"Here, let me take her," Dominic demanded, roughly squeezing between the preacher and his wife, pulling Odessa from Moira's arms.

"Don't be so rough, Nic!"

Nic ignored Moira and stared only at their sister. "You hold on, Odessa St. Clair. We are just minutes away. You hold on. This is where it begins, your new life. Wake up, wake up and see the mountains. See your new home. It's beautiful, Dess. Beautiful. *Wake up.*"

Beat this curse. Fight it. Wake up. Odessa considered his words from far away, as if she were a judge hearing both sides of a case. She could give in to this demon, let it spirit her away, so her siblings could bury her at the foot of the towering Rockies and be free to open the bookshop, live their lives without her as a burden. Or she could find the sword at her side and strike back at the curse of her family, this dark cloud that had stolen her brothers, that now came back like a foraging, hungry monster seeking more sustenance from the St. Clair fields.

She could not tolerate that. She could not bear the thought of her father, so thin, aging so fast, coming west to simply attend her funeral. She longed for hope, for light to again settle into the lines of his face. To see a smile and not that dim look of desperation, defeat. *I will fight,* she thought. The words gave her strength. *God almighty, You have the power of all in Your hands. Give me the strength to fight!*

Odessa opened her eyes and then quickly closed them, blinded by the bright, clear sun shining through towering windows all about her. She had a vision of brilliant white and wondered for a moment if she had already landed in heaven. Recognizing that the tip of her nose and cheeks were very cold, and supposing that heaven was bound to be warm, not frosty, she chanced a second glance through squinting eyes.

She was on a covered porch, all painted in white, upon one of ten beds—only two others occupied—and covered in ivory sheets and blankets. A porch, a blessed porch, and off that cursed train! She saw that two windows on either side of the long porch were open, letting a cool draft wander past. But she was laden with heavy woolen blankets that were tucked neatly on either side of her, cocooned against the cold. And she was propped up against several pillows.

Outside, towering pines gave way to the majestic mountains, purple in the light of morning's glow. One far outweighed all the others in girth and height; it had to be the famous Pikes Peak, the mountain that guided the way for the wagon trains heading west from as far away as Kansas.

They had made it. The St. Clairs had made it to Colorado.

She had survived, lived to awaken in the sanatorium where she might find the cure.

"Awake at last," said a voice from down the porch.

Odessa turned her head, suddenly aware that she must look frightful. She tried to give an older man, also cocooned from the chest down in his own bed, a small smile. It was an odd situation, this. Being on a porch alone with two men, even at a distance of twenty feet.

"You've been here three days. Doubt you remember most of that."

Odessa nodded and gave him a quick glance, not yet trusting her voice, uncertain of how to behave in such a foreign social situation.

He was a small man, with a wild, wiry gray beard and eyebrows that appeared to be taking over his forehead. His eyes, sunken and dark-rimmed from the consumption, were still alert, a spark of humor within.

He nodded at her, encouraging her to stay engaged. He seemed clearly bored with his hours of lying about. "Name's Sam O'Toole," he said. "I, too, came from Philly, but it's been …" He paused to cough, a long, hacking process that Odessa tried not to listen to. It made her want to join him. And although she couldn't take a long, deep breath, it was better than coughing and not stopping. She closed her eyes, tried to concentrate on the fact that she was alive, she hadn't died on the train; she was in Colorado Springs.…

"It's been twenty years," Sam continued at last "I imagine it's quite different now." There was a note of sorrow, separation in his tone. He was quiet for a moment and then seemed to remember himself. "Our companion here is my neighbor from down south, Bryce McAllan."

The other man, his cot set at an angle, was partially hidden by a canvas and easel.

Brown wavy hair. Kind eyes. He gave her a gentle smile and nod in greeting. He dabbed a brush in the paint somewhere that Odessa couldn't see, laid his head back as if summoning the strength to move, and then lifted an arm to place the color upon the canvas. But then he looked her way again.

Where was the nurse? Her doctor? Her siblings?

"You need not respond to Sam's idle chatter," Bryce said. "We know your struggle well." His smile faded and he returned his attention to the canvas. He dabbed his brush on the unseen palette, settled back among the pillows, took a few breaths, and then lifted his arm again toward the painting.

"We've met your brother and sister," Sam said, then paused to cough again. He leaned his head back, exhausted from the effort, but couldn't seem to stop himself from speaking. He pulled an age-spot-covered hand from beneath the covers and wiped his upper lip with a handkerchief. So he struggled with the fever, too. "Fine people. And I know your name is Odessa. I assume you know you arrived in Colorado Springs in the nick of time. They'll be very glad to see you awake."

Odessa moved a little and smelled the herbal poultice still upon her chest. Peppermint and sage and a deep, mossy scent that reminded her of the shady forest just after snowmelt. "My brother?"

"They'll return soon, I'm certain. They've hardly left your side. Your sister appeared faint herself, so he left to take her back to the hotel. She's been through an ordeal, between the journey west and their bedside vigil. Quite the beauty she is … almost as pretty as you, miss. If I was a few years younger—" He paused to cough and Odessa dared to glance his way, and further, to Bryce.

She fought the urge to squirm, touch her hair. She knew that he, too, was comparing her to Moira. She concentrated on the view outside instead. No wonder he painted it. Cloaked in springtime snow, the mountains were magnificent.

Bryce cleared his throat. His lungs sounded good, the way hers sounded on her best days. But she had seen the sheen of sweat upon his brow, how he leaned back among the pillows from the mere exertion of painting. She wondered so many things, how long he had been here, how many other patients there were …

Old Sam kept coughing, sitting up now to try to get on top of it.

As if reading her agitation, Bryce set down his brush and settled long, strong fingers around a glass bell. It looked desperately dainty and a bit silly in his big hand. She met his eyes, wide and blue, and then noticed his hair was streaked, his face weathered, as if he had spent many summers in the sun. He smiled, and his eyes crinkled again at the corners appealingly.

He was handsome. Terribly thin, but handsome. And only a few years older than she.

Blessedly, the nurse arrived then. "Oh!" she cried in delight. "Miss St. Clair, you're awake! The doctor will be so pleased. Let me go and fetch you some water—no doubt you are parched—oh, and Sam, you too …" She turned back to Odessa. "I'll make the doctor aware of your condition."

"Thank you," Odessa croaked.

"Not at all," said the nurse with a bob of her head, and with that she hurried out as quickly as she had arrived.

"Nurse Packard," Sam managed, still coughing as he grinned Odessa's way. "A saint in white."

"Everything is white around here," Bryce muttered.

A few minutes later, the nurse arrived with a pewter pitcher that was sweating from the blessedly cool contents within, and a tin mug. She poured a cup and set it against Odessa's lips. "There now, just a few sips. All right, one more. I know you must be terribly thirsty. But we must take it easy. We don't want it coming right back up now, do we?"

Odessa closed her eyes and pushed back a frown at the woman's words. She concentrated on the cold liquid she could feel slide all the way down her throat, easing, soothing, calming.

Nurse Packard set the mug on the table beside her, and Odessa noticed that she, too, had a bell beside her bed. "I'll return with the doctor," she said, and with another bob of her head, was gone.

"They'll bring food at some point," said Bryce. "More food than you've ever seen in your life. I've gained ten pounds in my two weeks here."

Odessa said nothing, thinking only of how perilously thin he must have been if he was already ten pounds heavier.

"Are you from the East as well, Mr. McAllan?" she said at last.

"Betrayed by the accent, eh? Bangor. But I've been in Colorado for five years running our horse ranch near Sam's land," he said easily. "It's in the shadow of the Sangre de Cristos. Have you heard of the Sangres?"

She shook her head.

"The way they rise off the valley floor, it makes these mountains appear as princes to their kings."

"They are taller than Pikes Peak?"

"Ten that rival her. Another couple of dozen not far short of reaching her height. But it's more that there is one after another, marching together as if in some grand parade."

"It sounds magnificent," Odessa said.

"This is a communal porch shared by all our patients." A short, broad-shouldered man in a white coat entered with Nurse Packard, no doubt the physician, but his words were directed to Bryce McAllan. "But I'll thank you to pretend that Miss St. Clair is not even in the room, Mr. McAllan. This is a medical facility, not a club in which to fraternize. Perhaps you'll be well enough to ride with the others tomorrow?"

Odessa heard no response from Bryce. She imagined he was irritated with the doctor's patronizing manner. But she understood his motivation. If they were to be ensconced in beds, all together as men and women … it was highly unorthodox.

"Is there not a separate porch for women?" she asked gently.

The doctor shook his head with a small smile and reached out a hand for hers. "I am Doctor Morton, Miss St. Clair. Forgive our arrangements, but we have twenty-two patients and only five of them are women. We are nearly at capacity. There is little choice but to intermingle our patients."

"Only five women? How is that possible?"

He gave her another small smile and a shrug of his narrow shoulders as Nurse Packard brought him a chair on which to sit. "You're in the West now. We have a preponderance of men, all intent on seeking their fortunes. And here, mining, ranching, farming, all subject them to uncommon levels of dust, weakening their lungs. They are primed for consumption. And others arrive from the East—those from coal mines or printer's shops. Still more that have lived in the shadows of factory smokestacks. We receive them all."

He took some papers from the nurse and gazed down at them. "I've seen to your welfare since you arrived on the train. We were expecting you, of course, but had hoped you would not arrive in such dire straits." He looked her in the eye. "It is fortunate you arrived when you did, Miss St. Clair."

"I am aware of that. Do you … do you believe you can help me? Heal me?"

Doctor Morton smiled more broadly and patted her hand. "We have brought you this far, haven't we? Back from death's door? I see no reason why you won't enjoy a complete recovery and live a long life. But it will probably have to be here, near the sanatorium, in case you experience any setbacks."

Odessa stared at him for a long moment. "I can—I can never go back? To Philadelphia?"

Doctor Morton's face sobered. "I would advise against it. I tell all my patients to settle here, make this your home." His eyes slid over to the men at the end of the porch and back again. He was quiet for a moment, carefully choosing his next words. "Your father did not tell you? I was quite clear about it."

Odessa barely shook her head, aghast when her eyes began to fill with tears. Papa had sent her off, sent her off knowing he might never see her again, that she might never return to him. How could he? *How could he?*

Chapter ❀ 2

Over and over, long after Dr. Morton had left the porch, Odessa worked the question and possible answers.

Her father had never said anything because he knew she might never have boarded that train if she had known the truth. If he had told her, she could not have borne the sorrow, the idea that she was abandoning her father, taking away his only remaining children, leaving him alone—possibly forever. His business kept him in Philadelphia. His desire to see his children prosper compelled him to send them West.

Tears ran down her cheeks and she began to wheeze.

"Say now," said Sam with a gentle warning in his voice, "don't do that, Miss St. Clair. I know how tears can lead to something worse."

She didn't look at him, but could see Bryce's movement in her peripheral vision. His brush hovered midair as he watched her too.

Embarrassed, Odessa turned her head away and felt the tears slide into her ear.

"Maybe you ought to tell Miss St. Clair about all that Colorado has to offer, Sam," Bryce said. "What she can look forward to."

They were trying to calm her, trying to ease her away from the precipice that all consumptive patients battled back from far too often. And they were right, of course, about the tears, the danger of giving in to them. But just once, this once, couldn't she purge herself of the tears and sorrow within her soul? She longed to cry until every tear was spent.

No. She could not. *I am here to get better. To live. That is the best gift I can give my father. Breathe in … breathe out,* she told herself, forcing away the niggling urge to cough.

After a few minutes, as her tears dried, she became aware of Bryce's mumbling words. She turned her head and found him on his knees, praying.

She quickly looked back to the windows in front of her. Never had she seen a man praying like that. Certainly not outside of church. It was oddly intimate. Like the time she'd walked into the parlor and discovered her father on his knees before her mother, his cheek against her taut, round belly, full of the baby girl that would soon die. They had been so happy at that moment, so full of hope.

Odessa swallowed hard. She had to think of other things, things that occupied her mind but not her heart. She'd find a way, some way, to draw her father west.

Bryce moved with some effort, like that of a man twenty years older, to his feet and practically fell into bed. "Bit too cold in here to be on your knees for long." His blue eyes sparkled, indicating that he knew she had seen him. He grinned. "I take it you're a Presbyterian, Miss St. Clair."

She didn't care for his assumption. He did not know her. He didn't know the first thing about her. But there was no way around it. She nodded stiffly.

"Methodist, myself. But the consumption has given me some Baptist propensities."

Odessa's mind was back on her church at home, on the girls her own age she had seen enter womanhood and get married. A few with babies of their own. Entering that church was like being surrounded by family, with irritating and exasperating and loving and laughing uncles, aunts, and cousins all about her.

Bryce settled wearily back into his pillows. "Forgive me, Miss St. Clair, I've made you sad again with something I've said. I'll keep my peace now."

"Nurse Packard will skin us faster than a Ute if we don't let the girl rest," Sam said.

"I thought the Ute were peaceful," she murmured.

"Pardon?"

She turned to look at the men. "I had heard that the Ute were peaceful."

Bryce smiled again and Odessa's heart skipped a beat. Odd. Such an odd situation, this! "Some are. Some aren't. Most are on their reservation, across the mountains and farther west, now. But some have held their own. Our ranch foreman is pureblood Ute, or *oo-tah,* as he says it."

"He's stubborn as a mule and not as pretty," Sam put in. "But he's a good man."

Odessa could feel her eyebrows rise in surprise. "You hired an Indian?"

"Sure." Bryce's smile faded from his eyes and his lips settled into a line.

"Is that wise?" she pressed.

"Tabito is one of the most loyal men I've ever met, and a better shot than most too. A good man to have around when you're on a ranch five miles from your nearest neighbor."

"'Specially if I'm one of your nearest," Sam joked, then laughed at his own humor, which set him to coughing again.

Nurse Packard returned, interrupting Odessa's next question about the Indian, and Bryce dabbed his brush into his palette as if Odessa were the furthest thing from his mind. The nurse looked from Odessa to the men and back again, obviously not fooled. "I brought you some broth. We'll work you up to the eggs and milk and meat that are standard here. You're terribly thin. How long since your last real meal?"

Odessa shook her head, trying to remember. "Some soup ... maybe a little bread on the train. But nothing really since we left home."

Nurse Packard nodded, her brown eyes kind. "Well, let's begin with this. A little soup will make you feel worlds better. And God's creation here in Colorado will do her wonders on your lungs. I promise, Miss St. Clair. You will find a new life here, and it all begins with putting a little meat on those bones."

"Odessa," she said, swallowing the broth. "Please call me Odessa."

But curiously, while she was glad for the woman's company, she felt herself speaking more to Bryce and Sam than to the nurse.

"Dominic, look," Moira said, pulling her small hand against the crook of his arm. They were on broad Pikes Peak Avenue, heading east to return to the sanatorium and their sister.

His eyes immediately saw what she was gesturing to, a new, unpainted structure with boards as fresh as a newborn's skin and a white "for sale" sign in the front window. Nic looked left and right, sizing up the location. It was near the end of any structures built on the street, but given the Springs' rate of growth, it wouldn't be that way for long.

"Not very convenient to the train station," he said.

"But probably going for a better price because of it," Moira returned. "And it's three blocks from the mercantile."

He smiled down at her and squeezed her hand. "I'll check on it. As soon as we know Odessa is on the mend, I can think about St. Clair business."

"Don't wait too long, Dominic," she warned. "I'm thinking buildings are sold fast in this town, or it's up to you to build it. Just consider it. If the structure is already complete, you merely have to fill it." Her eyes lit up with anticipation and she waggled her eyebrows in excitement. There was no negotiating with Moira St. Clair when she got like this. As the youngest girl in the family, she'd always gotten everything she wanted. And she wanted a lot. Spending the last few days at the sanatorium had left her restless.

They resumed their walk. Nic was grimly aware of the many appreciative glances Moira drew. Even in a city like Philadelphia, she had many admirers and men coming to call. Father had let her dabble, but intervened before anything became too serious; he wasn't yet willing to entertain potential husbands for Moira. But he'd failed to consider the vast number of men in this country. How was Nic supposed to fend them off?

Heading directly for them, two dandy gentlemen eyed her now. Dominic frowned. It was unseemly not to step aside and let a lady pass. Moira was chatting, talking on about how she had heard at the hotel that General Palmer intended to build an opera house—a real opera house!—in his burgeoning city. Already he'd planted hundreds of trees along the streets. If he could do that, and pass a bond to get the El Paso Canal flowing too, then surely he could knit together the funds.

Dominic pulled his sister to a stop and looked up suspiciously into the faces of the men before them. Both were impeccably dressed in long dark coats and vests. They had eight inches on him, but their black boots and pant legs bore the same spattering of fine street mud as his own. "Pardon me, gentlemen," he ground out. He moved to one side, to guide Moira around them, but the one nearest lifted a hand to slow their progress.

Dominic looked up, considering how he might protect his sister if this escalated into a scuffle, and then stared over at the man. He was taller, but Nic was broader. And used to brawling. These last years, through the pain and sorrow, he'd found relief in fighting, release for the anger and grief that welled inside, gratefully leaving each fight spent.

"Nic," Moira said in a whisper, head ducked, squeezing hard on his arm.

"Forgive me," said the man, moving his hand to the brim of his hat and removing it. "I simply could not let a moment such as this pass." He leaned slightly toward Moira and shook his head in wonder. "Permit me to say that never has this city seen a beauty such as you, miss."

Moira giggled. Such easy prey to charm! She lifted her chin. "This city is full of men, sir."

Dominic edged between the man and his sister. "I'll thank you to step aside and let me and my sister by."

The man, handsome, dapper, still stared at Moira with delight. "Your sister? Then, may I dare to hope, my dear, that you are unattached?"

"Consider her attached to me," Dominic said, edging nearer the man. He stared up at him, silently begging him to say another word and make a move against them. The man returned his look, sizing him up too, at first clearly thinking Nic was smaller, easily bested, but then taking into account the determination in his eyes.

The stranger cocked his head to one side and gave them a half smile. "Easy, brother," he said, an altogether different expression on his face now. He pulled aside his jacket and Nic caught the sight of a bright tin star on his vest. The sheriff? This was the city's sheriff?

"I make it my business to meet anyone moving in," the man said. "I'm Sheriff Reid Bannock." He tipped his hat, his eyes again only on Moira, "and this is Deputy Garrett Smith."

Dominic's eyes slid from sheriff to deputy. The deputy, Garrett, seemed hesitant, as if he didn't fully approve of his boss's forward ways.

"We don't permit brawling on our streets," the sheriff said coolly, looking down at Nic. "Maybe it was different in Philadelphia?"

Nic stared back at him, weighing his options. So the man had already checked up on him. How much did he know? He swallowed hard. "Pardon me, Sheriff," he said, forcing a smile. "Thought you were nothing more than a dandy prowling about. Must keep the sheep away from the wolves, you know."

Sheriff Bannock smiled, but his brown eyes remained curiously still. "A pretty sister like that would put any man on edge," he said, as if they were longtime friends commiserating.

"As you already seem to know, I'm Dominic St. Clair, and this is Miss Moira St. Clair."

"Pleased to meet you both," he said, sticking out his hand.

Grimly, Nic shook it.

The sheriff nodded at Moira. "Welcome to our city, Miss St. Clair."

"Thank you, Sheriff." She lifted the tips of her fingers to her throat and boldly gazed back at him.

Nic watched the sheriff force his attention off Moira and back to him. "What has brought you two to town?"

"Three to town," Nic corrected, clearing his throat and casting a narrowed-eye warning toward Moira to lay off the feminine charms. Did she have to flirt with everyone? "We are here to set up shop for my father, a book merchant, and to seek assistance for another sister, who is convalescing at the sanatorium."

The deputy raised a brow in surprise.

"Chasing the cure," the sheriff said, the edge of derision in his voice. But then he stopped, checked himself. "She as pretty as you, Miss St. Clair?"

"No," Nic interrupted, and led Moira around and away from the men. "Good day, gentlemen," he said over his shoulder. And tried to ignore their laughter behind him.

"You didn't have to be so rude," Moira said plaintively.

"You didn't have to be so flirtatious," he returned. "Saints in heaven, Moira. Father wants me to keep you safe. Can you help me out a little on that front?"

They strode along in silence, the sanatorium quickly coming into view. But all Nic could hear in his head were his father's whispered words in his ear before they boarded the train. *"Use your brain as well as your brawn, Son."* He swallowed against the dust of the street and the bile rising in his throat. He'd agreed to his father's proposal, to watch over his sisters, to open the first St. Clair bookshop, to stay out of jail and become, as his father put it, "a respectable man." If he could meet those terms, his father would allow him two years to travel, then enroll in a university of his choice—one that had not previously suspended him—to complete his education; at that point he could try his hand at another business, if he so chose. It would be up to him. That was their agreement.

Dominic knew his father hoped he would sow his oats, go to university, and then adopt the family business. But publishing was in his father's blood, in Odessa's. Not his. Colorado Springs would be his escape route, his path to freedom. Yes, after this year was done, he would be free.

"He doesn't have the demeanor of a merchant," Garrett said, staring after them.

Reid glanced at his deputy. "No. He won't last long."

"Doesn't seem the sort to give up."

"He will. For one reason or the other. He'll get the fever and head to the mines."

"Or die in some saloon brawl."

Reid smiled grimly. "You saw it in him too. That man's itching for a fight."

"Like half the other men in this city with all their pent-up frustration after failing at the mines."

"Or being away from their women. Too poor to stay. Too poor to go home. You ask me, General Palmer should be dealing with that issue, not getting so besotted with frivolous opera houses and such."

His deputy was quiet for a moment. Reid tipped his hat to a Mrs. Samson, plump and grinning like a happy cat, with a full basket on one arm, a child in the other.

"Think Dominic St. Clair was lying?"

"About what?" Reid feigned.

"When he said his other sister wasn't pretty?"

"Most likely. But this town isn't very big. It won't take long to find out."

Back on the ward, among eleven other men, half of them coughing in their sleep, the other half snoring, Bryce laced his fingers together behind his head and stared up at the planks of the ceiling. A lamp burned low in the corner, courtesy of the night nurse.

A knot in one plank reminded him of Odessa's eye, wide and the most curious shade of blue-green, like the island seas; the swirls of the wood grain reminded him of her dark hair, waving about her face like the ocean at night. She was pale and thin and terribly ill, but he'd never seen such haunting beauty in all of his years.

And she had gumption. Talking to Sam, even him a little—strangers—the way she had. She was cultured, pure, but she had the heart of a pioneer. He could see it in her.

But what was the sorrow lurking within? It was beyond home-sickness. He knew what that felt like, the deep, lurking pull of it, the ache below. There was a grief inside the girl, dark and menacing, threatening to suck her under. It was enough to battle the disease that threatened them all at the sanatorium; what else threatened Odessa St. Clair?

He sighed. How long until he saw her again? Her tears pulled at him, tying him to her. Had she lost someone dear to her in chasing the cure? Or would it cost her some dream to remain in Colorado?

Did she share his pain?

He closed his eyes in prayer for her again, praying with everything in him that Odessa would be safe. That she would find healing. And rediscover joy.

Chapter ❀ 3

The men down the porch were obviously trying to give the St. Clairs a measure of privacy, but Odessa was well aware they could hear every word. Yet she was in no condition to move.

"Oh, Dess, you look so much better," Moira said, taking a chair beside her sister and lifting her hand. "Doesn't she, Nic?"

"Pretty as a princess," he said, grinning at her shyly. "I told you you'd make it to Colorado."

"Always have to be right, don't you, big brother?" Odessa said.

"Don't have to be. Just am."

She smiled back at him. "Glad you were right about this. Now let's hope they can see me all the way to health."

"They will," Moira said, squeezing her hand. "I have such a good feeling about this place, Odessa. It's going to be good for all three of us, I know it."

Odessa studied her younger sister, the sparkle in her eye. Only two things delighted the young woman so: singing or a new suitor. Their father had sent her here to avoid both. "Moira, you haven't—"

"No, no," Moira said, looking away. "Stop it, Sissy. I'm merely happy to be someplace new. It's all so fresh here. So … raw. It's rather like a blank canvas, isn't it, Mr. McAllan?"

"I beg your pardon," Bryce said, looking their way. Odessa's eyes slid from him to her pretty younger sister and back again.

"The Springs. It's so new, so untouched, isn't it rather like a blank canvas?"

Bryce thought on that for a moment and then gave her a small smile. "I can see why you would say that, Miss St. Clair. But no, I don't agree. I believe this country has already been painted by the hand of God. We can cover it over with our own creations, but it will merely mar what is already perfect."

Moira's mouth dropped a bit and then she abruptly shut it. Odessa bit her lip. It wasn't often that a man didn't fall all over himself to please Moira. And she liked what Bryce had said.

"You young people need to hire some horses and take a ride," Sam O'Toole said. "See some of this country as Bryce here describes it. Where we hail from …" He shook his head. "The farther from any city you get, the more you'll see what he's talking about. You turn some corners, crest some hills, and the majesty of it is enough to make a grown man cry."

"Sam's right," Bryce said. "Before you get your bookshop going, spend some time riding about. Consider what it means to be on land that nothing but antelope or mountain lion or Indian have ever been on. Stare upon mountains that men have yet to climb. That's when you'll get a sense of Colorado."

He coughed hard then, and they all waited for him to stop. He leaned back against his pillow and closed his eyes for a moment, and Odessa wondered if he was done talking. She hoped not. She liked the low, soothing timbre of his voice. The confidence, the authority of his words, that belied his ill state.

Odessa looked to Dominic, who had been listening as intently as she. Moira's attention seemed to be fading. She glanced about as if looking for an excuse to leave.

"You don't want to see this city built?" Nic asked.

"City's already well on its way," Bryce said. "No stopping that, and that's not a bad thing. But I'm just saying that we who hail from the East have a propensity to want to re-create what we knew before, rather than letting the new place become our home."

"We crave the familiar," Odessa said.

"That's right," Bryce said, his eyes meeting hers. "And sometimes, God asks us to wrestle with the unfamiliar until it becomes our new familiar. Until we can …" He stopped, clearly trying to keep from coughing, and reached for a glass of water.

"Until we can breathe freely in that new place," Odessa said.

Bryce's smile grew. Odessa felt a slow blush at her neck and she looked away.

Sam laughed softly, as if he'd just been let in on an inside joke. Odessa ignored him.

"Let's do as they suggested, " Dominic said as they left the sanatorium. "Let's go to the stables right now and hire some horses and see some of this country."

"Nic, it's freezing. We'll catch our death."

"Ahh, the snow's nearly melted away. We'll stop at the hotel and bundle up. Our appointment with the building manager isn't for hours. Please, Moira. We've been here for three days and all we've done is visit Odessa and look for space for the shop. Let's explore a little."

Moira considered him and then glanced right, to the wooded hills that flanked the young city. "I don't know, Nic. Is it safe?"

"That's the point," he said, taking her arm in his and steering her down and around the corner, heading to the stables. "As McAllan says, it's unknown. Unfamiliar. And the only way to make it familiar, Moira, is to venture forth."

Sam O'Toole chuckled and then leaned to his right, looking down the porch at Odessa. "You'll get your opportunity soon enough to lay your own eyes on this land. They'll take you out and set you upon a horse and when you're not so sick that you think you're about to fall off, you'll catch a glimpse of what we're talking about.... Such pretty places for you to see, such grand experiences ahead, miss ..." He leaned back and looked over at Bryce, then back to Odessa. "You two. There's something special brewing here, yes indeed."

"Sam ..." Bryce warned.

"Bah," said Sam, flicking out his fingers in dismissal. "If an old man stuck in a sanatorium cannot meddle in the affairs of others, what else will occupy his mind? It's plain that you and the young miss "

"Here," Bryce said loudly, cutting him off. He tossed a Bible onto his cot. "Occupy your mind with that."

Sam laughed again. "All right, all right," he said, leaning back and opening the worn leather cover. "Now where is the Song of Solomon?"

"Sam ..."

But Sam just laughed. Odessa turned and feigned sleep, but continued to listen to their banter. Sam relented from his teasing as Nurse Packard came in to check on all three of them, refill water glasses, and pull covers up higher against winter's leftover chill. The men lapsed into musings about their beloved valley, wondering how much snow they'd gotten in this last storm, how Bryce's men and horses fared, how the neighbors were weathering a snow-laden spring.

Their easy camaraderie comforted Odessa, and she settled back, eyes closed, to listen. It reminded her of Papa discussing a favorite new novel with a colleague.

Bryce lowered his voice and Odessa turned slightly in order to capture his next words. "Sam, is there something else? You look like a stallion who has just discovered his own private meadow of sweet grass."

"I do? Nah. It's nothing."

"What, specifically, is nothing?"

"Nah, boy," he said with another laugh. "All is in order."

"In order for what?"

"In order for … anything."

In her own room, Odessa awakened in the deep hours of morning, long before daybreak. She shook her head and squeezed her eyes shut, half of her longing to recede back into the comforting eddies of sleep, half of her trying to make out the sounds she heard coming from the next room. With a start, she sat up straight in her bed.

Too fast. She coughed, which began one of her fits. It was always this way; once she gave in to the urge to clear her lungs, a terrible cycle ensued. Sometimes she was successful in clearing her throat and not fainting. Sometimes not.

Minutes later, when she finally regained control, she sat on the edge of the bed and reached a trembling hand to the nightstand. A nurse had left the lantern burning low. She turned it up, taking comfort in the warm glow that filled the room.

She listened hard for what she had heard earlier, but could only make out the dull pounding of her heart in her ears and the high whistle from her lungs.

But she had heard it, next door. The sounds of a man's muffled cry, rustling, as if in struggle. No one was coming down the hall to help; had no one else heard? She heard the squeak of a floorboard and the soft footsteps of someone hurrying away. Tried to hold her breath and hear. Failed. Coughed.

She knew Sam O'Toole was next door. Was he hurt? In trouble?

Odessa stared at the bell, thinking of the night nurse—what was her name? Not nearly as kind as Nurse Packard, but efficient. She reached for the bell but resisted ringing it. What exactly would she say to Nurse Carlson? What if she had dreamed the whole thing? It wouldn't be the first time her imagination had taken over, playing out so vividly she was sure it was true. That was part of why she had taken to writing … to make use of the stories that continued to spool across her mind. But what if it *wasn't* merely a figment of her imagination?

She looked about her private room—one of only six available at the sanatorium. "Only the finest for a St. Clair," Dominic had said proudly when she'd seen him the day before. In all reality, it was little more than a nun's convent room, stark and small. But her window faced northward, to the Front Range, the mountains that spread out from Pikes Peak like the ruffled skirt of a lady. On the wall was a simple cross. The bed was made up in standard-issue white cotton sheets and woolen blankets. And it was a relief not to have to share quarters with another.

Odessa lifted her chin, still listening intently. Silence, utter silence. A chill ran across her arm, and then another down her back. Her eyes went to the dying embers in her corner fireplace, little more than ashes now. It wasn't the frost of her window that caused her chill. It was death. She knew this shadow, the feel of this particular quiet, creeping up on her sunset in the deepest woods.

She swallowed hard. Still no movement, no sounds. *You imagined it all, Odessa. It's in your head!*

But it wasn't.

She had to find out.

She placed her feet on the smooth-planked floor, strengthened from her days in bed and on the porch and Nurse Packard's gently administered teas and broth. Holding on to the table, she rose on shaking legs and stood for a minute until her vision steadied. She hadn't been anywhere unassisted. Wasn't it time she tried?

She moved forward, reaching for the doorjamb, and looked one way and then the other. No one in view. She could hear the sounds of coughing fits, but they were downstairs or on the other side of the building. Nothing from next door. Shuffling forward, she rounded the corner, still clinging to the wall, until she stood in the doorframe of the next room. She realized dimly she was in little more than a night shift, far from the proper attire of a lady about to meet a stranger, but that thought quickly left her mind.

There was no light in this room, only the gray cast of moonlight from the window. His lamp had burned out or been snuffed.

Her eyes slowly adjusted. She could make out an old man with a white beard. Sam O'Toole. A gentleman's hat and cane on the bed-post at his feet. She crept a foot closer. He was under the covers, but his head was at an odd angle.

"Pardon me, Mr. O'Toole," Odessa whispered. She waited a moment for a response, then forced herself to take a step forward, reaching for his bedside table. A tickle edged her throat, and she willed herself not to cough. "S-Sam?"

She took one more step, until the man's head was in silhouette against the moonlit window. His chin was up, his mouth gaping wide. The pillow was on the floor beside him. Odessa knew that look, that expression of terror. He had tried, tried with every effort in him to take one more breath.

And he had failed.

She dimly recognized that she was wheezing, panicking. But as her eyes went to the dead man before her, and the pillow on the floor, and the sounds she had heard—his pitiful cry, the soft, muffled rustlings of bedsheets as if someone had been atop him—she spun around, every corner now holding deeper, more ominous shadows. What if? What if the White Death hadn't taken him? What if he had been—?

Odessa went down hard to her knees. Her hand cast about, try-ing to find a hold that would keep her from the cold floor, left to die beside the old, dead man.

As if she were ten paces away, she could hear the glass bell as it crashed to the wood and splintered into a hundred pieces. From far away she felt the shards cut her cheeks as she slid across the floor, spinning as if in a whirlpool....

Chapter ❀ 4

Dominic paced the floor at the foot of his sister's bed. Moira sat perched beside Odessa, holding her hand, tears slipping down her face. Dr. Morton stood on the other side of his patient's bed, looking over her paperwork from under a furrowed brow.

"We're fortunate that—"

"Fortunate!" Dominic exploded, covering the few steps between them in a breath. "I left my sister here yesterday, better than I'd seen her in a month, and come back to find her unconscious again and her face cut up! What happened?"

"As discussed, Mr. St. Clair, it appears she tried to get up out of bed unaided, knocked a glass bell to the ground, and then fainted upon it."

"Why was she up? In the middle of the night?" Dominic spat.

"Sometimes our patients get disoriented, particularly when they first arrive."

"I want a nurse with her, day and night," he said.

"Mr. St. Clair, we hardly have the nurses to cover—"

"Day and night, until she's significantly improved." He stood close enough to the doctor's chart to push against it.

The doctor raised his chin and glanced from Dominic to Odessa and back again. "Very well, Mr. St. Clair. We can see if we might borrow a private nurse from among ranks of the nuns of St. Francis.

For three days, until we see Miss St. Clair through the worst of this. Then we shall reassess. We will, of course, add the cost to your bill." With that, he turned and left them alone.

"I should stay with her," Moira said, picking up Odessa's limp hand and stroking it. "At least for a night or two."

"It's a good idea," Dominic said. He paused, took a breath, and seemed to relax, considering it. "You could stay with her at night, rest at the hotel during the day."

Moira nodded and stared at her sister. "But is this to be our life in Colorado? Always hovering over Dess? We leave her for a day and look what happens! How did Papa think we could possibly open a bookshop?"

Dominic sighed. "It won't always be like this. In a few days, Odessa will be better and begin to regain her strength. This sanatorium has a 90 percent success rate in getting even their worst patients up and on their feet and back into their own homes."

"Within three to six months," Moira said.

"I'd be happy if she was living with us in three months." He strode to the bed and took her other hand. "That's what we're hoping for Odessa. It was just—just a hard go of it, getting her here from the East. She needs some time. You know our Dess. She'll be fine."

He studied her pale skin, her shallow, labored breaths and wondered if he believed his own words. He tucked her cold hand under the blanket and turned away, sudden hot tears in his eyes. He ran his fingers through his thick hair and closed his eyes, feeling a weariness enter his very bones.

What if he failed at doing what their father had asked of him— to see to his sisters' well-being? What if Odessa died here, while he could do nothing but watch? His hands clenched and he punched the air in frustration.

"Nic?"

Dominic blinked slowly and turned to face Moira. She gazed at him with those big sea-green eyes, a common trait among all the St. Clair children. Her face was oval shaped, like their mother's, whereas Nic and Odessa had inherited the longer, patrician nose and sculpted cheekbones of their father. She looked so much like their mother, with her porcelain skin and rosebud mouth, the same look of consternation on her face that he remembered receiving from his mother after he had gotten into a fight with Robby Smits from down the hill, even though he knew how she disliked his scuffles with the other boys. "What is it, Moira?"

"I … I like it here. I do. But sometimes, I feel …" She looked down at Odessa's sheets. Long lashes made her look more like a china doll than a flesh-and-blood woman.

"Homesick?"

She nodded and sniffled and Dominic stifled a sigh. Her tears made him feel angry, helpless. He wanted to flee. Return his sisters to their father's doorstep and walk away. But Father had asked him to do this for him. For a year. For a year, he could handle it. Reluctantly, he placed a hand of comfort on her shoulder. "All right, Moira. That's enough now. We don't have time for tears."

"Tears aren't on a schedule you can control, Nic."

He pulled his hand away. "It's time to grow up, Moira. A grown woman knows there's a time and place for such things."

"Go away, Nic, and leave me be."

"Think about someone else for once, Moira. Think about me or Dess."

"I am!" She glanced up at him, green eyes flashing. She jumped up and pulled her shawl more closely around her. "Forget my offer to stay with Dess tonight. You have it all under control! Hire the nurse. Let Papa see the charge, wonder if he's made a mistake, leaving you to make the decisions about her care."

She strode past him toward the door, but he caught her arm. "That's a foul thing to say, Moira."

"No more foul than your thoughts," she said, wrenching her arm away and staring up into his eyes. "I'm simply more brave in giving voice to the truth than you are." With that, she turned and left the room.

Roaring in frustration, Dominic grabbed the oil lamp and imagined sending it crashing against the far wall. It felt good to hold the weight of it in his hand. It would be even better to hurl it across the room, watch it splinter and fly apart, see the oil spread into a dollop and slowly case down the pine wall. But it would only take the edge off his anguish. It wouldn't take away its source.

He paced back and forth, hands on his head, staring at Odessa. "Come on, Dess. Come back to us. I need you."

Bryce heard the man pacing on the floor above him and to the right. Somewhere near Odessa St. Clair's room. Or even Sam's, God rest his soul. Maybe even in it. For the first time since his arrival, he wished he had chosen an upstairs, private room rather than take a bed in the communal quarters. He'd been looking to save the money, but now he wanted nothing more than to duck his head out in the hallway and see what was transpiring above him. He heard a woman's light, hurried step and a man's heavy-footed stride down the hall.

They were odd sounds, urgent sounds. And considering Odessa had remained unconscious since finding Sam the night before …

He eyed the patient next to him, a young miner named Jared from Illinois, who shared a look of concern. Bryce threw back the covers and sat up, waiting a moment to make sure he'd not start a coughing fit. The same action a month ago might've ended with him passing out.

Then he moved out, listening hard for more noise coming from upstairs. But the wide stairs that began at the entrance of the sanatorium and split to take people up to two different wings in grand fashion remained empty. Taking a long, slow breath, he eyed the stairs with some consternation. He hadn't ever been up them; Odessa had been carried down to the sunporch they had shared on the west side of the house. Thoughts of the long hill between the stables and the cabin, of Tabito having to carry him up and to the wagon, as helpless as a baby, assailed his mind. But he shoved them back, choosing to think only of Odessa St. Clair and what might be unfolding above.

Where the devil was everyone? He wiped the sweat from his lip and began the climb up the steps, feeling as if he were climbing the Peak instead of a flight of stairs. Halfway up, the stairway curved, and he could see a bit down the hall, with Nurse Packard and a maid moving in and out. A younger doctor, in training under Doctor Morton, looked in with a vague disinterest in his eyes, then turned to move down the hall.

So Odessa was safe. But there was a lot of commotion emanating from her room. He knew the occupants of every private room—that was, up until old Sam had died the night before—and had guessed at which one might be Odessa's. With little to do but read and eat and sleep, he had spent a good amount of time thinking of such things, mapping out the place, imagining the movements of everyone present, counting the days until he could join the others on the daily rides into the foothills and canyons. He felt like an old woman in a small village, overly interested in the comings and goings of all. But it was so oppressively dull, what was a man to do?

He vacillated, now that he had a pretty good idea that Odessa was safe. What was right, what was proper? She was no business of his. They'd barely spoken. But Sam … Sam had liked her from the start. Said her eyes were like his daughter's, a daughter long gone. And now Sam was dead. One day sitting next to him on the porch, yammering on, teasing him, the next day in a pine box. His neighbor, the man responsible for getting Bryce himself to the sanatorium, to help, on the road to health, now gone.

Bryce turned to head back downstairs and then paused and headed upward again. He had to see her. Just a glimpse to know she was all right. That something worse had not transpired. "Not another one, Lord," he whispered, panting. "Keep the girl safe."

At long last, he made it up the stairs. He paused for several breaths, swallowing against the sudden phlegm in his throat. The maid left, bucket in hand, and passed him by with little more than a curious glance. The room was still and quiet, morning sun streaming across the floorboards and out into the hall.

Decided now, he stepped down the hall, felt the pull of leg muscles he hadn't felt in weeks, more alert, awake than he had been in months. His pulse raced; his temples pounded.

He passed by her room first, just glancing in. Sam's room was dark in comparison, the shades pulled down, the bed remade and empty. Bryce frowned. The old man had seemed better lately, as if he were making a recovery. But the White Death was like that … nibbling up people bit by bit, sometimes in hidden ways. Yes, sometimes it only took another swipe, a compounding infection, sometimes even a mere cool north wind, to carry off the barely standing wreckage of a consumptive.

But he had seen people leave this place, if not fully cured at least whole again. On their feet. He wanted to be among their numbers. Resolutely, he turned back toward Odessa's room and, seeing no one down the hall, peered in at her. He frowned. Her lovely face—a face begging to be immortalized by a sculptor—was covered in bandages. They had wrapped the cloth around her head, so that her dark hair lay flat beneath but sprang to life in swirling curls below, at her neck and around on the pillow.

Bryce realized his hand was over his heart. What was it about this woman that moved him so? What right had he to feel his pulse quicken in the face of her further injury? What had moved her to risk herself, rising unaided? A man lumbered down the hall and Bryce started, realizing now that he was within Odessa's room. He cast about his mind for a suitable explanation.

"McAllan?" Dominic said, brow furrowing.

"Forgive me, Dominic. I … uh … I know I have no business … Listen, I heard some commotion and after last night …"

"You wanted to make sure she was all right." Dominic's eyes moved from assessment to a softer understanding. He reached out to touch his sister's arm, tucking it beneath a blanket. "Dess has that effect on people. Always has."

"Yes, well. Now that I know you're here, I'll cease my meddling and be about my own business."

Bryce moved to pass him in the doorway but Dominic reached out to grab his arm. "They found her in Sam O'Toole's room," he said. "Do you have any idea why she would have gone in there?"

"No." Bryce shook his head, glanced at Odessa again. "How'd she get so cut up?"

"Swiped one of these glass bells off the stand as she was going down," he said, picking Odessa's up and stilling the ringer. "Just her luck to fall down on it." He set it gently back in place. "Doctor thinks she was confused, feverish. Wandering. Just happened to be in O'Toole's room after he died."

"And you?"

"Seems plausible," Dominic said, moving closer to Odessa. He looked up at Bryce. "I'm sorry for your loss. Your friend—the old man was kind."

"Yes, he was," Bryce said.

"Mr. McAllan!" Nurse Packard said, pausing in the hallway. "What are you doing up here? You get back down the stairs this instant. You're in no condition to be climbing them unaided!"

"No, I suppose I am not. I only wished to see Sam's room, wondered—"

"Ach, it's a pity the old man passed on. I understand you've lost a friend. But the man would've wanted you to go on to find good health and return home." She set down a tray on a hall table and then ushered him down the hallway and stairs, not waiting for the men to say good-bye. "The last thing we need is for you to take a fall down the stairs. Miss St. Clair's fall was quite enough."

❦

There Moira was. After his discussion with McAllan, and when Moira failed to return, Nic had left Odessa's side to go after her, and had been down one city block and up the other before he spied her, just ahead, speaking to three men on the dusty Wahsatch Avenue. On either side, fine homes were going up, spoils from the miners who labored in the mountains to the west. But Dominic's eyes were only on Moira, who was looking to the left and down—what she always did when she felt ill at ease. She had a pasted-on smile and obviously tried to say "good day" to the men, miners by the look of them, but when she moved to go around the last one on the left, he stepped in front of her.

"Hey!" Nic shouted. "You leave that lady alone!"

The man looked up, sized him up, obviously found him wanting, and said something out of the corner of his mouth to his comrades. The other two laughed.

It was all Dominic needed. He tore across the remaining fifteen paces and rammed into the miscreant who dared to waylay his sister. The second man grabbed him by the arms and bodily lifted him away, but Dominic tossed his head back and broke his nose, then found his footing and came forward with a solid right for the third man, who was descending upon him.

He could hear Moira screaming at him, then begging him to stop through her tears, but it had been too long. Too long since he had felt so strong, so alive. He wanted to stay here, among the living, feel vital, for as long as he could. No St. Clair woman would ever feel the need to fear for her well-being in this town as long as her brother was around. This was why Father had sent him with them. To protect them. He had said to use his brain *as well as* his brawn. Not his brain alone …

Nic lifted the first man from the ground by the collar, backhanded him, then punched him. The second man surprised him, bringing a mine-forged hand into Nic's back. He gasped as shooting pain emanated from his kidney; from far away he wondered if this was what it felt like to be Odessa, always trying to steal a breath like a beggar before. He rose, keeping watch, instinctively knowing the third man was on his feet, when that man pounded a fist past his cheek and almost into his eye.

Nic felt the flesh tear loose, and a warm gush of blood blinded him. Moira screamed and Nic braced for the next punch, again to his belly. He doubled over and the man rammed a knee up into his face. Nic's head spun and he fell to the ground.

"Please! Please stop!" Moira begged, and suddenly all three did as she asked, mumbling apologies, brushing off their clothes, moving away.

Moira sank to her knees beside Dominic. "Nic? Nic, can you hear me?"

He laughed, little more than a breath of folly. "How can I help but hear you? You're screaming in my ear."

"Nic, you can't do this. Not here. We can ill afford enemies and Papa isn't—" Her voice abruptly fell away.

He squinted upward when a new figure stepped between him and the sun. "A mere five days in my town," the newcomer said, "and you're already brawling, Mr. St. Clair? I thought we had words about this already."

The sheriff.

Nic set his head back down and swallowed some blood. And then he laughed, laughed as he had not for years.

Chapter �֍ 5

Odessa awakened late again, nothing but black at her window and a low-burning lamp in the corner.

"Oh, Odessa," came a voice beside her. "I'm so glad you are awake. I had no idea a person could sleep so long."

Odessa turned and studied her sister beside her. "Why are you here?" She moved again and for the first time recognized the pull of the bandages. Wearily, she raised a hand to her face and touched them. "What happened?"

"You fell—scared us all to death," Moira said, her tone moving from care to complaint.

"Didn't intend to," she said. Every word scraped out of her throat and out through parched lips as her memory of the event returned. "May I have a sip of water?"

"Of course." Moira stepped toward the bedside table and poured from a sweating pitcher into a pewter mug marked with the St. Clair "S" on the side. "I wouldn't hear of them leaving any more glass near you," she said with a smile, "and the tin mugs simply won't do. I unpacked a few of our trunks. I knew you loved those mugs." She wrapped an arm behind Odessa's neck and helped her take a sip, then another. Never had water tasted so good to her. It tasted of home.

"Ah. Bless you," Odessa said, leaning back into her pillow. "It's as if I haven't had a drink in years."

"Air's so dry here, I can't get enough. I imagine it's even more difficult on you."

Odessa glanced at her. Moira always preferred to steer clear of Odessa when she was in her "weakened state."

"Where's Nic?"

"Nic?" Moira asked, covering her mouth as she yawned. "Aren't I enough? I thought you'd be happy with your baby sister here."

Odessa sighed and closed her eyes. She struggled to make sense of her memories, of what had transpired. She'd been on her feet, intent on something …

A low snore sounded from the corner of the room. Odessa lifted her head from the pillow and gazed over at her sister. Moira was fast asleep in the rocker.

"You have to let me out!" Dominic yelled.

Could no one hear him? He shouted until his throat was sore.

He pulled back and forth as if he could pry the bars from their welded edge at top and bottom, then rested his forehead against the cool bars of the jail cell. His captors refused to even respond anymore. His fingers, stiff and sore from the fistfight, closed around the bars and he squeezed as if he could pinch them apart and free himself.

He had to get out … Odessa, alone in the sanatorium … Moira, all alone in the hotel … What would Father say?

Dominic turned and sighed heavily, collapsing onto the stiff cot mattress stuffed with old hay, and put his face in his hands. The sheriff had refused to give him more than a clean bucket of water and a rag to address his wounds. But Nic wasn't surprised. He'd been treated worse in Philadelphia. There, the law had come in and given him a second beating, saying it was "for his own good," thinking they could convince the *dandy* to stay on his side of the tracks.

But in Philadelphia, Father had always come and bailed him out.

Doctor Morton consented to let Bryce leave the next day and take part in Sam O'Toole's funeral. Bryce couldn't imagine his friend being lowered in a casket, with no one to pay their respects but people he'd met just a few weeks prior. Bryce wasn't family, but he was the nearest Sam had had. Riding in the wagon several miles out of town to Evergreen Cemetery taxed every ounce of his strength. He mused to himself that once they got Sam's body out of the wagon he'd have to get in it, flat on his back for the ride home. Sam would've laughed at that. The memory of his easy smile, his laughter, poked at Bryce and made him melancholy.

"Why's the cemetery so far out of town?" he asked the wagon driver beside him, a servant at the sanatorium.

"Hard for a city promoting herself as a 'haven of health' if the dead outnumber the living," he said.

Bryce smiled. Sam would've gotten a big laugh out of that, too. Finally, they arrived, and Doctor Morton, Nurse Packard, and several other patients from the sanatorium all unloaded from other wagons and carriages. A large man that Bryce deduced was the sheriff rode up and joined the small gathering that stood before the chaplain.

Chairs emerged for the ill and weakened patients and Nurse Packard, but the others stood through the ceremony. Out of respect for Sam, Bryce stood as well, but kept a hand on the back of his chair in case his head started spinning with the fever. The chaplain did a decent job of it, considering he'd never known Sam. But Sam had been a believer, had understood something far grander was ahead of him, and hadn't dictated anything fancy for his funeral service.

"When I'm done here, I'm done," he'd said to Bryce once, when it looked liked the consumption was going to take him. "No tears for me, boy. I'll be free. *Free.*"

He'd always been looking ahead, that Sam. Bryce smiled as the chaplain uttered his last *amen* and picked up a handful of dirt, sending it in a dusty drizzle down to the pine coffin below. They buried a box, a body. But the man—his friend, his brother—was ahead, on to the next adventure.

The group dispersed, heading back to their wagons and carriages, the service now over. Bryce remained, staring at that perfect pine box marred with dirt, imagining it covered, grass soon growing atop the mound. He looked out to the mountains, then back to the coffin. "Rest in peace, old friend," he whispered. "You shall be sorely missed."

"Pardon me," said a man from behind him.

Bryce turned, wondering if he was in the way. The man bore an extra thirty pounds and wore a fine suit that marked him as wealthy, but Bryce did not know him.

"Are you Bryce McAllan?"

"I am," he said, wrapping his arms around himself. He suddenly felt the bitter chill of the March wind.

"Then this is for you," said the man, handing him an envelope. "I am Mr. O'Toole's attorney. He specifically asked that I deliver it to you."

Bryce took the envelope and stared at the writing he knew to be Sam's.

"Is Miss St. Clair present?"

Bryce looked up at the man. "Pardon me?"

"A Miss Odessa St. Clair," the attorney clarified, looking back to a second envelope. "Is she present?"

"No. Miss St. Clair is in no condition to be out in this wind. She is back at the sanatorium."

"Ah, I see. It's a bit unorthodox, but listen—would you mind delivering this to her? I have pressing business and must be off on this afternoon's train."

Bryce reached out and took the second envelope. Again, Sam's handwriting. Odessa St. Clair's name on the front. "I will see to it."

"Good," the man said, clearly relieved to have seen his duty through. "I bid you good day, Mr. McAllan. And my condolences on your loss."

"Thank you," Bryce murmured. He stared at the envelopes and then up the hillside.

Only Doctor Morton and Nurse Packard stared back, waiting on him, clearly wondering what was holding him. They were cold, eager to get the others back to warmth, the safety of the sanatorium. He moved up the hill as fast as he dared, suddenly well aware of his weakness. He just might opt for the wagon bed, with a few of the woolen blankets to cover him. Yes, Sam would've laughed, said something like, "I just get out and you're trying to take my place." He glanced down at the envelopes and then back to the wagon. He'd open his later. And get Odessa's to her as soon as he could.

The sheriff refused to release Dominic, no matter how much Moira begged. Only one thing had convinced him to consider releasing Nic the following day—she agreed to accompany him to dinner.

Moira paced in her hotel room. Papa would yell and stand before the door, refusing to allow her out with a man they had just met, sheriff or not. Dominic, if he knew, would throttle them both.

But neither man was here. She was on her own.

She stopped and glanced in the long, oval mirror hanging in her hotel room. She was dressed in a fine teal gown, low at the neck, tight in the bodice, which showed off her narrow waist and the pleasing curve of her breasts. She had summoned a maid to assist her into the corset, and then into the gown. Then with shaking hands she had seen to her hair, pinning it to the top of her head, and applied light Parisian makeup. She ran her hands over the raw silk of her bodice. Nic wanted her to behave as a woman grown? Well, this was it. She could act the part.

Act the part. Was it within her, this role? Never had she been with a man who had not been approved by her father. But this was the West. And Papa was far away. And the sheriff had threatened to keep Dominic in jail for a week. Only her reluctant agreement to dinner had swayed him. One dinner. One dinner and Nic would be out in the morning, back in the adjoining hotel room tomorrow. And they could get back to the business of finding a proper space for the shop before Papa even got wind of what had happened.

Her heart fluttered as she thought of Nic on the ground and bleeding. She'd seen the repercussions of what their mother had termed "scuffles" before, bruises and scratches and cuts the day after, but never had she seen men exchange blows. It was … unseemly.

And oddly fascinating. She was drawn to the foreign force of it all, the scent of primal manhood.

She lifted her chin. There was nothing for it. It was time she acted the part of a grown woman, not that of the baby of the family. Even when her little brothers had been born, Moira had always taken a special place in the family as youngest daughter. And it was thrilling, freeing really, being here in the West and on her own, with neither Dess nor Nic to stand in her way. This sense of independence was what she had craved in Philadelphia, what had frightened Papa when he recognized it. "You are far too fickle, Moira. A creature of passions, drawn to dangerous men and dangerous pursuits."

"Dangerous men?" she had sputtered. "You mean James Clarion? I would think you would be happy to have a Clarion—of all people—court me. And dangerous pursuits? I've always loved to sing, Papa. To say nothing of acting … it can be a lovely thing. If you would only consider allowing me but a year in New York—send me there instead of to Colorado. Please, Papa. I beg it of you. Just a year. Only a year!"

He had stood there, face stricken. For a man of words, a publisher of books, he consistently ran short of them when in heated discussion with his daughter. "Moira, what makes your passions, your pursuits dangerous is that you do not yet know yourself. And the theater is full of passionate people liable to lead you astray." He sighed. "Without your mother to guide you … No. It is decided. You need to go West with your siblings. There you will have enough distance from all of this to become who you are meant to be."

She smoothed down her bodice again, although it was perfectly in place, and studied her image in the mirror. She scoffed at the memory of his words. Papa wanted her to become the person she was "meant to be," but he'd cut her off from the one avenue that would lead her to who she believed she was, deep within—an entertainer, an actress. She was nineteen years old, of age to marry, have children of her own. But Papa believed she did not yet know herself. She leaned toward the glass and stared into her own eyes. "Have some gumption, Moira St. Clair," she said. "Show your father just who you are." She leaned even closer. "Show yourself."

Despite the stern words she gave herself, a knock at the door made her jump.

"Yes?"

"Miss St. Clair, the sheriff is downstairs waiting on you."

"Thank you. Please tell him I'll be down shortly."

"As you wish, miss."

Moira went to the foot of her bed, wrapped the shawl around her shoulders, and gathered up her evening bag. And then she sat down on the edge to count to a hundred. *It'll never do to have a man think you're eager to see him,* her mother had said once.

Moira agreed. Particularly this man. This man was dangerous. Powerful. She pulled on her lace gloves slowly, watching as each finger slid into its pocket. Yes, she would need every weapon in her feminine arsenal if she were to keep Sheriff Bannock in line. Fortunately, her arsenal was well supplied.

Reaching a hundred, she rose and after one last glance in the mirror, slipped out of the hotel room and turned her key in the lock. It was good to be out of the room, really. It would be hard enough to sleep in there all alone, to say nothing of doing so after an evening of pacing within. And if she had to spend another moment at the sanatorium, it would make her scream. It was wise for her to get out, clever of her. She could ply the sheriff with compliments and free her brother as she helped Nic find the best retail space in the city. Who would know the city better than the sheriff?

She moved down the stairs, bending her legs to give herself the appearance of floating. As anticipated, the sheriff rose, a look of awe upon his face.

He pulled his hat from his head and held it to his chest. "You do me an honor, accompanying me tonight, Miss St. Clair."

He smiled and Moira had to admit he was handsome. His teeth were good and she liked the look of his carefully combed, full mustache that partially hid them. His nose was a bit big, but not too much so, and his brown eyes were lined with dark lashes, much like her own. He was a powerfully built man, obviously able to look after himself. This evening wouldn't cost her as much as she had thought.

Her mother's voice came ringing through her mind again as she accepted the sheriff's arm and he placed his hat back atop his head. *Never underestimate a man who has an eye on something he wants.*

Never underestimate a girl who has an eye on something she wants. Then she was immediately contrite with remorse for talking back to her dead mother. *I don't want him, Mother. But I need him. I need to set things back to rights, for Odessa, for Nic.*

No answering comment echoed through her mind, and for a moment, sorrow cascaded through Moira as freshly as when they had just lost their mother, nearly a year ago.

"Miss St. Clair?" the sheriff asked, looking back in her direction.

Moira started and shook her head a little, realizing she had paused, thrown back in time to a place, a day she could talk to her mother, reach out and touch her. She covered her embarrassment with a quick smile and then ducked her head. "Forgive me, Sheriff. I was lost in my own thoughts."

He led her forward, down the boardwalk to the restaurant where they would dine. "Those must have been entrancing thoughts indeed."

She said nothing. Most considered Moira beautiful but simple, pliable, malleable. But few knew how much she understood about others, thought about them, intuited how to guide their reactions to her. The sheriff was the sort of man who liked a challenge and enjoyed some secrets of his own. The way to wrap this man around her little finger was to make him think she was full of secrets. Which she was, in a way.

"How long have you lived in this town, Sheriff?"

"Almost three years. General Palmer and I go back. My father served under him in the last year of the war. They became good friends, and I served in the army as soon as I was able, due to his influence. I hailed from General Palmer's hometown, and he took a special interest in me. Twelve years later I was a sheriff in Minnesota, and General Palmer came through on the train. He asked me to come with him. Said he had the best job in the prettiest city in the state, and it was mine to make it what I would."

"So you left? Just like that? For Colorado."

He gave her a half shrug. "Three years ago. Said my good-byes, gave my notice. Did right by the town. But no, I didn't let any grass grow beneath my feet. Deputy took over for me and I joined General Palmer on the train the next morning."

"And did you find Colorado Springs to be all that General Palmer promised?"

"All that and more. Our city has a long way to go, Miss St. Clair, but she is well on her way."

"General Palmer sounds like quite the solicitor."

"He knows how to make the right deals," he said, nodding and looking slyly in her direction. Moira had the distinct impression that he was no longer talking about the general, but more about their dinner. They passed the wide windows of a large restaurant, the interior a buzz of activity between servers and diners. "Here we are."

She went through the door and paused, pulling off her heavy spring shawl as she waited for Sheriff Bannock to join her. The dull rumble of conversation paused for a few seconds as the townspeople considered their sheriff with a stranger at his side, but then slowly resumed.

Moira smiled at the hostess and followed her to a table, taking the seat that Sheriff Bannock pulled out for her. Their chicken dinner was delicious, the best meal Moira had enjoyed since arriving in this new city, and they were halfway through a slice of preserved apple pie when General Palmer, and his wife, Queen, arrived. Moira knew them on sight, having seen their portrait hanging in the Antlers Hotel. Reid immediately rose and waited for the Palmers to make their way through the room, stopping to greet every other table. She could see that although the sheriff had a good twelve inches on the general he deeply respected the man.

Her eyes went from one to the other as they shook hands. General Palmer turned to Moira. "Well now, where did our fine sheriff find a beauty like you?"

"General William Jackson Palmer, Mrs. Queen Palmer, I'd like you to meet Miss Moira St. Clair, newly arrived from Philadelphia."

General Palmer took her hand in his and bowed over it. She smiled and nodded at his wife, but the general wasn't finished with her. "Tell me, Miss St. Clair, how do you find our Little London?"

Moira swallowed and forced an admiring smile to her face. She had heard the founder called the Springs Little London because of the influx of settlers from England, but she had been to that great city, and she was fairly certain Colorado Springs would never quite reach its stature, even with the current rate of growth.

"Your city is beautiful," she deferred. "I am in awe of your mountains, the clean water, and my new neighbors, of course," she said, sliding a glance toward the sheriff.

General Palmer grinned and glanced at his wife. "The more you meet, the more you'll feel at home," he said. "My wife is here for only a short time. We have invited several to join us tomorrow evening at the Glen. You and the sheriff will join us."

"Oh, I—"

"Thank you for the invitation, General," Reid said. "We will look forward to it."

"Excellent," General Palmer said. "Good evening, Sheriff, Miss St. Clair."

They moved away, and Moira felt a bit faint and more than a little perturbed. How dare he accept the invitation on her behalf?

"Sheriff Bannock—"

"Please, call me Reid."

"Reid, I do not believe I can attend. My brother will not allow it without attending me himself."

"Your brother is in jail."

Moira glanced down at her pie, no longer hungry, then back to Reid. "It was my understanding that after our dinner together tonight, you would consider releasing him tomorrow morning."

The sheriff smiled. "You have just met the most important couple in the entire city, Miss St. Clair. Queen is hardly here anymore; due to a heart attack a few years ago, she and the girls live back East, for the most part. You can hardly say no to such an invitation. If for nothing else, think of your brother. You said you are seeking retail space. General Palmer is the man to know. You will need timely shipments, supplies. General Palmer is the man to know. You will need a reporter to cover your opening in the *Gazette,* our newspaper. General Palmer is the man to know."

"But my brother—"

"Your brother. Perhaps it is in his best interest to keep him longer. Perhaps another night will do him some good, remind him that he should approach others in a different manner here in Colorado Springs." He sat back and considered her. "And that leaves you free to accompany me tomorrow night to Glen Eyrie, right?"

Moira struggled to find the best answer among the options. "Glen Eyrie?"

"The Palmers' castle, a half hour's ride away. It is lovely. You will be enchanted."

She looked up at him, knowing he had her in a corner. She could muster no charm. "It seems I have little choice."

"No, indeed you do not," he said with an easy smile. "But trust me, you will not regret your decision."

She rose. "I'd like to go back to the hotel now," she said. "I must change and return to the sanatorium to attend my sister."

He stood, unruffled by her barely disguised anger, and set his napkin on the chair before straightening his jacket. "Then I shall take you."

Moira wished she could deny him that, insist she see herself back, but it wasn't safe, a woman alone in a new town, especially at this hour. Thoughts of the three miners who had waylaid her yesterday cascaded through her mind. Swallowing a sigh, she waited while Reid walked around the table and placed a hand on her lower back, gesturing forward.

"Moira—"

"Miss St. Clair," she corrected crossly.

He raised his chin and studied her down the length of his nose. "Tread carefully, my dear. This is not your town. It is mine."

Chapter ❁ 6

Odessa awakened to her doctor unwrapping her bandages and Nurse Packard on the other side of the bed. Moira stood in the corner and then moved to the bed to take her hand when Odessa caught her eye.

"Is it awful?" Odessa managed to ask, despite her terrible thirst. This morning, every muscle in her body ached, probably the result of her fall.

"Not so awful," said the doctor kindly. "The wounds are superficial. They will heal quickly."

Odessa accepted that information with some skepticism. But it mattered not—the damage was not something she could undo. Her thoughts cast back to that night, the night Sam died. Her memory had cleared, and over and over she relived those moments that drove her to her feet and into Sam's room.

Dr. Morton studied her, watching her chest move beneath her thin chemise, and then he bent over to listen at her mouth. He pulled down one eyelid and then the other.

"You must calm yourself," he said with concern. "Consider pleasant things, quiet things. Breathe in slowly, Odessa ... and now out ... That's it. Good girl."

He rose to depart and Moira cried out, "But Doctor! Is she all right? Shouldn't you do something else?"

He eyed her, then gave them both a warm smile. "Miss St. Clair, twenty years ago, Odessa might have perished. One in ten still die today," he said. His words sounded callous, but his eyes were kind as he turned toward Odessa. "But you, my dear, are in the finest care, in the finest city for consumption care in the country. In short, it won't be long until we have you up and on your feet. Then soon into a saddle and on the trail with the others."

Odessa remembered Sam telling her about the long train of twenty men and two women, many of them deathly pale, bundled and saddled up for their morning constitutional into the mountains—part of the sanatorium's prescription for health.

"I confess," she murmured, "it's difficult to imagine."

He met her gaze and then examined her cheeks again, turning her chin with his hand. "Most of the patients felt the same as you three days in. All are pleasantly surprised at what they can tolerate a week later. I find that your doctors in other places have not demanded enough of you, and in doing so have robbed you of the chance at proper health. Do you trust me?"

Odessa shifted in the bed, considered his question. "As much as I've learned to trust any other doctor."

He smiled. "Fair enough. You shall soon see, Miss St. Clair, that I am entirely trustworthy. And that you've placed your life in the right man's hands."

"I hope you are right, Doctor."

His smile faded. "Do not rise without assistance. Today you begin more advanced meal treatments. The sustenance will help you keep your feet when next you wish to try." He eyed Nurse Packard. "She is to be moved to the sunporch from one to four."

"Yes, Doctor."

With that, he was gone, already on to the next patient. Odessa met the nurse's eye. "What happened to Mr. O'Toole? How did he die?"

Nurse Packard raised an eyebrow and settled her covers again. "Well, it wasn't the consumption, that's for certain. He had made excellent progress." She looked at Odessa quickly. Clearly, she had shared more than she had intended.

Odessa nodded and frowned, wondering if she should confide what she heard that night. But something told her to keep silent. She gave Moira a little shake of her head, urging her to do the same, but her sister was frowning, thinking hard.

"What about you, Odessa?" Moira said. "Why were you on the prowl at such a late hour that night?"

Odessa shook her head, as if embarrassed. "Delirious, most likely. Perhaps I caught a chill, a fever even. That happened from time to time in Philadelphia." She looked over at Moira and her sister nodded, as if confirming her story.

Nurse Packard nodded. "Common enough among consumptives." She shook a finger in Odessa's face. "Just see to it that you stay put from here on out or we'll have to tie you down." She smiled over her firm words, but was there a note of true warning behind them? Odessa could not be sure.

Bryce watched Odessa enter the sunporch that afternoon on the arm of her younger sister. She glanced his way, lifted a hand as if she had just remembered the bandages on her face, and then quickly looked away. Her sister helped her into the cot, then efficiently covered her with the blankets, tucking her in so thoroughly that Bryce was sure she couldn't move. She remained still, trying to catch her breath for several moments.

"It's terribly cold in here," her sister complained. "Surely this cannot be entirely edifying for the patients." Her green eyes looked Bryce's way, and he noticed they were the exact same color as Odessa's. Like their brother's. *Family trait.*

"Take a blanket and wrap up," Odessa said to her. She tiredly glanced from him to her sister. "Mr. McAllan," Odessa said. "I ... I was most sorry to hear the news of Sam's passing. Please accept my condolences. He seemed like a kind man."

Bryce stared at the ceiling. "Thank you, Miss St. Clair. He was." He paused. "I gather you encountered some mishap of your own. Are you all right?"

"Fair to middling, as my grandmother used to say," she said. A smile briefly spread across her lush lips, but then faded. "I was up and prowling when I was ill prepared to do so."

"Ahh. I, too, have fallen victim to the consumptive's faint."

"Yes, well, I did it quite elaborately, don't you think?" She gestured toward her swathed face.

"Quite." He picked up his paintbrush again, intent on giving the sisters a sense of privacy, even if he could hear their every word.

"Odessa, what has come over you?" Moira asked in an undertone. "I am the dramatic one of the family."

Odessa leaned back into her pillow and closed her eyes and sighed. "I know not. Only that being here, so narrowly cheating death, then seeing Sam, so alone in his room ... there's an air of madness about me. It's as if I've lost any sense of propriety."

Moira remained where she was, silent. She pulled the blanket a bit closer around her shoulders.

"Where is Nic today?"

Moira looked down and to the left.

"Moira," Odessa prompted.

"He is seeing to business matters. Busy."

"Busy?"

"Indisposed."

"Indisposed? In what way?"

"Now, now. Don't get alarmed. It's not good for your breathing." She leaned closer and then glanced nervously toward Bryce. "Please, Dess. If the doctor finds I've upset you enough to send you into another fit, he'll never let me return."

Odessa nodded, silently urging her on, while taking her note of warning to be cautious, aware of her mind, heart, and lungs. "Please. Quickly. Out with it."

"He was fighting again, Dess. And Reid Bannock, the sheriff here, won't abide by any brawling. He's as firm on street fighting as General Palmer is on drinking in this town—they'll have none of it. High and dry, peaceful, orderly. That's how they like it here. And Nic … you can see that train wreck about to occur. He spent the night in jail."

"Jail?" Odessa sputtered, forgetting to keep their hushed undertone. "He spent the night in jail?"

"Don't fret, Dess. Sheriff Bannock only wanted him to remember the lesson. He assures me he'll be out tomorrow at the latest."

"How? How do you know all this?"

"From Sheriff Bannock himself. He took me to supper last night."

Odessa groaned and leaned her head back on the pillow. "Don't even speak of it, Moira. Tell me you were not out on the arm of the town sheriff."

Moira stuck her chin up. "Well, why not? Surely there are worse men in this town."

Odessa raised her head and stared at her. "You promised Papa. No suitors for a year."

"He's not a suitor. He's the sheriff. And he's holding our brother."

"Moira. Tell me what's happening."

"No, Dess." She rose, glanced Bryce's way and then back to her sister. "You know all you need to. I shouldn't have told you anything. I'll return tonight to stay with you, and tomorrow Nic and I will call upon you. You just concentrate on getting better."

"Moira—"

She leaned down to kiss Odessa on the forehead and then fled.

"Moira!" But she was already out the door.

Several long minutes passed by and Bryce began to believe she had fallen asleep.

"Mr. McAllan," she said then.

"Bryce, please call me Bryce."

"Bryce, do you have any siblings?"

"An older brother, back East. But we barely speak. Had a falling out some time ago."

"Ahh. There might be some measure of blessing in that."

Bryce laughed under his breath.

"Mr. McAllan—" she began, forgetting.

"Bryce."

"Bryce. Did Sam have any enemies?" Slowly, she turned her wide green eyes upon him and he frowned at her.

"Miss St. Clair—"

"Odessa."

"Odessa, why would you ask such a question?"

She continued to study him, measuring him with her eyes, weighing her decision. "Because," she said at last, "I think … I believe someone murdered him."

After Dominic's jailers had taken away his lunch tray, Sheriff Bannock approached the cell and grinned at Dominic as he tossed in a copy of the city newspaper.

Frowning in suspicion, Nic bent and retrieved the paper, then slowly rose. It had been neatly folded in six segments, the article about Dominic's arrest calling out to him with the headline, "Newcomer Jailed for Brawling." He sighed and pinched his nose, trying to hold back the rising anger. That's just what the sheriff wanted to see after all—him unable to control his fury, giving him further excuse for punishment. *Use your brain as well as your brawn, Nic.*

He handed the *Gazette* back through the bars to the sheriff with a thin-lipped smile. Just his luck to land in jail before the weekly paper went to press.

Sheriff Bannock raised his hands. "You keep it. Some reading material would probably be welcome 'bout now."

"I read enough. Shame the reporter—or his source—neglected to mention the three miners making inappropriate comments to my sister. Shame, too, that the sheriff didn't jail the men who started all of this."

The sheriff studied him. "No laws against a man flirting with a pretty girl. You, man, just have to figure out how to deal with that pretty sister, protect her, without resorting to fighting."

Dominic met his eye. "Agreed. Now can you release me?"

"Tomorrow. One more night in the cell. You'll be free at daybreak, providing that you can give me your word about the things we've discussed."

Dominic shifted, trying to maintain his composure. He licked his lips. "Sheriff, this has been quite enough to prove your point. And my sister Moira, she's pretty young to be on her own in a strange town. She must be frightened, all alone. That's how all this started—"

"I understand, Mr. St. Clair." The sheriff shook his head and then looked him in the eye. "But I don't want you to fret over your sister. I'll have no woman fear for her safety in this town. I'll be certain to look in on her myself. You have my word."

Biting back a retort, Nic gripped tightly to the bars and watched the sheriff saunter away.

He should be mollified, encouraged that Moira would be looked after.

Why, then, did he feel as though he had just been had?

It took Bryce several moments to say anything in response to Odessa's audacious claim. He glanced toward the door, then wearily pulled the blankets from his torso and came to his feet. This was not the sort of conversation they should have from across the room. And he had to give her the envelope.

Odessa glanced his way and then away as if she had forgotten she had said anything. A self-conscious hand went to her bandages and then she wrung her hands. He sat down in the chair that Moira had vacated. The hallway was still empty, quiet. "Tell me what you saw. Or heard. Please, Odessa. For Sam."

"I—I am uncertain. Perhaps … you know how this disease is. Half the time I feel as if I live in a fog. Do you?"

He rested his forearms on his legs and leaned forward, waiting. Odessa St. Clair did not seem the sort of woman to make idle statements for effect. "That night …" he led.

"I was feverish," she said. "I awakened, terribly thirsty, not sure where I was. I realized I was thirsty, but that wasn't what had brought me around."

"It was …"

"Sounds. Terrible sounds."

Bryce frowned. "What sort of sounds? Moaning? Shouting?"

"Gasping. Suffocating. Silence."

Bryce leaned back. "Odessa, Sam was old. It could've been his heart, the consumption—"

"And I heard footsteps, and a floorboard creak. And then saw a shadow, fleeing …"

Her eyes were wide and still, staring at the ceiling as if reliving the terror.

"Someone was with him," Bryce filled in.

Her eyes met his again. "Someone was with him," she returned.

"And so you went in there? You got up out of your bed and went in there?"

"After the other one departed." She gave him a humorless smile.

"I attempted it. But didn't get very far before I saw him, Bryce. Saw his mouth open, knew he was dead, and then there was no more strength within me and I fell. Must have hit my head on the way down. I have the goose egg right here to testify to my folly."

"It was very brave of you, Odessa. Foolish, but brave."

She smiled too and leaned back against her pillow as if weary and stared up at the planked ceiling.

"Odessa—you've had a rough go of it. Are you certain it wasn't a nightmare? A horrible nightmare that coincided with the terrible moment of Sam's death? Perhaps you heard him struggling for breath and your imagination invented the rest."

"I know what I heard, Bryce." She glanced at him, then lifted a hand to her brow as if battling a headache. "I wish I hadn't. I can't get it out of my mind. And I've told you because I could see you and Sam were dear to each other. He liked you, trusted you."

Bryce sat back and considered her, then gave her a brief nod.

"Who would gain from his death?"

Bryce shook his head, his eyes flitting about as if he was thinking it through. "I have no idea. Listen, before anyone comes—at Sam's funeral I was approached by an attorney. He gave me two envelopes, one for me, and one for you."

"For me?"

Bryce nodded. Nurse Packard came in then, saw Odessa take the envelope from Bryce. The nurse gave him a wise look and her eyes slid to Odessa and back to him. "Dr. Morton does not abide fraternization," she sniffed.

"I understand," Bryce said gravely. The nurse left and Bryce winked at Odessa.

She smiled and glanced down at the envelope, as if disbelieving that her name was across the center front. "Why …?"

"Sam had his own ideas about things. Kept his own counsel. No doubt he was up to some sort of mischief."

She slid her finger under the flap and opened it, then pulled out a single piece of paper. It took everything in Bryce not to ask what it said. She appeared to read it through several times before leaning back, her brow furrowed.

"Odessa?"

She started, as if she'd forgotten he was there, and glanced his way. "It's a poem, directions of a sort. Yours, too?"

Bryce hesitated for a moment. "The deed to his land. He left it all—a couple hundred acres and his cabin."

"He had no family?"

"None for some time. Guess I was as close as it came." He stared at her. "Odessa, I don't mean to pry, but Sam's poem for you—is there something in there that confirms your idea that someone took his life?"

"Yes," she said. "I believe so. Was Sam a wealthy man?"

Bryce shrugged. "He got along. Made his living as a sheep rancher. But once in a while, he'd spend money that surprised me. The private room here. A new suit."

Odessa considered that.

"If … if you're right, Odessa, does it place you in danger, having that note from Sam? Should we go to the sheriff?"

Odessa shook her head, raising her fingers to massage her temples. "No. He'll only remind me that I saw nothing. Only heard sounds that anyone could say was merely Sam, giving in to the consumption. No, I'd say the fewer people who know about this, the better."

Bryce paused. "What is it, Odessa, that makes you not fear me?"

Odessa glanced at him, knew she was blushing. "I am a fairly good judge of character. Let's just say that I feel inclined to gamble that I'm right about you."

She closed her eyes, intending to end the conversation at this most improper and forward juncture, but as she did so, she stole one last glance at Bryce. And he was smiling.

The sheriff flicked the reins over a fine black mare, and the horse lurched their small cart forward. In spite of herself, Moira was pleased to be getting out, to see more of what Colorado Springs had to offer, to "making familiar what was unfamiliar," as Nic had repeated. Reid drove her down Tejon Street, which was becoming the city's main thoroughfare more than the intended, flashier Pikes Peak. A few brick buildings were going up, standing in stark contrast to their smaller, more modest wooden neighbors.

Down one street, Moira caught a view of a massive building of limestone blocks. "What is that going up down there?"

The sheriff smiled proudly. "That's General Palmer's new opera house. It should open within the year."

"Oh! I had heard he was building it, and I simply could not dare to believe it."

Reid glanced down at her, curiosity rife on his face. "You like opera?"

"I do. I adore singing and always dreamed I'd be a part of the theater."

The sheriff nodded, a measure of concern lifting a brow. "After dinner, General Palmer and the men will retire for cigars in his den. But Queen, Mrs. Palmer, she always likes to take the ladies and share some music. I think you will enjoy it."

"Oh, I will!" Moira said, almost clapping, she was so happy. It had been weeks and weeks since she had enjoyed a nice evening of music, since the Frasier dinner party in Philadelphia, and before that, the Donnavon Ball, held at their estate just outside of the city. Just thinking about those two wondrous nights made her sick with longing. Despite the progress Colorado Springs was making, she could not imagine this town ever rivaling the fine society of Philadelphia. But if Mrs. Palmer cared to try, Moira was more than happy to support the effort.

They drove on a narrow dirt road, crossing Monument Creek, then joining a larger dirt road that paralleled the mountains, what the sheriff called the stage road. Soon, they passed amazing red rocks bursting from the earth. Above and beyond them was the blue, snow-covered Pikes Peak.

"Like it?" Reid asked, slyly glancing over at her. "That there is the Garden of the Gods. Used to be sacred land to the Utes."

"I can see why. They are captivating! Like a bunch of hands all thrusting their way toward heaven!"

Once they passed the Garden, the little black mare climbed a hill and then Reid directed her left, into a canyon. "General calls this 'Queen's Canyon.' This whole parcel of land belongs to the Palmers."

More red rocks jutted upward about them, like forgotten neighbors cast out of the Garden. Steep cliffs climbed on either side. To

their left, in the dusk of evening, stood a ram, looking back toward
the city as if he were a sentinel for others. To their right, a bald
eagle landed on a ledge, atop a monstrous nest of sticks. Beyond the
natural walls was the glen, made up of lovely meadows and twisting
piñon pines. "The Utes, they liked to winter down in here," Reid
said. "Natural protection, water source … some of the prettiest land
in all of the Springs."

"How long ago were the Indians sent away?"

"Back in sixty-eight," he said. "Most went with them to the reservation. Some stayed and learned the white man's ways."

"You mean I might see one? A real Ute?"

"Most likely," he said, mirth knitting his brows together.

"Are they dangerous?"

"Nah. Most are harmless. But there are beggar Indians, and I've
had to jail quite a few for stealing. Had to string one up once for
murder."

"Oh! How awful." She sighed dreamily. "I've always wanted to
see a real live Indian."

"Should've been here a couple of decades ago, then. You would've
seen more than your share."

The castle came into view then, as they crossed another small
stone bridge that led them over the creek. The home was a magnificent structure, made of coarsely cut rectangular bricks of limestone.
Beyond it, a red canyon fairly glowed, reflecting the last vestiges
of sunset on her walls. Here and there, a dusting of spring snow
clung to the shadowy crevices. But Moira's eyes were quickly drawn
back to the castle, with leaded glass windows and turrets climbing
upward and a massive courtyard facing the wondrous glen. They

went around the structure, then pulled to a stop in front. A man impeccably dressed in servant's attire appeared to help her down. Another servant came out and greeted them both by name, then led them up the walk to the entrance, while another took the buggy away, presumably to the carriage house they had passed. The horse would be brushed and watered and rested, so that when they were ready to return, she would be fresh for the ride.

Moira paused, imagining how angry Dominic would be if he knew she was here, intending to return home in the dark, alone with a man.

But Nic wasn't here. And he wasn't her parent, but a mere temporary guardian. And her mother wasn't here. Nor was her father. Besides, this was for Nic's benefit as much as for her own.

"Miss St. Clair?" Reid asked, turning back to study her in the entrance.

She shook her head. "Lead on, Sheriff. I am most eager to greet our hosts."

Odessa awakened at midnight, feeling a little sick to her stomach. She was certain it was the result of the two glasses of milk, three eggs, and large piece of meat the nurse's assistant had watched her consume for dinner. She didn't think she would ever eat again. But that was part of the regimen here at the sanatorium. According to Nurse Packard, it was what had made them famous. The massive amounts of food gave patients extra strength to battle the ailments of their lungs. Within a couple of weeks, they would expect her to double what she had consumed this night.

She sat up and let her feet fall to the floor. It was after nine o'clock, when Moira had said she would come. Where was she? Was she not coming? Was something wrong?

"Need something, miss?"

Odessa gasped and whirled, then saw the night nurse looking in on her from the doorway. "No, no, Nurse. I just have a bit of indigestion."

"Let me go and fetch some Manitou mineral water. It will settle your stomach quickly."

"That would be wonderful. Thank you."

The nurse scurried out and Odessa sat there, brushing her feet over the rough edge of the floor where two planks joined. Her eyes shifted from the dark hallway to her pillow. She considered how long it would take for the woman to return with her mineral water and, deciding to risk it, slowly eased the paper from beneath her pillow.

"Why me?" she had asked Bryce earlier, before they left the porch. "Why leave this to me?" He had shrugged. "As I said, Sam kept his own counsel." He shifted and Odessa saw that he colored a bit at the neck. "Probably his own crazy kind of matchmaking—give me the land, and you the rationale to find your way there."

Odessa's eyes ran over the now-familiar words.

> *Find two forgotten men*
> *Desperate for drink*
> *Perched over a river winding*
> *Never to reach her shore*
> *See God's finger pointing*
> *Southwesterly*

And a lady and child

Now pillars of stone

Who lead the way

Follow them to a valley sweet

Damp to her East

Wounds to her West

Land in my mother's name

Within an old sheepherder's cabin

In high hills of piñon pine

Chest beneath the floor

Wealth that burns

And that that is eternal

Hearing the nurse on the stair, she hurriedly folded and stashed the sheet of paper beneath her pillow again.

"Thank you, Nurse," she said, accepting the glass of bubbling water. She swallowed the first gulp and tried to hide her distaste. It smelled and tasted of sulphur, or rotten eggs. For heaven's sake, if the eggs of her supper hadn't managed to make her purge, this was bound to. Still, she gulped the rest down and sat there, staring at her glass.

"There now, did it help?"

Odessa considered it, then burped from the bubbles. The two women laughed together. "Oh, now I feel better! Thank you," Odessa said in dismissal. "Surely I can sleep now."

"Very good," said the nurse, and with that, she disappeared down the hall.

It was troubling, this. Sam had been doing better. Had he

somehow known he was dying, seen what others could not? Had he summoned the strength to have an attorney call upon him, draw up a will? It would've had to have been the day after they'd met! Why her? Was it because he merely wished to give her something, something to think about beyond this place, this time of healing? She had to admit that having something to occupy her mind during the long, languid hours at the sanatorium was a gift. Or had he intended to give her impetus to regain her health and make the journey south to the beautiful Sangre de Cristos? Or was it indeed some sort of mischievous matchmaking? She sighed and settled back under the covers.

But sleep felt far from her reach indeed. Because all she could think of was the night that Sam O'Toole had died. Over and over, she searched her blurry memory, trying to re-create the sounds that had drawn her forward in fear. She could've been wrong. She might've misinterpreted what she heard.

But if she hadn't, were she and Bryce in grave danger?

Chapter ✦ 7

At a table of sixteen in the massive dining hall of Glen Eyrie, all eyes hovered on Moira St. Clair. She held them with the ease of a vivacious teacher surrounded by devoted students, dragging her long lashes upward to meet the gaze of fascinated gentlemen, deferring repeatedly to Queen, her hostess, until the woman was as smitten as the men, and complimenting the others, easing them into conversation until each of them felt she was somehow *more than* just by being in Moira's presence.

How simple this is, Moira thought, well practiced in the ways of social etiquette and niceties, knowing how to make friends of both men and women. It was a dangerous walk, using coquettish ways with the men that made them puff their chests out like strutting animals, while befriending the women so they did not assume defensive positions against her. But by the time dinner was finished, Moira felt in command of her new little world, small that it might be. She knew that numerous invitations would follow to dine with the others, if not to return to Glen Eyrie. In Philadelphia, she had been the debutante to watch. If her future was to unfold as she wished, she would have to make sure all eyes continued to do so.

She laughed, listening intently to the older woman across the table. But she could feel the heat of a man's gaze upon her, and slowly, methodically moved her eyes across the silk-fringed tapestry tablecloth, past empty silver platters being lifted by uniformed butlers, to his chest, to his shoulders, and finally, his eyes. She let them rest there a moment, fully taking in for the first time another newcomer to the Springs, Jesse McCourt. An actor, of all things, en route to Denver, merely stopping for a night to visit a relative among them. Deliciously talking to the general about bringing his troupe here for the opening of the opera house.

He was lovely, a man who would fill several slots on her dance card at home, sporting a strong cleft chin and warm eyes that covered her with a searching gaze. His chin reminded her of Reid, and just in time, she looked up and to her left to catch the sheriff laugh at the end of Queen's story and then smile down on Moira.

It was then that she felt Reid's big hand move under the table and brush against her thigh. He was looking away from her now, but his hand pressed, skirted, and then clamped down around her leg. She froze, aghast at his forward move, and flitted her eyes about the table, feeling a sudden blush rise from her neck and begin a steady ascent up her face.

Jesse continued to study her. "General," he said, placing a napkin on the table as his host had done before him. "It is true you have in your possession the finest of Cuba's cigars, or is that mere rumor?"

General Palmer laughed and sat back against his massive, hand-carved chair, a diminutive king wielding his power. "As ever, Mr. McCourt, your timing is perfect. Come," he said, lifting a hand in the air in invitation, "let us retire to gentlemen's quarters and leave the women to their idle pleasantries."

Reid's hand abruptly left Moira's thigh and she rose in turn, wondering if his hot fingers had left wrinkles in her teal silk. He rose to follow his host, General Palmer. She eyed Jesse across the table and gave him the tiniest of nods before the men all headed off as a group. Moira turned to join Queen, taking her hostess's offered arm as she led the way to the blue room, the women's group following the men.

"Are you all right, my dear?" Queen asked.

"Of course. Why do you ask?"

"You appear a bit flushed."

Moira smiled over at her hostess, a small woman. "It must be all that fine food and drink. It really was amazingly delicious. I don't know how you can manage to bring all the comforts of the East way out here in the West. I feel as if I'm in a dream."

Queen smiled. "A princess in her castle? I confess I feel the same. I thought it a bit much but the general insisted."

"A castle fit for a queen," Moira deferred with a grin and a nod. "Your king must be sad indeed when you all depart." She thought of the three small children in stiffly ironed dresses and perfectly curled hair, paraded through the dining hall by a nursemaid. Later, they had peeked out from a loft, watching the adults at dinner as if observing a grand banquet play. They had been led off, all three faces glum, when their nurse discovered them again and pulled them into the shadows. It reminded Moira of her and Odessa when they were small, always wishing, wishing to be big.

"It is not as either of us had envisioned. But the doctors tell me my heart cannot endure this altitude, and my husband's heart has belonged to this city since the first day he laid out the streets with the surveyors."

"I am deeply sorry."

Queen eyed her with one eyebrow lifted and gave her a small smile. "We make do. The general will sojourn east to visit us. I fear I shall not return again."

"I hope that does not prove true."

Obviously growing weary of the subject, Queen said, "It is our understanding that the heirs of St. Clair Press wish to establish a bookshop here in the Springs."

"Indeed. My father wishes to expand his enterprise, not only publishing, but selling his wares. Since my sister was to come here for treatment of consumption, he thought it might occupy my brother while she convalesced."

"And it sounds as if your brother is in need of … occupation."

Moira paused, careful to choose her words wisely "It is always best for Dominic to be engaged, using his hands as well as his mind. Give him a hammer, nails, and some wood and he'd have our father's first bookshop built in a few weeks."

"He sounds like a true pioneer. But why begin from scratch if there is already something in place to be utilized? The general will enjoy having a fine bookshop in town," Queen said. "Come. You must meet Amy Brennan. Her husband owns three square blocks of land downtown and will aid you."

Moira smiled and squeezed her hostess's arm. "Thank you so much, Mrs. Palmer." She put a hand on her heart. "That would be an answer to our prayers."

They swept down the massive hall, then down the wide, cascading stairs edged with stone banisters, turning, then turning again until they were again in the grand reception hall. One corner of the wide entry led to the stairs, another to a small front parlor, another to the blue room, and still another to a welcome expanse of solarium glass and a warm, wood-paneled den with a massive fireplace. A fire crackled in the hearth already.

The men moved off with a wave and a nod to the women, while the women turned into a north-facing room lit with a hundred candles. As Queen entered, a woman at the grand piano began playing. Moira felt quick, hot tears lace her lashes. It was as though she were truly entering a grand home in Philadelphia—it made her miss all that she'd left behind. Perhaps she had been wrong about this rough, unsettled country. Perhaps there really was a place for her here.

"Here, Miss St. Clair, please sit with me and Amy," Queen directed, depositing her upon a small divan with the plain-looking woman she had met earlier.

"Mrs. Brennan," Moira said, giving her a warm smile. "I'm afraid we were seated at opposite ends of the table. Please, tell me all about yourself. How did you come to be one of Colorado's first residents?"

"I've always been a Colorado resident, Miss St. Clair," she said, eyeing her with the look of a woman on guard. Clearly, she was well used to the long nose and narrowed eyes of those from the East, scrutinizing pioneers as some odd specimens.

"You have?" Moira gushed, barely letting a breath escape. "You can teach me so much! I am desperate to learn about this new land. It is frightfully beautiful, but a bit overwhelming. Do you ever get used to it?"

"In time," Mrs. Brennan said drily, thawing just a little bit in spite of herself.

Moira kept up her efforts. "Please, grant me a bit of wisdom. What is the most important thing I must remember?"

"Keep the edges of your skirts out of the mud," Mrs. Brennan said.

Moira laughed as if they were sharing a private jest, choosing to ignore the patronizing snippet, and Mrs. Brennan relented a bit. "Mrs. Palmer said that you might be of assistance to me and my brother."

"Oh?"

"Yes," Queen said, rejoining them on the settee after seeing to the other women. "Miss St. Clair's brother is seeking retail space downtown for a bookshop. I think a bookshop would be just the kind of establishment that the general would like to see, don't you agree?"

"Indeed," Mrs. Brennan said with a nod, eyebrows raised. Moira could see she felt caught, like a fly in a spider's web.

"Mr. Brennan has that quaint little shop on Tejon almost complete, does he not?"

"I believe he does."

"Wouldn't that be a good location for a bookshop?"

"I believe it has a tenant already, Queen," Mrs. Brennan said, shifting now with discomfort.

"Oh," Queen said with a slight pout. "A pity, that. To whom?"

"A merchant of dry goods."

"Hmm. Another merchant of dry goods." She let the comment sit for several moments.

"Of course, I could speak to Mr. Brennan about returning the merchant's funds and selling him another plot."

Queen brightened and reached across to place a hand on Mrs. Brennan's arm. Moira noted the large ruby and emeralds that she wore across her short, stubby fingers, felt the visceral pull and might of the woman, and knew she was watching the skilled efforts of a mentor. "That is a fine idea, Amy! A fine idea. I always say you are one of the most clever of my friends here in Colorado. The general will be most pleased."

"You saw him hand off two envelopes to Bryce McAllan?" the man asked.

A shorter man nodded. "Day of the funeral. At the grave site."

"You think it's related to O'Toole calling him in?"

"Hard to consider many other options."

The first man paced, chin in hand. "You certain it's worth pursuit?"

The second man shrugged. "All I know is that O'Toole brought in the highest-grade ore the county assessor had ever seen."

The taller man nodded. "We have O'Toole's signature. We can get to the mine. It'll be ours before month's end."

"Unless he willed the mine to McAllan."

"Has McAllan laid claim to it?"

"Not yet. But he's not exactly in miner condition."

"No matter. While he's laid up, we'll just see if it's as good as the rumors say it might be."

"Only one problem."

"What's that?"

"O'Toole apparently hid the entrance."

"That's impossible."

"Maybe, maybe not. He didn't mine much of the ore.

Consumption made him too poorly. And that creek runs the full length of his property. All five miles of it."

"Five miles!"

"Five miles, winding tighter than a rattler under a rock."

The taller man began pacing again. "Head down now. See if you can find the entrance. Maybe it's not as difficult as they say."

"And if it is?"

"Maybe McAllan holds the keys." The two shared a meaningful look, and the taller man moved to the door. He was stopped by the other. "And when he returns, see if you can persuade the honorable esquire to tell you what those envelopes contained." He slid open a drawer, withdrew a pouch of coins, and tossed them to the other. "There. That ought to prove persuasive enough."

"You sing?" Queen Palmer asked, moving her head closer to speak in a tone barely discernible above Amy Brennan's soprano.

"Me? A bit," Moira deferred. "Forgive me. I was humming, wasn't I?"

Queen nodded, her brown eyes searching Moira's.

"It is a favorite of mine, this song. I could not help myself."

"Then you shall sing the next." Queen patted her arm.

"Oh, I cannot. I did not bring any music with me."

"Pay it no heed. My pianist knows all the best. Opera, hymns, folk tunes," she added in a conspiratorial whisper.

Moira's heart beat a bit faster. Opera? Hymns? Folk tunes? She studied the woman at the piano with renewed interest and tried not to cringe when Amy sang a flat when a sharp should have been met.

Reid had told her that Queen once sang opera, but had been forbidden to take on any duty remotely strenuous following the frightening episode with her heart.

The ladies applauded as Amy completed her song. Moira could hear the gentlemen down the hall laughing uproariously, their laughter fading like fog under sun.

Queen rose. "Thank you so very much, Amy. Would anyone else favor us with a song? Or a bit of drama?" She looked about, but no one rose to her invitation. "No? Then I must invite our newest companion, Moira St. Clair, to come and share her music with us."

Moira paused, deferential, poised, waiting for just the right second to rise and join her hostess. Her mind cascaded through the potential songs she might sing, dismissing one as too ostentatious, another as too vain. Amy had just sung opera, and it would be dangerous to set up a comparison, so she would select something less vaunted. She needed these people, every one of them, as her friends. It was then that it came to her.

Moira turned to the pianist. "Do you know 'Funiculì Finiculà'?" she asked in a whisper.

The young woman smiled and gave her a quick nod.

She paused. "I shall sing the English version, I believe."

"Understood."

"In honor of a new freedom I feel in this country," Moira said, "please permit me to share with you a favorite folk tune of mine."

She began to sing, noting the three Palmer girls in starched white nightshirts, now with hair pinned in curls to their head, peering in the doorway again, obviously delighted by the happy tempo. Moira smiled at them, again remembering happier days with Odessa, dancing together to the happy tune of "Funiculì Finiculà" in the center of the parlor floor, their mother at the piano, singing. She remembered her parents as young and hale and hearty, the boys constantly at play all about them, the future spreading before them like some glorious, undiscovered road. Had her mother known any heartbeat's pause, or had she always been of the ever-forward mind-set?

Some think the world is made for fun and frolic,
And so do I! And so do I!
Some think it well to be melancholic,
To pine and sigh; to pine and sigh;
But I, I love to spend my time in singing,
Some joyous song, some joyous song,
To set the air with music bravely ringing
Is far from wrong! Is far from wrong!
Listen, listen, echoes sound afar!
Listen, listen, echoes sound afar!
Funiculì, funiculà, funiculì, funiculà!
Echoes sound afar, funiculì, funiculà!

Moira remembered her mother, her distant father, remembered what it felt like to wrap her arms around each of them at once, nestled between them. She knew it forced an extra edge of desperate joy, a defiant choice to her tone, which added a jaunty attraction to it. She imagined her family again in that parlor, all together, all well. Before death. Before so much death …

Ah me! 'Tis strange that some should take to sighing,
And like it well! And like it well!

For me, I have not thought it worth the trying,
So cannot tell! So cannot tell!
With laugh, with dance and song the day soon passes
Full soon is gone, full soon is gone,
For mirth was made for joyous lads and lasses
To call their own! To call their own!
Listen, listen, hark the soft guitar!
Listen, listen, hark the soft guitar!
Funiculì, funiculà, funiculì, funiculà!

The song now complete, she let her arm drop to her side. There was a breath in the room, then two. Then grins and applause erupted in the grand hall of Glen Eyrie's castle, the men drawn out of their den—the children shooed up the stairs—the women rising to their feet.

And Moira St. Clair knew she had arrived.

Dominic stared at the newspaper on the cell floor, watching the shadows dance from its curling far edge. The only light was from the lantern on the deputy's desk. The man now snored softly in his chair, his head leaning against the wall behind him, his knees sprawled. The sound grated at Dominic's ears. He forced himself to stay still, to not get up and resume his pacing, worrying about Odessa and Moira…. He lay on his side on the cot, one arm tucked beneath his head. He looked about the wooden walls, devoid of any artwork, and thought of his home in Philadelphia, with its fine papered parlor and vast dining room that had harbored many an author or publishing associate. But those were memories of years past. More and more, the nation's publishing empires had moved north to New York, and the flow of visiting businessmen and authors slowed to a trickle. But still, his father remained as stubbornly attached to Philadelphia and St. Clair Press as he had been to Dominic's mother.

Friends had encouraged him to join them in New York, but still he stayed. The country was young, he said, too young to become so centralized in any industry. He turned a blind eye to the purchasing might that the combined conglomerate wielded, stuck, as if his feet had been planted beside his wife's grave.

And he not only expected Dominic to open a bookshop here in Colorado—Dominic sighed. There was so much Father wanted him to do. On his shoulders rested the hopes of five dead children. Of a dead wife. Of two daughters, now Dominic's primary concern.

But he was in a jail cell in his new hometown.

He stared at the newspaper, shadows dancing, laughing at him.

He closed his eyes, willing strength into his movements, and then he rose, bending over to reach for the paper that Sheriff Bannock had thrown in. Where was the good sheriff now? Looking in on Moira, as promised? Where? How?

He gripped the rough-ground paper, symptomatic of the West's paper poverty, and pulled it closer, eyes not yet focusing on the words.

Father, you knew I wasn't up to the task....

"Newcomer Dominic St. Clair, heir apparent to the St. Clair

Press enterprise of Philadelphia and hopeful book merchant in Colorado Springs, was placed under arrest today...."

I am a man. But a man who wants to make his own way ...

"St. Clair was arrested for disorderly conduct on Colorado Springs' Wahsatch Avenue, for brawling with three miners visiting our fair city from ..."

I cannot bear the entire burden of the St. Clair clan. I cannot be the one hope ... I've already failed you.

Chapter ✿ 8

"You are curiously silent," Moira said to Reid. The lanterns, strung out on arcing metal bands before the horses, barely illuminated ten feet in front of them. The miles between Glen Eyrie and the city seemed to crawl by, but Moira was comforted by a carriage both before and behind them, other guests of the Palmers who had declined their kind invitation to stay the night in the castle. The weather was unseasonably warm, the mud puddles no longer frosting over, even in the cool of night.

He smiled over at her. "Forgive me. Concentrating on the road. If we suffer an accident, my lone prisoner might throttle me."

Moira smiled, covering a pang of pain at his reference to Dominic. What were they to do if Reid refused to honor his promise the next day? They were on their own here in the West, something neither of them were fully prepared for. Moira constantly caught herself looking over her shoulder, looking for her father, who had always been there.

"I had no idea, Moira."

Moira focused on his words again, embarrassed to note he had been speaking and she had been too lost in thought to hear him. "No idea?"

"No idea you were such an accomplished singer. When you sang that song …"

Moira studied him in the yellow, pale light. He appeared visibly moved. But this was the man who had made inappropriate advances beneath the Palmers' table. Dangerous. Perhaps the most dangerous person she had ever met, capable of wielding power over her and hers that she did not care to fully acknowledge.

He coughed, clearing his throat, and glanced down at her again. "It was perhaps the most delightful thing I've ever witnessed."

She stared into his eyes, melting in admiration and pleasure, but knew that behind them was a steely strength that was a threat. She had to tread carefully here, like a mule on a high, narrow mountain path, a precipice on either side.

"You honor me with your favor, Sheriff," she said quietly, not too warm, leaning slightly away.

"The favor is unavoidable. You are as talented as you are beautiful, Moira St. Clair. There has never been a woman who has caught my eye as completely and suddenly as you."

Moira smiled. "Sheriff, I know many a woman would be so honored by your words. But I am … conflicted. Like a bird caught in a cage. Just as my brother is now in your cage." She stared at him until he again glanced her way.

He caught her eye and held it a moment, then looked back to the horses. "I'll go and release him tonight," he said, voice raw, naked, hopeful.

"No," she returned softly. "Tomorrow morning, as you promised. Then, with my brother's blessing, we shall see where this leads. He is the man my father entrusted with my guardianship. Would it be befitting to proceed without him?"

Reid glowered over his reins, not answering. He knew she had him. He had made gains this day, but in holding her brother, the brother she wished him to befriend, he had lost. How to free a prisoner and gain his permission to court his sister at once?

She could see him churning the idea over in his mind. But he was not like the boys at home who had lined up to court her, young men of means seeking a potential bride. He was a man. Life-hardened. Moira felt his experience, his age like an iron rod within him and knew she must proceed carefully.

Soon, the dim oil lamps of the Springs' downtown came into view as they turned around a curve in the road. In minutes, they had crossed the rough, narrow bridge and emerged on Cascade and soon reached the Antlers Hotel. Reid pulled his horse to a stop, and the mare stood there, breath crystallizing in the night air.

"I'll wait here and take you over to the sanatorium when you're ready."

"No need. My sister is surely long asleep by now. I'll attend her in the morning."

"Are you certain?" He seemed to be reluctant to let the evening come to an end.

"Entirely," she said.

Reid set the brake and came around the carriage. He lifted her slowly down. Moira pushed away, but he held her waist in his broad hands, staring down intently on her.

"I have serious intentions when it comes to you, Moira," he said.

She glanced up at him, playing up the flirtation to cover her unease. "One never knows where these things shall lead. Speak to my brother, Reid, and let time take its due course."

He bent his head as if to kiss her, but she tore away.

"I'm a patient man, Moira St. Clair," he called.

She moved up the hotel steps and then glanced over her shoulder. "We shall see how patient you are. Thank you for a delightful evening."

She moved into the hotel, his gentle laughter echoing after her, muted only by the closing glass door.

Dominic dozed on the cot but was instantly awake when the door opened.

It was the sheriff. He shook the deputy's shoulder, chiding him for sleeping while on duty, but immediately moved over to Dominic's cell.

Dominic swung his feet over the side and rubbed his head. He knew better than to stand.

"Probably wondering why I'm here so late," the sheriff said.

"Partly."

"I looked in on your sister. Did you one better, actually," he said, playing with the iron ring of keys in his hands, "and took her to General Palmer's for the evening."

Nic raised an eyebrow and nodded, not looking him in the eye. If he did, he knew the sheriff would see his fury. He had overstepped his bounds. Moira was young, so easily taken advantage of, regardless of her ability to manipulate people. There was much for her to learn.

"You didn't tell me she was a songbird."

"You didn't ask."

"She's as talented as she is beautiful."

"That she is."

"I came here to offer you a deal."

Nic paused. "I'm listening."

"Allow me to court her, and I let you out tonight, right now."

Nic let out a scoffing laugh. "Or else what? You'll keep me here forever? No judge will tolerate that." He looked up at the sheriff then, unable to keep the challenge from his voice.

"No," the sheriff said, still playing with the keys, rolling them around and around the ring. "But the judge agrees with me and General Palmer. We abide no drinking nor brawling. We don't keep brawlers in jail, but we have on occasion escorted them to the edge of town and persuaded them never to return."

Nic rose, unable to stop himself.

"You and I got off on the wrong foot, brother," the sheriff went on. "I'm hoping we can get past that. Frankly, I'm looking to settle down, have a family." He inserted the key in the lock and turned it, intently watching Dominic between the bars. "I'd like to see if Moira and I get on."

"My sister is not thinking of settling down yet. Our father does not wish her to take a serious suitor. Her mind flits from one fanciful thing to the next—and that includes men." He shook his head. "No, if it's a wife you're seeking, I'd look elsewhere."

The sheriff grinned and stood beside the open door. "Even wild horses can be tamed, in time."

"Moira is not a brute animal, a filly to be broken."

Reid cocked his head. "No. She's definitely more than that. But she needs a strong man's hand to guide her."

"Yes, her brother's."

"With some shaping, she shall be magnificent."

"Indeed she will," Dominic said. He bit into his tongue until he tasted blood and rather than challenge the sheriff further, looked away. *Use your brain as well as brawn, Nic. Brain as well as brawn.*

"So as I see it," the sheriff said, looking in at him, "you're at a crossroads, Mr. St. Clair. Stay here, make a life, build the bookshop, take part in the wealth that is to be Colorado Springs. All I ask is that you grant me permission to call upon your sister. I'll write to your father, ask his permission to formally court if we get on."

All at once, Nic could see the way out. He could grant Reid Bannock to call on his sister. But there was no agreement for anything more. *Moira or Father can refuse him....* She had certainly toyed with many other powerful young men as a favor to their father—and he always managed to extricate her from the courtship before it went too far. Could they not do that once more now? Here?

His breathing came more steadily now and a tiny smile edged at his lips. He reached out a hand and Reid shook it, each man staring the other in the eye.

As Dominic walked past the deputy and exited the building, he gave way to a full grin. Sheriff Reid Bannock had permission to call upon his sister. How would he like it when he discovered that only chaperoned visits and excursions were sanctioned by the St. Clairs?

Chapter ❊ 9

The next morning dawned cold and bright. As was the routine, every able patient assembled in the main parlor downstairs, watching as stable hands saddled horses. Ten or more patients rode in the morning, into the hills and canyons that lined the city's edge; the other half went in the afternoon, returning just before dinner. Every other day, a larger group—but not all—rode out for the entire day, often not returning until after nightfall, but usually bringing back a string of fish or a freshly killed deer to be gutted, skinned, and carved into fat venison roasts.

It was part of the therapy at the sanatorium. Long draughts of fresh, mountain air, air so dry that it made their noses bleed. But it was plentiful and clean. Exercise, as much as they could tolerate, building muscles long dormant as they battled to breathe. Given the countless canyons and old Indian trails at their disposal to explore, it was easy to keep the patients' attention on the path and off of their own breathing. Then hale amounts of food, vast portions of red meat, large trout, frothy fresh milk, eggs—fried, scrambled, or hard-boiled.

Once in a while, an attendant would return, bringing a patient who was coughing up blood or was too weak with fever and chills to continue. But by and large, Odessa had to admit, the patients did seem to thrive in the natural air, coming back with ruddy cheeks and bright pink noses and eyes alight with stories to tell.

They all began on the porch, taking in the air there, or if suffering a relapse as Bryce had done, returning there. Next they were
ensconced beside Monument Creek, or even in a boat laden with
blankets, fishing for hours on end. The sanatorium had dug out a
large pool beside a massive cottonwood, and the waterway flowed
gently into the chasm, creating a slow eddy. When Odessa sat upon
the boat in its center, she gradually spun around. It was lazy and
invigorating at the same time. It felt good to be doing something
useful when she brought in her first fish a week after she had arrived
in Colorado.

"Do they have fish in Philadelphia?" Bryce asked, recovering
from a coughing fit after his walk down the hillside to the creek. He
had his easel and paint bag over his shoulder, which he slowly set
before him.

She smiled at him from the boat. "One or two." Gently, she
pulled the hook from the brown trout's jaw and set the fish, wrig-
gling still, in the bottom of the boat. "My grandfather used to take
me and my brother out fishing on occasion. He favored a narrow,
deep river with a slow eddy, like this one here. He was always trying
to snag a massive, old bass that continually eluded him. Hooked him
a few times but never managed to bring him in."

Bryce laughed as he got the easel legs in place. "Always one in
every river, stream, pond, or lake."

Odessa decided she liked the sound of his laughter, deep and
warm. It was the kind of laugh that would make any house a home.
Her grandfather used to laugh like that. But she couldn't remember
her father ever laughing in the same manner. Was that because he
never did, or because he had lost the ability to laugh as each of their

family members died? Did she simply not remember? She searched her mind, wishing, hoping for the memory. Gentle, sad smiles she remembered. But no laughter.

"I've said something that has upset you," Bryce said, settling the canvas atop the easel and then leaning back upon his stool, gathering his strength. He had ridden out with the others on the previous day's trail ride and it had clearly taxed him.

"No." She sighed. She glanced over at him. "Your laughter simply made me remember my grandfather. I miss him. And his laugh." She cast out her line again, watching as the hook floated for a moment on the moving surface and then suddenly dropped.

"I had a grandfather with a good laugh too," he said.

"Where did he live? If I may presume to ask such intimacies."

"It's not presumptuous at all," he returned, as he uncovered his palette and dabbed a deep blue pigment onto the wood. "Both my mother's and my father's people hailed from Maine for several generations. But an uncle came west, here to Colorado. We've always imported and bred horses, and we needed more land."

"There's a lot of that here."

"Yes, indeed."

"Are your parents still with you?"

"No," he said, resettling his blankets around his shoulders. "They passed on."

"I'm sorry. And your uncle, he is at the ranch?"

"No, he died too, this past year. He was building a house, hoping to marry his love from Maine and bring her west, when he died."

"I'm so sorry. That is tragic."

"It's all right. He died doing what he loved to do—running

horses. Just hit a squirrel hole, fell and broke his neck. It was over fast …" He glanced up at her, as if embarrassed that he had shared more than he meant to.

"So it's just you? Running the ranch?" she said.

"Me and my foreman. It's a lot, running the ranch alone. We have quite a few ranch hands to help, but it's really Tabito who bears the brunt of it. And every time I head east or beyond to see to the business, I seem to come back sicker than when I left."

"You can't do this sort of thing—convalesce, recover—while on your own ranch? Seems to me all they do here is feed us and send us out to take in some fresh air."

He gave her a small smile. "I have a hard time not overextending myself when I'm home. They send us out on horses to ride a trail, sure. But at home, I'm out from dawn to dusk, working, not merely riding."

She nodded. "It would be difficult. To see the work and simply turn away. I suppose there isn't much time for painting there."

"No, there's not."

"Are you about done with your painting of the Peak?"

"Peak?"

"Pikes Peak," she said, waving over her shoulder. "Is that not what you are painting?"

He smiled and then shook his head. But he did not choose to elaborate on what he was painting. Curiosity burned so intensely in Odessa that she almost pulled herself to shore to see if she could steal a look at the canvas herself. She ventured a peek at Bryce, but he only looked to the sky before dipping his brush in the vivid blue and placing it upon the canvas. She sighed in frustration.

A servant who frequently was stationed by the pond to look after the patients tossed in his own fishing line. He immediately got a bite and expertly landed a beautiful fish, grinning with delight.

"I think I'll take it in, along with yours, Miss St. Clair, if you two will be all right for a moment," the man said.

"We'll be fine," Bryce said, smiling over at her. "If Miss St. Clair tips over her boat, I'll jump in to pull her out."

"I think I can manage to stay put for a few minutes and avoid that," she returned. "I'd love to have Cook fry my fish up for lunch."

The servant smiled and pulled on the rope that kept her boat firmly attached to the tree. He reached for her catch, took hold of it with a finger under its gills, and set off up the hill to present their bounty to Cook. Odessa remained in the boat, even pulled up onshore, comfortable in her layers of blankets and cozy seat. The eddy gently rocked her, like a baby in a cradle.

"Wake up, jailbird," Moira said, tossing one glove on Dominic's chest. She threw the second at his face. "It is almost noon."

"I might be a jailbird," he said, squinting one eye open to take in his sister, already dressed and with hat perched on her head, "but you had to be a songbird? You couldn't wait to show off your singing?" He tossed her glove back at her.

Her lips clamped shut for a moment, caught. "The sheriff told you, then?"

Dominic sighed and then sat up, letting his legs swing off the edge of the bed. He rubbed his head and looked up at her. "He's got his eye on you. Knowing you sing like an angel just made it worse. You know that, right?"

Moira walked to the window and stared outward. "He hasn't been exactly secretive about his intentions."

"He made me promise to allow his courtship of you in exchange for releasing me last night."

"What?"

"You heard me." He sighed again heavily. "I didn't see a way out, Moira. He threatened to drive me out of town, and then where would we be? Cut off from Odessa? No way to build Father's bookshop as planned."

"Maybe we ought to go somewhere else. Come and fetch Odessa when she is better."

"No. This is the place to be. Colorado Springs is at the crossroads of discovery and untold success. If the miners keep striking it rich, there will be no end to it. Don't fret over the sheriff," he said, rising and pausing behind her. She still stared out the window, giving him his privacy in his semidressed state. "I said he could court you. I didn't say you had to make it easy. And I didn't let him in on the fact that Father demands a chaperone on any excursion outside of the public eye."

She turned to him and grinned. "Well played, Brother," she said, with surprise and admiration in her tone.

"You know me, always using my brain as well as my brawn," he said.

She laughed. "Go and wash up, dress. I believe I've secured your new storefront."

"Truthfully?"

"Truthfully. But first we must stop in to see Odessa. She'll want to know that you're a free man again."

Bryce glanced over his shoulder at the departing servant and then set down his brush, leaning closer to her boat. "Odessa, are you … well? Have you heard anything? Seen anything?" He glanced over his shoulder again. "In regard to what we spoke of earlier?"

They hadn't had the opportunity to speak in private for two days. She dragged her fingers through the cold water, snowmelt from the mountains high above.

"Nothing more," she said with a shake of her head. "I keep running through the poem, wondering why he left it to me, someone he'd just met. What he hoped I'd do, exactly."

"He loved this kind of thing. Once, he sent our pastor and his wife on a hunt."

"A hunt?"

Bryce smiled at the memory. "He thought if they wanted his tithe, and God deemed them worthy, they could work a little for it. They had to visit eight homesteads and ranches to gather what they needed."

"Did they do it?"

"Nah. Pastor at the time was too proud. Refused to do it. Sam was just after a little fun. He tithed his money in time, but he made that preacher sweat it out for a bit."

Odessa considered that. "Bored, was he? Living all alone?"

"He found ways to occupy himself. You know what I think?"

She waited.

"I think Sam had the will drawn up, penned that poem he left you, months before he even came to the sanitorium."

"Why?"

"So he'd be ready. Just in case."

"In case?"

"The consumption proved too much to bear."

"But he didn't know me."

Bryce shrugged. "Probably figured he'd figure out who was to get his 'treasure' once he saw them."

"And yet you were surprised he left you the land."

Bryce let out a wheezy laugh. "Shouldn't have been. As I said, Sam loved surprises." He looked to the Peak, and then back to her.

"I've heard that some here pledge their land to the sanatorium as collateral against unpaid bills."

"That's true. I did the same when I signed the paperwork upon entrance." His eyes narrowed and he shook his head. "I see where you're going with that. But I checked with the administrator today, and Sam owed only $23. They let me pay it on his behalf."

"That was generous."

"Least I could do if the old man was going to go and leave me his land." They shared a smile.

She cast a line into the water, suddenly aghast at the quick camaraderie forming between them. Where was that servant? Flirting with the cook?

And that was when the screaming began.

Chapter ❀ 10

Bryce assisted Odessa out of the boat and they slowly made their way up the hill to see about the commotion. A young woman, small and wiry, but impressively strong for a consumptive, looked about with wide, wild eyes.

A man, likely her husband, pried her fingers from the wagon and carried her in the door, where he handed her to a guard, laid entry documents upon the front desk, and then turned to her, ignoring the gawking crowd. "Amille, this is the best thing for you. You can get better here, sweetheart, *better*." With tears rolling down his cheeks, he took her hands in his, kissed them, and then left her with the guard as he walked away.

Amille writhed and wailed, her hysteria sending her into a coughing fit that made them all fear she might fail to take another breath. But her husband continued to walk away, stiff-backed, as if making himself place one foot in front of the other, down the hill. Only her lack of breath kept her from continuing to scream, but steady tears rolled down her cheeks as the doctor and nurse attempted to calm her.

"John and Amille DeChant," Bryce said under his breath.

"You know them?" Odessa asked, struggling for a decent breath herself after their climb up the hill.

"Neighbors of Sam O'Toole's," he whispered. "Amille's mind's been slipping for some time. Their little girl died in the creek out back on their property, near Sam's, about a year ago. John found a silver vein while searching for her body. But no amount of silver will ever buy a mother's peace of mind."

The others gathered along the top floor balcony and staircase indoors, watching the newcomer. She looked about madly, a lost look in her eye. It was as if a person disappeared within their depths, as if she swallowed one whole, chewing a person up in an attempt to find an anchor-hold in the storm. But more than that, Odessa sensed the woman's terrible desperation and sorrow. She had loved her family, and now they were lost to her.

Doctor Morton and Nurse Packard saw Amille to a private room, presumably to Sam's old one. Odessa shoved aside the unease she felt at having the woman right next door, in a room that had already claimed one life. Perhaps she would find health again here, physically, and in physical gains, make mental gains as well.

"Please, God, let it be so," she whispered under her breath, wondering what it took to separate a woman so thoroughly from her mind.

"Odessa," Bryce said. "You're looking peaked. Come, sit."

She shakily took a seat beside Bryce on the porch. Gradually, the others drifted back to their rooms or the far side of the building, favoring the mountain views, or to the stables for their afternoon ride, since the morning group had just arrived back. Again and again her mind went to the young woman upstairs, and Odessa remembered her mother, so desperately sad after each of her sons died of the consumption. She had been so hopeful, believed so clearly that the new baby would somehow begin to level a drastically tilted universe. And then she was gone.

"You are sad," Bryce said quietly.

Odessa tried to force a smile. "Oh. Forgive me. Amille's sorrow simply reminded me of my mother and her own sorrow."

Bryce hesitated. "May I ask—what sorrow?"

"The family plague, this consumption. We've lost four boys, four of my brothers."

"Odessa," he said. She dared to look at him and his eyes held such grief for her! Never had she seen such empathy within a man. "There are no words," he said, shaking his head.

She felt her own throat begin to swell, tears rise, but swallowed hard. "There *are* words. Horror. Pain to the very marrow of one's bones. Ache. Endless waves of agony. Battered and bruised hearts—purple and barely functioning."

She rose, but Bryce caught her hand. "Your mother ... has she recovered?"

"She died trying to deliver my sister a year past." It felt strangely comforting to see that her words pained him, as if he were absorbing some of her own grief, taking it in, holding it for her. But talking about it made her feel irrationally angry, as if for the moment it was somehow Bryce's fault, these past losses.

Bryce looked her in the eye as Doctor Morton and Nurse Packard returned downstairs, Amille now eerily silent. Had they administered a sedative? Laudanum? Odessa was glad for the diversion. Better to think upon Amille's pain than her own. Did she now drift like a leaf on the river, appearing serene, but underneath, spinning, lost, far from home?

"It'll do her good, being here. You'll see," Bryce tried.

But Odessa did not believe his weak words. She slid her hand out from his. "They can heal her body, but not her mind. I've heard of people like this. They don't come back."

"You do not know that, Odessa," he said, disappointment in his eyes. Did he believe the best, hope for the best, in all things, in all people?

"No, I am no fortune-teller, no seer, but that woman is lost."

Bryce stared down the empty hall, at sunlight streaming through the open doorway. "But all that are lost can be found, Odessa. Every one. God calls us to life, to love, to healing. We merely have to find our way home."

Find our way home. Where was that, exactly, when she had left the only home she'd ever known and found she could never return? Suddenly, Odessa was overwhelmingly weary. The morning, their conversations, the arrival of Amille—all had taxed her. "I must go and take my rest," she said, already walking away.

"Sleep well, Odessa."

She didn't look back.

A week later, a maid helped Odessa don a second pair of stockings, carefully layering them over the long underwear she wore beneath her heavy woolen skirt and then stuffing her swaddled feet into her boots. She was barely able to lace them up. Odessa sat back in her chair and watched, already dreadfully weary from the effort. And they expected her to ride out on a trail today? For how long? Surely the other patients had felt better than she did at this moment, before the doctor demanded they mount up.

"Odessa!" Moira cried from her bedroom door. Nic peeked over their sister's shoulder.

Odessa turned and smiled at her siblings. "I'm so glad to see you both!" she said.

"The cuts are healing nicely," Moira said, gently touching her cheeks. "You should not bear many scars."

"No, I don't think I will," she said, shoving away the irritation she felt at her sister's constant fascination with appearances.

"You look so much better, Dess," Nic said, edging near, holding his hat in his hands and fiddling with the brim. "I mean, in general."

"I feel much better, but not as well as they seem to think I am," she said, aiming her words at the maid.

"What does that mean?" Nic asked.

"They intend for me to ride out with the others this afternoon," she said, leaning back again in her chair. "But I confess to thinking a nap sounds much better than a ride at this moment."

"Then you shall take to your bed," Dominic said.

"No. We agreed to submit to the doctor's care," she said. "I can't deny that I see improvements in almost all of the patients I see here. Day by day, this regimen seems to work. It's just that … toil and strain are a bit much for a consumptive who would rather be at her writing desk, if not in her bed."

People were moving down the hallway, assembling for the ride.

"Well then, you had better get through it. Perhaps it gets easier with each day that passes. Just think, Dess. The better you feel, the more you can write. The stories must be spinning in your mind, now that you're feeling better again, here in this new place. Maybe you can take your rides in the morning and write in the afternoon, emerge from this place with not only your health but finally a book we can publish at St. Clair Press."

"I've been too ill to even think of writing. It is enough to consider filling a page, let alone an entire book."

"You only seek to avoid sending it to publishers. I keep telling you, your stories are good. Brush one of them off and turn it into a full-blown novel."

Odessa let out an exasperated breath. "Of course, Nic. I'll see to it straight away. Right after I recall how to endure a horseback ride without expiring."

He stared at her, growing exasperated as they went through a well-rehearsed conversation. "It's Father, isn't it? You don't want to write so you don't have to face him and find out if he likes it or not." He lifted a shoulder. "So, don't send it to Father. Send it to another publisher."

"Nic, this truly is idle conversation."

"No, Odessa. It isn't. Here you will reclaim your life. And isn't part of your life doing something with the gifts God has given you? Doing something with your writing?"

Odessa considered him for a long moment. "And what if they despise it? The publisher."

"One man's poison is another's elixir."

Odessa sighed. "Enough. We shall discuss it another time. I am growing weary and must preserve my strength."

"What will you write?" Nic persisted.

"Maybe I'll write of a young man newly arrived from Philadelphia, taking on three men in the street and being jailed for it."

Dominic colored and frowned. "Cease. I've heard enough from Moira."

Odessa rose wearily and tapped him on the chest. "Then you stay clear of trouble. Show Papa that you have what it takes to be a responsible man in this family." She leaned close and kissed his cheek. "Show him what I already can see in you."

"We have a storefront," he said. He pulled away and stared at her perspiring face.

"Wonderful," she said, ignoring his worried look. "Papa thought it might take a good month. How have you done it in half?"

"Moira," he said, nodding toward their little sister. "She's already made friends in the highest corners of this city. She found us something already built. All we need are some shelves, a counter, and we can bring the inventory in."

Odessa smiled and shook her head. "Honestly, Moira, I've never known anyone who could move as quickly as you."

"I try," she said, leaning in to kiss Odessa's cheek. "When might we come and call upon you tomorrow? Given this new regimen?"

Odessa paused at the door. "I'm on the shorter afternoon ride until I'm able to handle the longer excursions. I expect I'll return to rest and then rise by midafternoon."

"Tomorrow, then," Dominic said. "We'll come by later. Be well, Sister."

"Take care," she warned both of them.

They watched her move down the hill toward the stables and disappear inside. Moira turned and looped her arm through Nic's. "Odessa has Mother's eyes," she said.

"I thought we all did."

"Not the color. The look about them. As if she can see everything we're thinking."

Dominic let out a humorless laugh as they turned in the opposite direction to depart from a side entrance. "She can see into people, understand motivation, passion. She's empathetic. It's what makes her a good writer."

"I wish she'd tell Papa of her desire to write."

"Maybe she fears the disapproval she's seen in him over my actions—or the way he consistently squelches your dreams. Ever since Mother … maybe it's better to hide dreams in our family."

"It's never best to hide," Moira said. "It's not right that we feel we have to." Their words were well rehearsed, but they never found an answer. All he wanted for his daughters was marriage, grandchildren. A good reputation and success for his son. Anything else was deemed unsuitable.

"We must send Father a telegraph on our way to the land purveyor's office," Nic said. "He'll want to know that Odessa is doing well enough to ride a horse today."

"Who would have believed it?" Moira said, taking his arm. "Perhaps this place really does hold the keys to the cure."

With several taking their first ride or recently recovering from a setback, it was announced that they would only travel a long loop around the Garden of the Gods.

Odessa sighed in relief and glanced at Bryce, mounted on the horse beside her. "Perhaps they don't intend to kill me after all."

He grinned. "Trust me, it does us all good."

"What if I cannot keep my seat and slide off the horse? Will that do me any good?"

"If you're feeling weak, hunch over like this," he said, miming the position. "It takes less strength and as long as your feet remain in the stirrups and your hands on the horn, you should be all right."

"You are not instilling a lot of confidence, Bryce."

"No? Well, you should be encouraged. I raise horses, after all. My mother used to say I was born on horseback."

Odessa smiled and he smiled with her.

"I suppose it was a stretch in the storytelling. But I was told she went into labor while straddling a horse. Most likely, she made it to ground before I came into the world."

Odessa looked away, hiding an embarrassed smile. Polite society did not discuss things such as childbirth. But she was intrigued. She wished she could stand unseen and listen to him talk.

"I like stories," he said as they got their horses in line and headed out. "I'd like to read your stories someday."

Odessa frowned. "My father's stories? You mean the books he publishes?"

"No, I'm assuming you write. A woman does not get that much ink on her fingers writing letters. Unless there's a beau back in Philadelphia."

"No," she said. "There is no beau."

"Then you are writing …" he asked, barely pausing for a beat, "a book of your own?"

"I like to spin an idle tale now and again. For my own enjoyment. Short stories, mostly. Nothing as audacious as a novel."

"Knowing you the little I do, Odessa St. Clair, I doubt they are idle stories. That brain of yours is always churning away, like a waterwheel in a constant, spring-fed creek. I can see it in your eyes."

She glanced over her shoulder at him. "You are entirely too forward, Bryce."

"Perhaps. Forgive me, Odessa."

Odessa clamped her lips shut and concentrated on the slow, rocking motion of her docile mare. She had to admit, it did feel grand to sit astride her horse—Dr. Morton would hear nothing of a sidesaddle; it was too dangerous, given their weakened state—and a nurse brought a specially made blanket that covered her exposed calves and ankles and added more warmth for her. Spring sun heated the back of her head even as snow-laden, awe-inspiring mountains rose ahead of them. In half an hour they had skirted the edge of Colorado City, a wild town where drinking was allowed, unlike her dry new neighbor, and reached the crest of a bluff, overlooking the Garden of the Gods again. Odessa knew from Moira's description that Glen Eyrie was just to their north now.

"Doing all right?" Bryce asked, from behind her.

"I am," she said, unable to keep some of her own surprise from her voice. Being outside, moving, seeing new things occupied her mind. For the first time in a long time, she realized she had not thought about breathing since mounting the horse. Her breath came now, high and wheezy, but she was getting enough air. The bit of exercise was simply pushing her to her normal limits.

"We'll rest down there, beneath the rocks," Bryce said. "You're doing great, Odessa."

And for the first time in a long time, Odessa believed she was. She shielded her eyes and looked up to watch a large gray bird circle high above them. So free, so easy were his movements, movements Odessa longed to echo. *Thank You, Father,* she prayed silently. *Thank*

You for this, a glimpse of health, not in a story, not in my mind, but in my real life.

Moira and Nic sent off their telegraph and then walked the remaining blocks to their new storefront. Entering, they marveled at the tall, bright windows and relished the scent of freshly hewn planks. Clear pine made up the twelve-foot-high walls and covered the ceiling, too. Upstairs was a bedroom and sitting room. A washroom and small kitchen were included in the back, beside the storage. "It will be perfect until we find a good cottage to rent," Nic said.

"Or house," Moira said, arching a brow in his direction. "It is difficult to entertain guests of a certain stature in a small and cramped parlor."

"Careful, Sissy. There's already one Queen in this town," he said, grinning over at her.

"But she's soon leaving again for the East." Moira smiled. From the basket on her arm she pulled a pen, paper, and bottle of ink. She set them out atop the counter, dipped her pen in the inkwell, and let it hover over a page. "All right. Let us begin our list of supplies. The sooner we can get this store in order, the sooner we can accept the shipment of books and open for business. Papa will be so pleased."

"Yes," Nic said with a sigh. "So pleased." He wandered to the front windows, wishing for the thousandth time that he was excited about the store. But to him, it was merely a project. Glumly, he saw himself, tying on an apron day after day, seeing to customers. How much better would it be to be one of the farmers outside, heading to land they had tilled, thinking of spring planting, or the workmen across the street, measuring and sawing lumber for the next building? He'd always been good with a hammer and nails.

"Nic! Where are you?"

"Oh. Sorry. We need shelving, lots of shelving, from floor to ceiling. I can take care of that myself, as well as a glass display case for more expensive items. Two rolling ladders to reach the higher shelves. Signage to designate the various categories of books."

School. Other than building the shelves, it sounded as dull as school.

"Paper. We'll be selling low-grade paper to most folks and high-quality stationery to your new *friends*," he said, pacing now, eager to be done with it. He wished Odessa were here. She would love this, this dreaming of the store, imagining it filled, thinking through all they needed.

"Papa is sending the cash register and a safe, along with the books," Moira said.

"Yes. We'll also sell ink of various colors, and pens. And maps. Everyone will be looking for the latest maps."

"We should sell chalkboards and chalk for the schoolchildren."

"Good idea."

"And primers."

"Perhaps you will sell a primer on courting the prettiest girl in town," said the sheriff from the doorway. He had entered unnoticed and stood there with his hat in hand. "Fine new shop you have here," he said, stepping forward. "I'll be eager to see it filled with your wares."

He spoke of books but his eyes were on Moira.

Dominic took in a breath and held it a moment, then slowly released it. "Sheriff," he allowed.

"Dominic," the sheriff returned. "Miss St. Clair," he said with a nod in her direction. "I came to see if I might call on you tomorrow afternoon. Take some tea with you and your brother, if you can spare a moment away from your work."

"I'd love to, Sheriff, but I'm afraid we haven't yet had time to buy as much as a teakettle since we arrived."

"I thought of that," Reid said, turning back toward the door.

Dominic watched his sister carefully, aware that she kept the counter between her and their visitor. She was afraid of him. He didn't think he'd ever observed Moira St. Clair afraid of a soul. His eyes returned to the sheriff, coming back in, arms around a midsized crate. He set it on the counter before her.

"Sheriff, what have you done?" she asked, pretending to be coy. She truly was a talented actress. She pulled the lid off the wooden crate and moved aside some packing straw. Out came a box that, when she opened it, held four china cups. Then another box, with a sturdy iron kettle. And a third, containing a matching china teapot. Moira studied them, set on the counter all together. "Oh, Sheriff—"

"Reid, I've asked you to call me Reid."

"Reid, this is much too generous. I cannot accept."

"Of course you can," he said with a grin toward her and her brother. "If I'm to come and call on you, I'll want a spot of tea. The general has me hooked on it. And I can't come and ask for tea if you have no means to get it for me." He winked at her and leaned over the counter, placing his hat back on his head. "It's the first of many presents for you, Moira. You deserve the best, of everything. So, until tomorrow?"

"Until tomorrow."

With that, he pushed off and left the building, pausing on the porch to straighten his jacket like a cock fluffing his feathers.

Dominic picked up a teacup, taking aim at the glass window and the sheriff.

But Moira was there, one hand on his arm, the other lifting the fragile cup. "There will be other days, other ways, Brother," she whispered. "Remember, we're buying time to get established before we dare to taunt the sheriff with a dismissal. Leave him to me."

Nic wrenched his arm away from her, still staring at the sheriff as he walked down their stairs. He turned toward her. "In all my days, I've never seen you fear a man, Moira."

She glanced down and to the left, verifying his assumption. When she did that, it signaled uneasiness, fear....

"What'd he do? What'd he do that night alone with you?"

She turned her beautiful eyes on him and stared up at him resolutely. "You leave him to me, Dominic. Do you understand? You make a move and you'll either cost us this shop or land in a jail cell again." She reached up and straightened his narrow tie. "Men I understand. Reid Bannock is dangerous, yes. Formidable. But underneath, he's still only a man."

They had taken their rest among red stones warmed by the spring sun, eating freshly baked hot cross buns and drinking strong coffee.

"Tell me of your horse ranch, Bryce," Odessa invited, leaning her head back to face the sun. It felt too good to worry about getting too much sun, like a farm girl. And the warmth of the spring sun felt wonderful after a long, dark winter of illness.

"It's the prettiest country you've ever seen," he said, leaning his head back against his own rock. "You can make your way up a canyon along the Arkansas River, then head south, toward Westcliffe. Small hills covered in piñon pine gradually give way to a long, wide valley, with those towering Sangre de Cristo Mountains on your right and the smaller Wet Mountains to your left."

"Is your ranch big?"

"We get by," he hedged.

"How many head of horses do you run?"

"Three hundred."

"Three hundred! You must have many acres."

"We get by," he said again with a grin. "But then we also have access to the mountains. Come summer, we drive the horses up into the high hills, where the grass is plentiful."

"Sounds idyllic," she said. She ran his words over in her mind, then raised her head again abruptly, catching him staring at her. He looked away, embarrassed, but she ignored it. "What did you say those mountain ranges are called?"

"The Sangres on her western flank. The Wet on her eastern."

Old Sam's odd poem rang through her mind. She sat forward. *Damp to the East* ... easily translated as the Wet Mountains. "Bryce, what does Sangre de Cristos mean?"

He picked up a rock in his hand and rolled it between his fingers. "It's an old Spanish name. In certain light they appear red, and there is a peak with a cross that appears. You can see it mostly in the winter, because—"

"So the translation is …?" she interrupted.

He looked her in the eye, obviously confused by her intense tone. "Blood of Christ," he said. "Why?"

"Damp to her East, Wounds to her West,' one of Sam's lines in the poem."

But why the mystery? If she could unravel it, so could others. To say nothing of the fact that Sam's name—or his mother's—was on the deed.

"Bryce, you've been to Sam's place, I take it."

"Almost every month for the last few years. He's only a few hours' ride from our ranch."

"Is it hard to find?"

"No. Why?"

"Merely curious," she said idly. "What about his mother's property? Is it nearby?"

He shook his head. "His mother's property? Sam never spoke of that."

"Someday soon, I'd like to see if we could unravel the mystery."

"Make it through today, Odessa," he said with a grin, "and you're one day closer."

Chapter 11

The trail nurse gave them the signal to return to their horses and Odessa rose quickly, too quickly, and instantly collapsed, her lungs short of oxygen, her head spinning.

Luckily, Bryce was there to catch her.

"Glad you're nothing but a consumptive sack of skin and bones," he teased as she came out of her faint. "Or you might have crushed me."

She tried to push away, but he held her tight as the trail nurse timed her pulse and observed her breathing.

"I just tried to get up too fast. I'm fine."

"I'll be the judge of that," the nurse said. "She's all right," she said to Bryce a minute later. "But we ought to get her back to the sanatorium. She needs to spend some more time out of doors, beside the creek, before we bring her on the trail again."

"I'll have you address me of my own health, Nurse," Odessa said crossly, succeeding now in pushing away from Bryce. "It is improper to address anyone but me." Again, the sudden movement made her woozy, but she attempted to cover it. Could they see the sweat beading on her upper lip? She refused to wipe it away.

"Pardon me, Miss St. Clair," the nurse responded icily. "I wrongly assumed that you weren't yet in your right thinking. Please, rise and mount up immediately." She stood and lifted her chin, knowing she was asking Odessa to do something downright impossible.

"Here, take my arm," Bryce said, offering her his hand.

She grabbed it like a lifeline, now too tired to feign independence any longer.

"Slowly, slowly," he said, as if whispering to a wild colt. "Take it from me. You'll be flat on your back again if you move too fast. Cracked my head open once on a rock."

"No one there to catch you?" Odessa asked.

"No, ma'am," he said, smiling his encouragement. "Now let's get you to that horse. I'm telling you, when you get back to your bed today, you'll sleep the whole afternoon away."

Odessa suddenly could not wait to return to her room, her white sheets and woolen blankets. For the peaceful spin into sleep. She barely could tolerate the time it took for Bryce to help her mount up and a servant to cover her with the blanket and tuck the edges around her legs.

She watched as Bryce moved toward his own horse and mounted as effortlessly as a noble equestrian, no longer a consumption patient. But once in the saddle, once they resumed their horse train back toward the city, he turned his face to her and she recognized the utter weariness of their shared ailment.

Consumption. Consuming. Consumed. Eaten alive.

Bryce's eyes, his manner, seduced her toward trust. Their shared struggle already bonded them all as if they were siblings, but this man looked upon her with eyes that bespoke more. Could they both beat this monster back, into submission, maybe even entirely out of their lives?

Her heart skipped a beat at the mad dream of it, the wild hope within her. What if she bested this disease at last? For good? What if her life did not end at a young age, as she had supposed it would? What if she could live to be ... old?

"Just go," Moira said, reading a book in the corner of the hotel room. "Your pacing the floor for an hour is about to drive me mad."

He looked over at her, obviously torn. "But you—"

"I'll be fine. I'll be a princess up in her tower, refusing to come to the door if anyone comes to the drawbridge. Just go and walk. Walk for miles. It will do you good."

"You promise? You'll stay here?"

Moira set her book on the small table beside the lamp. "If you will promise me that you will walk, not brawl. You know what it means to us, Nic. The threat of it. You must not fight."

Right. He understood the import of her words, knew the dire consequences as spelled out by Sheriff Reid Bannock. But it was that same man who worked him into a frenzy now. The thought of him making Moira so uncomfortable she actually feared the man ... that he had bartered off his freedom from jail in exchange for the privilege of coming to call on her ... Dominic longed to punch him, pummel him until he bled. Who was he to dare so mightily?

"Nic, go," Moira said. "I'll turn in early. But you remember your promise."

He barely acknowledged her, his need so urgent now. He paused outside her hotel door until he heard her turn the key in the lock, then practically ran down the stairs. Once outside, he looked left, then right, thinking.

This town was small, and it was Reid Bannock's town. A dry town.

What Dominic St. Clair needed was a drink.

He hailed a carriage outside the hotel and climbed in. "Colorado

City," he said, leaning forward in his seat. "Take me to your favorite saloon."

"Right away, sir."

They drove out of town and across the creek and into the next, arriving in minutes. It was a farce, really, this separation of dry town from a town full of saloons and whorehouses. But what General Palmer wanted, apparently, General Palmer got.

Dominic shoved down his feelings of guilt for being present here, shoved away the thought of how Father or Odessa, or even Moira would react. She had sent him out, after all. She saw in him his need for escape, release, freedom.

He entered the saloon, and several men at the bar and some at a couple of tables turned to look his way. But as he moved toward the barkeep, most turned back to their private conversations, private card games, private drinking.

"Whiskey?" the barkeep asked.

"Double," Dominic returned. While the barkeeper poured, Nic surveyed the saloon. Fine wooden paneling, now a bit beat up, testified to a wealthier age when Colorado City and the mines to her west were first discovered. Now she was the poorer neighbor, the forgotten relative, of a new, shinier prince of a town to her east. Well Dominic knew what it was to be less-than. Less-than-hoped-for. Less-than-imagined. The only living St. Clair son. Heir to a successful publishing company. An inheritance he did not want. "Live long, Father," he toasted in a whisper.

"Again," he said to the barkeep, patting the smooth bar with an open hand, and silently, the man poured another.

"Slow down there, neighbor, or you'll end up on the floor," said a man on the next stool.

Dominic, in defiance, tossed the second double back, studying the man with closed lips as the hot, burning liquid flowed down his throat. Slowly, he moved his eyes away from his neighbor in silent dismissal. "Another," he demanded. "This time, the good bottle." In tandem with his request, he placed a silver coin on the bar, the silent word of every saloon in the country.

The proprietor studied him for a half second and then reached behind him for a bottle of fine scotch.

This glass Dominic savored, letting the previous two glasses do their work within him. He felt the muscles in his neck and back relax, the familiar tension in his cheeks and forehead ease away. He let the scotch sit in his mouth and then slide down his throat, as he detected the undertones of smoke and licorice.

"New to the city?" asked another man, taking the stool on Dominic's other side. He lifted a finger, silently ordering a glass of the finer scotch Dominic was now drinking.

"Colorado Springs," he allowed.

"Interested in a game of cards, friend?"

"No. I have interest in the more physical games."

His new companion laughed. "Whores or the ring?"

"The ring," Dominic said. "Is there one in this town?"

"Always one in every town," the man said.

Dominic studied him, taking in the new suit, the groomed fingernails. Card shark. Traveling gambler. Nic knew the type, just as he had been clearly made as well.

"You're kind of small to be a fighter," said the man, a tone of jest in his voice that kept away the broad, sweeping hand of offense.

"That's what they say," Dominic allowed, taking another sip.

"Hmm. An underdog. I like to play against the odds. Shall I lead the way?"

"Please." Dominic drank the last of his scotch.

"The brother has left her, Sheriff. Took off for Colorado City, for the saloons."

Ah, yes, Reid thought, unsurprised. The young Mr. St. Clair had been clearly itching for another fight. If he wasn't careful, he'd get himself killed. The thought made Reid consider for a moment. Dominic wouldn't be the first man to find himself surrounded and sustain a beating that would eventually take his life. Especially in a place as rough-and-tumble as Colorado City. Yes, he thought, picking the dirt out from under his fingernails, if the man continued to be reluctant to accept his calls upon his sister, he might simply find an end to his miserable, frustrated life. It might be a relief of sorts to him, a blessing in disguise. Like a wounded racehorse that had to be put down.

"Did he go for a woman?" he asked, handing the man a coin.

"Drink, when I left him. But plenty of it."

"And we all know where such drinking leads us. Whoring. Debauchery. Brawling. All the worst in every man."

"Yes, sir."

"You can be on your way," he said to the spy in dismissal.

The man departed and Sheriff Reid Bannock slung his holster around his hips. He thought he just might stop by the hotel, not to drop in on Moira, necessarily. But just imagining her there, all alone. In her hotel room, pulling off her dress, her corset—

"Where you off to?" Garrett asked.

"Off to make sure the city is safe as she slumbers."

"You mean your future wife, don't ya?"

"Her, too," Reid tossed back.

The ring was like countless others Dominic had seen, little more than a wooden floor, four posts, and heavy rope between them. The pit was full of Irish and Chinese, laborers from the railroad or disillusioned miners, determined to earn their fortune here, if not out *there*. Dominic inhaled the heady scent of men's sweat, the mood within the room making him more alert, more alive than he had felt in weeks. The liquor made him fearless.

This was a constructive use of his skills as a fighter, he reasoned. A method to make a little of his own money, not Father's donations, and the means to release the inexhaustible anger and frustration that built within his belly.

He edged between the men, moving steadily closer to the ring until he felt the spatter of blood and sweat across his face as one man plowed another with a swift, iron-hinged uppercut to the right. The loser went down, falling to the wooden floor with a dull thump barely heard against the roar of the crowd. He stared at the man, whose eye was swollen shut from some earlier punch, lip bleeding. The man moaned, but didn't open his other eye, did not attempt to rise.

Dominic stared at him and yet felt no fear. Worse, he felt no glory for the winner. The crowd cried out, but it was as if Dominic had gone deaf. He could see their mouths open, hands raised in the air, but he could hear nothing but the sound of the loser on the floor, breathing, gasping from around broken ribs to breathe, just breathe.

Just like Odessa sounded. Wordlessly, Dominic moved forward, climbing into the ring and tearing off his shirt, popping the buttons off, tearing buttonholes in his frenzy to be free. It was then he could hear something beyond the beaten man, carried out of the ring now, passed off to stranger after stranger to rest and recuperate in some forgotten room or die in a weather-beaten hotel.

Now, he could hear again. Felt the ringmaster raise his arm. "I have a challenger here! What's your name, son?"

"St. Clair," Dominic said, looking about, no longer able to focus on individuals in the crowd, only searching for the man he would fight tonight.

"Shorty St. Clair!" called the ringmaster. "Who will fight the honorable Shorty St. Clair, newly arrived from—where are you from, son?"

"Philadelphia," he mumbled.

"From Philly! Shorty St. Clair from Philly! Who will fight this man tonight?"

Moira pulled shut the drapes of her room, preparing to undress for the night. But at the last moment, she caught sight of a man across the muddy street, a tall man with guns at either hip. No one but the sheriff and his deputies were allowed to carry weapons in town.

She closed her eyes as she turned to the side of the window, as if he could see through the drapes, wondering if it was her imagination, or if Sheriff Reid Bannock was truly standing across the street staring at her hotel room, arms crossed. She opened her eyes. She refused to peek out the same drapes she had just closed, refused to let him know he had a power over her, an edge of fear.

Resolutely, she walked to her door and paused, hand hovering over the key. She had promised Dominic she would not leave this room.

But she had to. She had to know. Just how great a threat was this sheriff? Would he truly go to such great lengths in his pursuit of her as to stand outside her hotel, watching her as a wolf observed a sheep in a farmer's pen? She had had hopeful suitors in Philadelphia who had walked past her father's mansion as if on an afternoon stroll, while casting pining looks in her home's direction.

This was different. The man stood across the street, watching, doing nothing but watching. Or maybe he was watching someone else, someone who posed a danger to the city. Simply doing his job.

Decided now, she turned the key in the lock and peered down the hallway. No one was present, all the hotel guests taking their supper or already happily ensconced in their rooms.

She moved into the hallway, wondering why her heart was racing. What was there to fear? She was in a hotel, not alone in some alley. Oil lamps flickered cheerfully all along the dark hallway. Moira had watched others arrive this afternoon. She was not alone within this hotel, regardless of how she felt at this moment.

Moira moved down the stairs, trying, inexplicably, to avoid the creaks. It was with some relief that she made it to the ground floor and peered to her left into the dining room, filled with guests.

She turned and moved through the downstairs hallway, squaring her shoulders as if she knew exactly where she was going. The laughter and hum of chatter in the dining room faded behind her, then the loud, clanking noises of the kitchen. She paused outside a door labeled "Office" and noted that no light peeked underneath.

Glancing over her shoulder to make certain no one approached, she turned the knob and raised an eyebrow when she found it unlocked. Colorado Springs was a young city, indeed, when an office manager left his office unlocked. She eased inward and closed the door, listening for several heartbeats to make certain she was alone.

It was utterly silent.

She turned and felt her way toward the window, pulling aside a heavy drape to peer outside.

The street was empty. Not even a carriage for rent or people heading home for the night. No one. Certainly no one across the street watching her.

That was when Moira heard the door open behind her and watched as Sheriff Reid Bannock's silhouette filled the doorway. "Now, Moira," he whispered, "why are you in here? What would the hotel manager say?" Her heart picked up a frantic beat.

He took a step inward, then over to her, barely visible in the soft golden light of the streetlamp from outside the window. The door swung halfway shut behind him.

Moira vacillated between trying to get past him and screaming, taking two precious seconds. He was in front of her then, perilously close. "I saw you outside," she stammered. "I thought you might be looking for a criminal, thought I might be able to better make out where you were looking down here."

"No criminals," he said with a smile in his voice. "Just a man with a woman on his mind."

He stepped closer. "Reid ..." she warned.

"I heard your brother is away. A woman ought not to be left alone." He was so close she could feel his breath on her bare neck.

"I don't mind being alone, actually," she said, turning away. "I told him to go out."

His voice softened and he turned away, running a hand through his hair. "My mama was alone too often. My father never liked to be home much. It was hard on her. When I heard Dominic left, I felt I ought to come over and keep watch over you." He paused and studied her. "I'll have to remember you might have a different mindset than my mama."

She laughed lightly. "I don't believe I've ever been compared to anyone's mother."

"No. No, I don't suppose you have," he said with a soft grin. "Come. Come outside. It isn't seemly, us being here alone."

Moira considered him in the warm light of the gas lamp. Perhaps her imagination was simply running wild. He was only out on this cold spring night to make sure she was safe. Perhaps he was a bit zealous, but she was moved by his attentions, his care. Surely a man who loved his mother as dearly as he loved his couldn't be all bad.

"Thank you for watching over me, Reid. But now that I know all is well, I think I will return to my room. I'm dreadfully tired." She kept her hands clasped before her waist.

He twisted his hat in his hands. "Then good night, Moira. May I call on you tomorrow?"

She hesitated. "I'll look forward to it. Good night, Reid."

She took a step away but he reached out and gripped her arm with a steely hand. Then, as if he had moved too forcefully, he softened his hold immediately. "Please."

"Pardon me?"

"Please, Moira. Just say that one more time," he said with eyes closed. "Say good night to me."

Moira paused, confused. He stood there before her, waiting, eyes shut. It was rather awkward. "G-good night, Reid." She moved quickly then, hand on the door before she glanced back.

He was grinning and placing his hat on his head again. "It has been a good night, Moira," he said. "Sleep well."

Chapter ✿ 12

Odessa awakened at dawn and immediately knew someone watched her. She turned quickly upon her bed and looked to the doorway. Amille DeChant stood there, shifting nervously, wringing her hands. She coughed, and it was then that Odessa could hear the deep wheeze of her breath. "My baby," she managed to say as she panted for air. "I can't find my baby. Can you help me ... find her?"

Odessa winced and coughed as she came to a sitting position on the edge of her bed. She reached for a glass of water, willing the coughing to not even begin this morning. "I am Odessa St. Clair. Your name is Amille, right? It's a very pretty name."

Amille stared at her blankly, then shifted back and forth. "They took my baby."

"Who took your baby?" Odessa asked, feeling the woman's pain.

"The men. The men who want the mine."

Odessa frowned and rose. "I'm sure your baby is all right, Amille. It's early yet. She's probably fast asleep, asleep in Jesus' arms."

Amille glanced at her quickly then. "No, she's not with Jesus. She's lost. I have to find her. Have to find her. Have to find her. Have to find her. Have to—"

"All right," Odessa said, holding up a hand. "We'll go look. But first we must get some clothes on. It's not seemly, going out in our night shifts."

"Not seemly. Not seemly. Not seemly. Have to find her. Have to find her. Have to find—"

"Here," Odessa said. "Let me help you choose a dress and then I'll come back and find my own." She sighed. Was she making a wise decision? Would it be better to stick to the truth, try and force Amille's mind back to reality? Her heart told her no. There would be a time and place for fact. For now, fiction would soothe.

"Thought I told you to keep away from brawling in my town," Reid said, leveling a gaze at Dominic, who sat across from him, barely able to see through two eyes that were nearly swollen shut.

Moira knew the sheriff was watching her shaking hand as she poured tea from the china kettle he had given her. Did he credit it to fear for her brother? Desire for him? She didn't like how he spoke to her brother, his total lack of respect, regardless of what Dominic had been up to.

"I wasn't in your town," Dominic returned. He lifted his cup. "Thank you, Moira. I'm certain our guest is grateful for your pouring as well."

"Yes, thank you," Reid ground out, still staring at Dominic. "If it wasn't in my town, may I ask where you found yourself in fisticuffs?"

"No," Dominic said with a cheerful grin, sipping at the tea. He stared through slitted eyes at Reid, then Moira.

The sheriff sat back, considering. It was then that Moira knew that Reid was well aware where he had taken his beating. Otherwise, he would be pressing him for a response. How much transpired in this town, or even the next, or the next that Bannock didn't know about? Or was it simply the St. Clairs that had captured the sheriff's undivided attention?

"This is fine tea, Moira," the sheriff said, eyeing her as she joined them at the small table in the center of the vast, empty shop floor.

"Thank you, Sheriff. I bought the tea leaves at Baxter's Mercantile." She dropped one sugar cube in her cup, then another, stirring slowly. "He said the tea had just arrived, the best that San Francisco importers had to offer."

"San Francisco," Reid said, shaking his head as if that was the most wondrous news he had ever heard. Moira had the notion she could utter unintelligible jabber and still the man would shake his head as if she had shared the most insightful comment possible. "Colorado is well on her way. Imports from the West, as well as from the East."

"Speaking of imports," Dominic said, "my father was sending a shipment of books and supplies to arrive soon after us, in the off chance that we might obtain a storefront already built." He waved about them. "Here we are, but without our wares. We've been here over two weeks. Do you know to whom we should inquire about a shipment set to arrive at the Colorado Springs Depot?"

"Joe Potosky," said the sheriff easily. "He gets such shipments all the time. I imagine your crates are awaiting you in the warehouse even now."

"Excellent," Dominic said, draining his cup of tea. He set it down in the saucer with a loud clatter. "Well, we appreciate you coming to call, Sheriff."

Reid leaned back in his chair, teacup still in hand, and did little more than raise an eyebrow. "I thought I might, if you will permit me, after we finish our tea, take you both over to the sanatorium to visit the elder Miss St. Clair. The streets are terribly muddy, hardly suitable for Miss Moira to trudge through."

"Oh, that's no trouble," Moira said, lifting a hand prettily to her chest. "Dominic can see me there safely. Though you should see my sister, Reid. Odessa has begun riding. I'm eager to find out how she is faring. You can't imagine how amazing this progress is, to our minds. She hasn't ridden in more than a year! And now she's to be astride a horse every day?"

"That Doc Morton knows how to handle his patients," Reid said, a comforting tone in his voice. "I'm certain Odessa will be only one of many he heals over the years."

"Oh, I do hope you're right," she said, setting down her teacup. "Talk of her makes me anxious to see her," she said. "Might you take us over there now, Reid?"

"Of course," he said, setting down his own cup and rising. He looked to Dominic. "Perhaps you should consider staying behind. Your appearance might upset your sister."

Dominic paused, as if the last thing he wanted to do was to send Odessa into one of her breathing attacks. Not when she had so recently made such good strides. But Moira silently begged him with her eyes to come along. "Your words are wise," Nic said to the sheriff. "I don't want to upset Odessa."

"But—" Moira began.

"But as we've said before," Dominic cut in, "our father does not approve of unchaperoned visits with his daughters. As the sole

St. Clair man present, I must see to his wishes. I will travel with you to the sanatorium and await my sister outside."

Without a word the sheriff rose and set his hat upon his head, eyed them both, and turned to lead the way. Nic winked at Moira as they walked out behind him. What would Nic do if he knew Reid had found her alone last night?

The trail nurse led them to a small canyon south of Glen Eyrie and told them to leave their horses to munch on the tender scrub oak trees' new leaves while they made their way upward on foot. "Slowly," she said, warning them needlessly. "Pause often to rest and rise carefully. You don't wish to take a tumble up here."

Odessa raised her brows at the understatement. On one side of the trail was a sheer cliff, rising high above them. On the other side was a sheer drop, falling down to a winding creek far below. Were they mad, bringing patients to such a place?

"Those who feel strongest, go first. If you pause, everyone has to pause behind you. We'll walk just a little way up, to a pretty waterfall."

Bryce looked back at her with a question in his eyes, but the nurse sent him forward, five people ahead of Odessa. Only one girl of sixteen was behind her. "Last of the pack, I suppose," she said to the girl. "What is your name?"

"Charlotte. Charlotte Hansen."

"A pleasure to meet you, Charlotte. I am Odessa St. Clair." The girl was as pale as her white hair, with the consumptive's classic, oddly flushed cheeks, as if someone had painted Parisian rouge upon them.

She had a sheen of sweat across her face and neck, an echo of what Odessa felt upon her own. "Just breathe, Charlotte. Be sure you take it slow and concentrate on your breathing. If you feel faint, go to your knees. The waterfall mustn't be far. Otherwise, we'd still be astride our horses." She looked ahead, frowning when she saw the trail nurse so distant. Shouldn't she be behind them all, with those who fared the worst? "They're aware we're ill-prepared for an arduous hike."

The nurse caught her accusing eye and paused, letting several patients pass her at a wider section of the path.

They continued on, taking several steps, pausing to catch their meager breath, then moving on, as pathetic a group of climbers as there ever was. The thought of them posing for some poster touting Colorado Springs' good health made Odessa giggle, but the laughter stole her precious breath, so she considered more sober thoughts. Like falling down the canyon wall to the river below. Or Amille's fruitless search for her daughter. Looking around the sanatorium had only succeeded in agitating the woman further, until she collapsed in a full-blown consumptive attack. Odessa was miserable as she watched Doctor Morton help a nurse to get Amille back to her room and sedated again.

In ten minutes they had reached the trail nurse, who dutifully then took up her position at the rear, and in another ten minutes they reached the small falls, a minor snowmelt-fed cascade of perhaps five feet in total. But it had a delightful sound and they all sat about and stared at it, panting as if they had just hiked for ten uphill miles, not twenty minutes.

They were preparing to go when a woman appeared on a trail above the falls and then made her way down beside it, a massive camera and tripod over her shoulder. "Ahh, my fellow consumptives," the big woman bellowed. "Keep it up. I know it's hard. But these mountains will heal you as they did me. I came here barely able to rise from my bed, thirty pounds lighter. Now look at me!" she cried proudly, patting her ample chest. "Your day will come too. Just keep putting one foot in front of the other."

She moved past the group and a man said to Odessa over his shoulder, "That's Helen Anderson."

"Helen Anderson, the author?" Odessa asked.

"One and the same."

Helen Anderson! The woman had eight books to her name. She'd made Colorado famous in her book *A Thousand Miles from Home*. Odessa had loved every word on every page.

"Mrs. Anderson!" she called impulsively. Bryce and Charlotte looked up in surprise and back to the woman who was quickly disappearing down the trail.

At the sound of her name, she turned and climbed back toward them. Bryce, Charlotte, and the trail nurse moved past Odessa to give them room to speak.

"Forgive me for interrupting your hike. I'm Odessa St. Clair. I had to tell you—I love your work. I've read all your books, your stories! Everything you've ever written."

"Well, not everything I've ever written. There is much that is not suitable for publication."

"I doubt that very much." She paused, feeling an urge to keep the famous author nearby for a moment longer. Just being near her made Odessa remember the feel of home, of St. Clair Press and Papa. "Is that your camera? Your very own?"

"My very own."

"Could I—if it's not too much trouble, might I gaze through it?"

"Of course," said Helen, with barely a pause. She reached forward, intuitively knowing Odessa could use a helping hand as she rose, waited a minute, watching as she caught her breath, then led her over to the camera. "Where are you from?"

"Philadelphia."

"Philly, eh? You're not of the St. Clair Press clan, are you?"

"Indeed I am," Odessa said, flushing with pride that the woman knew of it. "It is my father's company."

"He does fine work. I've admired what he publishes for many years."

"I'm certain he'd love to add you to his roster of authors." She bent down to peer through the camera lens.

"Would you like to take a photograph?"

"Take a photograph? Me?"

Helen laughed lightly. "What good is to look through a camera lens if you don't fasten in film what you have in memory? This is a momentous occasion, is it not? You, a consumptive most probably written off as good as dead, now hiking in the wilds of Colorado." She winked at that last phrase, fully knowing they were but an eighth of a mile from the stage road.

Odessa smiled. "Yes. I suppose it is."

"Then what would you like on film?"

Odessa turned and looked at the group by the falls, perched like pale, sweaty boulders all about it. "I'd like to take a picture of them."

"Excellent choice." Helen set up the tripod and unfolded the black cloth. "Put your head back under there, tuck it around your neck, and frame your view. Move the entire camera until you get the right framing, then remove the back of the camera, here," she said, guiding Odessa's hand, "to expose the plate. Got it?"

"Yes, I believe I do." Odessa grinned as she saw her trail comrades straightening clothing and running their fingers through their hair, preening for the camera. Only Bryce sat still, as at ease in these hills as he was anyplace, willing to be captured as she found him. She admired his long nose and strong chin, the wide brows that arched over his eyes with a twinge of sorrow in them.

"See anything?" Helen asked her.

"No … wait. I think I see a man's image. It's rather fuzzy."

"It's inverted. You get used to seeing it in time. Now we'll just cap the lens and you're done!" She folded up the cloth and secured it again, then pulled together the sturdy wooden legs of the tripod, setting the entire contraption back over her shoulder. "Come and call upon me when you're up to it, Odessa St. Clair. I live on Nevada Avenue. And I shall show you how to develop your photograph."

They pulled up outside the sanatorium as the horse train arrived with the afternoon crew. Dominic slid down off the carriage and eased into the shadows beneath the porch, watching from a slight distance, while Moira tensely waited for her sister to appear. There she was at last, nearly at the back of the line. She appeared as she had yesterday, peaked and sweaty, liable to fall off her horse at any moment, but she had a wide grin on her face, which Moira returned.

"Where were you off to today?" Moira asked, looking back and forth for a servant to help her sister down.

"Oh, just a short jaunt to a small waterfall, along a most treacherous path," Odessa returned.

"That sounds frightful!"

"It wasn't really, not once you saw it beyond a consumptive's view. And it was worth it. Moira, I met—" Odessa's eyes fell upon Reid, standing beside the new carriage. "Moira, where's Nic?"

The sheriff stepped forward. "I'm Sheriff Reid Bannock, Miss St. Clair. A friend of your sister's and brother's. May I assist you down off that horse?"

"I've got her," interrupted a thin but handsome, weather-roughened man. "Odessa?"

She reached out grateful hands to him and he lifted her down, holding on to her until she was steady on her feet.

Introductions were made all around. It did not take Moira's practiced eye to see that this Bryce McAllan had certain hopes about her sister. Nor did she doubt that Odessa made similar observations about Reid and herself.

"I beg your pardon, but the ride taxed me severely," Odessa said. "I must retire to my room. It was a pleasure meeting you, Sheriff. Moira, will you attend me?"

Moira turned and flashed a smile at Reid. "Thank you for the ride."

"It was my pleasure, Moira. May I come to call on you tomorrow?"

"Indeed."

The sheriff tipped his hat at each of the St. Clair women and turned away, striding as though he owned this town.

"So now the sheriff is coming to call upon you?" Odessa whispered, walking with one hand looped through Bryce's arm, one through Moira's.

"Trust me," Moira said in an undertone, "it was not my intention. There is much to tell you, Sissy. Not all of it good." She glanced to the porch, where Dominic was settling into an Adirondack chair, still unseen by their sister.

"Your man is setting up an easel," Moira said. She stood beside Odessa's window, looking down below.

"He is not my man." Odessa leaned back into the pillows, closing her eyes in pleasure. How did Bryce find the strength to go outside and paint? Perhaps that was the difference of several weeks in the sanatorium's care. Perhaps in a few more weeks, she, too, could look at an afternoon's activity with pleasure rather than wishing for nothing but a good sleep. Maybe even manage to write more than a few paltry sentences.

"He is a painter?" Moira asked, still staring outside.

"Apparently."

"You haven't seen what he paints?"

"He hasn't offered." Odessa knew her tone was becoming short, but she was so desperately weary! Couldn't her sister see it?

"You haven't asked?"

"I'd be prying. I assume it's the Peak he paints."

"He's facing the wrong direction."

"Oh, for heaven's sake. Then I don't know. What do you need, Moira? You are here because you need to talk. Out with it, so I can rest."

Moira gazed at her with a hurt expression, and a surge of guilt and sorrow waved through Odessa. She closed her eyes and tried to summon up the strength she needed to apologize, but it was no use. She was too weary to care. She opened her eyes to ask Moira to return the next day, to allow her to sleep and find the composure she needed to be a decent, caring sister, to bring Nic with her when she came … but Moira had slipped away.

Odessa sighed. It was so like Moira to act like a petulant child. No matter. She'd make it up to her soon. What she needed most, what they all needed most, was for Odessa to simply feel better. In feeling better, she'd have the strength to act better. Her eyes shifted to the window, a brilliant blue sky filling the white frame. She knew that below Bryce was again at work on his painting.

And if it wasn't the famous Peak that filled his canvas, what was it?

Chapter ✿ 13

Over the next couple of weeks, it became easier to endure the rides and Odessa began to see how the regimen worked. Doctor Morton forced them out as soon as possible. The excursions left patients tired, but hungry. They returned to eat the huge suppers provided and sleep for hours, providing sustenance and rest for their weary bodies. It was the same in many sanatoriums. Odessa had even heard of ranchers taking in consumptives, knowing that for some decent meals and a bed, they could get free work out of them. How many were trapped in small cabins or remote ranchlands, unable to escape? She was thankful for the sanatorium here in the Springs. Although Papa had neglected to give her all the facts—that she was going to Colorado likely never to return—it had been a good choice, a wise choice to send her here. Papa had sent them a letter at last, assuring them he was well, busy as ever at work, but eager to come and see his children in their new home.

April had dawned with a thin heat that blew upon the late, meager March snow, quickly melting it away, and with it went some of Odessa's fears for what had happened to Sam O'Toole that terrible night. Gradually, she had come to believe it was all a figment of her imagination, a consumptive's groggy mind. Amille, Sam's neighbor, had settled into life alongside the rest of the patients, and today was on a horse for the first time. Something calming came over the woman as she slid a boot into a stirrup and sat back into the saddle.

There was a new peacefulness about her features, as if being astride a horse comforted her.

"You've done that before," Odessa said approvingly.

Bryce moved up beside her and smiled at Amille too.

"It feels right," Amille said, speaking more coherently, calmly, than Odessa had ever heard her.

"Good, good," she responded. She moved her horse along the path, right beside Amille, and they walked down the sanatorium road and out onto the broader avenue.

"We used to ride. In the evenings," Amille said.

Odessa couldn't resist glancing back at Bryce. He looked as surprised as she that Amille was speaking coherently and in full sentences. "Who? Where?"

"John and I. We loved to ride out into the valley and look upon the mountains. But that was before we had Anna."

"Anna. That was your baby's name?"

Amille nodded. "But then they came and took her. Took her."

"Who?"

"The men. The men who wanted John's mine. They said if he didn't sign it over to them, they'd hurt us." She turned miserable eyes upon Odessa. In them, Odessa did not see a madwoman. She saw truth. She glanced back at Bryce in alarm.

"Amille," Bryce said, gently easing forward to walk beside them. "Anna died in the creek. She drowned," he said softly.

"No," Amille said. "That is where they left her." She shook her head suddenly, as if tossing away the bad memory. "But they didn't get what they wanted. John still has his mine. And Sam hid his entrance. No one will find it. Not there."

Odessa sat up straighter in her saddle. Bryce caught her eye, obviously wondering the same thing. "Amille," she said slowly, "you said Sam hid his entrance. Did Sam discover a silver vein?"

"Maybe my baby is here," Amille said, her eyes once again distant. "Do you think she's here? I've been looking for her. Looking for her. Looking for her. Looking for her."

Odessa sighed and let her go ahead, her heart aching for the woman as she slipped back into her familiar, incoherent world. Bryce pulled alongside her and reached out a hand to briefly cover hers. "What do you think that means?" Odessa asked, nodding toward Amille's back.

He shook his head.

"Do you think Sam discovered silver on his land?"

"Could be. His land abuts John and Amille's. It would make sense." He shook his head. "But he never said a word about it."

"Might he have been concerned? Frightened, what with this story about John and Amille and the baby?"

"John would've gone to our sheriff." He dropped his voice. "The girl—she was little, not quite three years old. Slipped and fell. Amille hasn't really been right in the head since she died. You can't take what she says as truth."

They rode for a while in silence. "Sam never mentioned anyone coming around?" Odessa asked then. "Anyone who wanted to buy his land? Anyone pressuring his neighbors?"

Bryce pulled his head to the side as if reluctant to say anything. "Mining … It's a dangerous business, Odessa. You break your back trying to see if there's anything but rock in your yard and if you're lucky, you find it. But that's when others come around. Most miners are alone. Easy prey. That's why many take on a partner."

"Or hide their mine claim."

He studied her intently. "You don't think …" His eyes moved to Amille and back again. They pulled up their horses, letting the rest of the group move on without them.

"You've settled in here to recover your health," Odessa said. "But is this thing about Sam ever far from your mind? I'd just about decided it was all in my imagination, that I was too ill to think clearly that night and misinterpreted it … but Amille—maybe God brought her here for us, Bryce. So that we might be reminded of the truth, the need to ferret out the truth. Justice."

Bryce let out a humorless laugh. "We have your memories from a night when you were desperately ill, an odd poem from a dead man, and the rantings of a madwoman. How are we to ferret out the truth?" He lifted a shoulder. "I don't know, Odessa. Maybe our minds are too long idle, jumping to conclusions. The storyteller in you is acting up." He held up a hand as she began her retort. "And even if it's true … we're not in any shape to go and track down any claim jumpers. Right?"

"Right," she said reluctantly.

"Think on this with me, Odessa. John DeChant is apparently well and working his claim, even as we speak. I hold the land deed to all of Sam's land—even any potential mine—and you perhaps have the key to finding the entrance, if it even exists. Until one of those pieces changes, I believe we need to treat all of this as conjecture. Agreed?"

"Agreed."

The sheriff took to escorting Moira everywhere in town and coming to call for tea almost every day in the shop's back room. His pursuit was evolving into full-out courtship, blessed by the family or not, and Nic and Moira struggled to find a reason or rationale to end it. They knew they had to—Reid was making Moira progressively more uncomfortable; each day it continued, it encouraged him onward. Today, Dominic was helping an elderly man with his selections from the stacks of novels, patiently waiting as the man moved to put on his eyeglasses and slowly turn the pages—perusing the words as he might a crate of fruit to see if they were palatable—while Moira and Reid remained in the back room.

Every time Nic excused himself, the customer asked another question.

Feeling Reid's heated gaze upon her, Moira hovered near the doorway. "I think he might need a woman's touch," she said to Reid, moving to grab her apron.

"It's I who needs a woman's touch," Reid said in a seductive undertone, taking her hand and pulling her to him. He stared up at her from his chair, reaching for the other hand, holding both in his. "I've been fighting it, Moira, this desire in me. I've been calling on you for weeks." He rose, towering now above her. "It's time. I've been patient. You have to say I've been very patient. Please, Moira. Give me a kiss. Just one." He pulled her hands up to rest on his chest and placed his hands on her neck, pulling her closer.

"Reid, this is hardly the place." She pushed away but he held her firm.

"Good enough to steal a kiss," he said, smiling down at her, moving his face to hers. "Thoughts of your rosebud mouth drive me to sleepless nights," he said in a husky whisper. Then he kissed her, softly, searchingly.

"Moira?" Dominic called.

Moira squirmed out of Reid's grasp and looked from him to the door. She patted her hair guiltily. "Reid, we really shouldn't."

He just laid a hand on the wall as if weakened and smiled over at her, rubbing a thumb over his lower lip as if he thought to draw her back in. "I beg to differ."

Dominic appeared then, looking from one to the other. "Can you come help me package Mr. Smith's books?" he asked, hooking a thumb over his shoulder.

"Certainly," she said, moving past him in a hurry.

"I'll be on my way," Reid called to the trio at the counter. "I'll be back at six to pick you up for the dinner at the Glen. Dress appropriately."

"I look forward to it," Moira said, coming around to see him to the door.

"Do you?" he asked, staring at her quizzically. "I can't seem to figure you out. One moment you seem to be my girl, the next you're a stranger to me."

"You know deep down who I am," Moira said sweetly.

He reached out as if to touch her face, caught himself and grinned. "Until tonight."

"About tonight," Dominic called, finally finishing Mr. Smith's transaction. The man took a step and then paused to peruse a display of books to his right as if seeing them for the first time. "Odessa is feeling well enough to accompany us—"

"The general graciously invited her to attend," put in Moira.

"We plan to pick her up at the sanatorium, so we'll meet you at the Glen."

"I could fetch her. Then we could all go together," Reid said. "It's our last night before I head out of town."

"No, no," Dominic said in friendly fashion. "It's way across town for you. We'll pick Odessa up and meet you directly at six thirty."

"Very well," Reid said with a smile that held appreciation but eyes that held disappointment. Moira knew he liked arriving at the general's with her on his arm. General Palmer had taken to her of late, seeming to think of her as a pleasant diversion in the midst of Queen's absence. Half the time the men ended up in the baroque blue room, listening to music, rather than taking their leisure in the general's den.

"Until tonight." She closed the door and watched the sheriff move down the stairs and into the street. "I can't maintain this masquerade, Nic," Moira said, as she waved good-bye at the window and then turned to lean against it, her face falling. She ignored old Mr. Smith, who was hard of hearing. "I hate that he is always around, and I think he's beginning to sense it."

"Just a little longer, Moira," Nic begged, coming over to her. "With all the invitations you receive, we're meeting the finest people in town. We can even call a few of them friends. We need to know we can call more of them friends before you break that man's heart and he comes to collect. Just a little longer," he said again, lifting her hand. "We'll find a reasonable excuse yet."

"Young love," said Mr. Smith as he passed them by.

With that, he left. And Dominic and Moira burst out laughing.

John DeChant sat on the old wooden chair, hands tied behind his back. "I'm doing what you wanted."

"No," said the man above him, slapping him across the face. Blood began to stream from the corner of his lip. "You've found one measly vein of silver, barely enough to keep your crazy wife in the sanatorium."

"You better pick up the pace, DeChant," said another man near him, gripping his face. "Or they'll throw her in the streets. How long do you think a pretty little woman like that would survive on her own, mad as a hatter?"

John wrenched his face out of the man's grip. "You promised me you wouldn't touch her!" He shook his head. "You want me to mine my claim, but you also want me to search Sam's property. I can't be two places at once."

"No," said the first man. "That's why we're taking over."

"Taking over?"

"There's two of us, one of you. We can be two places at once."

"And what am I to do?"

The second man lifted him from his chair and pushed him out the cabin door. "You, my friend, have a day to find the O'Toole mine entrance or you will die."

"No." John knelt down in the mud before his house. "Please. Amille. She can't take it. It will be the end of her."

The first man lifted him up gruffly and dragged him toward the path. "So be it. It'd make it far easier to purchase the property. But we're fair men, DeChant. Do as you promised, find the entrance, and we'll merely buy you out for market value and ship you and the missus off to a sanatorium in France."

John turned and stared at him. "No. No, I will not do any more. Any man who would take a child's life would not hesitate to take another man's. Kill me now, but I will not help you anymore."

The man laughed and looked at his friend, then laughed harder, shaking his head. "DeChant, I keep tellin' you that was an accident. She slipped and fell—"

"Running away from you," John spat out.

The man's face lost any hint of mirth. "You're forgetting Amille. You will help us, and help us now. Or we'll take your wife and make her last hours the most miserable she's ever experienced."

Dominic took Odessa to see Helen Anderson two weeks after they had first met. Nic seemed glum, burdened by the work of the store, not at all glad to see it do a brisk business from the first day it opened. Only the reprieve from Sheriff Bannock's constant calls seemed to buoy his mood. Whenever Odessa was with him, she watched as he paced and wrung his hands, lost in his own world of thought. Was it the sheriff's unwanted pursuit of their sister, or something else?

The bruises on his face, his grimace when he helped her down from his new carriage, as if in pain, were not lost on her. He was fighting again. How? Where? And the question the whole family had asked for years ... why?

They waited on Helen's porch, shielded from the sun. She answered the door herself and greeted Odessa like a long-lost friend—"My, haven't you made some gains these last weeks!"—and then shaking her brother's hand. "A bookseller by day, a fine trade, young man. But aren't you also a fighter by night? Shorty St. Clair?"

Dominic's eyes shifted away from her in embarrassed surprise and he shook his head. "I'm afraid not. Just a bookseller. Though my sister would tell you I've scuffled with one or two men in my life." He flashed them both grins, trying to charm them. "I wouldn't mind staying," he said, "but I must fetch the latest shipment for the shop down at the depot. Joe's expecting me. May I return for my sister in an hour's time?"

"Make it two hours," Helen said decisively. "We have some work to do and it can never be cut short."

Dominic was off then, moving as if he could not escape fast enough, and Helen stared at Odessa. "Keeps his own counsel, does he?"

"All his life," she returned.

"Come," Helen said. "Sit on the settee and I'll pour you some Earl Grey. The biscuits are from the bakery down the street, lemon! They're divine. Try one."

Odessa accepted a lemon biscuit and relished the tangy sweetness of the treat. "Mrs. Anderson, you said you came to Colorado Springs to chase the cure too."

"Call me Helen, please. And yes, more than fifteen years ago now." She reached down and showed off her bulbous waist. "Obviously, the wasting disease is long gone. And those biscuits are of no assistance. Ever since I was young, people told me to eat, that I was nothing but skin and bones. Now women actually ask me if I should eat at all!"

Odessa covered her mouth and laughed along with her hostess. It had been a long time since she had met a woman as free and vivacious as Helen. "What do you believe it is? What is it about this place that heals?" Odessa asked as she settled in her seat.

"It's all they tout. The clean, dry air. Maybe it's wandering land sacred to the Ute Indians. Or the mountain's shadow. Maybe it's the bracing exercise and good food that is part of the sanatorium's regimen, although there was no sanatorium when I arrived. I'd nearly died three times by the time I dragged myself here at a friend's invitation."

"You never left?"

"Too afraid to leave again."

Odessa thought of Bryce, getting sick every time he went East, of her own longing to return home.

"But Colorado is big territory to feel confined in," Helen said with a grunt. "Come, finish your tea and tell me about yourself and your family. You're obviously a reader, if you know my books."

Odessa studied her new friend, weighing what to tell her. "I am. And I ... I have ideas for a book of my own."

"Oh?" Helen asked, lifting her eyebrows in pleasure as she bit into another biscuit. "How lovely! What is it about?"

"It's a story, a story of a woman in a strange, new place, trying to find her sense of home again." Odessa hesitated, suddenly shy. "I'm only beginning. I have all these things in my mind, but I can't seem to get past page one. I write it over and over again."

"Force yourself to page two, then page three. When you complete the chapter, then allow yourself to reread and edit. But only once. Then force yourself to the next chapter."

"But what if the first is not right? If it doesn't meet my expectations?"

Helen sat back. "One can always go back and rewrite it yet again. But, Odessa, if you never have something ready for editing, something of substance, then you'll never get anywhere. You won't see your story as a whole, only a partial work. And partial works can never ever be done, correct?"

Odessa sat across from her hostess, absorbing her words. "Correct."

"It's a bit like the farmers used to say back East. 'Too much rain, bad crop. No rain at all, no crop.' You need a crop. Worry about the rain later." She sat forward. "What are you afraid of, Odessa?"

Odessa pictured Papa in his office, tossing a manuscript to the burn pile. "Worthless," he declared, over and over. Was that what held her back? Fear that her father would declare her work worthless? She glanced at Helen. "I don't know," she said.

"A bit to think about, eh? Well come, then. Let us be off to the darkroom where we will see your photograph."

She rose and moved off. Odessa followed her, lost in thought. The woman could cover as much territory in conversation as she could with her camera. Did she have Helen's courage, somewhere deep within her? Or did she really fear her father's disapproval so much that it kept her from moving forward? Might she find a way to write for her enjoyment alone, as God had created her to do, whatever the outcome?

The clean scent of the chemicals, liquid in vast trays, assailed her nostrils when they entered the room, lit only by a ruby lantern. "There, you see? Light enough for us to move in and do our work, but dark enough to not harm the photographs." Helen moved forward and removed the holders from the edge of the glass plate. "This was the last photograph I took from the trail."

She placed it film side up in the first tray of water, making sure it was well covered. Helen pulled several bottles from her shelves and mixed a concoction of water, potash, bromide of potassium, and a few drops of oxalic acid. She removed the plate from the tray and washed it with the solution she had just mixed. In seconds, traces of an image began to appear. "See the air bubbles?" she said. "You have to remove them or they'll distort your image." Then she moved it into a second tray of water, using a pair of metal tongs to hold it. After several more minutes, a picture of a beautiful waterfall emerged from a fog of milky white into a clear image. "That's just up from where I discovered you," she said, looking at Odessa. "Been there yet?"

"Not yet. It's wonderful."

"Best about this time of year. Encourage the trail nurse to go a bit farther next time. But it'll be spoiled for you, now that you've seen it in my fine photograph," she said with a grin. "Now, on to your first photograph." She moved back to the stack and tore the holders off the next plate. "Go on, hold it by the edges and ease it into that first tray."

Odessa did as she was told, then flowed the developing liquid over her plate, watching the image emerge. Was that a boulder? A man's shoulder? Impossible to tell yet. "Helen, why did you call my brother Shorty St. Clair?"

"That's his fighting name."

"What fighting name?"

Helen met her gaze steadily. "Take the tongs. Move it into the next tray."

Odessa did as she was told, but still waited for her friend to answer her question.

After a moment, Helen sighed. "Your brother fights for money over in Colorado City. He's quite good, actually. One of the best I've seen."

Aghast, Odessa glanced at the older woman again. "You? You attend … fights?"

"Indeed I do. It's thrilling." She shrugged. "I'm not particularly proud of my fascination. But there is something primal about two men in a ring. Something I'm trying to capture in my writing." She moved past Odessa and peered into the tray. "Thought you wanted to take a picture of the whole group."

"I did!" Odessa cried. "Did I make a mistake?"

"You tell me." Helen gripped the corner of the plate and lifted it, dripping, into the air.

It was a photograph of Bryce. Alone among the rocks. Casual. Thinner—he'd gained more weight since then. But with those smiling eyes …

"I can't take that back with me. They're all waiting for me to return with the photograph of the entire group."

Helen unsuccessfully tried to hide her laugh, giggling, a deep, rumbling sound within her barrel chest. "Who's the man?" she said.

"Bryce. A … a friend."

"Handsome friend. Must've happened when I told you to center your field of vision and then focus in."

"I, I uh …"

"Odessa, a photographer follows her eye, to that element or nuance or pose that truly draws her, much like a writer is drawn to certain words, something that becomes the epitome of what she envisions. You did that here. There's nothing here of which you should be ashamed."

"But I took a photograph of a man. There is something oddly … intimate in it."

"Isn't there?" She lifted her eyebrows in shameless delight. "We'll let that cure and dry here on the line. You may return tomorrow to fetch it."

"I can't take that back with me," Odessa repeated. Her chest was constricting. She could hear the familiar, high whine …

Helen closed a heavy black drape between them and the room bathed in red light, then opened the door back into the parlor. "Easy, Odessa," she said, leading her back to the settee. "Just breathe. Breathe." She stood back, hands on her hips, staring down at her. "You St. Clairs have quite the secrets, don't you? I can't wait to make Moira's acquaintance."

Chapter ❊ 14

Dr. Morton appeared beside Odessa one afternoon, where she practiced her archery with Bryce and Charlotte and five others, shooting targets painted onto a hay bale. "Miss St. Clair," he said, pausing, as if unsure of what to say. "Most unfortunate news has reached us," he continued. "Amille's husband has passed away."

Bryce lowered his bow and frowned. "John? What happened?"

Oh no, was all Odessa could think. While Amille's health improved under the doctor's care, her mind remained fragile. And something happening to John DeChant … she shared a quick glance with Bryce.

"Cave-in at his mine. The sheriff down there found him. Said he went to check on him after he didn't show up at church."

Bryce lifted fingers to his brow and rubbed, as if he might scrub the frown from his forehead. "John was a regular. Never missed."

"I was hoping you might come with me to tell Mrs. DeChant, Miss St. Clair. She's obviously taken a liking to you. Perhaps your presence will lend some comfort during this terrible time."

Odessa set down her bow and nodded, following behind the small man as they entered the sanatorium and climbed the sweeping stairs to the private rooms. She glanced over her shoulder. Bryce was right behind her.

They rounded the corner and on leaden feet, moved past Odessa's room and on to Amille's. The woman was dozing in a chair by the window, sunlight streaming over her shoulder. The doctor moved forward, but Odessa said, "Please. Dr. Morton. Perhaps—perhaps it will be better coming from me."

Doctor Morton considered her over the rims of his glasses and then stepped aside, gesturing toward the woman.

Odessa covered the remaining steps and knelt at Amille's feet. She was so fine boned, so fragile yet. And Odessa knew she missed John, missed her husband. Saying a brief prayer for courage and comfort, Odessa reached out a hand and took Amille's.

The woman stirred and then opened her eyes, looking into Odessa's. She immediately seemed to sense that something was desperately wrong. "Oh no. No, no, no, no, no," she said in anguish. How did she know? Did Odessa's face hold some of the sorrow that John's had when he had to tell his wife that he had found their little girl, that there was no longer any hope that she was merely lost or wandering?

"No, no, no, no," she said, tears already streaming down her face.

"Amille," Odessa said, nearly choking on her name, tears now running down her own face. "I'm so sorry, my friend. But John has died. He is gone."

Odessa remained with Amille through an hour of screaming, then another hour as the doctor's sedation moved through her body and coaxed her into a fitful sleep. Bryce hovered at the door, alternately pacing and sitting on the floor with his back against the wall. He left for a time and returned with a sketch pad and pencil. Odessa watched him, so intent upon his work. She wondered what he sketched now. He was obviously reluctant to show her, once outright refusing her when she asked. It had hurt, that refusal, but she supposed it was a bit like her own writing. She was not yet ready for anyone to read the words she'd managed to pen here, for it felt like an intimacy, allowing them near what was in her heart, her mind.

She dozed off and awakened only when Bryce shook her shoulder gently. "Odessa, I'll keep an eye on her. I'll send another woman in to sit with her. But you have to get ready, right?"

Odessa shook her head, as if to dispel it of the fog that had invaded, and then remembered. General Palmer's spring ball. The first real social event since she had begun to make her recovery. "Perhaps," she said, hesitating. "Perhaps you ought to come with us, Bryce. To keep Dominic company," she rushed on, realizing her suggestion was entirely improper.

"No," he said with a gentle smile in his blue eyes. "I'll stay here." He nodded at Amille. "If I'm here then you'll be more likely to relax, to enjoy your time at Glen Eyrie, right?"

"I suppose that is true." She rose but he did not move away. "Thank you," she said, looking up at him.

"You're welcome." He reached out as if to touch her cheek, seemed to remember himself, then turned aside to let her pass. She moved into her room and shut the door, curiously aware of Bryce's presence next door. She dressed and did her hair, then pulled on a fine gown that still hung loosely on her gaunt frame but looked lovely on her. Odessa moved out of the room and down the stairs, hoping Bryce would see her, then angry at herself for such hope.

Just what did she think was transpiring between them? They had become companions, spending much of every day together, at least in a group if not alone, and it tore at her heart to think of leaving not only Amille, but Bryce behind this night. But what foolishness! There was nothing spoken between them, nothing declared.

"Odessa," he said, stepping out of the shadows near the front door.

Her hand went to her breast as her heart beat double-time. "Bryce! You frightened me."

"Forgive me." He took a step closer, then stopped, curiously distant, as if holding himself aback. "You are like something out of a picture. You are like …"

She met his gaze, expectant, wondering.

"Like someone from a far-off country." He stepped away then, turned to go.

"Only Philadelphia," she quipped, hoping to see him smile.

He had paused, listened, but said nothing more. "Your brother and sister are here," he said, gesturing with his head out the front door. Then he simply walked away. It was difficult to explain how Odessa felt in that moment, but the only adjective she could think of was *broken*, the only verb, *tearing*, the only noun, *separation*.

Odessa accepted Nic's hand up and into the carriage that night, glad to be escaping the dark pall that covered the sanatorium. Was it fear that something sinister had happened to Sam and now John? Or fear for what was happening to her heart?

"Are you all right?" he asked, noting her drawn expression.

"Fine. It's been a rather difficult day, though. Word reached us that a friend's husband died."

"Oh, how terrible," Moira said, as Nic settled into the driver's seat and flicked the reins. "Was it the consumption?"

"No," Odessa said, looking over the edge of the carriage. "A mining accident. Cave-in."

"Terrible, just terrible for her," Moira said.

"It is. And she's not of the most sound mind. I fear for her future."

"We must pray for her," Moira said.

"Yes, we must," Odessa agreed, surprised at Moira's suggestion. Moira had always been content to attend church to see and be seen. Was she discovering something deeper, something more about her God as Odessa was, here in the West? She considered her sister. "Say, where is the sheriff this night?"

"We told him we'd meet him at the Glen," Moira said lightly.

"Insolent man thinks he needs to be with Moira every day," Dominic groused.

"Now, Nic, don't start," Moira said.

"Yes, you know how it goes for you when you enter a room angry about something," Odessa said. "Someone always gets hit. You can't do that at the Palmers'."

Dominic shook his head and swallowed a retort.

"Just say what you need to say, Brother," Odessa said, meeting his gaze. "And cease looking at me as if I was made of glass, about to shatter at any moment."

"Speaking of glass," Moira interrupted, "wait until you see the plate glass windows in the Palmers' house. And their crystal! Truly, you have not seen anything so fine since we left Philadelphia." Dominic's demeanor softened as the sisters idly chatted, Moira speaking of every person bound to be in attendance. It was a spring ball, heralding the arrival of greenery on the trees and the waning snows of winter. Moira sounded more free, more herself, than she had in weeks. Yet Reid was like a shadow, drowning out her light, using it for his own glory. Odessa could see it.

The St. Clair sisters made the same stir they had made every time they entered a hall together in Philadelphia, although it had been some time for Odessa. More than two years, Dominic thought. Two years since she had grown too ill to even consider going to a ball, even to observe. Moira immediately took the spotlight, but Dominic could not miss how many of the men watched Odessa instead. She was classically beautiful, with her pretty face—still bearing faint pink lines from the cuts she'd suffered—dark hair, and wide blue-green eyes. She had chosen a lavender dress that gave her more color than he had seen on her for months, even beyond the ruddy cheeks. Her illness had left her with a haunting countenance that made others look at her twice, trying to decipher just what it was about her that gave her beauty depth. And even though Odessa was gaining weight, filling the curves of the gown a bit as a woman should, Nic thought she might never lose that memorable quality. He had known men, fighters, who had stared death in the eye but still remained among the living. Odessa had that same look.

Except without the broken nose, he joked to himself. He was proud of her, proud of Moira, too. Proud of himself.

If only Father could see his children now, making their way here in their new city. Part of her finest citizens. He took a crystal champagne flute from a passing servant and continued to watch over his sisters. Reid emerged from the crowd at Moira's side, and she managed to smile and take his arm. He offered the other to Odessa, and after a half-second hesitation, she took it. He paraded them around proudly, introducing Odessa about the room. Dominic knew his sister's dance card would soon be filled, since her illness would keep her from accepting no more than three or four turns about the floor.

Odessa moved with the social graces her mother had taught them, sharing small niceties with one and then another. Gently complimenting their host on the fine delicacies served and the well-appointed, perfectly decorated room. But as the meal was completed and the dishes swept away, as the music began and she accepted an offer to dance from her second dance partner, all Odessa wanted was to return to the sanatorium.

To what? She thought with surprise. Every evening was the same. A large, crackling fire in the hearth. People sitting about, hacking, hacking, hacking as they coughed, trying to get a decent breath, others who were better, talking, laughing. Playing games. Reading books. It was a warm place. A welcoming place. She thought about each of the faces there, but in particular, dear little Charlotte. Half-mad Amille. Bryce.

The memory of him when he'd come across her in the hall as she left made heat climb her neck. What was it about that moment? Seeing her dressed in finery? The intense draw to each other, then the sense of separation. *Like someone from a far-off country,* he'd said. Had she become different to him? She was still Odessa St. Clair, the same Odessa he had fished beside, walked beside, eaten beside. Was it this? That she danced about the room in another's arms, and then another's?

Did he not know that she did it all the while wondering what it would be like to dance with him?

Reid led her to the edge of the room and then quickly around a corner.

"My sweet, I ask that you not sing tonight."

"What?" Moira asked, confused. It had become a tradition of sorts, her singing at Glen Eyrie. Every time, in the ten visits they had made, she had sung.

"There are too many people here tonight. It is too … public. We've been apart too much. I don't wish to share you. Let's depart early, steal some time alone."

"The general has already asked me to sing after the dancing is done. I agreed."

He glowered at her. "I care not. Plead a weak voice. Make an excuse. But do not sing tonight."

She stared up at him. He had seemed agitated all evening, moving to block one man's stare and then another's. It was as if she were a sheep and he felt surrounded by wolves. Was that it? Was he jealous? "You seemed happy enough, proud even, when I've sung before."

"There weren't this many in attendance. It isn't … seemly."

This from a man content to steal kisses—three to date—a man

with devilish thoughts on his mind as he touched her, never thinking to ask her how she felt, what she wanted, if she desired him in kind. He simply assumed. "We shall see how it turns out," she said, moving past him.

He grabbed her arm, squeezing it painfully. "I told you how it will turn out," he ground out. "You shall not sing."

"You are hurting me," she said between her teeth, frowning in surprise. He loosened his grip and she wrenched her arm away. "I am not your wife, Sheriff."

"You will be someday."

She scoffed at him. "That is not decided. You have no claim on me."

"You are my girl. That is claim enough."

Moira placed her hands on her hips. "No, Reid. I am your woman. But you are not my man."

He paused, confusion gathering in his face. Her heart caught a moment, then pounded so hard she fought the urge to reach out to the wall and steady herself. What had she just done?

"Sissy?" Odessa called down the hall. "Sissy? Ah, there you are." She came around the corner, Dominic right behind her. "They're calling for you. The general wants you to sing now," she said, her wide eyes going from Moira to Reid. "Ready?"

"Ready," said Moira.

"What is it?" Reid asked the man in the hallway after the St. Clairs had departed. Reid ran his hand through his hair, wondering about Moira's words, as the shorter man moved out from the shadows and to his side. Had she meant it? Or was it merely her female ways, toying with him? He watched Odessa turn the corner with one final, worried look in his direction, wondering if he should have chosen her instead. A weaker woman, a consumptive even, would have been easier to mold into a proper wife.

But he didn't want a consumptive as his wife. Who knew if she could even bear him children? He needed a strong, hearty wife, a woman to meet his needs.

"She's the one," the man said. "Odessa St. Clair. She was the one in the room beside O'Toole the night he … gave into the consumption. I saw her."

Reid stared at the empty hallway, hearing the musicians begin the first chords for Moira's song, a song he had just asked her not to sing.

"She was bad off that night, as I understand it. You think she heard anything? Did she see you?" Reid asked.

"She got up, fell. That's how her face got cut up. Why else do you think she rose, as poorly as she was?"

Reid considered his words, remembering the faint pink lines on Odessa's perfectly sculpted face. "If my future sister-in-law knows something of O'Toole, I'll know it soon enough. In the meantime, we go in different directions."

"As you wish, Sheriff."

As you wish. How he longed to hear Moira say those words. He would hear Moira say those words to him. Over and over again. One way or another.

Chapter 15

May

Over the weeks, Moira made an excuse to walk past the opera house almost every day, watching with delight as the last of the brickwork was installed and posters were placed outside, announcing the call for vocal talent. Again and again she wondered if she could find her way onto the stage, find the way to rehearse if she even got the part with the traveling troupe. She vacillated over whether or not she should confide in Odessa or Nic, but elected to hold her own confidences. Papa had sent her west to keep her out of the theater. Surely her siblings would feel bound by honor to tell him. No, she couldn't risk it.

"Miss St. Clair! Miss St. Clair!" called a boy. She turned and waited on him, then saw the general across the street, in front of the opera house. He tipped his hat toward her.

"Miss St. Clair," said the boy, breathless by the time he reached her side. "The general … he asks if you won't come and greet him."

Moira straightened her skirt and followed after the boy, waiting for a heavy wagon drawn by four horses to pass. At last she was with the general, who stood beside a man she hadn't seen in some time—Jesse McCourt. The actor who had saved her from Reid's manhandling at the Glen!

"Miss St. Clair," the general said in tender greeting. "I believe you remember my friend Mr. McCourt."

"I do." She smiled up at the handsome man, so dapper in his fine suit. He smiled back at her.

"Mr. McCourt has just accepted our offer to his troupe to play in our opera house as it opens, but we are still seeking a female lead. It occurred to me how your lovely voice seems to captivate all who hear it. Tell me, my dear, would you consider an audition?"

Moira's heart beat triple-time. "How I would love it!" Her mind briefly paused over the image of her father, his firm disapproval over the theater, then on to Reid. He wanted to stifle her, control her, own her. Yet neither man was here.

She lifted her face and smiled sweetly. "When would you like me to come?"

Odessa's father had been right.

They had chased down the cure and made it their own.

"I want you to take me with you tonight," she said to Helen as they worked side by side. Helen was teaching her how to use her camera and rode with their small group a couple of times a week. "Take me to watch my brother fight."

Helen let out a long, low whistle. "Sure that's a good idea, friend? It's one thing to watch a stranger get pummeled. Another when it's your kin."

"You said he's good."

"He is. But there's a reason he shows up with a split lip or a bruised-blue eye."

"I've seen him fight before," she said, sounding more brave than she felt.

"Street scuffles, I'd wager. It's a different thing in the ring. I'll ask it of you again—are you certain you're ready to watch?"

Odessa stared back at her friend. "It's part of who Dominic is. I don't want to. But I need to. Does that make sense?"

"Perfectly. But you bring your man-friend along."

"Who? Bryce?"

"Yes. A fighting ring is no place for a lady. You'll need him with you."

"But you go."

Helen laughed. "Honey, I haven't been a lady in a very long time."

She found him on the porch in the corner, again at his easel. He glanced up at her when she arrived and gave her a gentle smile.

She paused directly in front of him. "May I see it?"

"What?"

"Your painting. Come, Bryce. I've been asking for weeks now. Just a peek?"

He studied her for a moment, his blue eyes searching hers, as if he wondered if he might trust her with this work. Did he want empty flattery? Honest review? She thought about what it felt like to hand another her words on paper.

"Why do you want to see my painting?" He dipped his brush into the paint on the palette, twirling it slowly.

"If you do not paint to show others your view of the world, why paint at all?" she returned.

"I allow others to see my paintings when they are complete." He set the brush to canvas, cocked his head, added another stroke, and then looked again to her.

"Well ... I would hope so." Odessa sank into a chaise lounge in front of the window, suddenly weary and weak in the knees. How had she managed to dance just two weeks ago? She hated this disease, how one day she could be feeling better, and the next have to take to her bed again. She turned to her side, and after a moment to the other, facing him again.

Bryce set his brush down on the easel's ledge and leaned down to rest his forearms on his knees, hands casually clasped together. He looked relaxed, strong, and Odessa suddenly could see him with another twenty pounds of flesh, astride a horse on his ranch. "What is bothering you, Odessa? You're as skittish as a half-drowned cat. Is it Amille? John's death?"

Odessa eyed the empty doorway and then whispered, "Does it not bother you, Sam, Amille's claim about her girl, and now John?"

He paused, measuring his words. "I am troubled. I need to get down there, talk to the sheriff, see if I can find out—"

"Leave! You can't leave!" She felt swift heat upon her neck as the words left her mouth. "I mean, you are not yet well enough. And if there is a danger ..."

"If there is a danger, I'd rather find out down there, far from here." But he said the word *here* as if he was saying *you*. He was worried, concerned enough to want to try and keep her safe. Go out and face the enemy before he got too close. "But there is something else on your mind, Odessa. What is troubling you?"

"No, I ... I am merely feeling confined. Trapped. As if I should

go for another ride today, and yet I'm desperately weary. That's it!"
she said suddenly. "You are painting your horses."

"You are changing the subject." He watched her shift in her seat
again. "Tell me."

"You want me to trust you with my intimacies," she said in irritation. *You who would consider leaving me behind.* "On what basis?"

He hesitated. "Friendship."

Friendship. So that was all she was to him? She sighed heavily.
"Trains, you are painting trains."

He sat there, simply staring, waiting her out. If she didn't start
talking soon, she was liable to begin speaking and never stop. She
might tell him that she thought of him as more than a friend, as a
beau, blurt out that when he was absent, she felt lost, incomplete …
that she hated this new, curious distance between them, as if he had
stepped away.

"My brother," she hedged. "I'm worried sick over him."

"Dominic?" Bryce asked doubtfully. "He seems like a man who
can take care of himself."

"Sometimes too well. He is fighting, apparently for money now.
As a boy in Philadelphia, it always began as something else—a score
to settle, an injustice to be righted. But here in Colorado, he goes
about as book merchant by day, and ring fighter by night."

Bryce sat back, clearly aware that she was giving him just a part of
what was on her heart. "If the man wants to fight, why not let him?
He's been thrust into the role of book merchant by your father, yes?"

"Yes."

"But had his future been his own, what do you think he would
be doing?"

Odessa raised her eyebrows and thought about that. She had never considered it. All their lives, it had been understood that the girls would become wives and mothers and the boys would enter their father's business. With but one remaining male heir to the St. Clair Press fortune, there was never a question as to what Dominic would do when he came of age. Was this from where his anger stemmed? Rage that was the kindling to the constant, flickering coals within?

"I know something of a father's goals for his son. Come, look upon my painting."

Odessa stared at him, suddenly fearful of moving. What if … what if she despised what she saw? What would she say?

"Come," he said, gesturing toward the canvas and moving his stool to the side.

She rose on unsteady legs and slowly walked around to stand beside him. Her hand went to her mouth. It was unlike anything she had expected.

There on the canvas were three ships, racing upon a wind-capped sea. The colors, various shades of sea and sky and shadow, were vibrant. "Oh, Bryce."

"Speak. You must say more than that."

"It's magnificent." Her eyes shifted back and forth as if she could drink in the salt air, feel the sea's mist upon her face. "I am suddenly no longer in Colorado but upon the Atlantic." She waved to the sails. "How you capture the curve of the canvas on the wind—I can almost hear them billowing full and then snapping taut." She glanced down at him in wonder. "How … what …?"

"Twelve crossings to Spain," he said. "My father knew early on that I had a talent with the horses. Yet horses don't favor long stretches of ocean and nothing but a ship's planks to walk. I've stood alongside Spanish stallions and broodmares for weeks, with nothing to do but soothe them and study the ways of a ship. I fell in love with the sea, but my father, and this cursed illness, forced me in a different direction. Painting is as close to the sea as I'll ever be."

Odessa felt short of breath, so heavy was the sorrow, the loss within his tone.

"Please sit down. You look faint." He placed his head in one hand and rubbed his temples. "I know there are no answers. I've had this conversation with myself a thousand times." She sat down again upon the chaise and gazed in his direction. He gave her a half smile. "I love the sea. But I also do truly love horses. And the land they need is ever farther from the ocean's edge."

"My father has always said that life is a series of difficult choices."

"He is a wise man."

"A wise man who cannot see his son before him … only his own dreams living on within him. Much like what your father has done to you." She rose and paced. "Bryce, I need you to do something for me."

"What is that?"

"I need you to take me to see him fight."

He was already shaking his head, firm decision in his eyes. "It is no place for a woman, Odessa. Those rings—invariably, they are on the wrong side of town and attended by people that are not of *polite* society."

"You think I am so naive? I am well aware it will be shocking—"

He was shaking his head again.

"Please. I need to know what drives my brother. I need to know Dominic, see him, in ways … my family has never taken the time to do that with him. The hopes of four dead brothers rest on his shoulders. Perhaps that is what drives him to fight. I think if I could see him there—"

"Odessa, no. It would be ungentlemanly of me to escort you to such a place."

"Helen Anderson has gone. She will take me if you will not."

He scoffed and shook his head, rising in agitation. "You must not." His eyes held fear now, concern for her. "Women do not belong there. You should not go there unescorted. If Mrs. Anderson wishes to risk that, so be it. But you, Odessa …" He reached out and took her hands.

The feel of his strong fingers around hers made her heart pound. They felt sure, right. Slowly, slowly, she lifted her eyes to meet his.

"Please, Bryce. Take me to see him. Just once."

He winced as if she had cut him, then stared at her again. "You'll see I'm right, Odessa. I've seen men in the fighting ring before. They're there because something else has driven them to it. Power or anger, usually. It's not what God wants of us. You'll feel that. It's evil, attempting to pummel another until he's almost dead. This will not be two boys playing, wrestling. This will be two men intent on killing each other. You and I … we've talked about knowing death, sensing it when it edges near. Are you really ready to walk into death's parlor again? Invite it close?"

Odessa put her fingers over her mouth, listening. "Nic wouldn't kill a man."

"He wouldn't intend to. But every time he steps into that ring, he flirts with it."

"That's why … this is why I need to go. I need to see it for myself. Understand it." She looked up at Bryce with pleading eyes. "He's my brother."

"I've warned you," he said, sorrow invading every syllable. "You can't say I didn't."

"How many times must I warn you?" said the man. "Don't come here unless you have good news for me. Again and again you appear, telling me you're no closer to the silver than you were before!"

"The sheriff from Westcliffe is about often. It's as if he's on to us."

The first man scoffed at that. "Sheriff Olsbo? He has no idea what's happening in his backyard."

"He's suspicious enough that we need to keep a scout out while we try to excavate the miserable DeChant mine in secret. It slows our progress. We need outright access. I thought you were going to deal with the DeChant woman so we could buy the property outright."

"She'll let the disease take her in time. It won't be long. With McAllan there, we have to tread carefully. He knows too much about his neighbors. It'll be beneficial when he sees Amille failing, and then possibly die, under no suspicious circumstances." He paused to narrow his eyes at the smaller man, remembering his sloppy work with O'Toole. "It'll ease any concerns that Odessa might have planted with her visions of that night. We need him to engage back into his life at the ranch, accept our man's offer for O'Toole's land, and quietly go our own ways. But if he's suspicious, that's not going to happen."

"Can't the consumption get him, too?"

"Too obvious. Besides, he's regaining his health. Soon he'll be on his way, heading back to the ranch. It'll be best if all goes as planned. Otherwise, we'll just have to find a way to kill him, far away from the mines, so there is no association. Then we pick up the land when it comes up for auction. But that's liable to be far more expensive."

"It'll be worthless unless we can find the entrance."

The taller man considered Odessa St. Clair again. "Maybe O'Toole left Miss St. Clair something about how to find the mine. Any luck in talking to the attorney?"

"He said the envelope was sealed before O'Toole gave it to him. He never knew what was inside."

"So she might hold the key to our lock."

"And she's not faring so well that a relapse would be suspect."

"No." He grinned at his companion. "As long as we move in the next few weeks, she could be just another of the sanatorium's rare losses. But first," he said, waving a finger at the man, "we resolve the DeChant issue."

They borrowed a carriage that evening and went to pick up Helen, who kept the conversation lively all the way into Colorado City. Posters were everywhere, touting the night's fight pitting Shorty St. Clair against Mustang Mex. "It's good we're here early," Helen said. "Might not be able to see had we come a bit later."

They entered a saloon, an establishment Odessa had never been before. "Stay right behind me," Bryce said, taking her hand. "I mean it. Right behind me."

Odessa nodded in agreement. She liked the way his hand, dry and warm, covered her own. Hers felt cold and clammy as she looked about, two men at the bar nearly falling off their stools they were so drunk. Prostitutes, sitting on men's laps. Men with guns at their hips, ready to draw and fire. Men, staring after her in naked curiosity. This, this was Dominic's world?

He didn't know they were coming, and in fact, he and his sisters had never openly discussed how he afforded fine new suits, trading in their carriage for a newer model, buying furniture for their cottage. Father had provided for them, and the bookshop was faring all right, but his extravagance was beyond that.

Odessa realized that her silence had been a form of tacit approval, that she hadn't felt strong enough to wrangle with Dominic and keep an upper hand on her consumption. She wished now she had pressed Nic about it. Asked him how dangerous it was. Asked if there wasn't another way to prove himself or accomplish whatever he was after.

Helen stopped at a back door and handed a burly man some cash. He waved them in. Odessa struggled to see in the dark, and nearly choked on the heavy smoke that filled the room like a storm cloud. In the center was a platform, surrounded by a rope strung between four posts. They got to about halfway back, men shoving on either side of them, pushing them like a wave upon the sea, lifted, moved, set down again.

Helen turned to her, shouting to be heard as the crowd neared capacity and a drum sounded. "Remember, you can't let him see you," she cried. "Trust me, it will distract him, and that will be dangerous. Tell him tomorrow, if you must, that you were here. But not tonight."

Odessa nodded, her heart pounding. She tried to take a lungful of air and coughed against the smoke. Doctor Morton would throttle her and Bryce for subjecting their fragile lungs to such abuse, but the decision had been made. She was here and would see it through. It was so crowded, Odessa could not leave now unless all the men passed her over their heads and from the room. She took some comfort in the fact that Helen had come here before and lived to breathe another day.

A low rumble, a cheer, emanated from the far corner, gathering in intensity. Everyone shouted as the fighters took the stage, the ring, each dressed in shirts rolled up at the sleeve and light pants. Dominic was barefoot.

Odessa gasped, sizing up his opponent, Mustang Mex, even as her brother did the same. He was much larger than Dominic, lithe and rippling with strength. She knew her brother preferred the big, lumbering men, men who could not move as quickly as he. That was who he always took on in his brawling in Philadelphia, and it matched the description of the three he had fought on the streets of Colorado Springs.

But it was Dominic that caught her attention. Never had she seen him appear so intense, so focused. And yet his eyes were light, free, taking in his opponent from head to toe, watching him move, almost smiling in invitation.

Odessa felt sick inside. Nic was more alive than she'd ever seen him, but he was undeniably flirting with death. This was what Bryce had warned her of. This feeling, all around them. These men intended to pummel each other until one fell to the floor and did not get up. And looking at them both now, Odessa feared that would be her brother.

"Your brother's gone," Reid said outside Moira's new cottage door on Boulder Avenue. "I saw him ride out. Come outside and talk to me."

She said nothing, her back to the door. He pounded it again, nearly knocking her forward with the force of his blows. "Moira? Moira! Please, Moira. Things … things haven't been right between us since that night at the Glen. I just want you back. You've made me sorry over it. Now open this door."

He pounded at it again, paused, then walked off the side of the porch.

Moira ran to the far wall, wincing as she thumped against it, panting, even as she saw Reid's shadow form in the window beside her as he peered in.

"Open the door, Moira," he said lowly. "The more you make me appear the fool, the worse it will be. This isn't right. You know it isn't."

Moira stayed where she was.

"Is it that you auditioned for the opera? I know all about that. The general told me. I know you love to sing. I'll learn to accept it." He put his hand against the window. "It's just that it's hard on me, Moira, having you up there, pretty as can be. All the men can't help but want you for themselves. And without us married, they don't know you're mine. It's hardly proper."

Moira bit down on her lip to keep from screaming. She wanted nothing more than to be far away from the sheriff, safe, and here he was, liable to break through that flimsy glass window at any moment.

She could tell by his tone that he had begun to doubt she was inside, speaking mostly to himself, wondering if she wasn't inside, where was she? He didn't want her anywhere without him. When he left town, he practically made her promise to stay home, as if she were to sit here, pining for him, night after night. His shadow moved away from the window. He was giving up. For now. It was time to end the farce. She could act onstage but she could not continue this any longer. She could not continue to duck and cower, hiding from Reid in her own home, *her own home!* She had the general on her side now. And the general could keep Reid in line, if necessary.

Taking a deep breath, she moved forward and opened the door. Reid, almost at the front gate, turned at the sound and took a few steps forward. "Thank you for coming out, Moira," he said, hat in hand. "Please. Can we sit?"

She looked out to the street and saw the reason for the change in his demeanor. A couple walked past, arm in arm. "Certainly, Reid."

They sat down on a front porch swing. "Reid, it pains me to tell you that my brother and I feel this courtship is not in line with our father's wishes, especially since you have not even made his acquaintance."

He stilled and Moira could feel the waves of tension, disbelief emanating from him.

"Is … is there another?"

"No, Reid. There is to be no other. That was my father's wish."

"Then there is no cause to end it," he rushed on. "Courtship is an exercise in discovering if a man and a woman are right for each other. Is this about your singing?" He rose and paced before her. "I said I'd find a way to deal with that—"

"No, Reid. This is about you and me. And my father. And how we must now part, painful as it may be."

He hovered, utterly still, absorbing her words. She could feel his desperation sink into anger. "I'm afraid it's not a choice, Moira." His voice was low.

"Not a choice?" She rose, shaking in a rage that surmounted her fear. "It most certainly is!"

"Is it your brother? He told you to cut me loose, didn't he?"

"No, Reid, this is my decision."

"He never did like me; we got off on the wrong foot, with his brawling and all. But that's hardly my fault. You need to give me another chance. You just haven't seen it yet, seen why we're supposed to be together."

She turned toward the door. "Good night, Reid." She had opened the door a few inches when he shut it again, his arm over her shoulder. "No woman turns me down," he said in her ear.

A shiver ran down Moira's back. She took a deep breath, summoning up her courage, and eyed him from the side, swallowing a sharp retort.

"Moira, all I'm asking for is some time. The summer. If you decide it's not right come autumn, I'll let you go."

"And if I don't give you the summer?"

He dropped his arm and leaned back, waiting on her to turn and face him.

She did.

"Summer's a fine time in Colorado. We'll have some fun. You'll see what a good man I am, what you'll be missing if you spurn me."

"Reid, answer me. If I don't give you the summer?"

"Don't go that route, Moira. Don't do it. Bad roads lead to bad consequences. I'm offering you a good road, the high road. Will you take it?"

She paused, her confidence faltering. Just what was he threatening? "I'll consider it."

"Good," he said, clearly relieved. "Good. I'll see you tomorrow then." He bent down and kissed her cheek, a kiss she stiffly received. "Now get on in your house so I know you're safe."

Dominic danced around the newcomer, sizing him up. He particularly loved these moments just prior to a fight. He imagined himself an Olympian wrestler, wide awake, alive, his own man, skin glistening, testing his strength against another.

He moved left then right, observing how this Mexican moved, anticipating his strengths, his weaknesses. Right-handed, he noted, as the young man nervously wiped his brow, staring at him as intently as Dominic stared at him.

The crowd disappeared. He could barely hear them. It was as if his ears closed up, the closer to the fight he drew. He took note of his heartbeat, strong and steady. Tonight he would clean up. This man was strong, but no stronger than he. And he had the greater will, the more fervent desire to win. For the money.

For himself.

See me, Father, he whispered silently through the dark room, as if his words could reach his father in Philadelphia. *I am not a bookshop merchant. I am not a publisher. I am a fighter. This is me.*

The man who ran the fighting ring raised both of their hands. It was then that Dominic happened to glance down and see Mustang Mex's pocket bulge, as if filled with coins. He frowned. Who came out fighting with coins in their pocket?

The bell rang then. He threw a good punch, and his opponent came back hard, striking him twice. Nic pretended to wave as if already going down, then feinted to the right, driving his left fist into the man's belly and then his deadly right from across his body, sending the Mexican spinning.

Dimly, he heard a woman scream and the crowd roar, as if listening to them through a pond. His opponent came after him, and he shoved the sounds from his mind.

The Mexican drove him hard, pummeling his chest and belly, moving at just the last second every time to avoid Nic's punches.

It wasn't until he struck Dominic's jaw with a left he didn't see coming that Nic thought again of the coins in his pocket. It was no bag of coins. This man had a brass rod in his fist. Not knuckles. Knuckles would be seen by others and the fight would be declared Nic's. But a rod could be hidden. He'd heard of it being done. And the stiff consequences served … to the loser.

He glanced at the other man in the ring with them, the owner, but the Mexican hit him then again, sending him spinning. As he went down, he clearly heard a woman scream. He knew that voice. His eyes scanned the crowd.

It couldn't be. Not a woman. Here. Not Odessa.

His eyes locked on hers. There, in the middle of the crowd. Beside Bryce, who had his arm around her. She was crying, weeping. Sobbing! Did she not know he was good at this? Could no one in his family see, see what he was capable of? On his own? As a man?

With a growl he rose and went after the Mexican again, managing to land a fierce left hook. But then the young man grinned, lip bleeding, and came back at him, striking him once, twice, and three times with the same fist full of brass.

Dominic went down, hard.

And the world went black.

Reid Bannock leaned against the wall beside the back door of the saloon. He grinned up at the last full spring moon, wide and bright as it shone over his city, his fine city, in the distance. He disliked being here in Colorado City, but business was business.

The young Mexican exited, followed by two other burly, finely dressed Mexican men. Seeing Reid, the man nodded to the others to return inside. They did so without comment. The man stood there, black hair soaked with glistening sweat, air escaping his nostrils in twin, steaming streams.

"It's done?" Reid asked.

"Done," he said, dropping a wavy brass rod in his fist.

Reid raised it up, catching a bit of blood in the moonlight. Dominic's blood. Moira would know the truth of his words, that bad roads led to bad consequences. Nic sure knew it now. He'd tried to warn Nic, dissuade him from this path, but the man had refused to acknowledge it and choose a new road. Sometimes the only way to change a stubborn man's path was to make it impossible for him to continue. Reid sighed. The St. Clairs were merely young and inexperienced. They needed someone older to look up to, follow. Someone like him. It was good he had been here when they arrived. Beneficial for all of them. Another year with them and all would be in order.

He handed the man a wad of bills and turned away, fading into the crowd on the street, heading back to the city he loved, whistling, whistling for the first time in a long while. He had just done his future brother-in-law a favor, ending his fighting career. Now Dominic could settle into the life his father had intended for him, as a respectable bookshop merchant of Colorado Springs. That was a man well suited to be the town sheriff's brother-in-law. Not some man sneaking into the night. Why, Moira would not be able to sleep at night, worrying over him. Reid couldn't tolerate that.

No, he wanted her every thought to be about him. She needed to look to him for protection, guidance, wisdom. Not anyone else. And they had just taken one big step closer to realizing that dream.

Chapter ❀ 16

"Will he live?"

"If he awakens soon," the doctor said grimly. They had brought him back to the shop, and together, managed to get him upstairs to the extra room, not wanting the neighbors to see him in such a state, not wanting the general to hear of it. "If he's not awake by morning …" He shook his head in grim warning.

Odessa sank to her knees beside Dominic's bed. "No. No, no, no …"

"It is a concussion?" Bryce asked, taking charge.

"Severe trauma, besides a broken nose and eye socket. Besides that, he had two broken ribs. It will take him weeks to recover, if he does regain consciousness."

"Is there nothing further you can do?"

"He needs to remain still, sleep. We want him to awaken to a point, but the brain needs to rest and recuperate. I will return at daybreak and examine him again."

"And in the meantime?"

The doctor looked at each of them. "Pray. With all you have in you." He left then, and the three stared at the battered Dominic, no word of prayer upon their lips. For all the words within Odessa, she could not seem to link any two. They remained where they were for several long minutes, Moira crying quietly. Bryce came closer and put a comforting hand on her shoulder and his other on Odessa's.

"Father God, look upon us here," he said, his voice steady and low. Odessa closed her eyes, finding assurance, hope in his words. The St. Clairs were clearly condemned to misery. Perhaps the McAllans had a surer connection to the Almighty. "Come and lay Your healing hand upon Dominic," Bryce went on. "We ask it with everything in us, Lord God. Come and heal this man and help him live a long life."

He did not end with the traditional "amen" and all three remained in place, hanging on to his last word, letting it roll through their minds as if it were echoing through the room again and again. Life … life … life …

Moira greeted him at the shop door the next day. It was plain she had been crying. Her bloodshot eyes made her irises an even darker shade of teal. Dominic was nowhere in sight.

"Reid," she said, forcing a smile to her lovely rosebud lips. "I wish I could stop to take tea with you, but you can see I have customers."

He moved inward, feigning concern. "Moira, are you here all alone?"

"Dominic … he—he's feeling poorly. He's resting upstairs."

"I'm sorry to hear that," Reid said. "Here, let me help you for a bit. The town should be safe for a few minutes without me on her streets."

She hesitated but a moment. "If you could go and climb the

ladder to fetch Mrs. Chandler the medical volume she's seeking, that would be a great help." Moira moved off toward the cash register, where three other women waited to pay their bills. One woman looked from the pretty shop girl to the sheriff and smiled.

Yes, the stranger could see it as clearly as Reid. They were a good couple, a handsome couple. They were meant to be together. They had merely suffered a bumpy stretch in the road. It was common to all relationships. Now things would be straight. All part and parcel with molding Moira, shaping her to take the proper form as his wife.

There were bound to be some difficult times through that process. Probably would be a few more. But it was all worth it. Well worth it. Growth, progress, often took some breaking as part of the cycle. He thought of the fields, with deep-plowed channels for seed and water. Tree stumps, wrestled out of the earth. Cornerstones, set into broken, raw ground, declaring new rights. Yes, breaking was part of the process. But in time, all smiled and agreed it was worth it. Temporary losses for long-term gains.

He whistled and smiled down at Mrs. Chandler. "My Moira tells me you're seeking a medical volume," he said cheerily. "Just point it out and I'll fetch it straightaway for you."

"Why, Sheriff," said Mrs. Chandler. "I didn't know you were a man who favored books."

His eyes moved to Moira, who glanced his way and then pretended not to see or hear him as she tended the next customer. "Now, Mrs. Chandler," he said loudly. "If you were a red-blooded male and the book proprietress was as pretty as our Miss St. Clair, wouldn't you become a man intensely interested in the literary arts?"

Mrs. Chandler laughed and then fanned herself, blushing furiously. "Well, I guess I would. Good day, Sheriff."

"Oh, it is that, Mrs. Chandler," he murmured behind her. "It is that."

"Moira!" a voice called from upstairs. He could hear Odessa's hurried step even before she peeked around the corner. "Moira," she said, eyes bright with a smile. "He's awake," she whispered. "He's awake!"

The two women disappeared upstairs, ignoring the remaining customers, and Reid gazed at the empty doorway. So the boy lived. It was good, he supposed. A beating like that changed a man, broke apart a shell of bravado and awakened the core to vulnerability. And vulnerability was something another could exploit.

Yes, it was good, good that Dominic lived.

Eyeing the empty sanatorium hallway, Odessa moved to her bookshelves and slid out the photograph of Bryce she had taken weeks prior. She stroked it, as if touching his face.

A knock at her door startled her. Bryce.

"Forgive me," he said ruefully. "Didn't mean to frighten you."

"No, no," she said, sliding the photograph behind her back. She smiled. "So do you wish to lose at cards or archery today?"

He shook his head. "Someday we'll race on horses and you'll know what it means to lose."

"Threats are not gentlemanly, Bryce."

"Gloating is not gentlewomanly," he returned. "Is Helen coming by?"

"No, tomorrow."

"Good. Then I only have to lose in front of one of you." He pushed his toe into the floorboard. "Charlotte's heading home today. We should see her off."

Odessa paused. The girl had made such a rapid recovery … Odessa had thought that she and Bryce would be gone before her. She considered him, wondering why Doctor Morton kept him here. She hadn't heard him cough in weeks and she knew he was anxious to get back to the ranch, to see what he could find out about John DeChant, and Sam's land. And yet she feared asking, feared tempting the move she knew wasn't far away. "Bryce, I—"

He turned, seeing someone in the hallway. Amille. The woman wandered into Odessa's room and sat down on the bed, arms crossed about herself, rocking.

"Amille?" Bryce tried.

Odessa rose and moved to sit beside the woman. As rapidly as Bryce and she were healing, Amille declined. For the last week, she refused to eat a thing. Odessa wrapped her arm around the woman. "Amille, are you all right?"

"They killed them, killed them. Killed them," Amille said mournfully. "I want to be with them, in heaven. With my Anna. With my John. With them, with them, with them …"

"I know, sweetheart. You must miss them so much!" But Amille pulled away and was on the move again, rising to walk out of Odessa's room and down the hall.

Odessa turned to Bryce.

"Sam was your friend," she said, moving to her bookshelves again. She pulled out the poem from Sam O'Toole. "Aren't you curious to see what he left me? Here. Read it." She held it out to him but he did not reach for it.

"I don't want it. Neither should you." Bryce shook his head. "There's something bad going on over there, Odessa. I don't want you anywhere near it. Not until I figure it out and make sure you'll be safe. Put that thing away and make certain no one knows you have it. Understood?"

He raised miserable blue eyes to meet hers, begging her to accept his gruff demands. "This is still the Wild West, Odessa. We've come far, very far. But the sheriff's hold on the law—it's tenuous. People disappear all the time, never to be seen again, particularly in the far reaches of the county. Places like where Sam and John were mining." He lifted a hand as if to place it on her arm, then as if thinking better of it, lifted it up to run it through his hair.

"Bryce, you've made certain improvements, but you are in no condition to wade into a fight. I—I would fear for you."

He clamped his lips shut for a moment before he spoke. "I'm well enough to care for those I care about. To see about a man's business. Don't fret over me; I'll be cautious."

"And in the meantime, what am I to do?"

"Rest. Make further gains on your health. See to your brother as he improves."

"Rest? Sit back and simply wait? Sam O'Toole practically—"

Bryce stepped forward and hissed, "Keep your voice down!"

"Sam O'Toole," she said in a loud whisper, "practically gave me an invitation to his land with that poem. There is something there he intended for me to have."

"In time."

"If I wait too long, it might be gone!"

He shook his head. "Well, don't look to me to escort you," he said. "I'll have no part in it."

"Don't give it another thought," she said. "I wouldn't dream of asking you."

"Fine."

"Fine."

"Good."

"Good."

He left then, and Odessa closed the door softly behind him so she could cry as she had not in years.

It took days for them to speak again, but then it was as if they had both decided to shove thoughts of Sam and his poem and his mine out of their minds, unable to keep their thoughts from anything but each other. One day, they were out on the front lawn, Odessa attempting to learn how to lasso an object. "I'll make a cowhand of you yet," Bryce said to her. "You're pretty good, roping boulders and chairs. Let's see if you can hit a *moving* target," he taunted, handing her the rope again. "Pretend I'm a cow and you have to get me." He moved off, giving his best cattle imitation, mooing and pointing his forefingers off the top of his head like horns.

Pursing her lips, covering her laughter with concentration, Odessa walked behind him, letting out a laugh as he *mooed* again. She thought nothing of the other patients staring their way. It was highly improper, really. Mother would turn over in her grave if she saw them, but Odessa didn't care. For the first time in months, years even, she felt well. Happy, free. Barely aware of her breathing at all.

She swung the looped rope over her head, still following Bryce's moves, keeping pace with him as he had instructed. And then at just the right moment, she let the rope go sailing through the air, crying out with glee as it circled around him. Quickly, she pulled back, cinching it tight.

The patients behind them cheered, perhaps not as aghast as she had feared. Maybe in watching, they felt a part of this visceral thrill, this joy that Odessa was feeling.

"Got me," Bryce said, tossing her a grin.

She pulled up the rope, drawing him closer and closer.

"You got me in more ways than one, Odessa St. Clair." He stared down at her, unmoving, not freeing himself from the rope, simply staring with those deep blue eyes at her as if she were the most lovely thing on earth. As if he wanted to ...

Odessa swallowed hard. She was used to men looking at Moira like that, not her. "Bryce, I—"

"Shh, I know." Slowly now, he pulled off the rope and took it from her hand, lingering at their touch. She stared down at their hands as if they belonged to another, wanting him to take hers in his as he had only twice. "You're wondering what it might be like, Odessa, once we're out of here. If it will change. I wish we had time to find out. You have some months to go before Doctor Morton will want you any farther than town. But the doc released me today, Odessa. And I have to return to my ranch. I have to find out what's happened to Sam, to John, to Anna."

Alarmed at his words, she lifted her eyes to meet his again. He was leaving? Leaving *now?* She knew it made no sense—her sudden fear, her anger. It was the logical conclusion, the hoped-for conclusion. Arrive, heal, depart. That was the sanatorium's role.

"Odessa, we've talked about this. Surely you knew I couldn't stay here forever. That we'd both have to leave eventually. I wish …"

It felt like all the others … her brothers, one by one, her mother, and then her father. Sending her off on the train without even the courage to tell her it might be forever.

"It's good news, Bryce," she said, pushing the words out, willing a smile to her face, taking a step away from him, turning away from him before he could do it to her. "Let's hope there is nothing suspicious as to how John died. You can get back to your ranch, your life again. If you can't get back to the sea …"

"Odessa—"

But she was already stumbling up the hill, desperately holding back her tears, aching with each step she took away from him.

Chapter ❁ 17

He left without a good-bye, as she suspected he would, with nothing but a note and a wrapped package outside her door.

2 June 1883

Odessa,

> *Forgive me for departing in silence. I hope you know that if there was a choice, I would make it. Please accept this gift from me. I have always thought of you as a fine clipper, just waiting for the right wind. Keep your bearing, Sweetheart. The trade winds are just ahead of you.*

> *—Bryce*

Odessa's eyes went over the words again. There was no declaration, no promise of return. It was simply a last word of hope for her, a good-bye, achingly short. But her eyes went back to one word: *Sweetheart.* A man, especially a man such as Bryce, did not place such a word within his text without forethought.

With a sigh she reached for the package, covered by brown paper and a loosely tied string. She climbed back into bed and untied it and slowly set the package on the side table. Then she ran her fingers beneath the flap of paper, feeling canvas and hardened paint beneath her fingertips.

It was too small to be the piece he had been working on ever since she had arrived. She slid off the paper, every movement slow, as if it might delay her separation from Bryce, then turned the canvas in her hands. "Oh," she whispered.

It was a scene of a grand ship at dead calm in the distance, a mere speck on the horizon, upon a vast, still sea. It was painted in the same hues of blue as his big painting, with a touch of turquoise, as if upon the edge of the Atlantic, bleeding into the Caribbean.

He had told her once of the trade winds, strong and bracing along the far-off tropics. "There are dead calms," he had said, "when the ship barely moves upon the tide. It can be oppressively hot, so hot you believe you are suffering a consumptive attack. And then these winds arise, strong and cool off the water, and suddenly you are not only breathing, but you are moving again."

Breathing and moving again, Was this what he meant when he said, *The trade winds are just ahead of you?* Is that what he wanted? For her to be on the move?

Toward him? Or away from him?

How could he leave her? Before he even knew which way the wind would take her? Was it just his way of breaking away from her, using this excuse to seek out the true cause of John's death, make certain there was no wrongdoing? Was it merely a way to keep her away? She swallowed hard against sudden tears. The sense of loss, abandonment, was overwhelming, bringing back days of mourning her brothers, her mother, her unknown sister....

Bryce, how could you just leave me? Our story just began! How could you leave without seeing it to the end?

A nurse shouted and two men rushed down the hall outside her door. Odessa threw aside her covers and reached for her housecoat, pulling it on even as she joined others who were moving down the hall. Several huddled outside Amille's doorway, peering in, and it was then Odessa knew.

Amille was dead, succumbing at last to her sorrow or her disease, gaining her desire to join her family in heaven.

Her eyes moved to Dr. Morton and two burly men who served as aides, coming down the hall toward her, moving at an unhurried pace. Did they know it already? That Amille was dead? Odessa looked in the neighboring room, to Nurse Packard, and then to the patients huddled about. Who was in on this? Or was her mind playing tricks on her? Was it all in her imagination? Wasn't it a blessing, that Amille was at last free of whatever had plagued her mind? What hope had the woman had with a mind so broken? Wasn't this a relief, an answer to prayer?

But if all that were true, why was everything in her screaming to be away from this place?

Odessa was one of five people who attended Amille's funeral and burial. As their small group walked to a high hill behind the men who carried the simple pinewood casket, she felt the brisk summer wind drive past as if it intended to go through her. Their lonely procession made her ache for Bryce, for his strong arm around her shoulders. Instead, she hurried to catch up with two others from the sanatorium, taking small comfort in being beside them.

Conrad, a relapsed consumptive who'd been in and out of the sanatorium ever since Odessa arrived, was laboring to breathe. Many of the patients at the sanatorium claimed they could not attend for this reason, not with the strong winds coming off the mountains. But they were the same people who managed to go and fish or hike each day. Odessa knew it was that Amille had made so many of them uneasy, wary, uncomfortable. Some were probably even relieved she was gone, never to return to hover in their doorways or follow them down the hall.

"Her husband's death probably hastened her own, poor girl," Conrad said. "Her fragile mind could not endure such agony."

They reached the top of the hill, and Odessa noted Sheriff Bannock's presence. The tall man took off his hat and nodded at her. She nodded back, wondering where Moira was. She hadn't seen her in a week, her sister claiming to be terribly busy with Nic, who was back on his feet at the shop. Was it customary for the sheriff to be present at every citizen's burial? She glanced away hurriedly, pulling her blowing black veil back into place. She could still feel the man's eyes on her, even as the pastor began his short service, speaking words of the everlasting that Odessa hoped was Amille's future. She hoped that now she was free, her mind again intact, reunited with those she had loved. Free. Free to dance and sing and breathe.

They lowered the casket into the ground and the pastor knelt to take a fistful of dirt in his palm. He sprinkled it over the wood, and it appeared like a dark stain on the light pine. "From dust you began, and to dust you have returned. Go in peace, Amille DeChant. Go in peace." He began to pray and Odessa again ventured a glance in the sheriff's direction.

A slow smile spread across his face as he brazenly stared back at her.

Odessa stared down at the wood. Others turned away as the pastor said his last amen and the gravediggers began to shovel the dirt into the hole, laying Amille to rest forever, like a seed planted and ready to spring to life. Odessa watched for another minute, hoping the sheriff would go and she could follow behind him. But he did not. He just stood there, waiting her out.

With one last glance and a silent promise to Amille to find out what had happened to her husband and little girl, even if Bryce did not, Odessa at last turned and followed the group down the hill. She tried to ignore the sheriff, just steps behind her the whole way, eerily silent. But she could feel his stare.

Dominic flipped the "Closed" plaque over in the windowsill and locked the shop door behind him. Today, for the first day in weeks, he had awakened without a headache. He felt like a new man, almost able to forget his injuries other than the troublesome drag of his right foot. But even that was better. With concentration, and by holding his breath, he was able to almost keep it in alignment.

He was a block down the street when he spied the sheriff leaning against the front porch post of the El Paso County Land Office. Dominic looked away quickly, but could see Sheriff Bannock moving to intercept him. "Little early to be closing up shop," he said amiably.

"Just making a quick visit to the bank," Dominic said.

"Shop must be doing well for you to be making another deposit this week."

Dominic cast a glance in the man's direction. "Well enough."

"That's good, good. Say, I was wondering if you and I could have a chat."

"Certainly, Sheriff," he said.

Reid fell into step beside Nic. "I was wondering how you felt, and how your father would feel, about Moira singing at the opera house."

Nic took a few steps without speaking, weighing his response. He knew that the shop, and afternoon opera rehearsals that often lasted into the evening, had become a convenient excuse for Moira to evade Reid's company. But the more she avoided him, the more he seemed to come around, desperate to share any minute with her he could. And if their father got wind of the opera house ... "Moira's always had a grand talent for singing. Both our parents were quite proud of her gift."

"But the opera house. Singing in front of all those people. It's unseemly. Surely your father wouldn't approve."

"You don't know my father."

"I know many decent men, and the kinds of decisions decent men make to keep their womenfolk safe."

"Begging your pardon, Sheriff, but you're speaking of my womenfolk, not yours."

Reid took in his words and then said, "Thought my intentions concerning Moira were clear enough. It's been some time I've been comin' 'round."

"Comin' 'round doesn't make a woman yours. And for some time, Moira's seemed as if she wished things were different."

Reid reached out a broad hand and stopped his stride.

Nic paused and then looked up into his glowering face. "Sheriff?"

"Don't press me," Reid said lowly.

"Now I thought we were just *chatting,*" Nic returned, refusing to look aside.

"Tell her to quit the opera. Don't let her take this indecent road."

"She keeps her own counsel these days, Sheriff. Pulling her out of the opera would be like convincing a garden rose to return to a field of prairie weeds."

The sheriff's mouth twitched. "Your sisters are full of surprises, aren't they? Makes them all the more intriguing. Puzzles to unravel."

Dominic's mouth filled with foul-tasting acid. He didn't like how the sheriff said that. *Puzzles to unravel.* And since when had the sheriff had any interest in Odessa? His fists clenched and unclenched by his side.

"Good day, Dominic. I appreciate your time."

He watched the sheriff saunter away out of the corner of his eye and sighed. Here in the West, far from their father, Moira undoubtedly saw an opening in an iron curtain to pursue her dream. "The stage is not a place for a woman of substance," their father said to her again and again. But try as he might, Nic could not see why a woman such as she could not own the stage. She'd relished the limelight ever since she was small. Why not allow that to grow, flourish? Why not let her be the woman God created her to be?

Odessa could still feel Sheriff Bannock's stare upon her back hours later. She shifted in her bed and looked across her shoulder, fighting the mad idea that he was there in the room, watching her. But no one was there, of course. Only the clear pine boards that lined the room. She looked to the boards that separated her room from Sam's, later Amille's, remembering what she could of them both. She couldn't keep from thinking something was wrong, off. Amille had been in decline, but what if someone had murdered her, too? Right next door? In order to gain the DeChant mine?

She turned again, straightened the blankets, and sighed. For the hundredth time, she wished Bryce were here. He would be able to think it through with her. Thoughts of him made her feel empty. She forced herself to think about the present reality. She remembered the urge, deep within her the day before, to get out of this place. To escape. But she was making progress, healing. She hadn't felt this good in a year. Heavens, she was almost back to normal.

But the doctor had not discharged her. And she had no mine to her name ... only clues to Sam's. And no one knew about that. Did they?

Sighing yet again in frustration, she threw back her covers and sat up. She opened a drawer and pulled out a watch, holding it up to the low flame of her lamp. Past two in the morning. She would not fare well on the trail ride come daybreak if she didn't get at least a couple of hours of sleep.

She leaned forward, head in hands. *Please, Lord,* she prayed, *show me what I need to do.* A thought of the sanatorium files, down in the office, cast through her mind like an autumn leaf on the wind. Maybe there was something further within them that would help her tie Amille to Sam, make sense of the little she knew. Her hands drifted down to her mouth as she stared at the wall. But the offices were locked. She had watched the sanatorium's administrator lock up each night, pulling a key that she wore around her neck on a chain, and then tucking it securely back under her bodice. What would God have her do? Steal into the woman's room and slide the key from her body?

The front desk attendant. He, too, carried a ring of keys. And at this hour, he was routinely asleep. The consumptives all knew this. After sleeping much of the day away, they often could not sleep and would walk the halls at night like specters on duty. Some orderly keeping watch, they all joked. He slept more hours than they!

Decided now, Odessa rose and then reached out to the table. Too fast. Her dizziness passed, however, and she laid a hand on her chest. Her heart beat quickly, but it was nerves more than the illness. She knew if she didn't try and find out, she would be awake all night. If she was discovered, she was discovered. She would claim she was disoriented, and they'd usher her back to her room, worried that she was regressing. Or they might throw her out of the sanatorium if they were unconvinced. And wasn't she getting better anyway?

A darker thought passed through her mind. What if they claimed she intended to steal the files, and Sheriff Bannock arrested her? The feel of his eyes was again upon her and Odessa shivered. No, that would not do.

Her eyes went to Bryce's small painting and she studied the small ship, sails just waiting for the right breeze.... Was he not doing what he could to find out the truth? Couldn't she do the same, from here?

She was decided, then. Going to her chest, she pulled out a blue day dress she favored and hurriedly tossed it over her head. She brushed out her long hair and tied it with a ribbon, so it was out of her face. After a quick glance in the mirror, she moved to the door and slowly turned the glass knob, reaching for her lamp with her left hand. Thinking that the light might draw more attention, she set it back down, electing to leave it behind.

The hallway was empty and silent. The patients were all at rest this night, apparently. With no new patients in the last two weeks, there was no one who demanded around-the-clock care. Could she be so fortunate that all slumbered through the dark hours? Somewhere, a night nurse was making the rounds. But even she was known to give in to sleep, even atop her stiff wooden chair, arms folded beneath her head on the desk. Especially on such a quiet night as this.

Odessa moved out into the hall and closed her door. She winced as the latch made a click that sounded like a scream in her ears. She listened hard for footsteps approaching, but all she heard was the pounding pulse of her heart, along with a symphony of snores and coughing from other rooms. The night nurse's office was at the end of the hall, right by the stairs. She would check on her first.

Odessa moved down the hall on bare feet, feeling the chill of the night on her toes. But she could move like a dancer without her boots on, sliding down the smooth wood, easing past one doorway after another, getting closer and closer. Her mouth was dry. She tried to gather enough saliva to swallow, but failed. She hovered, paused, wondering if she should peek in at the nurse or attempt to walk by as she had on other nights when she had been unable to sleep. Shaking her head slightly, she knew she would be no good at a charade. It was Moira who excelled at such things, not her.

She held her breath and peered around the corner. The nurse was asleep, head on her arms, a pile of papers beneath her like a poor man's pillow. Odessa smiled and watched her back rise and fall. The woman was deeply asleep.

Odessa turned and moved back to the top of the stairs and eased down the first few, wincing again as a step creaked under her weight. She paused and held her breath, eyes wildly looking up and down, waiting to be discovered. But all was still quiet. She slid her hands down the railing until she could lean over to see the night attendant at his desk in the center of the front foyer.

He was dead asleep, snoring, drool glistening on his cheek. Odessa smiled and moved quickly down the rest of the stairs.

She was now on the main floor, just ten paces away from the guard. She moved as if she intended to walk down the next hallway, and then glanced back at the man's side.

There. The ring of keys.

Glancing left and right, she moved closer to him. She paused, watching him breathe. He abruptly closed his lips and swallowed, as if finally aware he was drooling, and Odessa stopped, heart in her mouth. But his breathing soon returned to the slow pace of deep slumber, echoing the night nurse high above them in her office.

Odessa stepped closer. The ring of keys was on his belt, but it was an open-C ring, easily removed with deft fingers. She was close enough now. She reached out her hand and grimaced when she noted her trembling. She bit her lip and moved more quickly, deciding she had to act like a woman on a mission if she was to accomplish her goal.

Her fingers closed around the cold metal. She was perilously close to the attendant now. Could he feel her breath upon his shoulder? Looking back to the ring, she moved it slowly, conscious she could not jingle the keys together or all would be lost.

The keys slid down the ring as she turned it, but made little sound. The attendant slumbered on. Just a little more to edge it off his belt ... there. They were free, but Odessa was paralyzed. Did she hear something upstairs?

Staying here, all would be lost. Her eyes went to the door of the office. She had to get in there. Now. She hurried over to the door on tiptoes and tried one key in the lock, anxiously looking back to the attendant. A cough upstairs. Someone was coming.

She tried a second, then a third. Her hands were shaking so badly now that she could barely try the fourth. The guard moved at the desk just as the key slid into the lock. Odessa's eyes opened wide with relief and she hurriedly turned it and then the knob, edging inside. She removed the key and slid the door shut, aware that her breathing was now coming in uneven, thin gasps. What if there was nothing here to discover? What was she thinking? What if she was found here? Would she be arrested?

The office was dark, with a sliver moon's light giving only the barest illumination. She cast about and her hands closed upon a wooden chair, which she sank into, concentrating on her breathing, trying to gain control. In ... out.... In ...out ... Gradually, she was able to find some semblance of calm and she opened her eyes to study the warm light from beneath the door, as she listened for other sounds and watched for a shadow to pass by. But there was nothing. No one came. No one appeared to be coming. She had to complete her task, return the keys to the attendant, and get back to her room.

Dominic tossed back a glass of scotch, feeling it warm his throat and then spread across his chest. He had come back to Colorado City to find out what he could about the Mexican and who had paid the man to try and kill him. Some men fought dirty to preserve their reputation; more did it because a benefactor with a certain financial investment demanded it. He wanted to know which it had been.

After a while, Amos Burry, the saloon owner, came around, thumping him on the back in greeting. In spite of himself, he had to match the man's wide grin and smiling eyes. "I thought you were gone for good," said Amos.

"You weren't alone in that thinking."

"Like a mule, a mule. You should come back, man. Beat out your frustration, even the score on the next contender. How 'bout Friday?"

"Not yet, Amos. Maybe soon. I'm here to find out about Mustang Mex. I want to know who hired him, who was behind him."

"Behind him? You mean the two Mexicans with him?" Amos shrugged. "I don't know who they were. Family, I guess. You sure you don't want to fight on Friday? I need a good fight on for Friday."

"No, not those guys. Someone else. Someone else paid him. He was carrying a rod, Amos. He was bent on trying to kill me."

"A rod? That Mexican had a rod on him? If that lousy no-account ventures north of Texas again—"

"That's fine, Amos. Fine. But I want to know who hired him. Did you see him with anyone that day before our fight? Did you see him meet with anyone you remember?"

Amos put his chin in hand and thought for a moment. A light flashed through his eyes, as if he had remembered something, but then shadow replaced it. "Nah. I don't remember anything."

"Amos ..."

"No, boy. Leave it be. You don't want to chase that scent."

"Whose scent?"

"Friday," he said, rising, clamping him on the shoulder. "Or as soon as you're ready. When Shorty St. Clair is back, we'll welcome him with open arms."

Dominic watched the saloon keeper walk away, chatting with a few customers. How many secrets did the man keep? And why wouldn't he tell Nic what he knew?

Odessa could see the dim curve of a hurricane glass atop a brass base. The lamp. From her pocket, she fished out a match and moved toward the desk. After removing the glass shade, she clicked the flint and watched as a spark connected to the oily wick, catching fire. Warm light moved through the crowded room, with piles of papers and books strewn about.

The doctor used this as his office, sharing it with the administrator, whom Odessa had only seen each eve as she departed, so often was the woman holed up in this office. On the shelf were books full of notes. In the corner, there were three crates of files. Odessa frowned. The administrator seemed to be behind on her filing. This would not be as simple as she had hoped.

She opened the closest book and scanned the top of the pages, then set it back on the shelf. It was from three years prior. She moved forward by several books and pulled the next from the shelf. Last year's. The next book was from four years ago, so there was no sequential order to them. Frowning, Odessa turned to the desk. There atop it was an open book. This year's?

She moved around the corner of the desk and her skirts caught and pulled off a pile of papers. The resulting sound wasn't as loud as a book might've been, but the cascading sheets sounded like a thundering waterfall. She paused, motionless, listening for the guard outside, waiting for him to rise, realize his keys were gone, and rush toward the locked offices. Her eyes scanned the room as precious seconds ticked by. There in the corner was a safe. What was inside?

Still no one seemed to awaken in the building. After two interminable minutes, Odessa dared to move, finally reaching the book. She scanned it by date, seeing her name periodically. But it was nothing but reports on the patients' health, dictation from the doctor to be transferred into individual patient files. Odessa tapped her lips and then looked about again, her eyes landing on the pile of crates in the corner, beside a filing cabinet. She assumed the cabinet was full, and a quick perusal proved her guess correct. So the most recent paperwork would be in these crates.

She edged the lamp closer and moved through them. Amille's was close to the front. She pulled it out and set it on the desk, then returned to the rest. The next crate held Sam O'Toole's. Out of curiosity, she pulled her own as well. With the three files in her arms, she was tempted to make her escape and read them thoroughly in her own room. But to do so meant she would have to return them. With one more glance in the direction of the door, she took a seat and began to scan each, beginning with Sam's.

On the left side was standard patient information: health history, health upon arrival, health progress. But on the right was additional information, including financial basis, means for care, arrangements if death occurred. Odessa lifted page after page. Toward the back, under assets, Sam had listed: wagon, two horses, two-bedroom wood-frame house, iron stove, acreage in Custer County. There was no mention of the mine or the claim.

She moved on to her file, saw her father's handwriting, granting permission for her care, accepting all expenses to be billed to him directly. Nothing out of the ordinary. Hurriedly, she placed both her file and Sam's back in the second crate. Now for Amille's. If anyone came, she could slide it back into the top crate in seconds.

She opened Amille's file and moved directly to the assets section. There. A claim to a mine her husband had named the Silver Bucket. Signed over to the sanatorium in the event of death and the absence of cash payment. Then a death certificate and note from the administrator:

Patient deceased 12 June 1883.

Amount on account due: $238.00.

Amount in bank account at time: $110.00

Shortfall of $128.00.

*By previous agreement, the Silver Bucket mine is now
owned by Colorado Springs Sanatorium.*

The note was signed by the sheriff, doctor, administrator, and
a county clerk. Odessa sat back. Was this normal business practice?
Could the sanatorium claim the mine based on a $128 shortfall?
How rich was the mine? Was someone working it even now, tear-
ing from the earth riches that rightfully belonged to Amille and
John or their remaining family?

She was about to shut the file when an extra sheet of paper
caught her eye. There beneath Amille's death certificate was John's.
Odessa scanned the words, then let the file fall from her hands as
if she could no longer hold it.

John DeChant had been found beneath the rubble of a mine
cave-in. But he also had a gunshot wound.

She turned to the next page and scanned Sheriff Olsbo's report.
*Cave-in at the Silver Bucket reported on 28 May 1883. Short excava-
tion into shaft reveals victim's body, identified as John DeChant ...
Decomposition of body makes it difficult to determine whether wound
was likely accidental or evidence of a crime ...*

Odessa tried to swallow, but again found her mouth dry.
She had to get water. Her throat was suddenly ticklish, terribly
scratchy. She closed her eyes, willing herself to calm. She was
panicking, but her eyes kept returning to two words—*gunshot
wound.*

Go. Run, Odessa. Hurriedly, she rose and returned Amille's file
to the crate, looked about to make sure everything was in place—
get out of here—and turned down the lamp's flame until it was

extinguished. She paused for a breath or two, heard nothing, and then quietly turned the knob and peered outward.

Her breath caught.

The attendant was gone.

Dominic swirled the tawny-colored whiskey in his glass. He watched it move like a whirlpool, slow, then still, thinking about how his father never imbibed, how his mother would have hated that he was drinking. But it was his choice; he was a man. And as a man, he'd been given few others. This was his. He lifted the glass to his lips again and took another drink, holding it in his mouth for a moment, feeling the vapors drift to his nasal passages, then let it slide down his throat, warming every inch.

He shifted in his seat. He'd arrived early so he could watch the fight from here. His eyes roamed every inch of the rope that surrounded the ring, the worn floorboards inside, rubbed raw from shifting feet. There were stains on those boards—blood and sweat that no amount of cleaning could wipe clear. His own blood was intermingled there with how many others?

It mattered not. All he wanted right now was to enter the ring again, to have a chance. The last was a fluke, a cheat. No man could've stood after Mustang Mex's punches, steel rod in hand. No man. He needed to enter the ring again, prove it to himself that he was right, that he was still good at it, still could see his opponent's plan a split second before it was in play. But his sisters had agonized over his injuries, fretted over him as he and Moira had over Odessa when she was so bad off. Could he risk putting them through that again?

The crowd gathered. The fighters emerged, climbing onto the shallow stage. Nic's blood pulsed faster as he studied the men from head to toe. He could take either of them. Either of them, right now.

His eyes searched the crowd. No one he knew. The Mexicans were long gone, probably having moved on to another city, another state by now. But who had hired them? Who wanted him beaten, or turned away from the ring, and why?

There were those who bet against him. Maybe he had cost someone too much. But the gamblers learned quickly who to bet upon; they would've put their money behind him soon enough.

His focus shifted from the fighters to the crowd, a mass of miners and farmers and merchants and a few dandies—those who had made a mint off the blood of those in the ring. He knew few of them.

Nic's mind went back to those who'd want him out of the ring or even out of the way forever ... Sheriff Reid Bannock. The sheriff wouldn't want him fighting. It was unseemly, undesirable, uncivilized. Especially as the brother of his intended. Hadn't he made that clear enough in his distaste of Moira's interest in the theater, in jailing Nic for brawling? How much worse was boxing in the City of Sin next door to the pristine and holy Colorado Springs?

But Nic had enough of people running his life, pushing him, pulling him. He should be able to fight if he so chose. To drink if he so chose. And Moira, she should be able to sing if she wished. Sing anywhere she wished. Odessa, growing healthier by the day, should be able to chase her own dreams. To write, explore, whatever. The St. Clairs were not here to be governed. They were here to chase the cure—to live their lives.

And soon, very soon, Nic would find the way to do that.

Odessa could hear them upstairs, the nurse and attendant conferring, even as she locked the office door. She moved across to the guard's desk, knelt and set the keys on the floor beneath, as if they had merely fallen. They were coming out of the nurse's office. Odessa tiptoed across the floor and leaned against the wall, out of sight.

"You probably just dropped them," the nurse said.

"I'm telling you, they're not there."

"Go look again, you fool. You sleep so soundly, I wouldn't be surprised if you found them in the front door lock. Probably were sleepwalking."

"They're not there," the man said, his voice rising in agitation now. "Somebody took them."

They were moving down the stairs. Odessa tiptoed down the hallway and hid in an alcove around the corner. The nurse and attendant moved past. "Go check the patients," groused the man.

"I won't go disturbing the patients if I don't have to. Do you realize this is the first quiet night we've had in ten? Ah, you see? I told you."

Clearly, he'd discovered the keys. "I'm telling you, they weren't there."

"You probably just missed them. They were down there, in shadow, where you couldn't see them."

"How could they fall down there without me hearing it?"

"You tell me. You're the night attendant."

The man muttered to himself.

Odessa paused, wondering if now was the right time, then decided there would be none better. If the man decided to walk the floors now, or the nurse decided to check in on the patients after all, they would discover her, which would make them more suspicious. And what had she to fear? All was in place in the office. She had taken nothing. The door was locked; she could hear the attendant checking it now.

She tiptoed down the hall and began walking toward them, praying for God to give her confidence, to veil her fear. She could feel sweat dripping down her face. But that could be attributed to the illness.... She emerged into the foyer and gave the surprised twosome a small smile.

"Miss St. Clair! What are you doing awake?" asked the nurse.

Odessa kept walking. "Can't sleep. Fever must be up. I'm walking the halls like the ghost of Christmas past."

The man's eyes narrowed. "How long have you been up?"

"Hours," she said, rolling her eyes, surprised at how guileless she sounded. It was the truth, which aided her. "Sleeping too much during the day, I suppose." She kept walking past them, as if intent on completing another lap down the next hall.

"Seen anybody else up this night, miss?" he pressed.

"Not a soul," Odessa said with a woeful smile. "It appears everyone is asleep but me this night." She turned away and kept walking, heading down the next hall, but not before she spied them share a glance. Her die was cast. She moved down the hall on trembling legs, intent on the water pitcher and tin mugs at the end of the hall. Once she reached it, she poured a mug from the sweating pitcher and raised it to her lips, frustrated by her trembling. She would need to return to the front foyer and climb the stairs, still pretending all was well. The nurse and attendant might have further questions. But at all costs, she had to continue her charade. She could not faint.

She returned to the front foyer, where the twosome continued to confer. They grew silent when she appeared again, and the nurse played with the hem of her apron while the attendant studied her. Again, Odessa tried to give him a smile. "I think I've walked every inch of this place," she said. "The doctor should hire me as night staff to join you."

The man gave her a half smile in return, a smile that did not reach his eyes. "You're off to bed then again, miss?"

"And hopefully to sleep," she said amiably, climbing the stairs. "There aren't many hours left before daybreak."

"No, there's not. Best to get back to your room and stay there, miss."

"I agree," she said lightly, ignoring his stiff tone. She was almost to the top. Her vision was tilting, her heart pounding so hard. She hovered on the stair, waiting for her vision to steady.

"Miss St. Clair?" the nurse asked.

"I'm all right. G'night," she said, pressing forward. Once out of their line of vision, she paused and leaned against a wall, trying to calm her breathing and heartbeat, waiting for her equilibrium to return. Gradually it did, and she moved down the hallway.

If they discovered Bryce was now the heir to Sam's mine, would he be next? For the first time, she was glad Bryce was away from this place. But if people were truly being murdered for their land, if John DeChant had been killed, was Bryce any safer in his beloved valley?

Odessa entered her room and closed the door behind her. She leaned her head against the cool wood and listened, but no one followed.

She had to get out of this place. As soon as possible.

Chapter ✿ 18

Bryce was digging holes with Tabito on the western boundary of the ranch when Sheriff Olsbo rode by at a canter. He pulled up, touched his hand to the brim of his hat. "Mighty glad to see you home, McAllan."

"Good to be back, Sheriff. You in a hurry? Or would you like to come back to the house for a bit? It's about time for noon meal. The men probably made enough to cover you, too. Can't attest to how good it will be, only that there will be plenty."

"Can't," said the sheriff. "I'm on my way to Westcliffe to file a report on the DeChant property."

"The DeChant property?"

"Yes. For all the good that sanatorium did you, they apparently couldn't turn Amille around. She died a few days ago."

Bryce reached out to the nearest post, hoping it didn't look like he needed it to support him. But he did. "Don't say. She wasn't faring well when I was discharged, but I had hoped …"

"We all did. That valley—and family—was cursed. And now, with the bullet found in John's body—"

"What?" Bryce interrupted.

"Ahh, yes," he said, as if reluctant to share bad news. "We found him in the cave-in. Thought his own mine had done him in. But as the undertaker was dressing him for the casket, he discovered it. Bullet wound to the chest."

"Murdered?"

"'Spect so. Most likely a claim jumper. John probably put up a fight and the louse shot him, then staged the cave-in so no one would know."

"There's some nice ore coming out of those hills. Bound to draw some attention."

"Yep. Fine ore, but no miners. Old Sam's property might be popular among bidders. Heard you inherited it."

"Yes. Surprised me."

"Sam liked his surprises."

"That's for sure. Still, I'm not entirely at ease with how things have gone down around there. Awful convenient for them all to die in such a short span of time. Did Sam talk to you, say anything about anyone that made you think twice?"

Bryce paused. "Not anything definitive."

The sheriff stared at the mountains. "Strange that both Amille and Sam died at the sanatorium, ain't it? What with all its grand reputation and all? They haven't lost a patient in some time, right?"

"Right."

"Sam seemed on the edge? You know, at the end?"

"He'd relapsed a bit. But no, his passing surprised all of us. But he wasn't exactly young. And Amille, she wasn't right in the mind. She was refusing to eat when I left. A body can't handle starvation and the consumption all at once."

"Right, right. I 'spect that is so. Still, as the new owner of Sam's property, keep your ears to the ground, will ya?"

"Will do. Come back when you can join us for a meal, Sheriff."

"That I will, McAllan. Don't have to ask me twice." He tipped his hat again and kicked his horse into a gallop down the road, a small cloud of dust rising behind him. Bryce stood there, running over his words, his heart leaping at his warning. He didn't know where Sam's secret entrance was. But Odessa's poem might hold the answer. Was she in danger? Did anyone know what she had in her room?

Odessa and Helen were high in the foothills of the Rockies, steadily making their way on horses to an inn near Divide. With the snow quickly receding higher and higher and the hint of summer's heat on the Chinook wind, they planned to spend the night there and hike and ride about, returning to some of Helen's favorite haunts to take photographs. It was glorious to escape town and the small cottage she now shared with Moira. Her sister fancied herself a nursemaid, but then acted as if she were burdened whenever Odessa asked for help.

She sighed. She would not think of Moira today. She would only concentrate on this pretty day and these gorgeous mountains. Thick stands of evergreens blanketed the hills about them, the scent of sap heavy on the breeze. But as soon as Odessa succeeded in casting aside thoughts of her sister, something else troubling replaced it in her mind.

"You're terribly quiet," Helen said, glancing over her shoulder at Odessa.

"I need you to hide something for me, Helen."

Her friend pulled back on the reins and wheeled her horse about on the narrow path. She rested her forearms on the horn and studied Odessa. "Not much good comes from hiding."

Odessa looked about, peering into shadowed ravines as if there were enemies about, even here. "I can't risk it, Helen."

"Risk what?"

"Moira is ... adjusting to life here. Nic is finally recovered from his *incident*. The store is doing well. If they find out I have ... Please. Will you just hold something for me for a while?"

Helen raised a brow. "Sounds like a hot potato. Might I get burned if I take it from you?"

Odessa paused, sighed. "I don't know. I don't think so. Well, perhaps ... No, forget it."

"Why don't you back up and tell me what's going on."

"No. Pay me no mind. I'm sorry I even brought it up."

"Odessa."

"No. You're right. I don't want you burned either."

Helen lifted a hand. "All right, all right. Come, tell me. I assume responsibility for all potential burns." She smiled a little smile. "I'm a tough old bird. I can take it."

Odessa considered the woman. And the potential relief in sharing her burden was too much to pass up.

She had opened her mouth to pour out her story when a shot rang out, the bullet passing so near Odessa's head, she felt it go through a loose strand of hair. It struck a tree to the left of Helen and left a gaping hole. Helen frowned, looking from Odessa to the tree again. Odessa was too stunned to move.

"Come on," Helen said, reaching forward to take Odessa's reins. "Lean low!" she cried. Another bullet came singing past, striking a boulder to their right.

Odessa leaned as instructed and then looked back, searching the heavily forested valleys on either side of the high mountain road. Where were the bullets coming from? Who would dare to attempt to murder them here? Did someone suspect she carried Sam's secret note? No one was visible on the road behind them. *Please, God …*

Another shot, this time from a different angle. How many were there? Helen's horse reared up, but Helen held on. But the mare lost her footing and was going over … coming her way! Odessa's horse shied and the sudden movement sent her one way and the horse another.

She landed on her back and for a moment, wondered if she was in a consumptive attack. But she had simply been winded. She paused, waiting for her body to remember the newly returned habit of breathing in and out, praying that she was not now an easy target for those who hunted them. She rolled to one side, looking up the hill for Helen, and yet another bullet barely missed her. Had she lain still a moment longer …

"Helen?" she croaked, gasping. It came in ragged droughts now, but at least it was coming. Breathlessness was something to which she had become accustomed, and dimly she supposed it didn't unnerve her as it might another. She dug her elbow into the soft soil and pulled herself up, knowing that every second was another for their enemies to lock and load, gather them in their sights, and pull back on the trigger.

Helen appeared then over the edge of the road. "Take my hand," she demanded, reaching down.

Odessa did as she was told and the older woman hauled her back onto the road. They bent low and grabbed their skittish horses' reins and rushed around a bend, then paused between three old pine trees. "How many?" Odessa panted.

"Two, maybe three."

"Highwaymen?"

"None reported here of late. I was confident bringing you up here." Her gray eyes met Odessa's. "Odessa, do you think it's related to your secret?"

"Could be," Odessa returned in consternation.

"It's that big, yes?"

"This would seem to say so."

"Then we better get out of here. Quickly."

"How?"

"We could send the horses on their way and pick our way out among the forest. I know these woods well. And I can make it difficult for anyone to track us. On the road, now that they no longer can wield surprise as a weapon, we'd have to outrun them. And that's a gamble … that our horses are stronger and faster than theirs."

"Decide, Helen. I trust you. But decide now."

She heard it then too, the pounding of horses' hooves.

"Take your canteen. And your bedroll."

Odessa hurried to do as instructed. Her fingers felt stiff and sore, and she felt as though she moved underwater. She could hear a man's shout. They were close, just a minute away!

There. The pack slid loose and she threw it over her shoulder. Helen was reaching for her rifle, leaving the camera— crushed when the horse came back and over—tied to the saddle. "Come on!" she cried, slapping her horse and sending it running ahead. She moved back to Odessa and pushed her toward the trees. "Get down behind those bushes!"

She whacked the mare's flanks and the horse went running after her own, then she practically dived across the bush and had barely turned when the three men came flying by, tucked and kicking their horses in mad pursuit. Thankfully, Odessa and Helen's horses were already around the corner, leaving only a teasing cloud of dust upon the road.

"Come," Helen said, lifting her by the arm. "It won't be long until they realize we escaped."

She rose and followed her friend down the hillside. Helen was apparently not yet attempting to hide their path, since one rock after another came loose in their mad descent. In minutes they had made their way down the rocky hill, sliding most of the way down, and reentered the forest below. The dust filled Odessa's lungs, and she labored to breathe. Helen leaned her against a tree and looked upward. "Easy, sister. Take it easy for a minute and let your mind remember how it is supposed to direct your lungs."

Odessa glanced back up the slope, eyebrows knit together.

"Let me be the lookout," Helen said. "You catch your breath. We're lost if you give in to an attack now."

Odessa nodded and closed her eyes, concentrating on breathing … in … and out. She imagined she was on a hill overlooking Bryce's ranch, with him beside her, a hundred head of horses running in a glorious herd beneath them, toward the mountains, a sun setting between the peaks …

"Good enough," Helen muttered. She grabbed Odessa's face, forcing her to concentrate upon her. "Be strong. We can't rest again until we put a couple of miles between that road and us. Do you understand me? We can't rest again."

Odessa nodded.

"All right. Now I'm going to step carefully, and I want you to try and match my pace. You're still lighter than a cougar just out of a winter's den, so make that work for you. If they find our trail, with luck they'll think we're a lone man, not the two women they seek. Got it?"

Odessa nodded again, still conserving every ounce of oxygen in her lungs.

"You might as well head out. Leave now, and you might make the noon train."

"What?" Bryce asked, leaning against his shovel.

"You've got the sickness," Tabito said, digging in again.

"What?" Bryce asked him. "I've just spent months at the sanatorium." He pounded his chest twice. "Never better."

"Not here," said Tabito, waving over his chest, over the lungs. "*Here*," he said, hand over his heart. His black eyes searched Bryce's. "Who is she? You've been thinking of her ever since you got back. You've been worthless." He waved down the row of fence posts. "You do one. I do ten. Is it the girl you paint?"

"She's ..." Bryce began. But he couldn't finish. How did one describe Odessa St. Clair? And do her justice? Every word seemed to fail his efforts. So instead, he had painted her, painted her as a woman, not a ship atop a sea. He painted her in profile, on a hill from far away, resting in the bottom of a rowboat, a fishing rod across her lap. "Yes, she is who I have been painting."

Tabito grunted. "She is strong, that one. A warrior."

Bryce smiled. "Any woman who faces consumption and beats it back is a warrior. But yes, that one is strong."

"Then she is your true companion. She belongs by your side. Go and get her."

"It is not that simple."

"Yes, it is." He stepped forward and turned Bryce in the direction of the cabin, the stables. "Go and speak to her father. Tell her you have many horses, good land. And that you have need of her."

Bryce laughed and shook his head. "Again, it is not that simple."

Tabito stared at him for a long moment. "You laugh at me—"

Bryce let out a breath of exasperation. "Tabito, no. I—"

"Is not love simple?" He poked him in the chest. "It is you people who think too much over it." He gestured back to the twelve canvases beside them. Then he turned and tapped him on the chest again. "You are a man of many horses. She is a woman who belongs by your side. Go and get her."

"Go and get her? And bring her here? To the house I share with you?" He laughed, looking around the tiny cabin. They each had a room, if one counted the blanket as a wall.

"Sell some horses. Finish your uncle's house. It is half done."

Bryce stared at him for a long time.

"My friend, a woman like this," Tabito went on. "She passes through your life like a dream. If you do not wake, catch her, she will disappear with the morning sun."

Bryce thought on that for a moment longer. All at once, he wanted to see Odessa, desperately wanted to reach out, touch her. Hold her. Be with her. What if something had happened to her? What if she had weakened in these last weeks, her consumption worse? He looked to the mountains, as the sheriff had done, as if they held the answers. He forced himself to ask the next questions, so heavy on his heart since the sheriff had ridden away. What if Sam and the DeChants had been murdered?

Worse yet, what if he had left her, and in the meantime, something awful had transpired? Had he left her when Odessa needed him most?

"Lunch is here," Moira said, nudging open the shop door. "I bet you're famished."

Dominic turned from the bookshelves and smiled at her. "Stomach's been rumbling for hours. What did you bring?"

"Some leftover roast beef and fresh bread from the bakery. And this ..." She reached into her bag and pulled out a perfect orange.

Nic pretended to suffer an attack and fell back. "An orange! I haven't seen one of those in months!"

"They say we'll have produce shipments all summer. Had to pay a pretty penny for this one."

"More like two or three."

"Never mind. We'll split it," she said, handing him a knife.

"I saw Odessa today. She and Helen stopped by on their way out of town."

"Where were they going?"

"A ride up to Divide. They'll be gone overnight."

"They're miracle workers, over there at the sanatorium." Moira leaned against the counter, cutting the orange in half. "Perhaps our family curse has ended. Perhaps we've found the cure."

Something she said reminded him of the sheriff. "Now if we could only cure ourselves of Sheriff Bannock's attentions."

She looked up at him and flashed him a grin, then waggled her light brows. "I found a way, Nic, a way out of our conundrum."

"And what is that?" He folded his arms across his chest.

"I've accepted an invitation."

"What sort of invitation?"

"An old suitor wishes to come calling."

"An old suitor? From Philadelphia?"

"Well of course, from Philadelphia, silly. Where else would I have found one?" She moved past him and the counter, heading to the pitcher of water and glasses.

"Who? Who is it?"

"James Clarion Jr."

Nic's breath caught. James Clarion. He had been the most wealthy of Moira's potential suitors back home, but Father had thought it too soon for her to marry, regardless of the beau's stature.

Moira took a sip of water and raised demure eyes toward her brother. But the sea-foam green orbs were sparkling with delight. Nic swallowed hard, his mind racing. What would the sheriff do when he found out? "I thought Father didn't want you accepting his company any longer. Accepting *any* suitor, Moira."

"I wrote to Papa, and he wrote back, saying he agreed. That if James cared enough to come all the way out to Colorado to see me, that it 'said something about the man.'" She moved toward Nic and straightened his jacket, smoothing the shoulders, then moved on to his necktie. "Don't you see, Nic? Who will be the happiest about my new beau when he finds out?"

Dominic cast about, trying to see where she was going. Finally, he shook his head.

"Who wants nothing more than the world to know about Colorado Springs? For the influential to flock here, invest here, stay here?"

"General Palmer."

"And as a railroad man with an eye toward expansion, who is in need of coal and iron?"

"General Palmer."

"And who holds our dear sheriff in the palm of his hand?"

"General Palmer."

"Exactly," she said, patting his chest. She grinned. "I can hardly wait for the moment when Reid finds out. When he knows I've found my way out from beneath his long fingers."

"Careful, Sissy. We've been down this road of hope before."

"Oh, I know it. I'm not completely the fool." She paced back and forth, nervous excitement rattling along her shoulders and back.

"How will you tell him?"

"It will be a severe disappointment," she said, pulling sorrow into her features. "Such hope dashed! Love, just at the edge of our fingertips! But it simply cannot be helped. It is out of my hands. You see, Papa has arranged it all. And I, being the dutiful daughter—"

Dominic let out a rush of air, laughing.

"The dutiful daughter," Moira repeated over his chortling, pretending to frown, "must abide by his wishes. There is no way 'round it. Given the choice between a town sheriff, successful or not, and the heir apparent to such a vast fortune, any man would make the same choice for his daughter. Even Reid himself. And if he doesn't, the general shall aid him in seeing what is best. He'll be thrilled to welcome young Clarion to town and delight in the fact that he courts a local merchant's sister." She grinned. "We are free, Nic. Free. Reid cannot touch us."

Nic sighed and shook his head at her. "But what of love? Do you love this young Clarion? I'd always heard he was a bit ... stiff."

"James? I suppose some might consider him stiff." She laughed lightly and leaned forward. "He will arrive to court me. But I doubt I'll have him. Don't you see? He is merely a means to an end."

Nic's breath caught and he stared hard at her. "Moira, you are playing an ever more dangerous game."

"Such is a woman's lot in life," she said airily. "We do what we can with our humble resources."

Chapter ❀ 19

If they hadn't been fleeing, Odessa thought she would like to make her way slowly through these woods of aspen and pine. After hours of walking in silence behind her friend, it felt as if their assailants were far behind indeed, and her heart resumed a normal beat. She wondered at her breathing, the steady rhythm of it, the absence of clogging phlegm. She inhaled deeply, the scent of fresh river water and thunderstorm-dampened forest loam rich upon the wind; she relished the fact that she could breathe in and out, and that the scents did not cause her to collapse, gasping for breath. So far she had come! Had this happened a few months ago, she would already be dead.

"Did you know any of them?" she dared to ask Helen when they paused for a drink from their canteens. She sank onto a boulder by the stream, and her friend did the same.

Helen studied her. "No. You?"

"No. Do you think they were highwaymen, merely intent on robbing us?"

"Most of the highwaymen I've heard about surprise their victims, not try and kill them from afar. Those boys didn't want to be seen."

"No, I don't suppose they did."

"Are you going to tell me now?"

Odessa stared at her.

"Odessa, what is it you wanted me to hide?"

"Some sort of treasure map," Odessa said, giving up. "Sam O'Toole was a sheep rancher who was in the next room at the sanatorium, next door to me before he died. Bryce's neighbor and friend. He left his land to Bryce and this poem to me, the clues in verse." From there, she went on to tell Helen every detail she could remember.

"Odessa, how do you know all this? All the details about the claims, the sanatorium?"

"Because I went to the administrator's office and looked through her files and books."

Helen whistled lowly. "That was a dangerous decision, Odessa. If there is a murderer about, you are waving a red flag before the bull."

"I know it."

"Did anyone see you? Did anyone see you enter the administrator's office?"

It was Odessa's turn to look to the sky. "Not in the office. But they suspected me."

"Who?"

"The nurse and attendant."

"The night Sam was murdered … did you see anyone near his room?"

"No. I saw no one but Sam."

"But someone else … they might be afraid you saw them leave?"

Odessa paused. "I suppose so."

"They know you're either onto them or have something they want. Maybe they've gone hunting in his absence but can't find the entrance themselves. So they wonder if you hold something that will."

"You really think so?"

"It's logical, isn't it?"

"We have to warn Bryce," Helen said. "If these boys are after us, it won't be long until they go after the only man who stands between them and whatever treasure is waiting on Sam's land."

Odessa's heart pounded, almost painfully.

Helen stopped and lifted her nose, sniffing the air like a wild animal. She raised a hand of caution. "Hear that?" she whispered.

It was utterly silent. Odessa shook her head and frowned at Helen.

"Exactly," Helen whispered, getting to her feet. "Come. If you're right, my young friend, these men have more reasons than one to find you. And few reasons to keep you alive if they get Sam's poem. We have to get back to town before they catch us."

"You know the way, right?"

"Oh, I know the way. The only trouble is I don't think we can get there before nightfall."

A messenger arrived, asking Moira and Dominic to join the general for a small supper soiree at the Glen that evening. After conferring with Nic, Moira sent back her reply with the servant, gratefully accepting.

For all her brave talk, Moira dreaded seeing Reid Bannock, feared how he might react to her news. Every time the shop door opened that afternoon, she glanced up, expecting the sheriff's large form to fill the frame. But it was Mrs. Byrd, and then Mrs. Crandell, and then a schoolmarm from Monument, and then Mr. Jewett. "Now, why hasn't Reid come around lately?" she mused to herself.

Nic overheard her. "Maybe he's taken my advice and is giving you some room to miss him. Or he's lost his feelings for you."

"That would be lovely. What do you really think is going on?"

Dominic shrugged and placed his pen back in the inkwell and rose. "I have no idea."

Moira swallowed hard. "Do you think he'll be at the Glen? Tonight?"

"Good chance of it," he allowed. "But then he could show up anywhere." He reached out and stroked her arm in concerned, brotherly fashion. "Are you prepared for that? Do you know what you will say to him?"

Moira glanced up at him and shook her head a little. "Not quite."

Dominic crossed his arms and stared at her. "We both know that the sheriff is a powerful man. He doesn't care to be trifled with. And this news … Moira, it will enrage him." He looked up to the windows, staring out toward the street, thinking. "We need to arrive a bit early. Seek out the general. Get his blessing upon your courtship with Clarion. With his protection, Bannock won't dare touch you again."

Moira smiled. "If I'm not mistaken, Brother, you're using your brain as well as your brawn today."

"Yes, well … don't spread it around," Dominic said, blushing a bit at the jawline. "Go now and fish out one of the new gowns that Father sent. How did you manage to wheedle it out of him?"

"It wasn't only for me, Dominic. There was a new suit for you and a dress for Odessa."

Dominic smiled. "Look at us. I'm suddenly using my brain and you're acting almost … thoughtful."

They were halfway down the mountain, according to Helen. But the Peak's long shadow had cloaked their progress for some time now, and dusk was fading fast. "Keep moving," Helen said urgently, searching the woods behind Odessa. "We can't stop."

"But we won't make it before dark."

"We can get closer anyway. We might make the Thompson ranch. They'd keep us for the night, given the circumstances." She turned and again pushed through the thick, low-hanging branches of two trees, holding one aside for Odessa. As Odessa came through, Helen's eyes widened and she pulled her closer. A shot came singing through the tree branches, the sound like pebbles entering water.

They'd been found.

"Run, Odessa. Follow me!" Helen said lowly, and took off, strong and nimble as a mountain goat among the rocks and trees.

They were making their way through a copse of aspen when Odessa dared to glance back.

She paused.

A man was but twenty paces behind, his rifle pointed at her head. "Stay where you are."

Odessa turned and ran, moving left and then right as more bullets passed perilously near. Helen was right. If they got to her, they'd merely kill her after taking Sam's note.

"Can you swim?" Helen called over her shoulder.

"What?"

"Can you swim?"

"Yes, but—"

Helen suddenly stopped beside the river, arms casting about as if to help her balance. Odessa came close to running into her. The men, two now within sight, were just exiting the aspen grove. In confusion, she glanced at Helen and then back to their pursuers, slowing down now, relief and pleasure sliding across their faces when they realized the women had stopped.

"It's a jump, but we can make it. Saw an Indian do it once."

"What?"

Helen gestured downward and for the first time, Odessa saw what was down the cliff. A pool. Terribly small, and thirty feet down.

"No, I—"

"Keep your feet below you," Helen said, pulling her to stand directly beside her. "Whatever you do, hit feet first."

"Turn around," yelled a man, horribly close. Maybe ten paces behind them. "I've never shot a man in the back. Don't want to do any less for a woman." Odessa could almost feel the gun in his hands, wondered briefly what it would feel like for a bullet to pierce her back. She wondered if it would hurt. If there would be much pain.

"You didn't seem to mind when you were taking shots at us on the road," Odessa called, hands out, buying time.

"Turn around! Now!"

Helen's gray eyes covered hers. "Nothing to lose, friend. Only opportunity here."

They could hear the second man arrive. Where was the third?

"Nothing to lose," Odessa repeated, feeling as if she were reading a book about what was unfolding here, not living it. But then, as she stepped into the air beside Helen and felt her skirts billowing up, past her waist, around her shoulders, she knew she was living it. It was Odessa St. Clair who was about to die upon the rocks beside the pool or plunge into its depths … or be shot on the way down.

Water ran beneath the several arched bridges that led to the castle of Glen Eyrie. Reid had told her that the waters came from high above, in Queen's Canyon—named for the general's bride—fed by snowmelt and deep springs that could meet the needs of the Palmers and beyond. It was a fine piece of land, here in the glen. Tall, rugged pines covered much of it in cooling shadow. A herd of big-horn sheep frequented the red-hued cliffs all about them. A pair of bald eagles nested on a ledge. This had been sacred ground to the Ute Indians, and for good reason. It was idyllic, really, like a far-off dream in a far-off land.

"Almost there," Dominic said lowly. "Ready?"

"Ready." Her eyes searched the carriage house and the castle beyond it, worried that they had arrived too late to beat Reid here. "We're an hour before the invitation. Will the general consider it rude?"

"No," Dominic said. "I sent word that you needed a moment of counsel prior to dinner. He's expecting us."

Moira glanced at him in surprise. "Papa was right."

"About what?"

"That being here in the West would be as good for you as it is for Odessa."

Dominic thought on that as he pulled around in the yard before the castle entrance. Despite the beating, the disappointment, the worry, coming here had been good for him. "And for you?"

Moira straightened her hat, took her skirts in one hand and the hand of a servant with the other. "It suits my purposes."

Dominic laughed. "Undoubtedly, Sissy. Undoubtedly."

She moved to take his arm and a servant opened the massive front doors. Inside, a suit of armor decorated one wall, a historic relic imported from England by the general, and their host moved down the cascading staircase and toward them.

"Dominic, Moira, it's so good to see you."

"Thank you, sir," Nic said, "for accepting our call earlier than invited."

"Not at all," he said warmly. "Come, my young friends. Let's discuss what's on your minds in the sanctity and warmth of my den."

Odessa plunged into the pool. She was breathless, in shock by the time her boots met water. She sliced into the depths and opened her eyes to look up to the fading light, high above her now. She cast out, trying to slow her descent, knowing, as only a consumptive could know, that she had mere seconds to obtain air.

A hand closed around her arm and she fought it off madly. It took a couple of slow moments for her to recognize that it was Helen, dear Helen, reaching for her, guiding her, already pulling her upward, to the surface.

But she was swimming backward at the same time, at a diagonal. Odessa frowned and tried to pull away. They had no time! She had to get to the surface, directly! But the woman's hand remained clamped upon her arm.

The thunder of the small waterfall filled her ears, louder and louder as they neared the surface. Helen was leading them toward it! Was she mad? If Odessa didn't die from this plunge, the falling water would drown her for sure.

She tried to pull away again, but at last, they reached the surface, each gasping for air. Wordlessly, Helen hauled her backward toward the cliff face, echoing her gasping breaths. All at once, Odessa knew what she was doing. Sheltering them behind the veil of the falls, hiding them from their assailants. She wanted the men to believe they had died, that their bodies were still deep below, held under by the falls or the swirling current of the pools.

Black spots clouded Odessa's eyes. Her breathing was ragged, unsure. "Helen, I—"

"Shh," said the woman, reaching the cliff at last and pulling her close before her, facing out. "Shh, I know," she said through chattering teeth. "Just rest. Catch your breath. We're not safe yet. But we have to wait here for dark ..."

They entered the small, cozy den, and General Palmer sat down in his chair before a roaring fire and stroked the head of his dog. He waved to the couch beside the chair. "Please, sit. You've been so intent upon your rehearsals, I've seen precious little of you, Moira."

"It is good of you to invite us again," Moira said, reminding herself again to stop wringing her hands.

"Not at all, not at all. So, Mr. St. Clair, your note said you were seeking counsel?" the general asked. He glanced at his pocket watch. Clearly, the night's festivities were on his mind.

"Indeed. But I will let my sister speak."

"Very well. Moira?"

"Thank you, General." She paused and then plunged forward. "Of late I have been receiving correspondence from a certain young gentleman that I have known for some time, a man that courted me right before I came to Colorado."

General Palmer stared hard at her, obviously disliking where she was going. Plainly, to him, she was already as good as married to the sheriff.

Moira swallowed hard and colored prettily. "It was not my idea," she said, bringing a hand to her breast and shaking her head. "My father has always favored this young man and encouraged me to receive correspondence from Mr. Clarion, even though I was quite clear that I had a beau here—"

The general leaned forward. "Clarion, did you say? James Clarion?"

Moira smiled. "Junior," she added, "of course. But as I was saying—"

"James Clarion of Clarion Iron?"

"Indeed. They are something of a first family in Philadelphia," Moira said, sounding almost dismissive.

The general sat back, but not before glancing at the ceiling as if seeking guidance.

"I know James. He's had his eye on Moira for some time," Dominic put in. "But she so recently came of age …"

"And so, my dear," the general said. "What has transpired? Do you find his attentions … acceptable?"

Looking appropriately miserable, Moira turned sad eyes upon her host. "More than acceptable. He is delightful. Quite ardent in his pursuit. A good conversationalist, having been schooled abroad. And most ambitious." She paused and sighed. "He is very interested in our little city. I believe he might journey west to visit us and see what all the fuss is about."

The general steepled his fingers before his chest, watching her intently. Several seconds ticked by. "And so," he said at last, "you are here to seek counsel on how to extract yourself from the sheriff's kind intentions so that you might be free to receive this new suitor."

"Yes, I thought, as the parent of three young girls, that you might have given thought—"

The general rose suddenly and turned, leaving a trailing hand on the back of his chair. He looked to the wall, then back to Moira. "You are a keen actress, young Moira St. Clair. But I am the director of this stage."

Moira realized her mouth had fallen slightly open. She abruptly shut it.

He moved the fringe of the carpet with the toe of his boot, soothing it into place. "I will speak to the sheriff myself, this night."

"I—do you not think I should have a word with him before you do?"

"No," he said. "You leave it to me."

"Thank you, General."

"Not at all," he said suddenly seeming tired, mumbling through his words. He appeared years older. "Please, my friends," he said, gesturing a servant forward and whispering in his ear. He turned back to them. "Take your leave here while we wait for the others to arrive."

"Thank you, General," Dominic said, rising and shaking his hand. "Once again, the St. Clairs are in your debt."

"Remember that, son," he said, patting him on the shoulder. "Remember that."

Chapter ✤ 20

Never had Odessa been more glad to see night conquer dusk. Helen had slowly hauled her from the water and remained where she was, perched precariously on a tiny ledge, stubbornly holding Odessa before her. Her meager body heat was blessed, keeping Odessa from giving in to the deadly chill, but neither of the women could pull their legs all the way from the water. There was not enough room behind the falls. Their feet had become numb and almost felt warm in comparison to the rest of their bodies, a trick of the mind.

"Do you think they are gone?" Odessa asked through chattering teeth, speaking as loudly as she dared to be heard over the falls.

"I think we have to move, or we'll die here of the cold," Helen responded. She paused a moment, obviously dreading what would come next. "There's no way past but through the pool again."

Odessa gazed at the black waters before them. They could see, where the water parted as a curtain for a few inches, that a few stars were now shining in the sky. "We can hardly get colder than this."

Helen laughed, the rumbling in her chest making Odessa smile. How glad she was that this woman, this capable, strong woman, was with her now! Helen's laugh faded. "Here's how it will go," she said determinedly. "We'll swim across. On the far right, the falls drop over another cliff, so steer clear of that. Aim for the left. Over there, the old Indian footholds can be found. Let's get to that side. Once feeling returns to our feet we'll make our way down. Good?"

"As long as we're not shot while we wait for it." Before she could have second thoughts, Odessa moved out, entering the water, surprised that it could indeed still feel cold. Her limbs clenched in protest. She had to demand they move, think through every inch of movement, much like she demanded her lungs take breath during a consumptive attack. At one point, she felt her mind slow, thicken, her thoughts turning toward giving in, letting go.

Not since that day on the train had she toyed with the whispers of death.

No, she whispered in her mind. No. *I have come too far, worked too hard to die this way! Father God, give me Your strength! Save me!* She was sinking, the frigid waters edging up her cheeks, then her nose, covering her eyes … A surge of strength came through her then, and she managed to move one arm forward, and then another, kicking all the while.

"Odessa!" cried Helen. She felt the woman's hand and clung to it. Helen hauled her the rest of the way to the pool's rim. She could feel the draining draw of the next falls and wearily pulled her body out of it and to the far side. She glanced up. Blessedly, all was dark. No moon. Only starlight. Even if their assailants wished to fire, they'd be doing so blind. And with the pounding sounds of the falls, there was little fear that they'd be heard.

Unless they were already down below them. Waiting.

"Come," Helen said, hauling her backward, her legs now out of the water for the first time in hours. "Rest here." She took the small pack from Odessa's shoulders, unrolling the bedroll, hoping for some dry areas. No luck. Both shivered uncontrollably. She placed a small leather pouch beside Odessa. Odessa touched the soggy material and leaned her head back against the rock. Inside was Sam's note, probably disintegrating by now. *Oh, Sam,* she thought, *is it really worth all of this?*

She closed her eyes, teeth chattering, and wondered what it would be, to be free of the consumption, feeling better than she had in a year, with nothing to worry over but Bryce missing from her life. She longed to be unencumbered, with little but matters of the heart to concern her. Had Bryce abandoned her for good? How could he have simply left her behind, forgotten what seemed to be growing between them? Was she a fool to have believed it was … love?

Odessa leaned forward, strained to see her friend in the dark. Her teeth were still chattering, but feeling was returning to her feet with definitive pins and needles. "Life is never … easy. Is it?"

Helen hovered near, quiet for several seconds. "Sister, I've lost most of my family, buried two husbands, and endured more than twenty years of consumption. I've moved many times, becoming close and then tearing away from people. I've had books that were well received and others, dear to my heart, that sold not enough to pay the publisher's costs. And now …" She laughed lowly. "I have a young friend who has drawn me into a curious battle for life. So no." She laughed again. "Life isn't easy."

She paused and then took Odessa's shoulders in her strong hands. "But *this* … *this* is life. Do you feel it? I know you've felt death near us this day, several times. When one recognizes death, she certainly also knows *life* better as well."

Odessa wished she could see her friend's eyes, draw strength from what she knew she'd see there. *Is she right, Lord? Is this a part of finding out what it means to live, to breathe? Can I find this tiny glimmer of hope and hold on to it?*

"I've talked to God, Dess. Had a little chat, just me and Him, when I was holding you across this pool. I'm convinced this is not the day that God has ordained we join Him."

Odessa swallowed past a swelling throat and nodded. But Helen couldn't see her. "Yes," she croaked through sudden tears. "Yes."

"Good. Now let's get moving."

Bryce McAllan rode into town almost three weeks after he had left. Every day, every waking hour, his mind had been on Odessa. It was dark, past supper, but he knew he had to get to the sanatorium, at least lay eyes on her before he could sleep. So he left the hotel and rode out into a dark night, riding by feel, if not by sight. His horse knew the way. She could've done it in her sleep.

The sanatorium was a beacon in the night, many of her rooms still lit, weary consumptives undoubtedly walking her halls. He coughed, as if reminded by the sight, of his own illness, his own weakness and fallibility. For the thousandth time, he wondered if he was the man that Odessa St. Clair needed.

Was he strong enough? Did not a woman battling her own illness need a man twice as strong?

He pushed away his doubts, the desire to see her again overriding any other consideration. Two weeks. Nineteen days.

Nineteen days, twenty-two hours too long.

He licked his lips as the sanatorium drew closer. His gut was in knots, fear and hope entangled. All he wanted was to hear that Odessa was safe, see her coming down to greet him. Bryce dismounted and tied his mare's reins to the front post. Then on stiff legs, he climbed the stairs to the front entrance.

The attendant opened the door. "Mr. McAllan," he said. "Welcome back! Feeling poorly?"

All at once, Bryce remembered how awkward it was, coming to call at such a late hour.

"No, I'm feeling well," he said. "I came into town today on business and decided I would come and call on Miss St. Clair."

The guard paused oddly and glanced back at the night nurse. "Miss St. Clair?"

"Yes," Bryce managed. Why was the man acting so strangely?

"Miss St. Clair isn't here."

Bryce frowned and took a step toward the guard. "Not here? Where is she?" Panic edged into his mind.

"I … uhh …"

"Where is she?" Bryce demanded. "Is she all right? What has happened?"

The night nurse put her hands out in a calming fashion. "Mr. McAllan, Odessa is fine. She's fine!"

Relief flooded through Bryce, leaving him weak where a moment ago, every muscle was strong. He took a breath and leveled a gaze at her. "Then where is she?"

"She has so greatly improved, she moved into town with her sister more than two weeks ago," Nurse Packard said. "Doctor and I check on her daily, but she only continues to improve. She stopped by today to borrow that mare she favors for trail rides. She and Mrs.

Anderson were heading up to Divide to take some photographs, as I understand it. They are not due back until late tomorrow."

Disappointment flooded through Bryce. "Tomorrow?" he asked.

"Tomorrow," she returned, eyeing him knowingly. "Surely you can wait one more day to see your Miss Odessa."

Reid arrived. Moira knew the general had had no time to tell him. He came to her directly, taking her hands in his and kissing each of them, looking her over with warm greeting and joy, as if it had been three weeks, not three days, since they had seen each other. She dropped her eyes, fear overwhelming her. "What's wrong, Moira?" he asked.

"Come along, Sheriff," the general interrupted smoothly. "I know Moira is entrancing, but we must all progress into the dining hall. If we tarry, the food will be cold! Queen never could abide by cold food. Even in her absence, I won't present guests with food that would disappoint her." Reluctantly, Reid turned from Moira and followed their host's lead.

Dominic was there then, offering his arm to her. He leaned closer and said, "Calm yourself. You must see this through. The general will break it to him at the right moment."

She glanced at the general as he talked to Amy Brennan ahead of them. Moira wondered if he could turn Reid, control him. Memories of Reid standing in the street before the hotel, watching her in the dark, or at her cottage, banging on the door, sent a shiver down her spine.

So they sat down at the table, an intimate party of eighteen, and were served sautéed vegetables and roasted pheasant and delightful rolls. Servants poured champagne and then wine, but it did nothing more than make Moira more ill at ease, the moment looming ever nearer when Reid would know. She was terribly quiet, making all around her glance in her direction, clearly used to her leading discussion about people, politics, parties. At one point, Nic nudged her under the table, trying to get her attention.

She jumped and let out a little gasp, then looked around the table in dismay. Dominic kept eating, pretending nothing at all was the matter, but others held their spoons and forks in midair, staring at her in concern. "Forgive me," she stammered. "I seem to have a cramp in my foot. Would you all excuse me for a moment?"

She rose, and all the gentlemen at the table stood as well.

"I will attend you," Reid offered from the far end, obviously anxious for the opportunity.

"No, no," Dominic said smoothly. "You see to your dinner, Sheriff, while it's warm. A quick turn around the grounds should see her foot to normalcy." He set his napkin down on his chair, the matter settled in his mind. "Probably those new Philadelphia boots on her feet," he said, arching one brow. "Not everything is better in Philly."

The people responded with chuckles and Dominic escorted her to the door and out into the wood-paneled hallway. "You have to *be* Moira St. Clair. *Pretend* all is well," he said with a growl. "You're not yourself, being so silent."

"I can't help it," she whined. "I keep catching him staring at me, and I worry about what is ahead. It's awful. Just awful."

Dominic sighed. "We simply have to get through this night, and perhaps it will be over."

"Do you think so, Nic? Really? Do you think he'll give up?"

They walked in silence for a few paces. "I don't know, Moira. But I hope so."

Get me through this night, Odessa prayed. *Just one more night, Father.* She was still cold, even after a couple of miles of walking, following Helen's lead through the dark.

She did not know how her friend knew where she was going, could not bring herself to ask. What if she was lost? What if they were no more near the Thompsons' ranch than before? With no moon to guide them, they might've been going in circles, if it wasn't for the downward slope.

Every sound of the forest made them jump. First an owl, then a deer.

Her feet, wet within her boots, chafed. She knew that massive blisters were forming at heel and anklebone. But there was nothing else to be done besides walk on. On and on.

"Look, up ahead," Helen said, pausing.

There, against a dark, low-slung hill, warm light poured from three windows of a small ranch house. "We've made it," she said.

Odessa glanced over her shoulder and shivered again. "Oh, please, God. May it be so. Hurry, Helen. I think they're behind us."

Moira slept at the shop that night with her brother, anxious to avoid Reid if he came to the cottage, especially with Odessa being gone.

He came, hours after they had returned, and banged upon the door. "St. Clair!" he shouted. "St. Clair! I know you must be here! Open up! St. Clair!"

"He's liable to break the glass if we don't go down there and talk to him," Dominic said in the dark. Moira was sitting up in bed. Nic had been outside, on the narrow settee, but now stood in her doorframe. It was so dark, she couldn't see him, only hear his voice.

"St. Clair! It's the sheriff!"

"As if we didn't know," Dominic said dryly, in a whisper.

Moira giggled.

"St. Clair! I know she's in there! Moira! *Moira!*"

"He must've tried to pay us a visit at the cottage," Nic said.

Moira tossed aside the covers and pulled on an overcoat, buttoning it up to the neck over her night shift. "He won't stop. Not until I speak to him. I might as well talk to the big, bad wolf and get it done."

"You're not doing it alone."

"You come down with me, but stay in the office doorway. Near enough to help, far enough to give us some semblance of privacy. Can you light a lamp?"

Dominic turned away and did as she asked, returning in seconds.

Moira met his gaze over the warm glow of the lamp. "God be with us," she whispered.

Chapter ❀ 21

Reid's dark form filled the glass door as they neared with the lamp. He looked weary, wild in the eye, and Moira was unable to halt a shiver down her back. "Tread carefully, Moira," Dominic whispered toward her as he unlocked the door.

But Reid already had a hand on the knob and opened it, roughly pushing Dominic backward, immediately moving toward Moira. "How long?" he asked through his teeth. "How long were you carrying on with this dandy?"

Moira swallowed hard and held her overcoat at the neck with one hand, her other arm wrapped around her waist. "He was a beau before I came to the Springs. We were corresponding all this time."

"So all this time, you've been with me but your heart has belonged to him?"

"I'm sorry, Reid. It could not be helped."

The sheriff smiled thinly, sneering, "Helped? You think I can't see through your plan?"

"What plan?" she asked in irritation.

"Do not act the innocent with me, miss. You forget how many people I've watched try and play that game."

"Reid, I know you are hurt, angry. If there was any other way—"

"There is a way," he said, pausing a second. "Marry me. Marry me tomorrow. We'll send word to your father afterward. The general will come to peace over it, once we show him what it means for us to be together. Your father, too."

"No," Dominic interjected. "I cannot abide by such a plan."

"Stay out of this, St. Clair. It is none of your business."

"It is all my business," he said, moving behind the counter. "Whether you like it or not."

"Moira, I—"

"Reid, I love him," she said quietly.

The sheriff quieted, snapped his mouth shut, and stared at her. "More than you love me?"

She turned away and paced a few steps, then looked back. She shook her head, as if in wonder. "It seems impossible, given what has been between us. But there is something right, *easy* between James and me."

"Right and easy ... like money," Reid growled, striding over to her.

"There is that. I confess I enjoy the finer things in life."

"I can give that to you too, Moira. I've made good investments here in the Springs. I have more than you might imagine—"

"No, Reid. Please. Stop. My mind is made up. Just go. Go now."

"You can't mean it. It cannot be over like this."

"I mean it," she said, raising her chin. "And out of respect for what we once shared, I ask you to behave the gentleman. In time, perhaps we can be friends."

Reid let out a humorless laugh and looked to the ceiling, hand on head. Then he looked to her again, his eyes more wild than before. "You fickle, fickle fool." He took a step forward and then another, backing her up until she leaned against the counter. "You are nothing more than a common whore, selling yourself to the man with the thickest wallet—"

Dominic laid a shotgun across Moira's shoulder, an inch away from Reid's chest, barrel pointed at his heart.

Reid slowly lifted his eyes to stare at Nic. "You lookin' to go back to jail, Dominic?"

"Sheriff or not, you are threatening my sister on private property. You've said your piece. Now it's time for you to leave."

Reid's eyes narrowed as he stared at Moira and Nic. "You might've made a deal with the general, but you haven't with me." He leaned closer to Moira, and she turned her face to one side. "Not with me," he repeated.

He straightened, slowly, wiping the spittle from his lips with the back of his hand and placing his hat atop his head. Then, with one last threatening glance at the both of them, he turned and left the shop, slamming the door shut so hard Moira was sure it would shatter.

Bryce had just finished his breakfast beside the hotel restaurant's window when he saw two riderless horses trotting through town. He frowned, thinking it odd, and then looked closer as they moved on by the hotel. He rose quickly, tossing a coin on the table and racing out the door.

One mare was the one Odessa favored from the sanatorium, with its distinctive star on her forehead.

The other was Helen Anderson's, a smashed camera still tied to its saddle.

Two men chased after the horses and finally stopped them two blocks down the street. The horses were skittish, unnerved. What had transpired with their riders?

The sheriff and deputy pulled up beside Bryce, already astride their own horses. "Mr. McAllan," said the sheriff, tipping his hat. "You're back."

"Odessa St. Clair and Helen Anderson were riding those horses," Bryce blurted. "Something's obviously happened to them! They were on their way to Divide yesterday."

The sheriff's face darkened at the sound of the St. Clair name. It was unmistakable. "Foolish women," he sneered. "Female and consumptive and out on their own."

Bryce frowned. "Something bad has happened. We must go after them."

"He's right, Sheriff," said the deputy, obviously as confused as Bryce by the man's behavior.

"One probably was thrown from her horse and when the other went to help, the horses rode off. Common enough."

"That still leaves two women up on the mountain on their own," Bryce said. "All night."

"Helen Anderson has spent more than a few nights out on her own in these mountains."

"But not horseless and responsible for another."

"Yes, yes. We'll go and see to them. Find your mount and let's be off. Garrett, take those mares to the stables for care and fetch a couple of fresh mounts for the *ladies*." He drew out the last word as though it were a French epithet.

Bryce frowned and looked to the deputy, but he just raised his eyebrows and shook his head. He rode off ahead of Bryce, toward the city stables. Bryce hurried along, worrying about Odessa and Helen. *Where are you, Odessa? Are you all right?*

By the time he reached the stables, Garrett had ordered his mare brought out and saddled. "What's going on with the sheriff?" Bryce asked him, watching the stable hand work.

"I reckon it's not Miss Odessa, but rather Miss Moira, that has him all riled up."

"Ahh," Bryce said.

A boy rode in then, bareback and barefoot. "Sheriff!" he called down the street over all the clatter and shouts of commerce and men and horses. *"Sheriff!"*

Garrett and Bryce shared another glance and both mounted up, heading toward the boy.

"They're shooting at the house, Sheriff!"

"That's Alexander Thompson, from up past the Garden," the deputy explained lowly.

"Slow down, boy," the sheriff said. "Who's shooting at the house?"

"Two, maybe three men. They're demanding my da' give up the women."

Sheriff Bannock frowned. "What women?"

"The women, the women that came to us in the night. Miss St. Clair and Mrs. Anderson!"

The sheriff's chin went back as he took in that news and then he looked to Bryce and the deputy.

"My da' can't hold 'em off much longer, Sheriff!"

"All right, all right, boy. We're on our way."

"I'll go get Dominic," Bryce said.

"We can't wait," warned the sheriff.

Bryce looked about madly. Spying another boy, he called him over and tossed him a coin. "Go and fetch Mr. St. Clair at the bookshop. Tell him his sister Odessa is in trouble and to bring a gun to the Thompson ranch, straightaway. Tell him to ride hard, that we can't wait on him."

"Straightaway, mister!" said the child, running off.

The Thompson boy had already wheeled his horse around and whipped her flanks with the ends of his reins. The sheriff and deputy were directly behind him. Bryce closed his eyes, praying for protection over them all, even as he urged his own horse into a dead run.

Chapter ❀ 22

"I'm rather weary of being shot at," Helen said, turning her face toward Odessa. Another shot came singing through the broken glass of the Thompsons' window.

"Me, too," Odessa said. She looked up to their brave host, young, small, and wiry. "How many bullets do you have left?"

"Five," he said, still staring outside.

Odessa looked over to the corner, where Mrs. Thompson huddled with their toddler, a girl. *Please, God, let our arrival not mean that these dear people die too....*

"He got out," Mr. Thompson said. "My boy. He's quick. I don't think they even knew he was in the barn when they came."

"But they'll soon realize why you aren't shooting back," Helen said.

"There's one now," Mr. Thompson said, squinting his eye to center the man in his rifle's sights.

"I'll give myself up," Odessa said. "Before your last shot is gone." She shook her head. "I won't be the death of you all."

"Thompson!" shouted the man outside. His voice carried as easily as the wind through the missing chinking in the log walls and broken windows. "Thompson! We know you're running out of ammunition!"

"Do you recognize him?" Helen asked lowly.

Mr. Thompson shook his head. "He's got a kerchief across his face. He doesn't seem familiar." He looked down to the women and over his shoulder at his wife and youngest child.

"Get off my land!" Mr. Thompson shouted. "I've got ammo to burn!" And with that, he shot at the man on the edge of the clearing in front of the house. He grunted. "Didn't even move. Hit an inch from his big toe and he didn't even flinch."

Odessa closed her eyes and listened to him reload. Four bullets left.

"Hand over the women!" called the man outside.

"The next one won't be a warning shot!" Mr. Thompson shouted back.

"There are three of us, and one of you, best we can tell. Give 'em up and we'll be on our way."

A rock came crashing through the back window. Mrs. Thompson screamed as glass shattered across her and the tiny girl. Mr. Thompson whirled and shot blindly through the frame.

Three bullets left.

Four shots came through the front door and near the window, leaving gaping, dust-strewn holes in the wood. Again, Mr. Thompson turned and shot back. He broke open his gun and loaded a bullet in each chamber, staring silently from one woman to the next.

Two bullets left.

"Here they come," Mr. Thompson said grimly, lowering his rifle to the base of the window. "Two of them. I've warned 'em."

Odessa shook her head. Even if he got one with each bullet, he would still be one short. She stood on trembling legs, suddenly wanting it over. She could endure no more death, not when she could do something about it.

"What're you doing?" Helen asked, reaching out to grab her arm.

Odessa shook her off. "What I should've done hours ago."

The Thompsons' door swung open, but no one appeared. Bryce's breath caught as the two attackers in front of the house paused, rifles raised to their shoulders.

The sheriff swore under his breath. "What are they doing?" He motioned to the deputy. "Get in position, Garrett. When you get the chance, take your mark down. Don't miss." He looked to Bryce and Dominic, then back to Garrett. "First man takes a shot, everyone else fire. Bryce, ten paces to the left. You take down the man in blue. Garrett, you have the man in brown. Dominic, you come with me. We need to find the third man." He crouched down and moved back into the scrub oak, circling the house. The Thompson boy was hidden in a copse of trees about a quarter mile away.

Odessa appeared then, in the doorway, hands up. Her hair was loose, falling in waves down her shoulders. Her dress was torn, muddy. Bryce's mouth went dry at the very sight of her. Even bedraggled and dreadfully pale, she was beautiful.

The men below stepped forward in unison. "Come toward us! Ten paces! Now!"

"We can't let them reach her," Bryce said lowly.

"We won't," said the deputy. "But we need to know the sheriff will get the third man."

"Thompson! Throw your rifle out the window and come out!"

The rancher hung his gun out the window and dropped it.

"Now," the deputy whispered, and took his shot. The man in the tan shirt whirled and fell to the ground.

Bryce took his shot, but in the split second, his mark ducked. Bryce's bullet hit him on the shoulder, but it was a glancing blow. He was still on the move. And instead of returning fire on Bryce, he was turning, aiming at Odessa …

The deputy fired again, knocking the man to the ground.

Dominic followed the sheriff to the back and they immediately saw the third man, edging around the house to come to the aid of his comrades.

"Stop right there," growled the sheriff. "Toss your rifle to the right and get your hands up."

The man paused, straightened, and did as he was told, still facing away from them.

Dominic dared to take a breath. It seemed all was under control.

That was when the sheriff shot the third man. The man gripped his chest, turned halfway, and fell.

Dominic sputtered, eyes widening, trying to make sense of what he had just seen. He looked wildly to the sheriff. "What? He'd given up! Didn't you want to question him?"

Reid gave him a cold smile and stepped forward. "Frontier justice. I had all the answers I needed. Colorado Springs won't abide by highwaymen attacking innocent women." He moved forward and nudged the man with his boot.

Dominic knelt and felt for a pulse. He was dead. "Why would highwaymen chase them all the way here?"

The sheriff shrugged. "You've lived with your pretty sisters all your life. You tell me."

Dominic frowned and moved away, his need to see Odessa, hold her, make sure she was all right temporarily overriding his confusion over the sheriff's actions.

Bryce crashed through the scrub oak, conscious that Helen was now beside Odessa, holding her. She had looked away from the bleeding, dying men, didn't see him yet.

"Odessa," Helen said, spying him and pointing.

Odessa turned slowly and looked across the clearing in wonder. "B Bryce?"

And then he was running, running toward her, hauling her into his arms, kissing her hair, her face. "Odessa, Odessa. Oh, thank God you are all right."

She accepted the kisses, standing motionless in his arms, bending slightly toward him as if she wanted to kiss him back. "Odessa, I'm so sorry. I should've never left you alone. Should've never left you, period."

She looked up at him, sea-green eyes filled with tears.

"Please forgive me, Odessa. I'll never leave you again. At least, not without your permission."

She studied him and then nodded. He cradled her close again. It felt good to have her in his arms, it felt right—her shoulders fitting beneath his arms, her head just beneath his chin. How could he have left this woman behind? Ranch or not?

"Odessa," said her brother now, just behind her.

She pulled away then, and Bryce shoved aside a shiver at her sudden departure. She whirled. "Nic? Nic!" She cried out and stepped into her brother's arms next. "Oh, thank you, thank you all," she said, looking from the Thompsons to the sheriff beyond Dominic, then to the deputy and back to Bryce again.

The deputy knelt and flipped one dead man to his back and then the other. The sheriff pulled the handkerchiefs from their faces. "Any of you know these men? Anyone recognize them?"

They all shook their heads.

"Do you know why they were so intent upon catching you, Miss St. Clair? Or was it you they were after, Mrs. Anderson?"

Odessa put a hand to her mouth and shook her head, sudden tears in her eyes, then she turned away, as if she couldn't bear the sight of the dead men's faces any longer.

"Highwaymen, up to no good," the sheriff said in summary.

"Judge, jury, and executioner, all in one man," muttered Dominic. Bryce glanced up at his odd comment. He could see that Odessa's brother was angry, disgruntled over something beyond the trauma of the day. He looked about to the others.

The sheriff was moving to Mr. Thompson, shaking his hand, ruffling the toddler's hair. Alexander Thompson came tearing across the clearing, jumping into his father's arms. The two clung together, and tears ran down the father's face.

But the deputy stood to one side, his expression vaguely wary.

Chapter ❀ 23

Odessa had insisted she need not return to the sanatorium, and remained at the cottage with her siblings. Doctor Morton and Nurse Packard visited her twice a day.

"Honestly," she griped to Bryce as the doctor left on the third day, "if I can survive a night like I did with Helen and not die of a consumptive attack, what will strike me down here in our sweet cottage?"

He watched her, admiring her lovely, stubborn curls, falling from the bun atop her head, the new curve of her cheek, symbolic of a few precious pounds regained. Today, her eyes seemed all the more bold—a lovely deep ocean green. She turned to him, aware now that he gazed upon her. The doctor had set off, and the street was empty. They were alone on the porch.

Unable to stop himself, he took her in his arms and cradled her face with one hand. "Odessa St. Clair, how did I ever bear to leave you?"

She smiled up at him, a hint of sorrow in her eyes. "I don't know. Some trifling thing such as a massive ranch and three hundred head of horses needing attention."

He returned her smile. "I can't bear it. Not ever again. Come back with me."

She frowned in confusion and pulled slightly away.

He went to one knee. "In the absence of your father, I've spoken to your brother. He thinks your father will approve."

Odessa lifted one hand to her lips. "Of what?"

"Odessa St. Clair, will you be my bride? I've left you once. I've pledged to never do so again. But I cannot remain here. I must return to the ranch. You know that, right?"

"I know, Bryce," she said, pain in her voice.

He shrugged and cocked his head to one side. "Only one route out of such a mess: Take you with me."

"You … you are asking me to marry you?"

He smiled. "Are you stalling? Looking for a way to let me down easy?"

"No. I mean yes! Yes, Bryce," she said, placing a hand to his cheek. "I think I've always wanted to be your wife. From that first day on the porch. And ever onward."

He rose and picked her up in his arms, spinning her around. Gently, he let her slide back to the porch, and he felt the heat of her lithe body. He bent low, then, and kissed her soft lips.

"Honestly, what will the neighbors think?" interrupted Moira, suddenly at the front door. "Odessa, I'm surprised at you!"

"Let them talk," Odessa said, staring up into his eyes. And then, with those three words, and a sultry, loving look in her oceanic eyes, Bryce McAllan knew she was really going to be his.

They set off for Glen Eyrie in high spirits indeed. General Palmer had wanted to honor the heroism of the Thompson family in saving Odessa and Helen and had quickly organized this gathering. Dominic was planning to announce Odessa's engagement to Bryce. The ladies were in exquisite gowns and tiny hats with feathers. Dominic was in his new suit and Bryce had obtained his own from the local mercantile—not with the fine fabric that Dominic's boasted, but a dandy indeed.

"Have to sell a few horses for that one, Brother-to-be?" teased Moira, straightening his lapel in her normal, flirty way. But Bryce only had eyes for Odessa. He stared at her as she arrived from the back room and pulled on her new black elbow-length gloves and then straightened the teal silk about her. She met his admiring glance with a grin. So handsome was her fiancé! So tall, and stronger than ever after these past weeks on the ranch. He'd lost a little weight even as she'd continued to gain it. Either she would need to cook for the men or find a good woman to do so for all of them. Ranch men obviously needed food, and lots of it.

"I cannot wait to see your ranch," she said, coming near. She loved how his hair curled at the ends, around his neck. It begged to be cut and yet Odessa knew she couldn't bear to turn scissors upon it. Instead, she longed to run her fingers through it.

"And I cannot wait to dance with you this eve," he returned, bowing over her hand.

"I like the sound of that."

He offered her his arm, and Dominic and Moira followed behind them. Moira had donned a new deep russet gown, a daring choice indeed. But she looked stunning. The men helped them into the carriage, rented for the evening, and then stepped to the front bench. They stopped several blocks away to pick up Helen, and Bryce gallantly moved up the stepping-stones to her door.

She appeared in the doorway, every inch the lady. Odessa gasped and grinned, offering her hand as the woman stepped up and into the carriage. "My friend, I've never seen you look so … womanly!"

Helen grinned. "I shall take that as a compliment," she returned, lifting a wry brow.

"What happened that day, up in the canyon?" Bryce asked his future brother-in-law quietly, his tone barely discernible over the horses' hooves. He didn't want to cast down the women's festive mood, but he needed the truth, this night, before they faced others involved. "Nic, why were you so disgruntled?"

Dominic stared at the road ahead of them for a few long moments. "No one wanted those men dead more than I," he said at last, leveling a gaze at Bryce. "But the third man, the one behind the house … he'd given up, tossed his weapon aside. The sheriff shot him in the back. There was no threat. He just killed him."

The two men glanced at each other. "Why?" Bryce asked.

"I've asked myself a hundred times. Is the sheriff a vigilante? Was it a way to manifest power?" He cocked a brow. "He was angry, very angry. The night before, Moira had denied him, ended their courtship. The general told him to give up his quest. Maybe it was fury's fire, needing to burn itself out."

Bryce absorbed that information, thought it over for a minute or two. He glanced back. Helen and Moira were talking; Odessa stared back up at him. "How'd she do it? Break up with him?"

Dominic let a subtle smile spread across his face. "She named a suitor, back in Philadelphia. A man the general would kill himself to have come to town and stay."

"Who?"

"James Clarion Jr."

Bryce pursed his lips and nodded. He glanced over at Dominic. "Sure your father will bless my union with Odessa with someone such as *that* on the horizon for Moira?"

"I dunno," Dominic said in a teasing tone, grinning. "Maybe saving Odessa from highwaymen will sway him." He paused for a breath. "The big ranch won't harm your argument either."

They rode on in companionable silence for a while. "So do you think the sheriff was somehow involved with those men? Shooting to silence them?"

"I only know I don't trust the man," Dominic said. "You shouldn't either. There's something wrong here. Something really wrong. And I either need to find out what it is or make sure my sisters are far, far from it."

A trio of strings was playing on the broad stone deck outside the castle. Bryce escorted Odessa out of the carriage, his hand covering hers upon his arm, as if he didn't want her to slip away, or was afraid someone might try to pull her away. Odessa didn't mind. His arm felt strong and sinewy beneath her glove-covered fingers. And it was thrilling to be beside him, knowing she would always be beside him.

A day after his proposal, she could still hardly believe it. She glanced up at him, lean and handsome, a head taller than she. He looked fine in his new suit and she felt safe. Knowing he was steps away, as she had once known he was just downstairs at the sanatorium, comforted her. Their experience in the canyon and at the Thompson ranch had left her jumpy, ill at ease. Only Bryce's presence seemed to calm her nerves. It felt odd that Papa wasn't here, that she hadn't heard from him that he approved of Bryce McAllan and their impending union, but it was the nature of things here in the West. In time, she would receive a letter from him, answering her own. And she was confident he would approve.

Maybe as the new bride, as Odessa McAllan, with Bryce standing behind her, she could also come clean with her father and tell him she longed to write, to submit her work for publication. Or perhaps she could simply leave that identity behind, put it to rest alongside Odessa St. Clair and move on to embrace her new identity as Odessa McAllan, writing as Helen had encouraged her to do—from her heart, for her God, for herself, never worrying about who else might read it.

She looked about at all the fine ladies, watched as Moira flitted about between them all, already the center of attention, dragging Dominic along. She had always thought her younger sister would be the first to marry.

Odessa's recovery thrilled Moira, made her more joyful than she had seen her sister in some time. As much as she liked being the belle of the ball, she didn't really wish to be the only St. Clair woman. Some might dismiss her as shallow, self-serving, and there was definitely a selfish nature to her sister, but she was mostly, simply, *young*. There was much she had yet to discover, learn, many ways in which she was yet to grow. And without their mother alive to teach her, Odessa wondered where she would learn it.

For Odessa was soon to leave this place for a ranch, high and wide, sheltered by the steep Sangre de Cristos Mountains to her west. *Damp to her East, wounds to her West* … Sam's poem came to mind and she wondered how long it would be until they explored the valley, tried to find what he'd left behind. Or would such a search merely leave them open to attack again? She glanced up to Bryce again, thinking she never wanted to risk losing this curious painter-rancher again; not if she could help it.

Bryce greeted an acquaintance and led her off to the walled edge of the deck, to look out upon the Glen. It was cool outside, but they would remain outside until dark, when they would proceed into the ballroom upstairs in the castle for dinner and then dancing.

"You are quiet," he said, looking out beside her, then down at her.

"I am deep in thought," she returned.

"May I ask about what?"

"About your ranch."

"*Our* ranch."

"*Our* ranch and more. We've spoken at length about my father and his approval of our union," she said in a whisper, "but what of your family? Their approval of me?"

"It matters not. My choice of a bride is up to me. As long as I continue to breed and raise horses for them here in the West, and send them East for sale, I am fulfilling my end of the bargain."

"But you long to see the sea again, to live upon her shore. Can you really stay here in Colorado forever?"

He turned slightly toward her and for a moment Odessa expected him to lean down and kiss her. But he refrained. "Odessa, I glimpse the ocean every time I look into your eyes. And we both know that our health, our very lives, depend on us remaining in a land where we can breathe. We've found renewed health, renewed vigor, and love … I am a satisfied man."

She smiled up at him, in wonder at this miracle of love, weaving its way between them. "And I am a satisfied woman."

"That is good, my love, because soon, it will be public knowledge that you are my bride-to-be."

"Let's not wait long," she said suddenly.

"Make that my eager bride," he amended, a wry grin lifting one eyebrow.

She blushed, could feel the heat of it upon her cheeks. "It's only that … the consumption … then those men …"

"Death's shadow has made you hunger for life's light?"

She smiled. "Who is the writer and who is the artist?"

"We are of like mind, sweetheart. We shall marry as soon as your father arrives and I can get the house ready for you. We've already begun."

"So … July. We'll wed in a month." Odessa looked away as the memory of the mountain attack again recaptured her mind, as it had frequently since the event.

Bryce seemed to sense this. "You don't need to be afraid, Odessa. Married or not, I'm here to keep you safe."

Her eyes slid out toward the Glen.

"Odessa?"

"I don't want you to fret, Bryce."

"Tell me."

"Dominic told me the sheriff killed the third man. Shot him in the back." She shuddered.

"Dominic should not have burdened you with such a story," he said.

"It isn't merely a story. And somehow, I can't help but think," she paused to glance about them and lower her voice, "that it is somehow tied to Sam. What he's left us."

Bryce returned her stare. "So … you believe the sheriff is behind the attack? Really? Why would he do such a thing?"

"Greed? Power? I don't know, Bryce. I only know I don't trust him."

"That could be the sister in you speaking, Odessa. Because the sheriff overstepped his bounds with Moira, jailed your brother …"

"Yes. I admit, you might be right." Odessa stepped forward and scanned the crowd now milling about the Palmers' castle deck.

Her eyes finally landed upon Reid, who stood at the wall, arms akimbo, supporting himself as he stared down upon them. He gave her a small nod, a smile, but Odessa turned without returning a look in kind. "Or you might be wrong." She looked to Bryce, who seeing her expression, searched the deck and found the sheriff. "There is something wrong with that man, Bryce. Something deeply wrong."

Reid Bannock stared down at Odessa and Bryce, in animated conversation among the trees. Never had he seen Odessa look lovelier, but she did not look upon him with favor. She stared at him with indignation, judgment. "She knows," he said lowly to his compatriot who emerged then, from among the trees.

"Knows what?"

"She's putting it together somehow. There's just something in her eyes that tells me she knows." He turned and leaned against the wall, searching the crowd for Odessa's sister, the beauty in russet red. There she was. A picture. A lady worthy of portraiture. It burned still, her spurning, her abrupt departure. But part of him was all the more enticed. A hard-won woman was worthy....

"If you're right, we need Odessa St. Clair gone."

Reid considered her again. "What if O'Toole's map is gone, lost in the river?"

"Then you will have to force her to tell you what she knows, prior to some unfortunate accident."

"Pity to find the cure and then meet another death head-on."

"Pity," the man agreed in a mutter, then moved away, blending into the crowd beyond them.

Reid looked again to Odessa, and then Bryce. It would be more difficult to get to her with a fiancé nearby. And Moira would be so deeply grieved over her death. If they were to ever reconcile, he'd hate to see her in mourning black for a year.... Perhaps the map had somehow survived. Was it on the woman even now? Did she carry it in her bodice? Surely she hadn't left it behind in the cottage.

Another man moved to stand beside him. "Go to the St. Clair cottage and search every inch for the map, anything from O'Toole."

"Done. May I have a glass of Palmer's champagne before I go?"

"Please," Reid said, eyeing the general across the porch, still feeling the slow burn of his betrayal. "Have two. But don't miss our map if it's there."

"And if it's not?"

"Then," he said, sliding a grin toward the man, "we'll just have to search Odessa St. Clair herself."

Chapter ❀ 24

Moira walked up to Odessa, who was standing in the middle of the cottage floor, looking ill at ease. "Are you well, Sissy?"

"Yes, I—"

"Can you unbutton me?"

"What?"

"The buttons—will you help me?"

"Oh, yes."

Moira could feel her sister's fingers upon her back, but she stopped there. "Honestly, Dess. What is it? Are you in such a dreamy state over your engagement that you cannot even move?"

Odessa said nothing and moved over to a picture—the one Bryce had painted for her of the ship upon a vast sea—hanging crookedly on the wall. Frowning, she straightened it. Then she turned to a small table beside the settee and straightened the tablecloth.

"It's a bit late for housework, isn't it?" Moira asked.

"Someone's been here."

"What?"

"Someone's been here."

"The door was locked, Dess. It's highly unlikely …"

Odessa leveled her eyes at Moira and then strode over to her. "Come," she whispered, and ushered her out the door, where Bryce and Dominic stood on the porch, talking. Both men looked their way.

"Someone's been in the cottage," Odessa said.

Bryce was immediately on the move, with Dominic right behind him. Together, they moved from the parlor and into one bedroom, then the next, and finally the kitchen. They returned to the porch and Dominic shook his head. "No one here now."

Odessa let out a long breath, and Moira realized she had been holding her breath too. "I'm so relieved."

They returned to the parlor and the four stood in a circle.

"Why do you think someone has been here, Odessa?" Bryce asked.

"The painting, it was off-center. The tablecloth, too."

"We could've brushed by either on our way to the Glen," Moira said.

But Odessa was shaking her head. "No. I mean, right. It could've happened that way. But it's more a sense that someone else has been here. Smell." She lifted her nose and sniffed the air. The others did the same.

"No one but our fragrant brother," Moira teased.

He smiled and reached out as if to grab her and choke her, but Moira ducked, laughing.

"Someone else has been here," Odessa said, staring at Bryce.

"All right. Someone else has been here," he returned. "Not likely that they're coming back, with you home now. Anything missing?"

Odessa turned and rushed to her room. Fearing for her jewelry, Moira rushed to her room as well. Thankfully, all was in place as she left it. She returned to the parlor just as Odessa did, smoothing her hair. "Everything as expected," she said softly.

"Good, good."

"Together we have a small fortune in Mother's jewels," Moira said. "Surely any intruder would've taken them, right?" She reached out to wrap an arm around Odessa's waist. "Right?"

"Right," her sister returned, after an odd pause.

Dominic stepped beside Bryce outside. He liked his future brother-in-law immensely. He liked how he treated Odessa, treasured her really. He liked how he interacted with others—always warm, respectful. After these last couple of months, he had never asked Dominic why he chose to fight in the ring. He just accepted it.

"Think it's in her head?" Dominic asked him.

"No. I think someone was here, Nic."

Dominic frowned. "Why?"

Bryce glanced over his shoulder and then up and down the street, as if he could see in the dark. "If anything happens to me and Odessa, get to the authorities in Denver and insist they investigate. You cannot trust anyone here in the Springs. Tell them to begin with the death records at the sanatorium, the DeChants and O'Toole, and see what ties they can make to mine claims among those deceased."

"Mine claims."

"Yes, mine claims."

"I'm not liking the sound of this, Bryce. Is this what led those men to chase Odessa and Helen down?"

"We think so."

Dominic thought on that a moment. "Do I need you here tonight?"

"I don't think so. They won't attack you here in the middle of town."

"This from a consumptive rancher who is about to wed my sister and take her a hundred miles from any town."

Bryce returned his grim look then and swung up into his horse's saddle. "I'll be back in the morning, first thing. Keep one eye open tonight, will you?"

Nic said, "Probably both."

They watched the man arrive at the hotel hidden in the shadows across the street. "You searched every inch of the cottage," Reid said lowly.

"Every inch. I'm telling you, Boss, it isn't in there. Either the woman carries it or it's gone."

"Could they have given it to him?"

Both studied Bryce again, dismounting and leading his horse toward the stables. "Could be."

"We need to determine if the mine is as rich as we suspect. One way or another, we have to find out if McAllan or Odessa knows where the hidden entrance is. And McAllan won't let us near Odessa, so we may as well start with him." Decided now, Reid turned to the shorter man. "Take him outside city limits and determine if he already knows how to find his way into the mine that O'Toole left him. Maybe the old man showed him."

"And then?"

Reid studied Bryce as he rode down the street. "I'd prefer he died far from here, but at some point he must, so our *investor* may purchase the O'Toole property. Dispose of the body where no one will ever find him. Understood?"

"Understood."

Bryce was halfway down the alley to the stables when he heard the horses, coming fast.

He pulled his horse up short and listened intently. Two, maybe three … no, there were definitely four.

Acting on instinct, he urged his horse away from the stables and down another alley, and around the corner of the next building, a mercantile. In moments the group reached him, barely discernible in the dark, feigning ease but clearly on the hunt. It was the way they moved, their silhouette that said they were alert, not heading in for the night.

His horse shifted and whinnied as they passed, and Bryce froze. But they rode on by, never pausing, intent on their end goal, whatever it might be.

He waited there for another few minutes, laughing at himself over his paranoia. It was probably nothing. Nothing. If they were after him, they'd be back by now. No, they were just men coming in after a night's foray into Colorado City.

He made a low sound to his horse and stepped forward, intent on a clean bed in a good room.

That was when the first man rounded the bend, filling the alleyway.

Bryce frowned and turned back, just in time to see a club come down upon his head.

Chapter ❀ 25

Bryce came to; he was slumped over the back of his own horse as the group trotted along the road. It was too dark to make out where they were and Bryce didn't want to alert his captors to the fact that he had regained consciousness. He carefully reached for his gun, but both holsters were empty, his revolvers confiscated. But he knew from the pressure at his belly that the knives remained hidden at his waist.

He tried to judge how far they were from town, but he had no idea how long he had been out. Soon enough, however, the leader signaled the group to pull off the road and into a stand of piñon pines. Bryce eased a hand beneath his shirt and grabbed hold of the small knife.

"Get him down," demanded a man, and shortly thereafter, Bryce was hauled from his horse and deposited roughly to the ground. He heard the sound of a cork and then quickly detected smelling salts as they wafted beneath his nose. It was easy to feign that he had just come to.

He opened his eyes groggily. Four men. All with handkerchiefs about their faces. "What? What do you want?" he groaned.

The leader leaned in and grabbed hold of his hair, forcing his head back. Two others grabbed hold of his arms at the same time. "You're being robbed," sneered the leader. "Search him."

They went through his pockets and then ripped open his shirt, discovering the remaining hidden knife, but not the small blade in his hand. He fingered it, glad for the deep darkness of this night and the short, squat blade of the weapon that allowed it to remain undiscovered. *Please, Lord,* he prayed, *help me find a way out of this.*

"Take all I have," he said. "Then let me go."

The man nearest him lifted his hands toward the leader. "Nothing. Nothing but his purse."

"You have my money," Bryce said, fully aware of what these men truly sought, "now leave me be."

"You're in no position to order us about. Do you have it? The map to O'Toole's claim?"

"O'Toole? You mean Sam? I have no idea of what you're talking about."

"Give it up, McAllan. Either you have it or your pretty fiancée does. You better pray we don't have to go after her again." He laughed. "Not that I'd mind." He came closer and yanked Bryce's head back by taking a handful of hair in hand. "Trust me, she wouldn't escape *this* crew."

Bryce gritted his teeth. "There is no map. No letter. Odessa would have no idea what you're talking about."

The punch came then, from the left, meeting his eye and sending a cascade of light shooting across his head, as if he were witnessing Chinese fireworks. But then, nothing. He could see nothing from that eye. "I don't have it!" he cried.

The men around him laughed. One even patted him on the shoulder. That was when Bryce struck, ramming his knife into the man's kidney and then whirling to slash the other across the face. He laid hold of the man's pistol, but a third man hit him across the cheek with a powerful punch that doubled the pain in his eye, following

up with two punches to his ribs. Bryce went down. But as the fourth
man came near, he flung his knife and heard the man gasp and falter.
Bryce whirled, disappearing into the trees.

"Find him!" shouted the man.

Bryce had no illusions. They meant to kill him.

And then they'd go after Odessa.

The man closed the door at the jailhouse, hat in hand.

Reid rose from behind his desk. "What are you doing here?" he
hissed. "You know I don't want you seen with me, and my deputy's
due back any moment."

"I know it," the man said, clearly miserable.

"What is it? What happened?"

"I'm sorry, Boss, but he escaped."

"Escaped?" Reid swore under his breath. "How'd one man escape
four of you? Four!" He hit his thigh with the palm of his hand and
paced away.

"He had a knife hidden on him. Caught us unaware."

"I'll say," Reid said, shaking his head. "How bad? You lose any
men?"

"One. Two injured."

Reid ran a hand through his hair and stared out the window, the
hint of dawn on the horizon. "Now I'll have to find a way to fix it.
Dispose of the body. Take your injured to Denver to seek care. Find
a doc who won't ask questions. Understood?"

Garrett walked in then, and paused when he saw the stranger.
His eyes shifted back and forth between the sheriff and the man.

"Thanks for your time, Mr. Smith," Reid said smoothly, reaching out to shake the man's hand as if they had just met.

"Any time, Sheriff." He placed his hat on his head, nodded at the deputy, and departed.

"What was that about?" Garrett asked him when the door shut.

"Reporting some shooting up on Mount Hermon."

"Before sunup?"

"Dedicated citizen, I guess. We'll have to check it out tomorrow. What've you got?"

"On my way in, I ran into two drunks hauling in a man who was beaten pretty badly. Found him on the road to Colorado City."

"Who is it?"

"Bryce McAllan."

"Bryce McAllan! What was he doing out at this hour?"

"I don't know," Garrett said. Reid didn't care for how his deputy was looking at him, studying him almost. "We've awakened Doc Ramsey and he's seeing to him now."

"How bad is it?"

Garrett winced. "Pretty bad."

Reid walked to the door and took his hat from the peg. "I best go inform the St. Clairs."

"You prefer I do that, Sheriff?"

Reid paused at the door, back still to his deputy. "Why?"

"You know …"

"When I want your help, Deputy, I'll ask for it." And with that, he shut the door firmly behind him.

Pounding at the door awakened all three in the quaint cottage on
Nevada Avenue.

Odessa sat up and tossed aside her covers, pulled on her housecoat, and went to the door. Dominic, thankfully, was already dressed.
She could smell the burned odor of boiling coffee, so he'd been up for
a while. Moira emerged from her room too, hair in similar disorder
to Odessa's, but Nic was already opening the door.

Sheriff Reid Bannock stood outside, hat in hand. "Mornin'," he
said, his eyes lingering over Moira, covering her from head to toe,
then shifting to Odessa.

Nic stepped into his line of vision. "Sheriff?"

"I apologize for the early hour, Miss Odessa," the sheriff said
somberly, looking over Nic's head. "But last night it appears your
beau set off toward Colorado City."

"No, no. Last night he was with us. He left us quite late."

"Yes, that makes sense. I believe it was quite late when this
occurred. He must've gotten it into his head to go and get a drink at
the saloon and set off down the road."

Odessa glanced at Nic. Surely not. "There must be some mistake.
He's not the sort of man to go out drinking. Especially at that hour."

"Maybe he was after something *else*. All I know is that he was on
the road at an hour beyond the realm of respectability."

Odessa could feel her chest tighten, her breath coming in quick
pants. She didn't like his tone. "What *happened?*" Nic cut in.

"What?"

"What happened to Bryce? Quickly, tell us," Nic repeated.

The sheriff stared back into his eyes without blinking. "It appears
he was waylaid by highwaymen."

"Highwaymen," Nic said, his brow furrowing in disbelief. "An awful lot of that going around lately, don't you think?"

"We're a prosperous and growing town. We're doing all we can."

"Was he robbed?"

"Appears so. Nothing on him when he arrived." He eyed Odessa again. "He's been beaten. Pretty bad."

"Where'd you take him?"

"Doc Ramsey's. Some drunks found him and hauled him in with them, during the wee hours this morning."

Nic looked at Odessa. "It will be all right, but we need to get to him. Go and get dressed. Moira, you, too."

When Odessa turned to go, she saw Moira had already disappeared into her room. In minutes, they met Nic outside, waiting with the carriage. He helped them into the back. Reid was gone.

There was none of the gaiety that had surrounded the night before, Odessa thought gloomily. By now, Father would have received their telegram, would be making plans to come so he could attend the nuptials. But if he came now, before Bryce was fully healed, if he thought him the sort of man who was foolish enough to head out for Colorado City in the dark of night … She shuddered. Her father would be furious, and rightly so.

Lost in her own concerns, she barely saw the town as it slid by. Suddenly, they were in front of Doctor Ramsey's, and Nic pulled the carriage horse to a halt. Reid was standing outside the door, one boot against the wall, arms folded across his chest, casually waiting on them. *He wants to bear witness to our grim tragedy unfolding,* Odessa thought. It brought him pleasure, this. Some sort of justice to assuage the pain rent by Moira.

"Shouldn't you be out be chasing the highwaymen, Sheriff?" Nic asked drily.

"No point. Already long gone, I'd wager."

"I see," Nic said, clearly saying by his tone that he didn't. He walked past the man and opened the door for Odessa and Moira. Reid remained outside.

Inside it smelled of fresh linens and pine, antiseptic potions and ... tea. Odessa was instantly comforted. She had met the good doctor and his wife at the Palmers' home, and thought him both knowledgeable and kindly. The doctor emerged from behind a curtain, with his wife right behind him. Both were in white aprons, making the bloodstain at his waist all the more apparent.

"Miss St. Clair," he said, moving toward her. "You are looking so well, my dear. The sanatorium and Doctor Morton have done a fine job, have they not?"

They nodded at one another in greeting, anxious to get along to news of Bryce. Doctor Ramsey hesitated.

"Please, Doctor," Moira said, wrapping her arm around Odessa's waist, "just tell us what you must."

"He arrived unconscious and was beaten pretty badly." He shook his head in wonder. "He could lose an eye. We won't know for some time if it will heal completely."

He studied them to judge how they were taking it, and then plunged forward. "He has a broken rib, which I've wrapped, and that will heal. But obviously we're most concerned that he regain consciousness. Once that bridge is crossed, we'll hope that the eye will heal as God wills."

"We must pray that the young man returns to you," put in Mrs. Ramsey.

Odessa glanced up at the doctor, the depth of concern slowly sifting down into her consciousness. "He might … die?"

The kindly doctor paused, looking to her and her sister from beneath sagging lids. And then he nodded. "We've done what we can. The rest is indeed up to the Lord."

"And good medical care," Nic said. He wrapped an arm around Odessa's shoulders from her other side. "Can we see him, Doctor?"

"Straightaway." He turned and held back the curtain, allowing them entrance to the other side of the room. There, they saw three pristine white beds, one of which Bryce occupied. They moved over to him slowly, as if in procession, wanting to be near him but fearing the worst.

They stopped, Odessa beside him, Nic and Moira behind her. Odessa reached out so she could touch him where it might hurt the man least. "I will pray for his recovery," said Mrs. Ramsey. And then she disappeared behind the curtain again.

Bryce was bandaged, but it was evident that he was grotesquely swollen and bruised.

"I … I don't have the words," Moira said, looking toward her sister in misery. Twin tears tracked down either cheek.

"I do," Odessa whispered, bowing her head. "Father God, be with us now, here. You once heard Bryce pray for me. I ask that You hear my prayer for him now. Please, please, God. Do not take him. Heal him. Make him whole again. Restore him to consciousness, give him complete sight. Heal his wounds." Odessa was crying now. She sank to her knees and ignored Dominic moving away. "We beg You, Jesus. I beg You. Please."

"Please," Moira whispered in echo.

Chapter ✤ 26

Bryce awakened the next day and felt Odessa's hand in his. He smiled, wondering if he was dreaming, if she was truly here, if he was truly alive. And then he remembered.

He sat up. Too fast. Pain shot through his head and he was instantly nauseous.

"Whoa! Whoa, whoa, whoa!" Odessa cried, a hand now on his chest, another at his back, easing him back to the blessed crisp sheets.

"Odessa," he panted, eye shut now. "Are you all right? Where—where am I?"

"Shh, shh, Bryce. You must rest. You were attacked but you're safe now. You're at Doctor Ramsey's. Please—"

"Odessa!" He forced his good eye open and focused on her. "You're ... we're in danger."

"Who's in danger?" Sheriff Bannock was in the room. He hadn't seen him.

Bryce groaned. He forced his eye open again and stared at the man. "The men—"

"Who were they, McAllan? Did you recognize them?" Bannock asked.

"No. They had masks over their faces. I didn't recognize any of them."

"What'd they want?"

"I—I'm uncertain. I can't—I can't remember."

"They were highwaymen. You were robbed and beaten and left for dead."

Bryce closed his eye and lifted a hand to his head as if it ached. He shook it slightly. "They robbed me?"

"Nothing on you when you were brought in, anyway. Could've been the highwaymen or the drunks who rescued you. Hard to tell."

"Do you remember anything of the men?" Odessa asked. "What they said? Anything about their horses? Something that could help the sheriff find them?"

Bryce paused and then shook his head. "All I remember are trees. And the dark."

"What were you doing out there, McAllan? At that hour?" Reid asked.

"I … I don't know."

"Well, give it time. Maybe your memory will come back as you heal." He placed his hat on his head and nodded at Odessa from the door. "We'll find the men responsible for this."

"I hope so," she said. She remembered her manners. "Thank you."

Reid exited the doctor's office and eyed Moira and her brother, sitting on a bench. "He's awake."

Both rose, but Reid paused in front of the door, blocking them, but staring down the street. "I imagine your Clarion will soon arrive."

"He's due on the afternoon train, with my father," Moira said softly.

He still didn't look her way. "The last time you two saw McAllan was late last night?"

"'Bout eleven," Nic said.

"See anyone else? On the street?"

"No."

"Did you see anyone else on the way home? Anyone suspicious?"

"No."

"I'll ask it again … Know why he'd be on his way to Colorado City at that hour?"

Nic met his gaze. "Not my future brother-in-law," he said levelly.

"No telling what happened, then," said the sheriff. "Until his memory returns, I'm afraid we're all in the dark."

They watched him lumber down the steps and down the street, joining his deputy to converse about a block away.

"What do you think he'll do when James gets here?"

"Nothing. The general will see to that." She paused. "Right?"

"Let's hope so."

James Clarion climbed down the steep steps of the passenger car and paused to direct a servant toward his cases and trunks. He was as splendidly refined as Moira remembered—sandy-haired, thin but strong—and yet with a new air of maturity about him. She wondered if he sensed the same about her as they neared each other. He took her hand to kiss it, then rose to smile into her eyes. "If it isn't the lovely Miss St. Clair, Wild West adventurer."

"The Wild West is one thing. You've been to two or three continents since we last kept company."

"And do I have stories to share!" he said with a twinkle in his eye. He tucked her hand into the crook of his elbow, as if they had been courting for months, and turned to her brother to shake his hand. "Dominic, Colorado appears to be as beneficial for you as it is your sister."

"It's a fine place, a good place," he returned. His eyes shifted over James' shoulder, looking for their father. He squinted in confusion and then looked at James again. "Was not my father on this train with you?"

James looked from one to the next and Moira watched the twinkle fade in his eye. "I'm afraid he was not. Come, let us move on to someplace more suitable and I will tell you all about your father. If Miss Odessa is in good condition, she ought to be present too." He turned as if to look for her, then added, "He sent several trunks for you—" He turned away from them to speak to the servant again and counted his luggage. Moira shifted her weight from one foot to the other and back again—what could have detained Papa? "There now, all is accounted for. I do hope your carriage is large. Since I come bearing gifts, I am rather heavy laden."

"James," Moira said, reaching out to touch his arm. "Please. Is Papa all right?"

He looked upon her with genuine sorrow and concern. "For now, Moira. But he is ailing. It is rather dire, I'm afraid. Please, let us get to your sister and I will share all I know."

The telegram arrived three days later from the St. Clair Press attorney, Francis Bonner.

> *Regret to inform you of the death of Clarence St. Clair,*
> *at 2:10 am 10 July 1883 STOP Funeral to be conducted*
> *15 July unless otherwise directed STOP Request Dominic's*
> *immediate presence STOP Bonner*

Odessa had read it so many times it quickly seared into her memory as clearly as Sam's poem. But in this there was no light, no hope, no intrigue. Only darkness, despair, death. James told them that their father had been having difficulties with his heart for some time, suffering a minor stroke right before James departed for Colorado, which finally convinced him he should not travel. She sighed heavily as she walked down the street to Doc Ramsey's, wondering again if her papa had been alone when his heart beat a final time, if he had called out for her or one of her siblings or his wife. Only the knowledge that he was at last reunited with his beloved bride, her little brothers and tiny sister in heaven gave her any sense of comfort.

Doctor Morton had refused to consider the idea of her returning home for the funeral. Not even for a few days. "The train ride itself would be too strenuous, Odessa," he'd said. "You'll spend three days en route there, and three days back. Think of the last time you made that journey. You've made too much progress to risk regressing now. Please, your father wanted nothing more than for you to find health. You've done that here in Colorado. You honor his memory more by remaining."

In the end she had agreed, knowing her place was here, with Bryce. Moira stayed to attend to the shop and James Clarion, while Dominic journeyed home to be present at the funeral and see to the estate and their father's affairs. He'd reach Pennsylvania tomorrow and the funeral would be the day after that. She didn't know if he'd return—or when. He and Moira had come to loathe the time they spent at the store and had hired the schoolmarm, Kathleen Price, to assist during her summer break. Odessa, conversely, loved every hour she spent in the store, but found she did not have the stamina to remain more than a few.

She climbed the steps of Doc Ramsey's, nodded at his wife who peeked through a doorway to a kitchen, and proceeded to Bryce's bedside.

He smiled softly when he saw her and opened his arms wide. "Come here, sweetheart," he said quietly, reading the grief in her eyes. She moved toward him and sank to her knees beside the bed, resting her head on his chest, and gave way to the sobs she had been holding in for days.

He said nothing, merely stroked her head and hair and patted her as she cried. Even when her tears were spent she remained there for a time, drawing comfort from his warmth, the steady beat of his heart, the strength in his hands. At last she straightened and wiped the tears from her cheeks and returned his tender smile.

"Now you're looking better and I'm a sight," she said.

"You're beautiful," he said, tucking a strand of hair behind her ear.

"No, Moira could always cry and look somehow fetching. I get splotchy and puffy-eyed."

"All the more testament to your beauty. I'd meet you down that church aisle at this very moment and count myself blessed to have you as my bride."

She laughed off his compliment and studied him again. He was more coherent in his speech and seemed more like himself today. "Tell me how *you* are, Bryce. How's your head? Have you remembered anything more?"

"How's the shop?" he asked, trying to deflect. "Is Moira staying put at all, or merely looking to you and Kathleen?"

Her eyes narrowed and she moved to the chair beside his bed. "Why did they do it, Bryce?" she said in a whisper. "Tell me. I cannot bear the fact that I almost lost you and my father in the same week. Tell me what you remember."

"We've been through this, Odessa. I don't remember. Not a thing."

"They took your money, but not your watch. It makes no sense."

"Maybe they were angry I only had a few dollars on me. Few dollars among four men isn't much."

Bryce moved his head back and forth on the pillow and closed his eyes. "Leave it, Odessa. This will only make things worse."

"Tell me what you remember. *Tell me,*" she urged.

"No. No! It's bits and pieces. It makes no sense, even to me. Please, stop. It's making my head throb."

Odessa sighed and leaned back in her chair, catching her breath, letting Bryce's heartbeat return to normal. She didn't want him to regress … but this was important. "Bryce, do you think they were after you because of Sam's poem? Did they ask you about the mine? About me? About anything in particular?"

Bryce frowned and then slowly opened his eyes, staring at the ceiling. His left eye was still horribly bloodshot, but at least it wasn't as swollen. And the double vision had ended. The doctor had hope now that it would heal completely. "My memory is sketchy, but yes, I think they were after the map."

She reached forward and took his hand. "The map—Sam's poem. They thought I'd given it to you for safekeeping. Worse, maybe they meant to kill you, make it look like a robbery, because you now own the O'Toole mine."

He grabbed her hand and forced her to stop pacing again, then sighed. "It's been a terrible week for you, Odessa. First me, then your father. It's you I'm worried about. I have to get you out of here. Marry you and take you back to the ranch. We can see anyone coming from a couple miles out. Too many corners, too many ways for a man—or woman—to be ambushed here."

"You really think that?" Odessa asked. "You think we'll be safer on the ranch?"

"Absolutely."

"What about the DeChants? If Amille wasn't completely mad, if they would go to such lengths as to kidnap and murder their child— then murder John and make it look like a mining accident … why do you think we'll be safe?"

Bryce leveled his good eye at her and waited for her to cease pacing. "Because DeChant didn't have ten ranch-hardened men on the premises dedicated to keeping him alive." He reached out to her and she took his hand. "You'll be safer there, Odessa. We'll see to it."

Chapter ❧ 27

"You're telling me that my father left everything to me?"

"Everything. The house. St. Clair Press. Even his bank accounts are at your disposal." Francis Bonner, a small man with a long beard, pushed the documents across the desk to him.

Dominic picked the top sheet up but stared at it with unseeing eyes. With his other hand he untied his tie and unbuttoned his collar. It was stifling hot in Philadelphia. The funeral service, although short, had seemed interminable in the sweltering church.

"He never updated his will. This was drafted the year after you were born. I urged him to revise it every year, but the matters at hand always proved more demanding of his attentions." He paused and eyed Dominic. "I must say, I'm surprised at your reaction. It is common enough—and to your obvious favor."

Nic pinched his temples with the thumb and third finger of his right hand and set the document back on the desk. "What about Odessa and Moira? What do they receive of the estate?"

The small man coughed. "Well, that is up to you, of course."

"I could take it all?"

"You could, although you and I both know that would not be within your father's wishes."

"Yes, well, if it was up to my father, I'd stay here at this desk and keep running St. Clair Press. Work myself to death, just as he did, not living life, just *reading* about it. But it's no longer up to my father, is it? He's dead. *Dead.*"

Francis blanched and stared at him with wide eyes.

Nic rose and paced the office floor. How many times had he been in this office, trying to have a word with his father but having to wait for ten others to speak first? How often had he been reprimanded in here, told what to do? "Set straight," again and again? He ran his fingers over leather-bound editions of St. Clair Press's best-selling books. "He sent us West to find our way," he said aloud. "He knew it was ahead of us, not behind us."

"Pardon me?"

Nic shook his head and turned toward Francis. "Sell it. All of it."

"What?"

"I'll pack up the things my sisters would care about and send them to Colorado. Then you will see to selling the house, the remaining items within, and St. Clair Press. Reserve a portion of the proceeds to care for the family grave sites for the next fifty years. The remaining estate, in total, will be divided into thirds, with a third to be given to each of my sisters and a third to me."

"This will take some time," Francis said, rising, flustered.

"Of course," Nic said easily, his confidence growing by the moment. This was the answer, his escape route, hope. "But as you work out those details, I want my father's bank accounts immediately transferred to my name. Deduct it from my portion once the sales are complete, but I plan to depart Philadelphia within a few days and wish to have access to those monies."

"I must say, I believe your father—"

"My father had ample opportunity to pursue his dreams," Nic interrupted. "Now it is my turn to shape my own future."

"W-where will you go? Back to Colorado?"

Nic moved toward the door and set his hat on his head. He turned to flash the attorney a grin. "I have no idea. But I very much look forward to finding out."

On the eve of their father's funeral, Moira and Odessa stood on a cliff above Garden of the Gods, dressed in black and clinging to each other. James Clarion stood at a respectful distance behind them, and Bryce was in a carriage just beyond him. The young women leaned their heads together as they wept. One shared a memory and they would cry for a time, then the other would share yet another story, and they'd cry again. They had come here, to this place, because they had talked about bringing their father here when they saw it for the first time—the brilliant red rocks shooting toward the sky, the towering Pikes Peak, a lovely purple contrast above them.

"He would've loved it here," Odessa said.

"He would've loved seeing you looking so well," Moira said. "At least he knew you were back on your feet, Odessa, safe. That must have made him so content."

"I owe him my life twice over," Odessa mused. "He wanted nothing more than to know that all three of us were well."

They stood together in silence, watching as the sun set over the mountains. "What will become of St. Clair Press?" Moira asked at last as they turned to go. "Do you think Nic will remain in Philadelphia?"

"I don't know," Odessa said. "I hope he returns soon—even for a time. I want him to be here to give me away at the wedding, and there is much for us to discuss."

Moira spent much of her day on James' arm, at his insistence, weathering dull, long meetings in which he seemed to do little but stare at sheet after sheet of numbers. He was doing some investing for his father, principally in land, particularly land that might yield valuable commodities at some point. Her ears perked up during cloaked conversations, heavy with implied meaning and unspoken promises, innuendo meant to propel one man after another toward James' way of thinking. He was a master at deal making, and Moira reveled in watching him close each one.

After the meetings, the two would rehash the conversations, dissecting and disseminating what they thought was vital. James listened to her with some bemusement on his face, as if she were a beautiful toy that delighted him, but he also seemed to take her points under serious consideration. Moira blossomed in the light of this attention, this sense of respect that she had never found except in flaunting her beauty or singing.

They were on their way to dine together, alone at last, nine days after his arrival, and Moira believed she felt the faintest niggling of love for the man beside her. He had been very attentive, especially after her father's death. She smiled and held his arm even more tightly. He looked down at her. "Happy, pet? I mean, even in the midst of your mourning can you find a bit of contentment in this, this courtship?"

His nickname irritated her, but she shoved it aside. It was common enough. She nodded. "Very. I'm so glad you are here, James."

"As am I. Tell me, what was so important today that you could not remain with me at Dannigan's?"

"I've been meaning to tell you, James."

"Oh? What is it?" He pulled her to a stop, a block shy of the restaurant.

She paused, considering her choice of words. "I ... you have complimented my singing, in the past."

"Indeed," he said, reaching out to touch her cheek. He looked lively, boyish. A young man in love. His mossy brown eyes sparkled.

"James, I have a little adventure, here in the Springs. A place I've found to sprout my wings. I do so hope you'll approve."

"Anything, pet. Ask me anything, it's yours."

"I'm to sing, James. At the opera house. As the lead, opening night."

He frowned, hesitated, and Moira rushed on. "It's something I've always longed to do. To sing in front of a crowd. To ... entertain."

As his frown deepened, she knew that last word had been wrongly placed. "It is a fine opera, and deeply meaningful to me and my family, because it centers on something that brought us here, in the beginning."

"What is that?" he asked distractedly.

"Consumption. The heroine has consumption."

"Does she die?"

"What?"

"Does she perish?"

"Well, yes."

"No," he said, shaking his head, and breaking away to pace back and forth. "No, Moira. You are ill-cast. Imagine, beautiful you, dying, in front of all those people. It is oddly ... intimate. Unseemly."

"Well, yes, James. That is the point of all good theater. To let the audience in. Close. But it is all illusion. Make-believe."

"Not to me." He took her hands in his. "I cannot bear it, even watching your death in a false world. Please, do not do it."

Moira pulled her hands from his. "James, please do not ask that of me."

"Did your father approve of this?"

Moira shifted and then met his eyes. "My father did not know of my plans."

His mouth settled into a grim line. "It is settled, Moira." He laughed, a hollow sound. "Listen, I beg for your forgiveness over this disappointment. But we are courting; you are my intended. Your father is gone, unable to guide you. We will find other means for you to share your gifts."

She turned slightly away. "And how shall we do that?"

He took her hand and tucked it in the crook of his arm. "Come, let us eat. We'll both feel better after a good meal. We'll discuss it later."

But Moira knew their conversation was over. In James' mind, Moira was set to tell the director the very next day she could not take the part, and she would never set foot on the stage again.

She would just need to convince him otherwise. James Clarion was a good man, a man of the world, educated, a patron of the arts. Not anything like Reid Bannock. Surely, in time, he'd see things her way.

"I'm selling it. All of it."

"All of it? You mean the house—"

"I mean all of it," Nic said, looking from one sister to the next. "Wellington Press has put in a good bid for St. Clair Press—"

"Papa never wanted to sell to them," Odessa said, shaking her head. "He didn't care for how they did business." Bryce took a seat beside her. James stood behind Moira, leaning against a wall, listening, chin in hand.

"Francis Bonner thinks it's a decent bid, a fair bid, but we're waiting for another. I expect to receive a telegram today on it."

"What about what we want? Why did you not consult us?" Odessa asked.

"Come," Nic said dismissively. "You are to be wed tomorrow and Moira has never been as drawn to books as you and father were. Right?"

Moira nodded, reluctantly.

"If anyone was to take over St. Clair Press, Odessa, it would be you. But women are not publishers and—" He held up a hand when she began to interrupt him. "*And* as I've already said, you are marrying a Colorado rancher *tomorrow*. Right? *And* you can't return East even if you wished to do so. Right?"

Odessa rose and paced. "But, Nic, shouldn't you have discussed it with us first? It might be the right decision, but didn't you consider that Moira and I would want to be a part of it?"

"It wasn't yours to make. It was mine. Father left it to me."

"The decision," Bryce said.

"No. He left the entire estate to me. It's all in my name."

"He left no provision for the girls?" James asked.

"Bonner says he simply never got to it. The will is old, dated soon after I was born." He held up his hands when they all began to speak at once. "Look, we all know Father's intentions would have been to divide the estate between us, at least to some extent. So while the decision remains mine to make, I've asked Bonner to divide it in thirds."

"So that is it? It's done? There is no discussion?" Odessa asked. "Wellington will run St. Clair Press into the ground. I don't—"

"No. There is no discussion," Nic said. "It is done, Odessa. It is for the best."

"How much?" Moira asked. "How much money will we each receive?"

"Enough to buy you a nice home and keep you in fine dresses and food for decades to come. Father worked hard—"

"Worked so hard that in an instant, at the first opportunity, his son could simply sell it," Odessa said.

"What would you have me do, Odessa?" He rose to glare back at her across the table. "I don't want it! I never wanted it! I don't wish to be a bookseller or a publisher. I want to do something else. And now I have the opportunity." His face softened. "I know it disappoints you, Dess. The press was dear to your heart in so many ways. I'm sorry. I wish there was an alternative. But don't you see? This is my chance. Your chance. Moira's chance. To make Father's dream each of our own. It's a gift, really, unique for each of us."

"He's right, Odessa," Bryce said. She sank into the seat beside him and he covered her hands with his.

"And it would be nearly impossible to run it from afar," James said. "Even with a good manager in place, a business can be destroyed in months without solid oversight. I've seen it happen—mismanagement of talent, siphoning of funds. It's wise to let it go if there is no one capable or interested enough to remain."

"Wise, but sad. Just another ending for us," Odessa said, grief evident in every syllable she uttered.

"But endings leave room for new beginnings, right?" Bryce asked her. "You finish the last page of a book, aren't there then ten new tales to choose from? That's what Nic wants. A new opportunity. The chance to choose his own book. Write his own script. Surely you understand that."

Odessa glanced from him to her brother. After a moment, she nodded. "I do." She reached out to Nic and Moira and they came around the table to take her hands. She looked up at each of them. "Just remember that this money is Papa's final gift to each of us. Don't waste it," she pleaded. "Make it count."

"I will," Moira said.

"As will I," Nic said.

They were married on a bright and sunny July morning at the First Presbyterian Church, one of only three churches in town, and refused any party afterward. Under the shadow of her father's death, the sale of St. Clair Press, and mindful of the still unnamed thugs who had nearly cost her her husband, Odessa had not wanted a lot of fuss and bother; she didn't want to dance and drink champagne; she only wanted to be with Bryce, wanted to absorb what it meant to finally be his *wife*. Desperation to escape the threatening cloud that covered the Springs propelled her forward. And the idea that Bryce could both oversee his ranch again and introduce it to her on their honeymoon had been hers. Their plan was to travel to some dry clime on belated holiday come winter.

So she had donned a simple, but elegant, ivory silk gown, gathered a small, elegant bouquet from the sanatorium gardens, and walked the aisle on her brother's arm, but with none other than Moira and James, Helen, Doctor and Mrs. Ramsey, Doctor and Mrs. Morton, Nurse Packard, and General Palmer in attendance.

But it felt right to Odessa, to stand before this small, select group. She keenly felt the absence of her father as Nic stepped back, but then was warmed by the arrival of her groom. Bryce smiled down at her, delightfully handsome in a new black suit and crisp white shirt, his sparkling eyes—both now blessedly clear—captivating her as they always had.

"Ready?" Bryce whispered, and Odessa barely choked back a laugh. What was she to do if she wasn't? Run away? But she didn't want to run away. No, this was exactly where she wanted to be. The vows were spoken, the rings exchanged. And never, ever, had Odessa seen such love and joy in her beloved's eyes. It made her take a breath, as if gasping. But it was more a desire to inhale, to hold it within her for as long as possible, imprinting this precious day on her heart as if it were one of Helen's photographs, deep within.

Outside, under joyful, clanging bells, as she bade farewell to everyone she had loved longest, and new friends who had made this place home, a sudden sorrow echoed through like the last peal of a bell hanging in the air. But it was a short-lived pain that soon faded upon the euphoria she felt at officially being Mrs. Bryce McAllan. And the two of them were escaping, running away to his beautiful ranch to explore the land, and each other.

A distant train whistle blew. "We don't have much time," Bryce said lowly.

"Here," Helen said, handing her a camera and then setting a picnic basket beside it. "I'll expect to see some fine photographs from your new abode."

"Helen, I can't —"

"You can. There are supplies in the trunk. Happy marriage, friend." She pulled her close. "I've been married twice now, happily. Treat your spouse as your best friend. Remember that."

"I will. Do come and see us soon."

Odessa turned to Moira. "Stay out of trouble, Sissy."

Moira laughed. "James will see to that."

"I'll be back in a month or two to check on you."

"Yes, yes. You concentrate on being Mrs. McAllan."

"Mrs. McAllan," Odessa said, cocking her head to one side. "That'll take some getting used to."

"Take care of my sister," Dominic was warning Bryce with a solemn expression.

"With my life," he returned immediately.

The two shook hands and then Nic turned to kiss her on both cheeks. "Take close care, Dess."

"You take care too, dear brother. Stay off the roads at night."

"Upon my honor," he pledged.

A train whistle blew again, just as a beautiful white carriage, pulled by a team of black horses, drew up in front of the church.

Mud coated the side, but it mattered little to Odessa—only the thoughtfulness of her husband filled her mind. He grinned and gestured grandly in the direction of the carriage and she moved toward it, pleased to see her trunks already packed beside Bryce's in back. Those attending the wedding added their gifts to the back and stood around shaking hands with Odessa from across the carriage door.

And then they were off. She huddled close to her husband, leaning her cheek on his shoulder. "The last time I was on a train, I almost died. It was that dire, my consumption."

"I remember." There was a shiver in his voice. "And now you board a train, a woman with a new name, new identity."

"But I am still Odessa."

"Oh yes, always, gloriously Odessa. My Odessa." And with that, he leaned down and stole his second kiss as her husband.

"Should we stop somewhere, Bryce? I need to change. I don't want my gown to be ruined, sitting on a dusty train for hours."

"No need," he said mysteriously. They reached the train station, Bryce turned to direct the men on the platform with their baggage, flipping them each coins, and hurried to board the last car, an elegantly painted and appointed car with the words "General William Jackson Palmer" on the side. He lifted his hand to her as her mouth fell open. "The Palmers' wedding gift to us. We might be spending our wedding day on a train, but it's in a borrowed, private car like no other."

Odessa squealed and took his hand. They climbed in and Odessa's eyes opened wide in wonder. Rich mahogany covered the walls. Black lacquered cabinets with hand-carved ivory handles were on one end. Soft ruby velvet covered overstuffed chairs and benches

along the side. Tables with carved acanthus leaves and the heads of
nymphs were on either side.

Bryce was grinning, opening cabinet after cabinet. "We have our
choice of what to dine upon. There are crackers, canned sardines and
oysters, even caviar. Oranges, fresh oranges. And the general's cook
and Helen both packed us picnic baskets."

"We won't starve," Odessa said.

"But that's not the best part," he said. He took her hand and led
her to the back of the car, then opened two pocket doors. To one side
was a bed fit for a queen.

She glanced up at him. "We couldn't possibly," she said, hand on
her heart. "Look at the windows! I don't care to have ranchers and
whatnot gazing in upon us."

"We'll be moving just fast enough for privacy," he said moving
behind her and bending to kiss her ever so softly on the neck. "And
there are drapes anyway. Lots and lots of drapes."

"Drapes might work," she allowed, closing her eyes as he continued his trail of kisses to her ear. She felt weak, light-headed.

The train conductor called out, "Final call! All aboard!" and a
servant ducked into their car. "Sure you don't want a servant aboard
your car, Mr. McAllan?" The man averted his eyes from their intimate kiss, and Odessa turned away, her face aflame.

"No, thank you," Bryce said, a laugh under his tone. "We will be
just fine on our own."

"You surely will," said the man with a grin, and then he was
out and closing the door up tight. She shared a smile with her
husband and, feeling self-conscious, turned to pass the bed and
go out to the small rail and deck that protruded from the back of

the train. She looked across Colorado Springs, what she had called home these last months, and recognized that she wasn't yet home, that it was ahead.

Bryce joined her at the rail as the train blew its whistle and lurched forward, then slowly began to gain speed. He handed her a glass of champagne, bubbly and light and sweet upon her tongue, and toasted her. "To Mrs. McAllan and our new life together."

"And to my husband, Mr. McAllan."

They stood there, trying to drink their champagne, but the ride was already bumpy, jostling them about. "Want to go in?" Bryce asked, meaning deep in his eyes.

He moved toward her and kissed her, his lips becoming more and more searching, his questions and sentences broken up by kisses he couldn't stop himself from making, nor could she refuse. "Do you mind, Odessa? Very much, I mean? That it's here. Now. On a train?"

"What does it matter?" she asked. "Whether it be in a hotel … or a train … or a tiny cabin … right?"

"Right," he agreed, moving behind her, unbuttoning a gown her sister had buttoned up only hours before.

Sheriff Reid Bannock dolefully watched as Bryce McAllan whisked his bride away. It chafed, seeing a St. Clair girl in white, when he had thought it was going to be him as groom, Moira as bride. But instead she was there, accepting James Clarion's arm, looking up at the dandy in adoration.

The map was not in the cottage, nor on her brother-in-law's

person. Was it with Moira? His eyes returned to the train, small now, in the distance. Or Odessa? Or had it been lost when those fools chased her and Helen Anderson into the water? And if that was the case, did she remember pertinent details? Was it all in that pretty head of hers? What delicious torture might it take to extract it?

Another rider came up, joining him in the shadows cast by the swiftly climbing sun. Reid's grim smile faded. "All is in order?"

He nodded swiftly toward the train in the distance. "The men aboard will watch the McAllans day and night to see if they find their way to O'Toole's mine. Once we have the location, we uh, *clear the way* to purchase the property."

"McAllan will be more cautious than ever, given that beating he took."

"I've thought of that myself. We'll have to lie low. Give them the impression they have been forgotten, that they're safe on that big ranch. When McAllan relaxes, we'll move."

"Good. Long-term goals demand long-term plans. We can wait a few more weeks." He looked back to the wedding crowd still lingering. "What of Clarion? He's met all the appropriate people?"

"He has. And there's something else. Telegraph operator let me know that the St. Clairs received a message late last night. They sold the press. Word on the street is that Dominic plans to close down the bookshop and move on. They're cashing in."

Reid lifted his head in surprise and then dismissed the man.

So the St. Clair heirs had sold their inheritance while their father's body was still cooling. The girls would not have had the stomach for such a move. It had to have been Dominic. On second thought, Moira might have encouraged him. The selfish wench had big ideas in her head, plans. Would she now toss Clarion aside? He both hoped for it as much as he dreaded it. For if she severed her courtship with Clarion she was bound to move on, leaving Reid behind as well. There would be no opportunity for reconciliation … or retribution.

His eyes shifted to the horizon. It was time to face facts. Moira would never have him. She had never had serious intentions about him. And for that, she and her family would pay dearly. The McAllans would soon die and the O'Toole fortune would be partially his. With such funds in his bank, he would retire as sheriff and track Moira down. She was still young, foolish, bound to make poor choices with liquid assets at her fingertips. He'd find a way to exploit her, leaving her vulnerable, just as she had done to him. Then, in her most dire hour, she would fall to her knees, begging him to take her back, to rescue her.

He grinned, the thrill of promise, hope, surging through his limbs. Would he take her back then? Make her his bride or merely his mistress?

There would be plenty of time to consider both options. But at that point, it would be his decision, not hers. Moira St. Clair would be entirely at his mercy. He laughed under his breath. Yes, long-term goals demanded long-term plans.

Chapter ❈ 28

"So I'll see you both this evening," said James Clarion, standing beside a fine gray horse and preparing to ride away for yet another meeting.

"Tonight, at six," Moira agreed, from beside her brother. She flashed a smile toward him, and for the first time, Nic wondered if she truly felt something for the man. Moira and Nic climbed the shop steps while James rode east, out of town. Dominic wished he could switch places with James, have business that carried him in one direction and then the other, varied, wide, ever expanding. Or even with Bryce, to a ranch that presented new challenges each day. He couldn't wait to be divested of the bookshop, which, to him, felt like two wagon wheel ruts through a vast, endless prairie. He could barely stand this process of closing it down. He wished he could hop the first train through town and see where it took him.

A sudden thought came to him. A deep amber shot of whiskey. Then another. His mouth watered at the thought of it. In the whiskey, he could find the patience he needed to see the sale of the shop's contents through. Perhaps he would reward himself this night....

"Nic, I have to head over to the opera house soon for rehearsal," Moira said.

He frowned. "I thought you were going to help me here. There is so much to be done, Moira."

"I needed James to believe that. But I thought you knew I had daily rehearsals from now until opening night."

He shook his head. "You should shoot straight with James. Tell him now you're doing the opera. He's not the sort who will favor a surprise."

"I know it," she said ruefully. "But I cannot find the right words to convince him. If we can just get to opening night, if he could see me onstage, how much I love it, what it's like—"

Nic shook his head again. "I'm telling you now, Sissy. You should tell him the truth before opening night."

"He'll be frightfully angry," she said. "He might be so angry that he leaves town, pulls out of the business deals he's been working on. And that will infuriate the general."

"And so you're concerned that if the general is infuriated, he'll replace you in the opera? Are you more concerned about losing the role or the man?"

"Both. What if James walks away from me?" She ran her fingers over the countertop, thinking about it. "I think it would be dreadfully upsetting."

Nic shrugged his shoulders. "He's a good man, a nice match for you. And he certainly has access to enviable bank accounts. But you're a woman with your own means now, Moira. Your future is what you choose to make of it." He reached out to pinch her chin. "You are beholden to no man. Except me," he teased. "Until you've helped me see this shop emptied of its contents, that is. Then? You want to go and chase the stage? I say do it. You certainly have the beauty and talent it would take."

"You think so? Really?"

"Really."

"But if I could get both … launch my career and win the man, wouldn't that be the best?"

"The best, yes, but I think it's impossible. You must convince James to let you sing. Don't surprise him. That will not go over well."

Moira stared at him. "I'll consider it. I will. But now I really must be off. You can manage without me?"

Nic clamped his lips shut for a moment. "I'll manage. But you owe me, Sissy." He waved his finger in front of her face. "I expect you to rise early and come to help, first thing in the morning."

"First thing," she agreed, and kissed him on the cheek as she turned to rush out the door.

Moira walked out onto the stage, still mulling over her brother's words. The modest opera house was not anything like the glorious theaters of the East, but it was still something. It had two tiers of seats, spread in gentle arcs like the bottom of a seashell and offering prime acoustic advantage. The stage was wide and nicely lit, with the aid of candles and lanterns placed in just the right locations. And when they were all alight! Oh, it was magical. She couldn't wait for her costumes to be complete, for the glory of opening night.

In the back of her mind, she knew that there was a good chance that it might be her *only* night. After her final bows, a last curtain call—*please, Lord, let there be a curtain call!*—James would undoubtedly storm in. Perhaps he'd convince the general to toss her out to the sidewalk. Or maybe, just maybe, James would see in her that this is what she longed to do; he would be proud of her performance; she would win his approval as well as his love. Wouldn't it be grand? They could travel the world together, he seeing to business while she filled various roles on the stage.

But James would not convince her to turn down this opportunity. She would leave him. He was interesting, intriguing, and fabulously wealthy, but no man would own her, manage her, control her. She was talented, the director said. Fabulously talented, said Jesse McCourt, the male lead.

She needed no man, really. As Nic had pointed out, she now had her father's money. It would give her the start she needed.

Because this was just the beginning of what she wanted to do.

The mere beginning.

She attacked the rehearsal as if it were opening night, digging deep for every low note, clawing toward every high one. She became the heroine, Camille, imagining Odessa at her most dire hour in every anguished move. She magnified the role, giving it life, even as her character succumbed to death. She felt the power of it within her, knew it was moving. Her excitement grew at the ease of it all, how it flowed from her mouth, her steps, her eyes. She became Camille for a period of time, so lost in the role was she, as if she had fallen asleep and awakened to find herself another.

Instead of barking orders, the director was silent for the first time in weeks, watching one scene after another unfold. The other actors were equally quiet, each becoming more absorbed in their own characters even as Moira fell more deeply into the well that was Camille. By the end, two women near her were weeping, as was the director.

The death scene wound to a close, each breath becoming more difficult for "Camille." Moira thought of her mother, taking her last breath, then considered her father, feeling his heart thud to a stop as if it were now in her own chest. She became Odessa in the sanatorium, once so pale, almost translucent, with such long pauses between breaths that they thought they had lost her. She emulated Odessa in those dark days, held her breath, took another sudden, shaky breath, held it … and then another … and then stopped breathing altogether.

The cast about her and the director paused, holding their breath, waiting for her. The other actors completed their final lines, sniffing and teary, and Moira could feel their eyes upon her, could feel the tension in the room as if they were worried she had actually expired. Finally, the last line had been spoken, but still she remained.

The stage was silent.

"M-Moira?" the director dared, climbing the stairs.

"That went well, don't you think?" she said brightly, sitting up upon her settee.

The cast laughed nervously, and then applause burst out all about.

And never, never had Moira felt more gratified.

Their car was transferred to the next train in Cañon City, a narrow gauge, and from there they climbed the dry brown canyon dug over the millennia by the Arkansas River, far below. Sparse vegetation clung to the cliffs, and Odessa wondered for the first time if she was heading to a high desert valley rather than the lush valley she had pictured.

The river was high but receding, curving one way and then the next in a silky blue snake's shape as it rushed downward, ever downward. And still they climbed, the rails sometimes precariously close to the riverbank. At a tiny station—little more than a platform and water tower—the conductor drew the train to a stop and Bryce and Odessa disembarked, both sorrowful to be leaving the Palmers' lovely car behind. Several men unloaded their trunks and placed them into a waiting wagon with the Circle M brand on its side. A couple of men brought Bryce's horse out of a freight car and handed her reins to Bryce. And then the train pulled out again, heading for the mining camps higher up.

Bryce led the horse to water, but Odessa watched the train as it rounded the corner, the locomotive gone, then the first car, then the second … three more cars and then the Palmers' car was turning the bend. And then it was gone. All at once, she could hear nothing but the rush of the Arkansas River upon the rocks below and Bryce talking lowly to the horse, who balked at the idea of hauling a wagon after her recent weeks of freedom from such chores. Eventually, Bryce got her in the harness and turned to look upon his bride with a tender expression.

"It's a little isolated out here for a city girl."

"I think I can manage it," she said, lifting her chin.

"Yes, for now. In a few weeks you'll be begging me for a trip to the Springs—or at the very least, Cañon City."

"Few *weeks?* I can last a few months, at the very least!"

He smiled and drew her into his arms. "Is that a wager on your lips, Mrs. McAllan?"

"No, Mr. McAllan," she said, kissing him slowly, softly. "My family does not abide by gambling."

"No money will exchange hands," he said, the dare in his eye. "I'm just saying you won't last three weeks before you're begging me for a city fix."

"Three weeks is nothing," she said, scoffing. "Say I last *four* weeks. What will be my prize?"

"That's to be decided," he said.

"New fabric for our window curtains," she said. "And other girlish things I say we need. I don't trust you to have outfitted our new home with much more than a table and two chairs."

"Oh no," he protested, wrapping his arms around her again. "There's a bed, too. A big bed. We just need our bedroom done so we have someplace to put it."

She giggled and accepted his kisses. "Take me home, Husband."

"Lead the way, Wife."

"Right away." She stepped into the wagon and picked up the reins. "Which way is home?"

He smiled and took the reins from her, crossed the train tracks, and they began to climb a narrow dirt road with one sign: WESTCLIFFE. "See now, there's a town. That won't count in our wager, will it?"

"Trust me, Westcliffe is no Cañon City, and a far cry from Colorado Springs."

"Small-town life. I'll get used to that."

"Small towns are one thing. It's the ranching life I'm worried about," Bryce said.

She laughed off his concern, but inside, she wondered. Had she ever really been more than a mile from another? In Philadelphia, there were five hundred people inside a square mile. In the Springs, still a hundred. On the road—the road toward Divide—she and Helen had been fairly isolated. But still, there had been other travelers, people heading in the opposite direction ... and others. She closed her eyes, trying to drive out the memory of the men who had chased them, tried to kill them.

"Are you afraid?" Bryce asked, taking her hand in his.

"Afraid?" She feigned ignorance.

"Afraid. Being here. Near Sam's land. Near Amille and John's mine. Are you afraid they'll come after us?"

"Are you? I thought you felt safer here, on your ranch."

"I think you're safer here. Between me and Tabito and the other ranch hands, no one will get to you. And if you're safe, I'm content."

Odessa leaned into his shoulder, hugging his arm and looking up, intent upon only pleasant thoughts that pertained to the day, the potential in her future. Not the past. She searched the rocks as they left the river behind, some perched precariously atop others as if barely maintaining a balance, erosion creating odd shapes of others. And then she saw it.

"Stop, Bryce."

"What?"

"Stop."

He pulled the horse to a halt and turned in his seat, giving her a curious look as she stood and then climbed down, moving back up the road a bit. "We don't have much time to dawdle," he said, "not if we want to make the ranch before nightfall."

"Come here, please," she murmured, staring upward.

Wearily, he set the brake and laid the reins aside, then climbed down to stand beside her. "Rocks, and plenty of them."

"No. 'Two forgotten men, desperate for drink.' Sam referenced them. See them?"

He looked for several long, quiet seconds and then laughed under his breath. "There they are, 'perched over a river winding, never to reach her shore.'"

She grinned and then looked elsewhere. Nothing resembled "God's finger pointing" to the southwest. "Know of any rock that looks like God's finger, in this direction?"

"No. But I know the way to Sam's land, of course."

He helped her back in and they resumed their drive up, up, among piñon pines and scrub oak, rough, dry country that reminded Odessa of the true Wild West. The road ran beside a small ranch—"the Schaefers, fine folks," Bryce said—and then back through a series of hills. Here and there, the road had been washed out, which took them more time to cross, but then Odessa glimpsed it—a tall, snow-covered mountain, more glacial and clean-edged in appearance than Pikes Peak, which tended to ramble out more as a hulking mass than an elegant presence. And then she saw another, and another. In minutes, they crested the last hill and a vast valley spread before them.

Bryce pulled to a stop. "Pretty, isn't it?"

"Magnificent," Odessa said, fingers to her lips. She shivered against the sudden wind, a wind that seemed to lift from the snow high above and rush down to cover them like a wave from the sea. But she was not eager to move. The beautiful peaks appeared as mighty ladies, shoulders jutting toward the valley and then dissolving in long, smooth purple skirts. They wore capes and hoods of snow as if it were the tip of fashion, and Odessa knew they would appear bare, unclothed, without it.

"Later in the summer, they still have a bit of snow here and there. But they become more red than purple," he said. "At certain times of day, they appear crimson, which gave them their name."

"The Sangre de Cristos," she whispered. "Far more beautiful than I could've believed."

"Even though I told you?"

"Maybe if you had painted it I would've believed you," she said with an impish grin. "Where is your ranch? Can we see it from here?"

"That's it," he said, nodding to their right. The mountain range ran southward, but here at this corner edged a bit northwest. A vast valley, her belly full of lush spring-green grass, spread out before them.

"That's ... all of it? That is all yours?"

"Ours," he said with a grin, then cocked his head. "With a small portion owned by my father."

She looked at him hard then. "Bryce, how many acres do the McAllans own?"

"Ten thousand."

"Ten *thousand?* How? How could you have acquired such a massive tract of land?"

"Well, my uncle left me his property in his will. We homesteaded some. Bought some more. Pretty much every penny I've earned out here for the last five years has gone back into the land. People ... people find it hard out here, Odessa. The wind, long winters, short summers. High and dry is good for ranching, but not for farming. I've lost some fine neighbors who tried their hand at tilling the soil and nearly starved to death."

"But then you were able to buy their land at a bargain price."

"True, but I would've gladly traded it for their company. Even I find it isolating out here, Odessa."

"Hopefully a wife at home will help ease that."

"Already has."

They moved out again, and Odessa gestured to another mountain range. "Are those the Wet Mountains?" They wouldn't be going that direction, but it wasn't far away.

"'Damp to her East, wounds to her West,'" Bryce quoted.

"So it's that way, somewhere."

"Yes."

They rode on in silence for several minutes.

"Odessa, I want you to stay far from that land. There's a lot you need to learn, a lot you need under your belt right here … and there—" He paused to glower toward a far valley. "I've lost some more fine neighbors. Friends. I don't intend to lose my new wife. I don't care what Sam's mine holds. I know you're dying to unravel the mystery, see where it leads. But I don't think it's worth the risk. This," he said, taking her hand again and looking into her eyes, "is all the treasure I've ever wanted. Whoever is after Sam's mine … let's leave it to others to figure out. We have a *life* ahead of us. When a body has struggled to simply gain a decent lungful of air, life is enough, isn't it?"

"Bryce, I'm not going anywhere without you," she said, her tone sounding suddenly like her mother's hushing an agitated child. "I promise."

But as they turned a bend in the road, heading northwest, she couldn't help but glance back over her shoulder to the miles and miles of territory. And somewhere, nestled among those low-flung hills, was Sam O'Toole's treasure.

Chapter ❦ 29

They entered a new road through two lonely posts with the Circle M brand on either one, and moved northwest as the sun set behind the Sangre de Cristos. A half hour later, they crossed a hill and she could see it, the outline of their new home, nestled among the trees, near a small but tidy cabin, smoke curling from its chimney. Over the hill, she spotted the raw lumber of the two-story house, almost completed, and a white barn a short distance from it. Beyond that, among the fenced fields, was a long line of wall and shallow roofing, perhaps a windbreak or snowbreak for the horses.

"Good man, Tabito," Bryce murmured. "Either he's in that cabin, forgetting we're coming, or he's gotten it all ready for us."

Odessa smiled, but inwardly wondered where they'd all sleep in a cabin so small.

"Don't worry," Bryce said. "He'll join the men in the barn. There's a room in there that isn't half-bad. Once we move into the big house, we'll build a proper bunkhouse for the men, and Tabito will take the cabin as his own."

"How come you never built him a place before?"

Bryce shrugged. "No need. You come in after a day on the range, all you want is a basin of water, a mug of coffee, some meat in the belly, and then a good straw tick. You're out in seconds."

"But now …" Odessa led.

"With a woman on the premises, we all have to behave more like gentlemen."

"Do they know I'm coming?"

"I sent word a couple weeks ago. 'Bringing a bride home, finish the house. And don't forget the horses,'" he said with a smile, then pulled the wagon to a stop outside the cabin.

Bryce called out and the small cabin door opened. A short man, powerfully built, emerged. He reminded Odessa of Nic in stature.

"Tabito," Bryce greeted him. "Meet the new mistress of the ranch, Odessa."

"Mrs. Odessa," he said. He smiled at her with warm brown eyes. His face was like tanned leather, deep with wrinkles, although he didn't seem more than sixty years old. His hair was jet black. She offered her hand and he took it in both of his, bowing. "You're cold. Come inside."

"Thank you." She followed him, ducking a little to enter through the doorway.

Bryce had to duck even lower. "Keeps the wind out," he explained.

"I have some venison stew on," Tabito said.

He had a curious way of speaking, as if he didn't want his lips to move that much.

"It smells good," she said, leaning over the fireplace and lifting her hands toward the flames to warm them. Never had she been this close to an Indian before. But it didn't seem foreign, not like she thought it would. She sensed his stare and glanced at him.

He *hmphed* under his breath.

"Something wrong?"

"You are pretty. Too pretty to marry that ugly one."

She smiled. "I don't know. I think he's pretty handsome."

Tabito *hmphed* again. "Love. It makes the mind useless." But he gave her a smile that let her know he was joking. "Now, eat. You are too skinny. How will two skinny people fill that big new house with babies?"

She blushed at such intimacies, especially from a stranger. The door closed and she looked up to see that only Bryce was left.

"He never says good-bye. Just up and leaves."

"Ahh. Is that a Ute custom?"

Bryce shrugged and pulled up a stool to join her by the fire. "It's that Ute's custom."

She dished him some of the stew. "How long has he been with you?"

"He's been with me ever since I came to the ranch. He was a trusted hand on my uncle's ranch, the first spread that abutted my homestead."

"How big was that spread?"

"Two thousand acres. The people who owned it had been here for ten years. But smallpox killed most of the family. Only a couple of the children left, barely able to look after themselves, let alone a ranch. Tabito, he loved those children. But he wanted to stay with the land. He says it's something deep within him—the Indian in him—needs room to roam. Land and animals to care for. We still get a letter now and then from the children."

Outside, they could hear him unloading the trunks beside the front door, then speaking lowly to the horse. Eventually, the wagon creaked away, presumably en route to the barn.

"That's so sad! Where did the children go?"

"To an aunt in Boston. They're all right. And we paid them well for the land. It will see them into adulthood and beyond." He reached out to caress her shoulder. "What do you think of the cabin?"

"It's snug, warm, comforting." She looked about. Shelves with canned goods and sacks of coffee, sugar, and flour lined the wall near the fireplace, along with a few other blackened pots of various sizes. On the other side was a rocking chair, and behind them, two beds, with a curtain strung between them, but pushed back. Both were neatly made. She rose and reached out to touch the one nearest them. "Is that a bear skin?"

"Grizzly," he said, suddenly beside her. "My father shot it in the Sangres a few years ago."

"It's massive."

"Grizzlies are about the biggest bear out there." He set down his bowl and took hers from her hands. His eyes were warm, full of passion, desire. His hands moved to her hair and began pulling the pins from it, letting one coil drop and then the next. He was terribly, wonderfully close to her, and yet not touching anything but her hair. He moved slowly, clearly appreciating the moment as much as she, dragging out his seduction. Odessa closed her eyes. The cabin smelled of wood smoke and cedar and must and coffee … and her husband.

Backstage, after Moira changed back into her own clothes again, she rushed to the door, intent on getting back before she was missed, but then paused. No, she couldn't ignore the pull of the theater, and finally turned and went down one hallway and then the next until she emerged into what would soon be the completed lobby. Metalsmiths were fitting the ceiling with copper tiles while a host of painters lacquered the raw wood in a rich obsidian black. A team of seamstresses moved among three rows of chairs, installing cushions. The opera house was taking shape nicely; this would soon be a grand room, a lovely room where people like the Palmers and the Brennans, among others, would see and be seen.

General Palmer had told her that there would be fine people from as far away as Denver and even Santa Fe to take part in the opening-night ceremonies. Reporters, dignitaries, politicians ... it was perfect, simply perfect!

She moved through the big room, past the workers, the acrid smell of paint hanging in the air. In the back, she pretended to stop and speak with one imaginary couple and then another, gracious, holding herself just so.... She held out her hand, as if accepting a gentleman's kiss, and then she heard it. A real man clearing his throat. Moira whirled.

"I believed rehearsal was over, but here you are, still preparing for the big night."

It was Jesse McCourt, tall and slender, with that lovely mustache and deep sideburns that accentuated his handsome face. And when the man sang ... when the man sang, all Moira wanted to do was close her eyes and listen for hours to the notes that left his mouth. It was enough to make her want to ask the director to double the length of their rehearsals.

"You have me at a disadvantage, Jesse," Moira said. "It is never proper to spy upon a woman without announcing your presence first."

"I beg your pardon," he said regally, bowing low at the hip. He rose. "I intended to announce my presence, but I was captivated by your performance."

"Jesse, really," she said dismissively. She well knew that he was laughing at her expense. "Have you no shame?"

"Little, if any," he said dryly.

"Well, I really must be off now."

"Good day, Miss Moira," he said, tipping his head a bit toward her. "I shall very much look forward to your performances tomorrow, be they on or off the stage."

She tried to come up with a retort, failed, and whirled, rushing off. Behind her, she heard his deep, baritone laugh filling the room.

Odessa awakened beneath a bear skin, her nose nearly frozen, but the rest of her body warm and relaxed. She squinted and opened one eye, took in a swift look about the cabin, and closed her eye again. It was all real. She was Mrs. McAllan. She lived on a ranch. And for now in a snug little cabin that her husband apparently liked to keep at Arctic temperatures. He was over by the stove.

"If it's this cold now, what are the winters like?" she asked.

He laughed, a warm and welcoming sound. "Good mornin', Wife. We'll find a way to fend off the cold."

She smiled and watched him take a pot from the stove and pour. She sniffed. Coffee. She squirmed with pleasure.

He sat down on the edge of the bed. "It will go best for us if we play by the sanatorium's rules. Lots of fresh air."

"Absence of dust?" she teased. In the light of morning, she could see a thin layer covered every surface.

"That's a battle out here on the range. But in the new house, it will be a bit easier. I'm building with dust and wind in mind."

"Lots of physical exertion ... that won't be difficult here, I'd wager."

"No." He reached out and touched her cheek. "I have to go out with Tabito. But I'll be back in a few hours and we can look at the house together and have some lunch. Will you be all right here, making yourself at home?"

"I'll be fine." She sat up.

He paused, staring at her. "You are a vision, Odessa. God has blessed me."

"And me as well."

They smiled into each other's eyes for a long moment. "I hate to leave you, but I must," he said with chagrin as he rose. "Rifle is locked and loaded, right above the door there. I want you to lock the door behind me. Two of the boys will be nearby and on alert."

Odessa frowned. "Bryce, don't you think it's a bit much? As you said, we'd see anyone coming for miles."

"They'd have to be pretty dedicated to come this way. Chances are, they'll move on to other ... opportunities now that we're out from under their noses. But as you said, they knew Sam lived just down this valley."

"I don't want to live in fear."

"Nor do I. It'll be just for a time, Odessa. Until we're sure."

"Until we're sure? How long will that be?"

"We'll know it when the time comes." He put on his hat and pulled on a coat.

She reached for an overdress and pulled it over her shoulders, then rose from bed and padded to stand before him. "This is our new home, Bryce. I'm sure all that is behind us."

"I hope so," he said, stroking her face. "But for today?"

She sighed and then lifted up on tiptoe to kiss him. "For today."

He smiled at her and then was off. She peeked around the door, watched as he met Tabito and two ranch hands. Then she shut the door and placed a worn board over it so it could not be opened from without.

She turned and looked about the room, wondering what to do with herself for the morning. *Bread,* she decided, and as she waited for the dough to rise, she'd heat water to clean. Tabito had done a good job getting the cabin ready for them, but it needed a woman's touch. She wanted the windows to sparkle and to know that she had washed every surface with her rag, even if it ended up with a layer of dust again by day's end. It would make it hers, somehow. Home.

She smiled.

She was a wife.

She lived on a grand, sprawling ranch beneath picture-perfect mountains.

And she was making her husband something to eat.

If only her parents could know.... Never had she felt this happy in all her days.

Moira was miserable. Absolutely miserable.

"What is wrong with you?" asked Dominic, crossly pulling another misshelved book from its slot and then sliding it into its proper place.

"Nothing is the matter," she said.

But he didn't believe her. "Look, we have just three days before the sale. I need you to *concentrate*."

She had planned on telling James that Nic needed her here at the store today, which was true, and then telling Nic she had to go to rehearsal—but when she arrived at the store, Nic reminded her she'd promised him the whole day. "There's too much for me to do alone. This will buy our freedom, Moira. We'll get the cash from the store now, and soon, the additional funds from the sale of St. Clair Press. But this allows us to immediately pursue our goals. Are you with me?"

Moira had forced a smile and agreed, but all morning long, she wondered how she might escape and avoid the director's wrath for skipping. And tomorrow, there would be no choice but to attend the full-day rehearsal. How on earth might she manage such a feat? Dress rehearsals were only three days away, opening night just a week away. She fiddled with a stack of stationery, straightening it again and again.

It all would be easier if James would simply return home. Concern over Clarion business had called him north to Monument, but he seemed reluctant to leave Moira in the Springs. And she had to admit she enjoyed being with him, appreciated the respect others gave him that reached to cover her, too, when she was on his arm. But his presence complicated things.

She moved to a jar of pencils, putting each of them right-side up so the mark was at the top. The shop was dreadfully slow this morning, with only one customer so far. Where was everyone? The entire town seemed quiet, as if everyone were away, or onto more important tasks.

"Quit fooling with those, Moira, and help me price these books." She walked to the stacks of books that had just arrived in a shipment their father had sent before he died. Reluctantly, she picked up a novel and held it in her hand. "Are we doing the right thing, Nic?"

"What do you mean?" he asked, setting another volume aside and picking up the next. He didn't stop to look at her.

"Selling the shop. You selling the press."

"A third of the profits will make those worries go away, I promise."

She knew he was keeping something else from her, but her head was too full of her own complexities to give it further thought.

Moira sighed. She wished she had gone north with James, who was meeting with three landowners there and to look over a potato farm he was considering purchasing and then subleasing to share-croppers. If she had been with him, she could've pleaded a headache again, but then how might she have returned home unaccompanied? It was difficult at times, being a woman. She wished she had the freedoms that men held so easily in their hands. Or simply the freedom to decide when and where she would spend her days. How was it that she had to now report to not one, but three men in her life? Her brother. Her beau. Her director.

And then she saw it. Nic was making his own choices. Plowing his own road, making his way to his own glorious future. "Nic, I need to borrow some money."

"For what?" he asked, eyes narrowing.

"To hire my replacement," she said.

"Replacement?"

"Here. You need someone to help you get ready for the closing sale. See through the sale itself. I need James to think I'm here and yet still get to rehearsals."

"When are they?"

"This afternoon. All day tomorrow and so on like that until opening night."

"Why not just come clean with James now? Tell him you're taking the part in the opera whether he wants you to or—"

"No!" She moved over to him and took his hand in hers. "Don't you see? If he finds out I've gone against him, there's no telling how he'll react. If it goes poorly, he might convince the general to force the director to give my understudy the part."

"I don't understand. He might do that as soon as the first show closes. What do you gain?"

"Opening night. One perfect, free night when I can show the world what I'm capable of. There will be critics here from Cheyenne, Denver, and even Santa Fe. Let them hear me, critique me, and I have my start."

Nic sighed. "All right. Maybe the schoolmarm will take some extra hours. She's quick and can double-check my math."

Moira grinned and gave him a quick kiss on the cheek. "Thank you, Nic."

He shook his head. "Hope you know what you're doing, Sissy. You've entered a high-stakes game."

"Going for broke," she said lightly, over her shoulder.

Chapter ✥ 30

The next day, Bryce remained home with Odessa. He was at ease now that he had laid eyes on the horses, looked in on those that were ailing, and conferred with all his men. There had been cougars sighted near the mountains, and they had lost a few prize mares last year, so they were keeping nearer the stables. Soon, however, they would need to move them up into the high country to find enough grass.

Odessa loved watching the horses move together as a herd. The young colts, now weaned, still didn't venture far from their mothers. She leaned on a railing and rested her chin on her arms. "They're as magnificent as the ranch."

"Yes they are," he agreed.

"Are they for racing?"

"Some are used for racing, most for the finest riding horses available in America."

"Says the breeder."

He grinned. "You'll have to pick one, as yours to ride. Any of them catch your eye?"

Her hand went to her chest. "You mean it?" The mare she'd ridden at the sanatorium, a sturdy, steady, older horse, was dear, but had no spirit. It meant a lot that Bryce had understood without being told, that he was immediately about rectifying that trouble.

"Of course. I'll choose about ten that I think would be a good match for you, then you can take it from there."

"I'd like to watch them for a while."

"Always a good idea," he said. "You'll get a sense of their different personalities soon enough. They'll be in the stable corrals by tomorrow. Come, I must introduce you to the men. And I imagine you'd like to see your new house."

"I'm a little curious. Shame on you, making me wait a day."

He smiled impishly. "I wanted the mason to complete the fireplace before you saw it."

"And he's done now?"

"Near enough. Come." He offered his arm and she took it. They moved down a small hollow, and Odessa spied the big white barn and stables. No wonder the men slept there. It was lovely, a building reminiscent of any gentleman horse farmer's in the East. Clearly, this was where Bryce McAllan had focused his spending. On his horses, of course. And land for them to roam, far and wide.

The man swore and rolled over to his back, handing the telescope to his partner. "McAllan never leaves her alone. If he heads out, he leaves two ranch hands nearby. I don't know how we're supposed to get to her."

"Give it time," said the other, staring through the lens. "They don't know we're here. He's taking precautions, sure, but he's not acting like a man with an enemy at his gates. Few more days, they'll ease up, slip up, give us an opening. Just wait and see." He grinned, eyes still against the scope. "That's a big ol' house. And over the hill from the stables and barn." He turned to smile at his partner. "A girl might find some trouble in a house that big, and the boys down at the stable might not even hear her cry."

The first man smiled and nodded. "With the wind in the right direction, that just might be true. Give me that," he said, rolling back to his belly and reaching for the telescope. He studied the barn, the stables, the house across the hill, and lifted a wet finger to the stiff breeze. Even now, the wind was in their favor. He smiled. "Oh yes. Oh yes, indeed."

Chapter ❀ 31

They crested the hill and Odessa gasped. Their house was far more beautiful in real life than the hurried sketches Bryce had done for her, modest in size but much larger than anything she'd seen in the valley. It was nestled into a grove of aspen, looking out across the ranch land to the mountains above them.

They moved into the house, and Odessa hung back, moving slowly, wanting to memorize every moment of this glory. There was a small front foyer, with a staircase that climbed directly above. Bryce pulled her to the right, into a room that was already large and warm, graced by a massive fireplace. "This will warm the room nicely," he said, running his hand down a new mantle. "And the stone is from our creek out back."

"It's gorgeous, Bryce. Perfect. And they've done so much in so little time!"

On the far side of the room was a large dining hall, already occupied by a table that could seat fourteen. "Tabito made it. And I was kind of hoping you could feed the boys once a day. We can get you some help," he rushed on. "It's only that they've been eating their own slop for years. They'd think they'd died and gone to heaven if there was some real cooking on this ranch."

"I think that can be arranged," she said with a smile.

They moved from there into the kitchen, a large space, with a big wood-burning stove with six burners. There were cupboards and drawers and larders and big bins of flour and sugar by the back door. "And running water," she said moving to the pump.

"Upstairs and here," he said proudly.

Beyond the kitchen was a small sitting area where she might read or write or perhaps someday entertain other ladies from around the valley. Back up front again was a large room, bright and airy. "A study, don't you think?" he asked. "Where we can see to paperwork and whatnot?"

"Paperwork like novels and whatnot like paintings?"

He grinned. "Fine by me. Along with the occasional ranch ledger."

"Oh, that. Yes, I think we can work it in."

They moved upstairs. There was a water closet, with room for a washtub, and four bedrooms. "Heavens, what will we do with all this space?" she asked.

He wrapped his arms around her and kissed her hair. "As Tabito said, I hope we can someday fill it with babies."

Odessa took to riding out with Bryce and the men in the mornings, eager to learn how the ranch was run and loving the opportunity to sit back and watch her husband work. He was gentle and easygoing with the men for the most part, and then strong when he needed to be. But by and large, the men clearly respected Bryce and Tabito and deferred to them. It was clear that most had worked with them for years, since much of their work was completed without comment. There were more than three hundred head of horses on the Circle M, half of them bound for export come fall. Every year, Bryce shipped more than fifty head to his father in New York, fifty to a trader in Chicago, and fifty to Denver. All clamored for more, so he had plans to expand the herd, but carefully. Having enough grazing land was a perpetual issue.

In the last few years, more than a hundred mares birthed live foals; some even bore two. Of those foals this past spring, a hundred and ten had survived to romp together in the fields, becoming more and more independent from their mothers. Half were males, and Bryce had little need for more than ten of the finest as studs. He would sell the others for a fine profit as studs for other herds, and a few as racehorses. Those brought the largest profit of all.

"I'll have to teach you how to ride fast," he said.

Odessa watched him in bemusement. "Why is that?"

"It's how we know if a horse is of true value. The best racehorses want to do nothing but run. If you run past them, they'll join in for the sheer pleasure of it. You can see a lot in their form, the length of their legs, the strength of their muscles, but until you see them run … you just don't know."

"What makes you think I cannot ride fast?"

His eyebrows shot up in surprise. "Can you?"

"Fast enough. Once we choose my new mare, I'll show you."

He grinned. "Getting any closer?"

"It's between the black and brown ones over there."

"Two of the best," he said. "Either would be good. Let's release the rest tonight and spend some time in the corral with just the two of them. I bet you'll soon see which is your horse."

"I'd love that, Bryce."

"But for now, if you're really going to be a ranch woman, you need to know another vital skill."

"And what is that?"

"Mending fences."

She laughed. A few days on the ranch had clearly shown her that the bulk of the men's time seemed to be occupied with this task, mending fences. On a ranch this size, she supposed it made sense. Much of it was not fenced, but a good portion was. And horses who liked to rub against fencing, scratching their flanks, were hard on it, to say nothing of the elements that beat it to withered, rotting bits. The colts even gnawed upon the wood, cutting teeth. "Doesn't the fact that I'm cooking supper for ten men each night relieve me of fence duty?"

"Your biscuits aren't good enough yet."

She laughed again. "Watch it, or your cook will throw in the towel. Baking over a fire takes some time to learn."

"Apparently."

Odessa swatted him. "I bet it took *you* some time. You couldn't have been any better than I!"

He grabbed her hands easily and took her into his arms. "You can take all the time you want, Mrs. McAllan."

Moira bit into a light, flaky biscuit and closed her eyes in pleasure. James had even brought along a jar of honey on their surprise picnic on a cliff above Garden of the Gods, and she didn't hesitate to add a thick layer to her next bite.

"Will you not eat any of the chicken?" he asked, lounging beside their picnic basket. "Or are you intent on making a meal of my biscuits?"

"You have to admit that Miss Marla makes the best biscuits you've ever eaten."

"It's true," James admitted. "They'd almost be enough to keep me here in the Springs and eating at her restaurant every day." He looked her over with an appreciative eye. But then he suddenly righted himself and looped an arm around one knee. "Moira, I must tell you something."

"Oh? What is that?" She tried to ignore the sudden triple-time beat of her heart.

"With your father gone, I'd like to speak to your brother. It is my hope we might come to an … agreement. You and I practically courted in Philadelphia. We've known each other for years. Being here, with you," he said, reaching out to touch her face, "has only served to convince me. My instincts were right, Moira St. Clair. I think you're the woman for me."

The biscuit was becoming a wad of dough in her mouth. She kept chewing, hoping to be able to swallow, but failing repeatedly. Agreement? She swallowed at last. "James, you see our union as some sort of contract? Why not simply call it a business merger?" She wiped her mouth with a napkin and stood. "Honestly, that is the single most unromantic thing a man has ever said to me."

James frowned and rose, then reached for her hand, but she pulled it away. He looked upset, devastated really. "I … I thought you would be pleased, pet."

"Don't call me that. Don't ever call me that."

Now he looked extremely confused. "I thought you liked that."

"No, I do not," she said, turning around to stare at the Garden, and above it, Pikes Peak.

He was silent behind her for several long seconds.

"Am I to understand," he said lowly, "that you are not interested in any long-term arrangement between us?"

She half-turned back toward him. "Oh, James. Cease your fretting. Did our courtship not resume but a month ago? I am still very intrigued with you, brutish as you might be when it comes to affairs of the heart. But I am young," she said with a laugh, reaching out to lightly touch his chest. "As are you. There is no need to rush this, right?"

James looked down. "I was brutish, p—my love. Forgive me." He reached over and succeeded in taking her hands in his. "And yes, yes, we can take all the time we need. I had only thought … only wanted to … it matters not. I will simply see to my business at home for a time and then return to you."

He leaned down, passion thick in his eyes, as if to kiss her on the lips, but she presented her cheek instead.

James pulled back, hurt apparent in his eyes. But she ignored it. She had a bigger dream for her life than even James Clarion, a dream he threatened. She cared for him, could well imagine herself as the future Mrs. Clarion, but not if he couldn't love her and support her as she planned to love and support him.

No, men might take a fancy to Moira as their potential bride. But Moira intended to choose her groom. It would take a special man to be her husband. And she was not at all convinced that James Clarion was the right one.

Opening night would be telling for more reasons than one.

Chapter ❀ 32

Odessa chose the black mare as her own, naming her Ebony. She needed a big name, an elegant name to fit her. Astride her perfectly formed back for the first time, Odessa immediately felt regal, absorbing the young mare's strength. Every movement was rife with power, and she knew that Ebony would run as fast as she would allow. Odessa wondered about the animal's ancestors, undoubtedly the steeds of Spanish emperors or conquistadors, reigning conquerors. She was a fine horse, a beautiful horse, and as Bryce gazed upon them both, riding about the corral, she felt more a part of his world than ever.

"Bryce, please open the gate. I want to do more with her than ride in a circle."

He hesitated, studying her and then the mare. "She's pretty green, Odessa. Barely accepting a rider. She might break and run."

"I can handle her if she does," Odessa said, reaching down to run her fingers through Ebony's glossy, obsidian mane, then pat her neck. "I already know her, Bryce. I can't explain it better than that."

"I understand," he said. "But be ready. Hold on to those reins or you might not stop until you get to Westcliffe."

"That's a longer ride than I was—"

Bryce had barely opened the gate two feet when Ebony lurched into a gallop, nearly throwing Odessa. She felt the tension in the horse's flanks, the slight drop backward, but didn't react in time to be prepared. Ebony was up the hill and tearing across the cabin clearing in moments. They moved so fast that Odessa couldn't even look back or shout a response to Bryce. She had lost one of the reins, exactly what Bryce had warned her about. And without the reins, would the young mare really run as far as Westcliffe? There was only one way to find out.

Odessa settled into the cadence of the horse's gallop, thankful she had donned an old pair of pants from Bryce before beginning the evening ride. Her legs felt strong, as if they could cling to Ebony's flanks for hours, the gift of hours of sanatorium-sanctioned hiking and riding all spring long. And she felt the horse's power become her own again, the thrill of it elongating each muscle as she bent and gathered a fistful of mane in each hand. Her grandfather had taught her to ride bareback as a child. Granted, it had been an old, swaybacked nag, but there was still something familiar, comfortable in the action.

All of the St. Clairs had been taught to ride properly as children. The boys had received more lessons than the girls, and the girls had spent most of their time sidesaddle, but Odessa knew horses, loved horses. And so although she feared the speed at which the ranch road disappeared beneath her mare's hooves, she loved the freedom of it, the breath-stealing glory of it. She concentrated on matching Ebony's movements with her own, leaning down as the wind passed woman and horse like a sheet over one body, not two.

This occupied her mind for many minutes, but as she saw the ranch's front posts come into view and then slide behind them, she felt a more serious strain of fear. And yet there was no stopping this horse until she was ready to stop or Bryce caught up with them. She dared to glance under one arm and thought she saw him, far behind.

But she couldn't get a good look. She nervously watched the path before them. If the horse stepped into a ground squirrel's hole, or one of the many rain ravines in the road, she might twist her ankle and both of them would be down, possibly forever. Odessa could urge her a little one way or the other by pulling at her mane, but their fate was largely up to Ebony's choices.

Odessa could hear the heavy churn of the mare's breath. What were her lungs like? How big were they? They must be perfection, clean and free to power her long, churning, endless strides.

Odessa leaned a little closer to the mare's neck. "That's enough, Ebony. That's enough," she murmured, hoping to move into the horse's realm of conscious hearing, understanding that Odessa was mistress and she, servant. But that might take a little more time—

The horse hit a hole and stumbled, slowing her gait a little, and almost tore Odessa's fingers from her mane, but then she was back into the same rhythm and speed as before. They passed the stage road that led from the train platform to Westcliffe and kept moving, eventually veering southwest. Odessa dared to glance again under her armpit. Bryce was gaining on them, and two ranch hands were right behind him.

But Ebony was fast, a possible breeder to future racehorse stallions. They passed a homestead and a woman hanging out clothes over a line. She gazed up in surprise as they tore by. Then they passed a herd of sheep with a small boy tending them, and a burned-out rancher's cabin. They crossed mile after mile, and still Ebony did not slow, seemingly energized by her success, her speed, her freedom. *You can claim me, name me,* she seemed to be saying to Odessa, *but I am still my own glorious creation.*

Before them the Sangre de Cristos stretched out in a straight line, intent on running south until they met the untamed lands of Mexico. To her left, the Wet Mountains began as sunbaked piñon and scrub-oak-covered hills, but Odessa could see the taller peaks in the distance, peaks that as the minutes passed were getting larger and larger.

As they took shape and grew closer, Odessa struggled to hold on. Her fingers and thighs and calves ached. They felt frozen, bent on holding their positions, but consequently weaker, more fragile, as if—

It was then that Ebony lurched to halt, frightfully fast, and there was no way for Odessa to cling to her back any longer. She flew forward, over the mare's head, watching as if in a dream as she somersaulted in the air and was then flying feetfirst. She braced for impact, holding her breath, wondering how long it would be before she hit....

She never truly hit the ground.

Because she was then going down, down the side of a hill, sliding, grasping ... wondering if she would ever hit bottom. And then she did, the sudden stop jarring her, sending a wave of pain from heel to head. Slowly, she opened her eyes and dared to look about. She was in a ravine, an arroyo dug deep into the earth by the force of spring rains and floods, about twenty feet from the rim and thirty feet from the bottom. Her foot had struck a small, rocky ledge, one of the few visible on the chalky, dusty cliff face.

Odessa heard the others arrive up top, the horses whinnying traded greetings, Bryce calling out to her. She tried to call back, to let him know she was all right, but no sound left her mouth. She realized then that she was wheezing, panting. A consumptive attack. *It's all in your head,* she told herself. *You have been fine; for weeks you have been well, in fact. Get ahold of yourself!*

"Odessa! Odessa!" Bryce was right above her now, peering over the ledge. "Oh, thank God. Sweetheart, are you all right?"

She nodded, hoping he could see her.

"If I throw a rope down, can you grab it?"

"I ... I think so," she said in a whisper.

"Odessa?"

"I think so," she said a bit louder.

"All right," he said. "Hold on a minute."

The stiff rope fell beside her a second later. "Don't reach for it!" Bryce called. "I don't want you to fall any farther." The rope disappeared and then a moment later fell across her belly in a loose loop. "Put it around you," he called.

She swallowed a retort about not being some cow to rope. But there was not enough breath or time for wasted words right now. The large rock beneath her foot was loosening. She could feel it move every time she shifted her weight.

"Do it fast, Odessa," he said. "Then hold on to it. We'll have you."

Odessa gasped for a breath, lifted up her shoulders, and let the rope's loop fall around her body. At the same time, the rock gave way. The men called out from above, but Odessa froze, squeezing her eyes shut and holding tight to the rope.

She was hanging there on the steepest incline.

"Odessa. Odessa, open your eyes."

She did as she was told, looking up at her husband.

"Try and put your feet against the side. We'll pull you up, but it will go easier if you use your feet to try and walk at the same time. Got it?"

She nodded, trying to breathe with the rope latched tightly around her chest. She was feeling faint, a bit dizzy. But she did as she was told, putting her boots against the dry and grassy bank, trying to find purchase as the men hauled her upward.

They had her up in seconds, the two men gazing at her in triumph and relief. Bryce pulled her into his arms, loosened the rope, held her cheek in one hand. He was smiling, half laughing, half fearful. "Are you all right?"

She nodded, and he kissed her, over and over he kissed her. "Oh, thank You, God," he said, cradling her close, looking up to the sky and rocking back and forth. "Thank You, thank You."

He stepped back again to examine her. "Odessa, your lips are blue. Are you breathing all right? Odessa?"

She smiled weakly. "I'll be fine, Bryce. Just give me … a minute."

"I'll put that horse on the train. She's too wild, too—"

"No," Odessa said, pushing herself out of his arms and upright. She stared up at Ebony, who didn't appear the least contrite. "She's perfect."

Bryce helped her to her feet and together they stared out over the ravine. "I don't know what I would've done, Odessa, if anything had happened to you." He took off his hat and hit it against his leg, then wiped the corner of his eye with the back of his hand, as if he had some dust in it.

Odessa glanced back to the ravine, suddenly seeing the negative space as form. "Bryce. Bryce, do you see it?" She stepped forward, looking slowly left, then right. She glanced up at him.

He recognized it too, a clue from Sam's poem. To their right, the ravine was like a huge arm, complete with the bend of wrist and bulge of fist, right below them. To their left was a finger outstretched, as if pointing. *See God's finger pointing ...* They both looked up into the mountains. "The Wet Mountains?" she said, already knowing the answer. "Think we can track down land 'in my mother's name'?"

"You're not going to let it rest, are you? Until we look?"

"Just once. Show me his property. Let's see if we can find it. Aren't you the least bit curious?"

He hesitated and looked toward the mountains. "Just once?"

"Just once."

"I don't know, Odessa. I told your brother you'd be safe here."

"And the only danger that's presented itself is my new horse—a danger we'll soon tame. Come now, it'll be an adventure. You go to the land office and see if you can find out anything about Sam's mother and land nearby. Then we'll see what we can see."

"And if we don't find anything? You'll let it rest then?"

"Most likely."

"Uh-huh. That's what I thought."

"Well, I can't commit to what I'll wish to do five steps down the road if we haven't taken steps three and four, right?"

Bryce took a deep breath. "Right."

"So we can take a few steps together, see what we see, then decide *together* where we go from there. Deal?"

He studied her through narrowed, amused eyes. "A *preliminary* agreement. A *temporary* agreement. No *deal.*"

She smiled. "I'll take that."

Chapter 33

Moira had sent James a note, to be delivered within the hour at the hotel.

> *James,*
>
> *Tonight you will be thoroughly disappointed with me for being unforthcoming. I beg you to understand that I could not pass up this opportunity. Never again will I have the chance to know what it means to stand before so many others and sing. It is what calls me, completes me. And so I will try this night as "Camille." If I fail, I will know I tried. And if I succeed, we will have more to discuss. Come to the opera house. Decide for yourself if I have the talent, and what that means for us.*
>
> —*Moira*

Moira pulled on her gloves and stared resolutely into the mirror. If James cast her aside, so be it. There were always other potential beaus in the wings. The general would be furious if her subversive choices cost him business with the Clarions, but he would recover. If she succeeded in winning good reviews, then it would bring further accolades to Colorado Springs, and that would ease the general past his hard feelings. She might no longer be welcome at Glen Eyrie or even in the Springs, but if she succeeded, she would move on to sing in Denver, San Francisco, New York … maybe even Paris. The world was fascinated with the success of miners and the people from mining towns alike. An opera star rising out of a western town? She'd be the talk. Moira St. Clair would be on the lips of newspapermen and society women everywhere. She smiled at her reflection in the mirror. Yes, it was a gamble. But it was a good gamble.

Nic sighed, weary but gleeful after reviewing the day's numbers in the ledger. The city's citizens had swarmed the store and picked it clean like locusts after a hearty corn crop. By tomorrow, the shelves would be empty. He rolled his shoulder slowly in the socket. It still was not completely healed.

"Hurt yourself?" asked Kathleen, the schoolmarm. She set a steaming cup of tea down beside him and leaned against the counter.

"A while ago. Better than it was," he said with a small smile in her direction. She was a few years older than he, brusque in her mannerisms, but more efficient than the brightest men at his father's publishing press. If it hadn't been for Kathleen, Nic wouldn't have been able to pull off the sale, even if Moira had stuck it out.

"Thank you for your work, ma'am. You saved me."

"It's been my pleasure," she said, running a hand over the counter. "Only wish I had had the funds to buy the store. It saddens me to see our only bookstore in town close down so soon after its opening."

He closed the giant ledger book, watching as dust floated up in a cloud and then settled back to the desk. He tapped his knuckles lightly on the wood table. "Yes. It was a good idea, a fine idea. It just wasn't my idea for how I want to spend my coming years."

"What will you do instead?"

"Not sure yet." He shoved his chair back and moved out of the office, back into the great storeroom, watching as people moved back and forth along the street, either heading home or conducting end-of-day business. The wind had kicked up, as it so often did here in the Springs on a hot afternoon, bringing with it fierce thunderstorms and lightning such as Nic had never seen anywhere else.

His eyes scanned the skies. He decided he'd better change and get to the opera house if he didn't wish to arrive as wet as a drowned rat. He'd purchased a ticket weeks ago, intrigued to see how his little sister would see this act through and what it would mean for all of them. She was already entertaining offstage. Was the world fully prepared for Moira St. Clair onstage?

Moira heard him coming. Heard Gerald delay him and James' raised voice. Heard a third man join the group, trying to waylay him, protect her.

She closed her eyes. Her makeup was on, heavy for the stage. Her gown was buttoned up and they were just about to begin voice warm-ups. She had hoped James would wait to do this later, afterward. She had hoped he would give her the chance to shine, to show him and this town what Moira St. Clair could do.

The shouting escalated outside her door. She rose and opened it, hands clasped before her. James stilled at the sight of her and the two men holding either arm released him. "Come," she invited sadly.

He moved forward as if on feet of lead, but onward he came, refusing the seat she offered with a gesture from her hand. "How could you, Moira?" he asked in a hoarse whisper.

She closed the door slowly and turned to face him. "You gave me little choice."

"Choice? I thought we agreed!"

"No, you *decided* it was for the best. But it was only best for you, not for me. Don't you see?"

"How is it not good for you?" he sputtered. "How is it not good for *you*, nothing more than a *St. Clair*, to be on the arm of a *Clarion?*" He was shaking a finger at her, stepping closer to her. "How can you be willing to trade that for ... this?" He waved about the room, devoid of anything but mirror, table, makeup, chair, and candelabra. He reached forward and she willed herself to remain still, to not cower in the face of his wrath. He pinched her cheeks between forceful thumb and forefinger, dragging both down through her heavy makeup. "How can you wear the makeup of a whore and expect me to stand by, idle?"

She brushed his hand away. "It is theater, James. Opera. Everyone wears the makeup. It is entertainment. Diversion for the masses. A delight. And not merely idle delight—"

A man rapped at the door. "Five minutes, Moira."

She turned back to James. "Not merely an idle delight, but an opportunity to experience something different through another's eyes, to understand. It is story, onstage. And we learn, are improved, are *challenged* by them, James. If we are not strong enough for such challenge, we are weak indeed."

Moira bent down, peered into the mirror, and fixed the makeup he had damaged, then straightened and faced him again. "I know this is not what you wanted. And I am sorry for going against your wishes. But we are not married, James. Not even engaged. And I am my own woman. I would be my own woman even if we were married."

"So what are you saying? That you might not be the woman for me?"

"I did not say that," she said softly. "You did." She raised her eyes slowly, knowing she was using them to the most captivating effect. "James, please. I beg you." She moved over to him, took his hands in hers and raised them to her chest, never letting go of his gaze. "Please don't let this be the end. Give me a chance. This one chance."

But his eyes were steely. Resolute. "No. Then you would ask for another night, and still another. If you refuse to accept my proposal tonight—"

"What proposal?" she asked in bewilderment.

"If you get on that stage and sing, it will be the beginning of a long slide for you, Moira." He pulled her closer. Moira's heart skipped a beat. "You are young, impetuous. This is why your father did not want you to yet court."

"James, you are but two years older than I," she scoffed.

"In the absence of your father," he went on earnestly as if he hadn't heard her, "you've made a poor decision. One that will affect the rest of your life. You don't know this world you're stepping into. There are many who will lie in wait, ready to take advantage of you.

You are barely of age, and now with some means at your disposal. The wolves will come at you in packs, Moira."

She let out a humorless laugh. "So that is it? Threats of potential dangers? A half proposal from you to *marry*? And I'm supposed to walk away from the biggest opportunity in my life—"

"I'm the biggest opportunity for you, Moira! How can you not—"

"You expect me to settle into singing in drawing room parlors for the rest of my life? Find satisfaction in being the pretty bauble on your arm? Mindless? Sightless? Without any true voice at all?" She pulled her hands from his and stepped away. "Wouldn't that be like any other woman you've ever courted, James? Isn't my independence what drew you to me?"

A knock sounded at her door again. "It's time, Moira. Everyone onstage."

James seemed to recognize that she was stepping away from him. He gazed at her in wide-eyed surprise. "Yes, it is part of what drew me to you. But everyone knows that a woman gives up her life in service to her man. It is what makes you all the more a prize, Moira. You are so ... much. So vibrant. So alive. Grant me your life and I shall shelter you, protect you, lead you."

She laughed, no humor in her voice. "You don't understand. That isn't what I seek."

"Miss St. Clair!" shouted the director from down the hall.

She leaned closer to James. "I want love. Admiration. Support. Passion."

"Miss St. Clair!"

James shook his head in wonder. "How ... how could I have been so wrong?"

"I don't know, James. Go. Go and do what you must. And I will do the same."

The carpenters had finished their bedroom, kitchen, and dining room, so Odessa had elected to move in even as they continued working. It was much easier cooking in her big, new kitchen for the men than in the cabin, and truth be told, she couldn't stand to wait any longer. She loved the smell of fresh-hewn pine, the clean walls, the empty space waiting to be made a home. It called to her to sit down and write, even as men sang and hammered and sawed a room or two away.

This morning, they had run out of lumber that passed Bryce's muster—he wanted clear pine, with no knots—and left for Westcliffe for more. Bryce had promised to stop at the land office and see if there were any properties listed under a female O'Toole. And with most of the hands driving the horses into the high country over the next few days, her cooking duties were at a sudden minimum. She could give herself to writing, dipping pen in inkwell and watching the words form upon the page and begin to build upon the beginning of her story, her first story as Odessa McAllan. She would see it through, see if anyone considered her words worthy of mass production. The idea that her father would not be able to review it made her want to both hyperventilate and breathe freely at the same time.

She looked through her bright kitchen window to the mountains, where an afternoon thunderstorm was blowing in. Many of their men were up there with the herd, seeking the high meadow grasses. Peter and Nels, the men who had remained behind, were somewhere about—probably the stables.

Utter silence surrounded her. She wondered how long it had been since she had been so alone. The words in her mind swirled until she could barely wait to get to her desk, dip her pen, and begin chapter four.

She picked up the heavy rifle Bryce had left for her, then set it back down on the kitchen counter. The doors were locked. She'd sit at her desk by the window and would clearly see if anyone came down the road, long before they arrived. No, her mind was on her story; the rifle only yanked her back to present potential realities. It could remain where it was.

Chapter ❀ 34

It had been glorious, perfect. People swarmed Moira after the show, complimenting her on her fine performance. The director was ecstatic, the opera house manager claiming they had sold all the remaining tickets—for every performance—before the theater was empty.

Box office success was all that mattered. She knew enough about theater to know that. James would go home, lick his wounds, and find a new bauble to adorn his arm. Or he'd regret leaving her, recognize his mistake, and return for her.

She was pulling on her gloves and coat to go, every nerve still singing with the glory of the evening, when a knock at her small dressing room door drew her attention. Smiling, assuming it was one last admirer, she opened it. Her smile faded as she studied first the director's sober expression, and then General Palmer's. "Might we have a word, Moira?" the general asked.

"Certainly," she said, gesturing inward. She didn't know how she might fit two men inside her tiny dressing room, but she was anxious to put some wood between them and the curious glances of the rest of the cast outside in the hall.

"Moira—" the general began.

"General, how I wish Queen might've been here tonight! She would have delighted in it, wouldn't she?"

"Moira, stop. You and I both know that you've played a dangerous game here."

"I'm afraid I don't know what you mean."

"You know exactly what I mean. You came to me and asked for my blessing upon James Clarion's courtship. I gave it, risking a friendship with Reid, to support you both."

"Come now, General. We both know it was a benefit to you as well. James will bring commerce to your city, undoubtedly to you …"

He took a step to the side and leaned against her dressing table. "Ah, and therein lies the rub. James Clarion, and his father, are enormously important to me, now more than ever. There are deals in the works that are …" He paused to shake his head, then stared at her. "Young Clarion has not taken your spurning well."

"I did not spurn him, General. I merely refused to do anything but sing. I had to sing … you've seen how people respond to me, and I to them." She rose and paced a step. "I couldn't do anything else, regardless of what James wanted me to do. I thought, I thought that if he loved me, he'd support me in this. Encourage me. Dare I say applaud me along with the rest?"

"Yes, well, be that as it may, it's clear that you and Clarion will not continue your courtship."

"No, I would assume not. But you needn't fret over me, General. I will be all right." She waved about the room. "It's not much, but I find it glorious. There's no place I'd rather be."

The general and the director were silent.

Moira's heart skipped a beat. Dread made her scalp tingle.

"I must see these deals with Clarion through to completion. As much as I enjoy your presence on my new stage, those contracts mean more to me and this town."

Her hand moved to the base of her neck. "What does that mean?"

The director cleared his throat, began to speak, paused, and then started again. "Moira, you are dismissed from the opera. I will send you off with references. I'm certain you have a bright future ahead of you—it simply cannot be here." He uttered every word in misery, obviously compelled by the general to do this.

"I … see." She found that her mouth was hanging open, and she resolutely clamped her lips shut and tossed her chin. She had to handle this as a gracious woman, not the silly twit everyone assumed she was. "I understand. Please accept my heartfelt thanks and my apologies for forcing you into this position. You two have given me the confidence I needed to pursue my dreams. Despite the fact that it is ending now, far earlier than we expected, I'll always appreciate it."

The general's eyes gentled. "Moira, with your father gone and Odessa down south, and Dominic poised to move away, perhaps you ought to wait a bit, consider all your options. You could journey east and be a companion to Queen, a governess for my girls for a season, a year even."

"Oh, thank you, General," she managed to say. "You are most kind. But I feel the time, my time, has arrived. Be it here or elsewhere, I shall find my way."

Having completed chapter four of her novel by early evening, Odessa was elated. She glanced out the window, noted the angle of the sun through heavy clouds, and thought she had better get a start on supper—even with just three men to cook for, she was tardy and would have to rush. She moved into the kitchen and opened the back door, and then went down into the cellar, just outside. The rows of supplies that Bryce had brought home with him from Westcliffe and placed on the shelves only an hour prior gave her a satisfied feeling of preparedness. News that he had discovered a small parcel under the name of Louise O'Toole—directly above Sam's property—made her all the more happy. Now if she could simply pry her husband away from the ranch for another day ...

She grabbed a sack of flour and sugar and climbed the steps to the porch of her new house, setting down the heavy bundles on the counter for a moment to check her breath. She inhaled and exhaled several times, hand over her thumping heart. She smiled. Nothing more than a little exertion. No wheezing. No faintness.

She turned back to the doorway and admired the sun beginning its slow descent down toward Eagle Peak, dusted from a high mountain snowstorm, even in the middle of summer. Briefly she mused over the men and horses up in the meadows of those mountains, but she knew they were well versed in the shenanigans of mountain weather. High clouds caught the first hints of a setting sun, turning a lovely gold against a brilliantly blue sky. Odessa took a deep breath, thanking God for this place and time to find healing, love, a new home. This was just where she needed to be, as healthy as the mares in the fields.

She opened the back door and brought the sacks of flour into the kitchen, kicking the door shut with her foot. She set them down and then filled a bucket of water from the hand pump, then turned to chop some carrots and potatoes. The blade was dull and broken in places, no sort of proper instrument for one bent on making a quick and hearty stew—and she had no time to waste. She wiped her hands on her apron and went to the front door, where she kept her purse. Inside was her pocketknife, a gift from her father. It was too small for chopping, but too small was certainly better than too dull. Maybe Bryce would remember to purchase a few new knives for her in town next time he went, or get the old ones sharpened.

Odessa walked into the hallway and halted in confusion.

Slowly, fear took hold. The front door was wide open, with muddy footprints leading inward. She leaned down, gazing at the tracks against the fading light from the window, hoping they were only her own, telling herself they were.

But her prints were beside them, much smaller than the others. These new tracks led away, to the stairs. Bryce was in the stables—and he never came in with muddy boots. The carpenters or ranch hands would not come in without invitation. Once home, Bryce had sent Peter and Nels after a floundering mare in the north quadrant....

She straightened quickly, trying to control her breathing, to not give in to panic, feeling already the familiar constriction across her chest. If she had an attack now, there would be no way for her to escape. Maybe she was wrong. Maybe Bryce had returned from the stables....

She called her husband's name, trying to make her voice light.

No response. But a floorboard creaked directly above her.

And then another in the spare room. Someone else was in their bedroom.

She backed into the parlor, where Bryce had so recently been pounding nails into wallboards.

It was then Odessa knew fear more potent than any consumptive attack had ever brought on. It was the same as the night that Sam had been killed, back at the sanatorium.

Her enemies were here. In the house.

She could feel them.

And this time, they were coming for her.

Chapter ❀ 35

The men tore down the stairs and Odessa lost a precious second or two trying to think, torn between escape and the rifle, which was still on the kitchen counter. She could get out of the house, get to the stables, find Bryce, or if he wasn't there, mount Ebony and ride to the men in the north quadrant. Or if she could reach the rifle, she could hold them off, even force them outside, but that might endanger Bryce.

That was when she caught sight of her husband, walking down the hill from the stables. He was coming. She had to warn him. Had to reach him.

One man was already halfway down the stairs. She caught a glimpse of his hulking form as she narrowly avoided the other man reaching for her. She heard the slam of the front door as she ran into the dining room, the kitchen, then toward the back door … freedom. Too far to reach the rifle, she had to get out, make the door.

A man reached her then, grabbed her around the waist and pulled her back roughly. She tried to scream, but his hand was there, covering her mouth. She writhed and kicked, but he easily picked her up into the air and pulled her backward, out of sight of the kitchen window and her husband.

"Shh," the man said, "Odessa, quiet down now or we'll have to kill your husband as soon as he walks in that door."

She stilled. Who was this? Who would dare to steal into her house? Who knew her name? And moreover, who would threaten to kill Bryce? She stared at the back door in horror, praying that Bryce would be distracted, remember something he needed back in the stables ...

It was then she saw the doctor in the corner of her eye, in the corner of the kitchen, arms folded across his chest. Doctor Morton from the sanatorium. All at once she remembered what was familiar about this man holding her. She didn't need to turn to recognize him.

It was Sheriff Reid Bannock who held her and threatened her husband. Reid!

"I think you know why we're here, Odessa," he said lowly in her ear. "You stole something out of the sanatorium. The good doctor wants it back."

Doctor Morton moved to a window and peered out. "Looks like Bryce has been waylaid. He's heading back to the stables." He motioned to others behind Reid that she couldn't see. "Go. Make sure no one interrupts us."

Odessa closed her eyes, half in praise that God had heard her prayers, half in utter terror that her husband was not coming to her rescue.

"Don't scream," Reid said in her ear. "If you don't scream and you cooperate, you'll live to the end of your natural days in this house."

He let his hand fall an inch from her mouth, testing her. He left his arm around her waist, holding her in place.

But Odessa was staring at the doctor, the diminutive, kind

doctor of the sanatorium. She shook her head in disbelief. "Not you. You can't possibly be in on this. Tell me you're not."

"Odessa," he said. "Please. Forgive us for frightening you. All we need is the document you obtained from Sam. Sam died owing the sanatorium a good amount of money. It is ours legally. By rights. And it will go a ways in rectifying his accounts."

"I have nothing to give you. And Bryce rectified his accounts while we were still patients at the sanatorium." She shook her head. "You murdered Sam," she said softly. "Or had him murdered. I heard it."

"Murder? That's a tall accusation," Reid said, releasing her.

She whirled and took a step away from him, but he reached out and grabbed her arm as if to say *no, not too far*.

"The ears can play tricks," Reid said, "especially as ill as you were about that time. Though I must say you're not looking ill any longer. Marriage agrees with you, Odessa. I once had ideas of marrying your sister …" He reached out as if to touch her face and she backed away again, but he pulled her back roughly against his chest.

"Sheriff," warned the doctor. He looked at Odessa. "We need the document. If you give it to us, we will not file our suit against you and your husband."

"File suit?" she scoffed. "Sam left it for me, not you. He owed you nothing. He paid a good deal to the sanatorium, more than enough to cover the *care* he received."

"And how is it, my dear, that you would know such a thing?" He stepped toward her now from the other side.

"It matters not."

"No? Could it be that you broke into the office and looked at private documents?"

She said nothing.

"Sheriff, is that not a punishable offense?"

"Breaking and entering," he said, grinning down at her in delight. "I'd say that'd do it."

"Not that you would have found anything illegal, had you been reading our files," said the doctor. "Everything we do is perfectly legal."

She leveled a look of disbelief at him. "So what are you doing here, a day's journey from the Springs, in my house?" She looked up to the sheriff. "And you. Just because you are a sheriff does not make you immune to the law. Speaking of breaking and entering ... you broke into my house, threatened me. I can press charges of my own."

He smiled down at her, unperturbed. "The door was open. And we are merely encouraging you to relinquish what is ours. Maybe you found that document in the administrator's office. Maybe it was in the file and you stole it."

"I stole nothing," she spat. "It's mine. Sam left it for me!" She regretted the words as soon as they left her mouth.

"So you do have it," Reid said. He lifted her chin. "You know we will not leave without it. Go and fetch it. Now."

She glanced at the doctor, vainly hoping for help, but he stared back at her with the same steely determination as the sheriff. "And if I do not?"

"Come, Odessa. This need not be difficult. Give us the document and we will be on our way. You can resume your life."

"You'll simply walk away?"

He continued to smile. "Go and retrieve the document. Quickly now, before your husband tries to return. It will be easier for all if we can see this through without further … discussions."

Odessa hesitated. Bryce would be back any minute. They all knew it. But she would die if anything happened to him, if she were the cause of it. And there were two of them, both carrying a gun. Two others outside, between any of the ranch hands and the house. Chances were good that Bryce would be injured in a gunfight. She had to get them to leave, right away. "Sam's note is gone. It was destroyed in the water when Helen and I were chased, presumably by *your* men."

Dr. Morton studied her. "We are merely here to claim what rightfully belongs to the sanatorium."

"Of course," Odessa nodded. "You don't want to confess to sending killers after us."

Dr. Morton sniffed. "Please, Odessa. Since you stole the note—"

"I stole no note. It was left for me. Handed to Bryce for me by an attorney. It had my name on it! The lawyer can testify to it!"

The doctor reached up to tap his finger to a lip. "I believe Sam O'Toole hired an attorney I know—and he moved away about three weeks ago." He looked to the sheriff. "Did he mention where he was moving, Sheriff?"

"Don't believe he did."

"Pity, that. There goes your alibi. Meanwhile, my night nurse and attendant are prepared to testify to seeing you steal out of the administrator's office. We still have yet to determine what all you took from the files." He raised one eyebrow. "Perhaps there was more than just one document."

Odessa's mouth dropped open. "What? They did not see me anywhere near the hall! I took nothing!"

He stepped toward her and lifted a hand in an amiable gesture. "Ah, you are not very good at this game, Odessa; obviously, you did manage to make your way in. Come now, this does not need to be as messy for you as it has for others. I presume Sam left directions to his mine? I'm afraid I hadn't had the opportunity to carefully study his file before," he paused to cough, "you visited the administrator's office."

"I told you, he left me the document."

"And for your sake, I do hope you remember what was on it if it, as you say, no longer exists. He gave you directions to find his mine?"

"He said nothing so specific."

"What did he say, exactly?"

Odessa hesitated, but Reid pulled a revolver from his holster and removed the safety, then casually lifted it to point at her. With shaking voice she recited, "'Find two forgotten men desperate for drink, perched over a river winding, never to reach—'"

"He left a *poem?*"

"Of sorts."

A horse whinnied outside and Reid moved to the front window. "One of your ranch hands is coming." He glanced at the doctor. "Think he spied our horses up on the hill?"

The doctor looked nonplussed, but didn't answer. "The men are still out there. Whoever approaches must appear harmless."

She glanced out and frowned. If one was coming, where were the others? "It's Nels. He probably just wants to tell me what's keeping

Bryce and ask about supper." She swallowed hard, again thinking that she might be the cause of an innocent man's death. "I can send him away."

Reid studied her. "Do it." He pointed toward the door with the gun. "Carefully."

Odessa turned and walked to the front door. When she laid her hand on the knob, she felt the cold steel of the gun tip between her ribs. Reid was at her side, behind the door, and Odessa opened it, peeking out. "Evening, Nels!" she called, as he rode up. "How did it go in the north quarter?"

The thin man gazed up at her with a shy grin but slowly shifted his eyes to the crack in the door. "Mare's back on her feet. Much improved. Came to tell you Bryce is just getting her settled in the stables and then we'll be in."

"Oh, biscuits won't be done yet, I'm afraid. Please tell Bryce that it'll be another half an hour—and that I'd love it if he took a look at Ebony. She threw a shoe when we were out."

"We'll do that, ma'am," he said, searching her eyes.

"Thank you. I'll see you in a bit." She forced a smile and shut the door, then looked up at Reid.

He moved the gun to her chin and traced it slowly to her ear and then back again. "Nicely done. Now how 'bout you pick up a pen and write down that poem in your pretty head?"

"And then you will leave," she said, staring into his eyes.

"That depends on you—and what old Sam had to say, exactly."

He followed behind her up the stairs to her writing desk, too close to be polite. But he obviously didn't care. What all had Moira endured while he had courted her? No wonder she despised the man!

He followed her into the bedroom, leaning against the doorframe, watching her.

She sat down. Then with shaking hands, she pulled a sheet from the cubbyhole of the desk, uncorked the ink, and picked up a pen.

"Don't forget a word, Odessa. Moira's going to know, someday, the cost of disappointing me. Don't you go and do the same."

Moira. She swallowed the fear at his unnamed threat and wrote as quickly as she could. *Damp to her East, wounds to her West, land in my mother's name …* In her mind she whispered apologies to Sam as she wrote it out.

"Sheriff!" called the doctor from down the stairs. "We need to be on our way. Do you have it?"

"She's working on it," he called down casually. "Our boys will keep the men from coming around again." He left the doorframe and moved over to her, then placed a hand on either side of her, leaning down until his chest brushed against her hair, until she could see him looking at her. "I chose the wrong St. Clair girl, I think. All I wanted was a pretty bride. A woman of caliber. Substance. Moira failed me."

"Yes, well, I'm sorry for that," she said. *Within an old sheepherder's cabin, in high hills of piñon pine …*

He reached down and pulled a curl away from her temple, fingered it. "Do you think you and I might've had a chance? Had I met you first instead of Moira? There's something about your face, your eyes, something about you that sticks with a man."

Bile rose in her throat. *Wealth that burns, and that that is eternal.*

She bent forward and blew on the sheet, then lifted it with the tips of her fingers. "This is it," she said, shoving her chair back, forcing him to take a step. She rose and turned to face him. She hadn't beaten consumption to let this man bully her. "Take it. Leave and never come near me or mine again."

A slow smile grew across his face and then he gave her a hard stare. "So you're giving me the poem, just like that. What else was there?"

"That was it. Follow this and I'm certain you will find what you seek. I had planned to."

"I have a better idea." He took a step forward and pulled her closer. "I think I'll take you with me."

He ran his hand down one arm slowly, plucking Sam's poem from her trembling fingertips. "Yes, we'll need you with us for a bit, anyway. You can come home as soon as your husband signs over the deed to old Sam's land." He grinned victoriously and tucked the note into his vest pocket. "Come along," he said, pulling her roughly toward the door.

But Bryce was there, rifle raised to his shoulder. "Evenin', Sheriff."

Reid slowly eased his hands in the air. "Evenin', Bryce. Guess now that we're all together, it'll save me a trip back. It's just as well."

"What're you talking about?" Bryce stepped forward until the rifle hovered a foot from Reid's chest. Veins bulged and pulsed at his temples. "You break into my house, threaten my wife—"

"Bryce—" Odessa began.

"Settle down there, brother," Reid said. "I didn't do anything to your wife. I simply *encouraged* Odessa to return something that rightfully belongs to the doctor."

"Lots of ways to threaten a woman, Sheriff. But I don't need to tell you that. You're obviously well versed on the subject."

For the first time, Odessa saw murder in her kind and loving husband's eyes. "Bryce," she said with a quavering voice, "they have what they came for. Send them on their way."

"Yes," Reid said. "All I need is for Odessa to show us to Sam's mine, make sure she didn't leave anything out of Sam's poem, and a quick signature from you on the deed."

A bead of sweat rolled down from Bryce's temple, streaking through the trail dust on his cheeks. "You're in no position to make demands. Keep your hands up. Turn around."

Reid did what Bryce asked, turning and sighing. "You're making a big mistake, man." Keeping his hands in the air, Reid tossed Odessa a lazy grin. "Better talk some sense into your husband before this gets ugly."

"You're the one that brought ugliness into this house," she ground out, moving forward to reach for the poem in his pocket.

"Don't do it, Odessa," he said, eyes narrowed.

She took it from his vest and crumpled it in her hand, just as Bryce grabbed one gun from his holster and then the other, tossing them to the carpet beside them. "Now move downstairs."

But Reid was staring at her. "You know that poem by heart. You *know* where it is. Have you seen it? Been there already?"

Bryce grabbed his shoulder and pulled him roughly around. He brought the gun up to his chest. "You will leave my wife and my house *now*."

"Oh, I'll be back for her, McAllan, and you can be certain there won't be anyone in my way. She has something that rightfully belongs to us. And I'll get it from her," he said with a leer back at her, "one way or another."

Bryce whipped the rifle around and brought the butt of it swiftly into Reid's sternum, making him gasp and bend over. Bryce jabbed the rifle against his cheek. "Move. *Now.*"

Slowly, the sheriff rose and put one foot in front of the other. They reached the top of the stair, first Reid, then Bryce, then Odessa.

Odessa looked about the front entry, the parlor, in confusion. "Bryce, there are others! Where is the doctor? The other men?"

"Nels has the doc. What other men?" he tossed over his shoulder, concentrating on the hulking sheriff before him. Nels moved forward from the kitchen hallway, the doctor ahead of him, hands in the air.

A shot sang through a bright, new parlor window and slammed into Nels. He whirled and fell to the ground, clutching his shoulder. Another came right behind it, narrowly missing Bryce's head.

"Move!" Bryce yelled at Reid, shoving him forward down the stairs. Reid stumbled forward, then righted himself to move slowly again. More shots came through the windows, splintering above their heads. "Get down, Odessa!" Bryce cried out.

Nels managed to make it to his knees and return fire through the windows, shooting blindly into the hazy light of dusk. The doctor leaned down and cruelly rammed his fingers into the man's bullet wound until Nels could do nothing but drop his revolver and fall, ashen-faced, to his back.

Bryce pointed his rifle toward the doctor, but Reid turned on him, whipping the gun from his hands. Reid backed away toward the window and raised a fist, an obvious signal to cease firing. As ordered, the bullets stopped. Bryce moved up several steps, between Odessa and the interlopers, as if to cover her.

Reid ran a hand across his upper lip, wiping away the sweat. "Figure neighbors heard those shots?"

"Too far away," Bryce returned, levelly. "No need to kill us yet."

"Well," Reid said with a thin-lipped smile. "Not all of you, anyway."

Chapter ❧ 36

"Wait," Bryce said, when one of Reid's men raised a gun and leveled it at his temple.

Odessa panted through her nose for breath, Reid's hand across her mouth to keep her from screaming.

"She knows the clues that might help you find Sam's mine. But I know the rise and fall of Sam's land," Bryce said. "Been there a hundred times. You need both of us. And we won't help you if you kill my man." He tipped his chin toward Nels, unconscious now on the floor, a pool of blood spreading from his shoulder. "Bind him, but leave him behind."

"Can't risk it," Reid said. "Take him out and get rid of him."

Odessa squirmed in his arms, crying now, as she watched two of Reid's men grab hold of Nels and carry him out, presumably through the back door of the kitchen. Her heart thudded, waiting for a telling gunshot.

"We'll take you both with us. But only because I can use one of you to get the other to do as I wish," Reid said. He leaned toward Bryce. "After all, it'd be easier to buy the O'Toole property off a dead man."

Bryce clamped his lips shut and moved as if to lunge toward him, but the doctor moved in front of him. "Come now, Bryce. Let us see this to its—"

A shot reverberated through the air, through their chests, as if it had been shot at them.

Nels. Dear, decent Nels.

Odessa's knees gave way.

"Whoa, whoa," Reid soothed in her ear, lifting her. "It's all right. I've got ya."

Bryce turned eyes full of misery toward his wife, unable to do anything to free her from the brute.

Doctor Morton cleared his throat. "As I was saying, let us see this to its conclusion at last, shall we? Soon all will be in order. All in order." He gestured toward the front door and Bryce opened it, then moved through, the doctor directly behind him. Reid urged Odessa forward, and on leaden feet she moved toward Ebony, in a new, small corral near the house.

"No, no," Reid said, pulling her toward his horse. "I'll not have you on that racehorse. My men have seen how fast she moves." He raised a hand and his men moved out from the trees and jogged down the hill to join them.

Where was Peter? She glanced at Bryce, silently asking the question, but he looked away. He didn't want these men to know Peter was anywhere near. Reid mounted and leaned down to take her arm, easily lifting her to sit behind him. "Better hold on tightly to me, Odessa," he said, but he was looking at Bryce, taunting him. "Don't want you falling off."

The doctor urged his horse forward. "Come, Bryce. Show us to Sam's property and where the mine is hidden."

Bryce dragged his eyes from his wife to the doctor. "There's no guarantee we can find it."

"I do so hope you are wrong, Bryce. Because if you are not, there will be no reason to keep either of you alive. You'll meet some unfortunate accident; we will obtain the O'Toole property and resume our search until we find the treasure Sam left behind. One way or another it shall be ours. Why not allow it? Have you and Odessa not battled for life? Why give it up now?"

"What guarantee do we have that once you have it—the entrance, the deed—that you will leave us to live our lives?"

The doctor sighed. "Despite what you may think, Bryce, I wish for you and Odessa to live long and healthy lives. If we can come to an agreement as civilized people, I see no reason not to abide by it."

Bryce shifted his flat gaze to Odessa. He did not believe the man.

They had to find a way to escape.

They moved out from the ranch gates and down the road. Odessa prayed that someone would be coming the opposite direction, but there was not another living soul about. She prayed that the woman she'd seen hanging sheets outside the cabin the day Ebony had gone tearing toward the ravine would be outside again today, but the house appeared empty as they passed, not even a tendril of smoke rising from the chimney.

Where are You, Lord? she asked silently, glancing up at the mountains that towered over the valley. *Why bring me so far, to let me die? Why now? Please, Jesus. If one of us has to die this day, take me. Save Bryce. Please, Lord. Not my Bryce. Not after all he's been through. Please Jesus, Jesus, Jesus, Jesus, Jesus …* She shivered, suddenly realizing that she was crying.

"You weeping, Odessa?" Reid asked over his shoulder. He patted her hands, hands she had reluctantly wrapped around his broad torso, only to keep from falling off. "I could be a comfort to you, if you'd allow it."

"You are vile," she ground out. "I can't get away from you fast enough. Now I know why Moira couldn't stand you." She felt him stiffen, but could not stop herself. "You killed them. The DeChants. Even their little girl. And Sam. Who else? How many have you killed, Sheriff?"

"Those are terrible things to say, Odessa, terrible. I'll remind you I'm a lawman, well thought of from Denver to Albuquerque. Better not level such accusations again, or it'll come back to bite you and yours, understand me?" He patted her hands again and tipped his head toward Bryce, who stared furiously back at them. "Understand me?" he repeated.

"I understand," she said. "Pause up ahead."

"At the arroyo?"

"Yes." They pulled up alongside it. "Sam's poem? He wrote, 'See God's finger pointing southwesterly.' See it?"

"I see it," Doctor Morton said. He moved off ahead of them.

They rode for some time, entering a winding trail up between two steep cliffs that bordered a stream. "Dess," Bryce said, nodding up and to the left.

"What is it?" Reid asked, looking up to the rocks.

That was when she spotted it and murmured, "'Lady and child, now pillars of stone, who lead the way.'"

"Very good," Reid said. "Very, very good. If that part of the old man's poem is correct, perhaps the rest will bear out too." He glanced back at Bryce. "But you know the way, McAllan, already, don't you? Stay ahead of us here, where the path narrows."

Bryce moved ahead of him, and Doctor Morton and the two men trailed behind. In minutes, they reached a ramshackle homestead and a mine, worked by what looked like ten men, mostly Chinese laborers. "The DeChants' old place," Bryce said over his shoulder to Odessa. "Apparently, someone else has laid claim to the mine. The sanatorium?"

"Just keep moving and keep your mouth shut, McAllan," Reid returned.

But Odessa's eyes covered the men moving in and out of the mine. They each nervously glanced their way and either picked up their pace or scurried to work, clearly recognizing and fearing Reid and Doc Morton. Reid kept his eyes on Bryce, but Odessa was thinking about the sanatorium files, of the claim upon the DeChant land for a debt of less than a hundred dollars. She thought of Amille, mad with worry for a child long dead, of John and his stooped, heavily burdened shoulders as he walked away that day, of a small child, innocent.… If these people were willing to kill the entire DeChant family, why would they keep Bryce and her alive?

She considered it now, no longer weeping, but with a certain distant, factual process after she could no longer see the mine laborers. *You brought me into this world, Lord. You gave me brothers and You took all but one of them away. You gave me love, when I could not imagine anything more than survival. And You gave me life again, when I thought I was to die. Just as You did with Bryce.* She moved to look over Reid's shoulder at her husband, ahead of them.

As if he could feel her, hear her prayers, Bryce turned in the saddle and looked back at her, his eyes wide and sad, saying goodbye, *I love you, Dess. I've loved you with everything in me.*

She closed her eyes, unable to bear the wrenching sadness of such a silent parting. *You gave me that man to love, Lord. You gave me love and life. And with every breath I take, it is Yours to do with what You wish. I am giving You myself, Jesus. I have borne sorrow most have not had to, but I understand I have also been granted a gift most never receive. I understand what it means to breathe another breath and be thankful solely for that. I dreamed for more, Lord. A life. A future. But in this moment, on this day, in this place, hear me when I say, I am Yours. Save us, or welcome us into Your kingdom. I am Yours.*

Reid shivered, squirming beneath her grasp, and glanced over his shoulder. "What are you doing, woman?"

"I am praying."

"Well, quit it. We're not in church, and where we're going, I'm all the god you need." He laughed then at his own joke.

The path widened before them, and Bryce paused. Beyond him was a small cabin beside a stream. Sam's home.

"What is it?" Doctor Morton asked.

"We need to go up, higher," Bryce said, eyes on Odessa.

"Sam's poem," she said. "'Land in my mother's name, within an old sheepherder's cabin, in high hills of piñon pine.'"

"Louise O'Toole was her name," Bryce said tiredly. "Part of Sam's estate, now signed over to me, along with Sam's property."

"Why, that clever old coot," Reid said, shaking his head in admiration. "That's why we couldn't find it. You know how to get there?"

"Up until this week, I thought Sam's property ended here. Judging from the poem and the land assessor's description, it should be just over that rise and around the bend."

"Lead on, then." He chuckled, his chest rumbling beneath Odessa's hands. So he was about to get to what he wanted. What he and the doctor so desperately desired. They moved up the path, the horses working hard now with the steep incline. Odessa glanced back and saw the mountain ranges rising above these piñon-clad hills—the Sangres in the distance, the Wet Mountains just above them.

They rounded a bend and there it was, a decrepit old cabin with a roof that appeared ready to cave in with the first snow. Reid looked around. He gestured to the men. "I want you on either side of this place, arms at the ready while we're inside. Understood?"

"Got it, Boss," said one. The other just nodded.

Doctor Morton pulled his mare to a stop beside them and immediately began to dismount. Bryce was already tying his horse to a tree near the tiny structure. Reid dismounted and reached for her, but Odessa kicked her leg over and slid down on the opposite side. She ignored his low laugh, concentrating on her husband, who reached one arm out to her. She hurried over to him, nestling underneath, closing her eyes as he wrapped it around her, as if she could memorize the feel of it.

"After you," Reid said, gesturing forward.

Bryce climbed the rickety stairs and opened the door. "Go on, Dess. It's all right," he said, saying more to her through his eyes than his words.

She stepped forward, wishing he could read the love in her own.

"Get going," Reid said, pushing Bryce and then her inside. Doc Morton followed behind.

They looked around. But the room was entirely empty.

Reid knelt and started knocking. He glanced at Odessa. "I

remember. 'Chest beneath the floor.' Something about wealth, right? Help me."

Doctor Morton immediately began his own search in the far corner. Odessa and Bryce, acknowledging the inevitable, joined in.

"Here," Bryce said, going over a section again with one knuckle. He reached for his knife in his back pocket, realized it had been confiscated, and looked up at Reid. The sheriff reached for his own knife, glanced at them all, and then pried up the first board.

They could see it immediately. Three more boards and it was half-uncovered. Five more, it was totally free. A trunk, as if brought over from the old country decades before. Reid brushed off a thick layer of dust, unlatched the lid, and slowly pulled it open.

Bryce laughed aloud.

Inside was only a Bible.

"Wealth that is eternal," Odessa muttered.

"What?" Reid asked, jerking his head toward her.

"Wealth that is eternal," Odessa said with a small smile. She knelt and gingerly picked it up, then opened the cover. "I think it's in Gaelic," she said.

"Appropriate for an O'Toole," Bryce said with a grin.

Reid pulled the trunk out and flung it to his left. He dropped down into the narrow crawl space and peered around, as if he expected to see a trapdoor or an opening. His face grew flushed, and when he did not find anything, he stepped out of the hole and glowered at Bryce and Odessa. "What else?" he seethed, taking a step toward Odessa.

Bryce stepped in front of her.

"What else?" Reid roared. "What else did O'Toole write about this?"

Odessa shook her head, finding it hard to breathe in the face of his wrath. "'Chest beneath the floor, wealth that burns, and that that is eternal.'"

He bumped into Bryce and Bryce shoved him backward.

"No!" Odessa cried. "That's it. I promise. There was nothing more."

Doctor Morton took the Bible from her hands and rifled through the pages. He threw Reid a helpless look. "She's right. It's all in Gaelic."

"Any messages on the inside? Notes?" Reid asked, pacing now, running a hand through his hair.

The doctor glanced through it again. "Nothing. I see nothing but the text."

Reid stopped suddenly, paused, and then stared at Odessa. "There is something more." His hand went to his revolver and he pulled it from the holster, just as the doctor set his own gun against Bryce's temple.

Odessa shook her head, backing up until she hit the wall. The doctor drove Bryce sideways, clearing the way for Reid. He didn't stop until the gun was centered between her brows, until she could feel the cold ring of it. *Dear God, are You waiting for me? Please don't let me feel alone as I die, Jesus. Hold me close. My life is Yours. My very breath is Yours, Savior.*

"Odessa!" Reid roared again. "Where is it? He told you something else, didn't he?"

She focused on the sheriff. He was shaking in his fury, his pupils unnaturally dilated. He abruptly holstered his gun, grabbed her wrists, and slammed both up against the wall until his face was right beside hers. He was so close she could feel the heat emanating off his body.

"Odessa." He waited for her to look him in the eyes.

"Get away from her!" Bryce screamed.

Reid's eyes shifted to her husband. "Maybe she told you where it is, Bryce. What will it take for you to tell me?" He touched Odessa's face and gave her a lopsided smile, but his eyes went back to Bryce, seeing how his action was affecting him. His finger traced down, past her jaw to her neck. "The greatest fear of a consumptive is suffocation, right?" He pinched her throat a little.

Bryce, no longer able to remain idle, immediately pushed past the doctor and a shot rang out. It was so close that both Bryce and Odessa felt the bullet go past them. Both froze.

"Tell me, Odessa," Reid said, tightening his grip on her throat. "Or do you no longer fear death? Maybe it'll take you watching me place your beloved's head under the stream until he ceases writhing. Is that what it will take?"

Lord? Please, God. Not Bryce. Please don't let them take Bryce.

"Tell me," Reid whispered, letting up on the pressure at her throat. "Tell me what I want to know, Odessa, or Bryce will die first. I'll make you watch."

She closed her eyes and panted in fear. *Not that, Jesus. Please don't let them take him first. So much death, Lord. Please don't make me endure this, too, Father. I can't endure it.*

You can endure all things with Me at your side. Lean on Me, child. I will give you strength.

Her breath quickened at this word. Was she imagining things? Or had God spoken to her?

Outside.

"Outside. It's outside." She closed her eyes, wondering at where the words were coming from. Moreover, she wondered where the sudden hope was coming from. She felt a burst of power, a thrill raise the hairs of every inch of her body. Hope. As surely as if she were surrounded by God Himself. It can't be....

Reid released her throat and backed a step away, as if repulsed. As if—"What are you doing?"

"Doing?" She moved forward and glanced over her shoulder. "I'm showing you the way." Boldly, she continued walking, dimly wondering if a bullet would pierce her back at any moment, but unable to stop her momentum. She paused at the door. "Coming?"

Reid frowned, but the doctor was already pushing Bryce ahead of him. Slowly, Reid followed.

The four of them stepped into the bright light of a summer afternoon, brilliant blue, cloudless skies above that Odessa hadn't noticed on the way here. A man moved on her left. The guard. She glanced to the right. There was the other.

I got them outside, Lord. Now what? She waited, but heard nothing. Had it all been in her head? A fervent dream made real? God didn't speak to people anymore, did He? Had she slipped into madness like Amille DeChant?

A gunshot sounded, and then another. Five more, in rapid succession. Odessa felt the impact of a man's body, felt herself going down as if she were no longer in her own skin. Was she hit? Dying? Is this what it would feel like to give in to the death that had hunted her for years? The monster that had taken her brothers, her mother, her father?

From far away, she heard more gunfire, looked for her husband ... discovered him beside her ... gazing down at her. He took her face in his hands. She could see him mouth words. *Odessa. Breathe.*

Breathe.

Breathe, Odessa, echoed her God. *Live. You are Mine.*

As if remembering that it was what she was supposed to do, she made herself pull air in through her nostrils, felt her lungs inflate, saw Bryce smile, saw hope enter his eyes. And then she did it again. And again.

Chapter ❀ 37

Odessa stayed in her husband's arms, down on the ground, but her eyes were on the doctor. The man who had healed her. Brought her life. And others death. Blood rapidly spread across his white shirt and his hand was inside his jacket lapel where he reached for his handkerchief; he was unarmed. "I'm a doctor," he said pitifully, looking into her eyes. "This was not what I had imagined … I only—"

He did not finish his next sentence. His eyes stilled and grew blank.

Odessa shivered and leaned against Bryce.

After a moment, he accepted a man's hand up and then lifted his wife to stand close to him. It was then that Odessa recognized who had come to their rescue.

"Peter. God bless you, man," Bryce was saying. "And Sheriff Olsbo. How …"

"You all right, Mrs. McAllan?" The older man stared at her with kind eyes from beneath bushy brows. "Up at the Shaefers' today, they said they'd seen some men about that they didn't know, for days now, up on the bordering hills. After the trouble at the DeChants', we thought we'd better look into it. We ran across Peter, hightailing it from the ranch, bent on seeking help. Appears he was right, since there was a kidnapping taking place—near murder to boot."

"Nels?" Bryce asked hopefully.

Peter shook his head and glanced away. "Gone," he said with a shaking voice. "Saw them take him out back and shoot him. Knew it wouldn't be long before they did the same to you." He managed to look at his boss again.

"Glad you kept them from doing so," Bryce said, reaching out to clap him on the shoulder. "We won't forget Nels. We'll honor his memory, what he did. I promise you, man."

"He'd like that," Peter said with a nod, his voice high and thin, as if fighting tears.

"It's Reid Bannock who will pay for his death," Bryce ground out. He spoke to Sheriff Olsbo, but Odessa knew Reid could hear.

"That's *Sheriff* Bannock," Reid called. He wore iron cuffs behind his back and stood beside one of his men. The other was dead. The deputy led both to a wagon just pulling up, down the road.

"I'll be out before morning," Reid said over his shoulder. "General Palmer will see to it."

"I don't think so," said Sheriff Olsbo. "General Palmer is a good man, a righteous man. I don't believe his Christian upbringing will allow him to look the other way. He'll want you to face justice."

"There's legal rationale for almost everything I've done here today," Reid said.

Sheriff Olsbo ducked his head to the side. "You'll get the benefit of assumed innocence, Mr. Bannock, same as anyone. But as a sheriff, I think you'll see the problems you face—breaking into the McAllans' house, kidnapping them, threatening them."

"Oh, that wasn't me. That was the doctor who arranged that."

"And he was all alone on that call, eh? Rest assured, we'll get the story straight from everyone before we're done."

"I'll want a lawyer from the Springs," Reid said, as they forced him into the back of the wagon.

"Yes, yes. We'll get you any lawyer you want. The truth will bear out," returned Olsbo.

Reid laughed under his breath and leaned back against the boards, as if making himself comfortable. He eyed Odessa and laughed softly again. "In time. Yes, sir. In time, it will." He laughed yet again, no sign of defeat in his eyes as the deputy whipped the horse and turned the wagon around on the road. Was it nothing but bravado? Or did Reid still hold some unseen upper hand? Bryce wrapped a protective arm around Odessa and together they looked up at the sheriff as he mounted his horse.

"You two come in tomorrow. I'll get a clerk to come by and take down your statements."

"We will," Bryce said.

"Think they were acting on their own? Or are there others we should question?" The sheriff's eyes slid from Bryce to Odessa and back again.

"As I see it, it's just these two," Bryce said. "The doctor had the access. The sheriff had the power. Odessa was attacked in the mountains above the Springs before we were married, and those who attacked me … I think they were hired men. Working for cash, not long term."

He looked to Odessa for confirmation and she agreed with a nod.

"Still. After you testify, you might want to take this pretty bride and head out on a honeymoon. Leave here for a spell while things simmer down. Give me a chance to ferret out any other no-accounts in the tunnels. Don't want you two in danger."

"I appreciate that, Sheriff. We'll talk about it more tomorrow in town?"

"Tomorrow in town." With that, he gave his deputy the signal. Odessa turned away before she would see Reid Bannock and the dead doctor, laid out in the back of the wagon, once more. She wanted them out of her mind as fast as possible.

The next morning in Colorado Springs was unusually warm. Most nights, the temperatures cooled to "good sleeping weather," as their father had put it, but last night had remained uncommonly hot. They met up in the kitchen. Nic silently poured coffee from the tin pot into Moira's tin mug. The china gift set from Reid had been sold with other unwanted items at the store. "You sleep as well as I did?" he mumbled.

"Probably," she said, running her fingers through a mass of tangled blonde hair. "Not that I would've slept well even if it had been cooler. Too much going through my mind."

"Mine too. You all packed up? Ready for the train station?" He took a seat at the small dining room table and she took one across from him.

"Ready. The boys will come by? Get the rest of our crates and put them in storage?"

"That's the agreement."

"Think we can trust them?"

Nic let a slow smile spread across his face. "Do we care?"

Moira matched his smile and reached across the table. She shook her head. "I've never felt this free in all my life, Nic. Never."

"Me neither." He raised a brow. "Think we'll find the happiness Odessa has?"

"I hope so. Can't get closer to it unless we try, right?"

"Right."

"I'll miss you."

He pulled his hand from hers. "You'll be just fine, Sissy. And we'll keep in touch through Odessa. We'll always make sure she knows where we are, all right? She's the settled one. She'll be our touch point."

"Always."

They gazed at each other for a second longer, then Nic, uncomfortable with the tension, shoved back his chair. "We'd better go and dress. Our train will be here in two hours and I won't miss it waiting on you."

"I'll be ready," Moira said, rising too.

They separated, dressed, and Nic gathered Moira's remaining trunk and carried it outside. He closed the door of the cottage and they stood there a moment, each lost in their own silent good-byes and thoughts of what had transpired here for them. Then they turned together, silently climbed into the carriage for hire—their own had been sold—and watched as the Springs disappeared past the rolling wheels, each wondering if they'd ever be back.

"This is good, right," Moira said, taking his hand again. "Right, Nic?"

"Right." But he was sure his stomach churned as much as hers. Was she ready to be on her own? Without him to watch over her? What would their father have said?

She giggled. "Why do I feel a bit like the prodigal, heading out with my fat purse?"

"Because we're making our own way, not Father's way," he said quietly. "Let's make him proud in the long run, all right?"

"All right."

They reached the train station, and Nic paid a man to carry their luggage to the train. In twenty minutes they were aboard and settled. "Leaving here feels better than arriving," Moira said.

"I'll never forget that day," he said, leaning over her to look out the window. "We almost lost her. It was worth it, coming here. Just to see Dess safe."

"Yes, it was."

They stared out the window together, ignoring the other passengers who crowded in across from them. Their minds were on Denver, where they would separate. Moira was heading west to San Francisco to try her luck on the stage there. Dominic would travel east to New York and beyond. He planned to sail on the first ship that caught his fancy. Bryce's paintings had whetted his appetite to experience the sea—not just the transatlantic crossing they had taken as a family to London—but deeper, farther exploration.

"She'd have our heads if she knew we were doing this," Moira said.

"No," Nic said, turning to look into his sister's blue-green eyes. "She would understand the need to breathe freely, make each lungful our own."

"She'll fret, once she knows."

"Yes. But it will be all right. Someday, someway, we'll all see one another again."

"Oh, I hope so. The world feels a bit big now that I'm heading out into it."

"I know," he said with a twinkle in his eye. "But doesn't that feel exactly right? All my life, I've wanted something more, something bigger, something I couldn't name. Now I get to go and find it."

"I hope you do, Brother. I hope we both do."

Odessa and Bryce sat on the back porch of their house, watching the sunset spread brilliant peach and pink streams of light into the pale blue heavens above the mountains. He wrapped an arm around her, resting it on the back of the chair. "Maybe we ought to head out on that honeymoon 'bout now. Get away. Catch our breath."

"No, Bryce. You're needed here on the ranch. Get the horses shipped come fall, let me get my house finished and settled, and we'll go to Mexico or California. Right now, I just want to stay here, with you. Settle into life as Mrs. McAllan."

He pulled her closer and kissed her head. "You're not afraid?"

"No," she said, really thinking it through. "I'm at peace. Morton and Reid were the ones with the power and incentive to try to get Sam's mine. They had the access. No one else. I think it ends there."

He considered her words and then nodded. "All right. But I don't plan on ever seeing you that close to death again. We've gone through too much, journeyed too far to take such chances."

"Our life is not our own," she said, leaning her head on his shoulder. "That's what God taught me through that whole ordeal. That every day is to be celebrated, but our lives ... it's not up to us, Bryce. I'm thankful for each hour here with you. But I will trust and praise God, regardless of what comes, regardless of how many hours we have left. We are His, first."

"Amen," he said, raising an eyebrow. He smiled.

She did too. "Amen."

They sat in companionable silence for a while, watching the sky change. "Did you notice it, even after all that commotion?"

She shook her head. "What?"

"Your breathing. And mine. No attacks, no relapse. Still right as rain."

Odessa put her hand to her chest and smiled. "Not a wheeze nor a whistle," she said in wonder. "I'm breathing better than I have in years. Even after all that excitement."

"There's more ahead."

"What do you mean?"

"Been looking at that Gaelic Bible of Louise O'Toole's."

She edged away from him to look him in the eye. "You know where the mine is?"

"Might. Something to explore, anyway. If we want to." He caught her questioning expression. "We're ranchers first, Odessa. Do we have the stamina to be miners, too? Do we want to? Or would we rather leave it? Take what we have rather than chase what we might?"

She thought over his words for a moment. "I kind of like that it's there if we want it. *Wealth that burns and that that is eternal.* I'd like to know what Sam meant by that phrase, at least. Is that a clue or a warning?"

"Maybe both," Bryce said.

But as they sat there together a while longer, watching the last vestiges of the setting sun behind the Sangre de Cristos, Odessa knew that for now, being here, beside her husband, unmoving, *abiding,* was exactly where she wanted to remain.

She inched closer to him, this man God had made her husband, lover, partner, protector.

And together, they breathed in and out and in again.

... a little more ...

When a delightful concert comes to an end,

the orchestra might offer an encore.

When a fine meal comes to an end,

it's always nice to savor a bit of dessert.

When a great story comes to an end,

we think you may want to linger.

And so, we offer ...

AfterWords—just a little something more after you

have finished a David C. Cook novel.

We invite you to stay awhile in the story.

Thanks for reading!

Turn the page for ...

- **Author's Note**
- **An Interview with Lisa T. Bergren**
- **Group Discussion Questions**

AUTHOR'S NOTE

Thanks for reading my book. For the sake of the story, I took some liberties with historical fact, either moving the dates or "revising" history (and in some cases, geography) just a bit. But I have attempted to incorporate as much as possible to remain true to Colorado Springs' history. Here are some facts to be aware of:

- The Opera House in Colorado Springs opened in 1881 (depicted as 1883), but did truly open with a performance of *Camille* by a traveling company on its way to California. It was seen as a poor choice for a community full of consumptives, but it was what the traveling actors had rehearsed to play, and so they had little choice.

- The Antlers Hotel opened in 1883 and remained a dominant structure in the area for decades; it was destroyed by fire in 1898 and rebuilt in 1901.

- Inspiration for the character of Helen Anderson was drawn from the famous writer Helen Hunt Jackson, who settled in the Springs after struggling with tuberculosis for years, and the photographer Anna May Wellington, who traveled all over Ute Pass around 1890, taking pictures with glass plates and a view camera.

- Tuberculosis wasn't named as such until after this era—which is why I referred to it as "consumption" or the "White

Death." Some historians have said that up to one-third
of Colorado Springs residents came here to seek the cure.
Doctors figured out around the turn of the century that
the disease was highly contagious, adding to the growth of
sanatoriums in an effort to isolate patients. But as early as
1870, a Mrs. Teachout had opened her property to TB suffer-
ers, allowing them to set up tents on her ranch and providing
meals. And there are reports of smaller sanatoriums built to
house those struggling with the disease. Resting outside—
regardless of the weather—eating three hearty meals a day,
plus drinking six raw eggs and eight glasses of milk, was a
popular treatment plan.

- Queen, General Palmer's bride, did indeed have a heart
  attack at age thirty and was advised to move from Colorado
  Springs' high altitude. She moved to Newport, Rhode Island,
  for a time, and then to New York before moving in 1882
  or 1883 to England. I do not know if she ever returned for
  a visit, as I depicted, but General Palmer did travel once or
  twice a year to see his family, even venturing across the seas
  when he had been paralyzed from the neck down and was in
  a wheelchair. His attention and devotion undoubtedly speak
  of a very great love and a tragedy of absence. Queen died in
  England in 1894 but her ashes were disinterred and brought
  to lay beside the general's in 1910.

- The Sisters of St. Francis of Perpetual Adoration arrived in
  Colorado Springs in the summer of 1887 from Lafayette,

Indiana. Their first mission was to care for patients. In the spring of 1888, they opened a new hospital known as St. Francis Hospital. The sisters were outstanding nurses and administrators who also tended to the spiritual needs of their patients. For the purposes of this novel, I "moved up" their arrival to 1883.

AN INTERVIEW WITH LISA T. BERGREN

Q: You've written contemporary romance, nineteenth-century fiction, general contemporary fiction, and a medieval suspense series. Why return to the nineteenth century?

A: There is something intriguing and reassuring about the 1880s to me. It's both a vibrant time in the world with the Industrial Revolution well under way, but also somewhat simple and innocent, too. Sometimes I wish I lived in the 1880s, but with a computer, vaccines, appliances, and indoor plumbing everywhere.

Q: You're a travel junkie. Why place this series in your Colorado backyard?

A: People love Colorado. I love Colorado. It's visually beautiful, of course, and it's been on my mind and heart to set a series here for some time. And when I learned of how so many people came to Colorado Springs to seek the cure for tuberculosis (in the early years, about a third of our residents), I knew it had to be here. But I have to say my eye is wandering back toward Europe for my next series. Can't keep me home for long! I'll stay put for *Sing* and *Claim* but then I'm outta here, baby! Luckily, *Sing* takes place in the Sangre de Cristos and the gold camps of Colorado; *Claim* will take place near Ouray—a fantastic, gorgeous place to visit. And Moira and Nic are on the move—around the world—so I can do some exploration, too.

Q: Your fascination with travel has even led to a new business, hasn't it?

A: A hobby, mostly. Tim and I launched a Web site with friends, www.FamilyTripster.com, to encourage families to travel together. We love hearing how other families manage it—and to share tidbits on how to make it easier for all to navigate a city, foreign or close to home.

Q: How much did you have to research for this series?

A: I read several books about the history of tuberculosis and many first-person accounts. It's a terrible way to die ... a slow suffocation. Then some general history books about the 1880s to refresh my memory. And I always love the local books that have pictures and accounts of our forefathers; it makes it come alive for me.

Q: What did you learn about yourself in writing *Breathe?*

A: I love to learn along with my characters. It's part of the ride as an author. For me, the "aha" was the same as Odessa's. I think that I'm slowly coming to believe, understand, and embrace the idea that God really does hold my life in His hand. And that's okay.

I trust Him … so if He gives me another sixty years or sixty seconds, I'm good.

Q: What are you working on next?

A: *Sing*, the next book in this series. And a couple of children's books.

Q: How can readers find out more about you and your work?

A: My Web sites: www.LisaTawnBergren.com; www.BusyMomsDevo.com; www.GodGaveUsYou.com; www.FamilyTripster.com are the best way. And If a reader signs up on www.LisaTawnBergren.com to receive my monthly e-newsletter, she'll receive a new devotional each month inside it. My heart goes into those, in between novels. You'll get a glimpse of the good, the bad, and the ugly in my life—and how Christ somehow redeems it all.

GROUP DISCUSSION QUESTIONS

1. Have you ever endured a life-threatening illness or been close to someone who has? What was that experience like? What did it teach you?

2. Are you afraid of death? Why or why not? What would be the hardest part about saying good-bye to loved ones? What would bring you comfort?

3. Do you think you could have survived in the 1880s? What would you miss the most: Internet, television, or a washer/dryer?

4. If you are a woman, how would you deal with the traditional role of women in that era? Would that be a comfort or chafe?

5. In this time, people left family behind to move West, and often never saw them again. If it meant never seeing your extended family again, would you have moved to have a chance at prosperity or health? Why or why not?

6. Odessa comes through a lot to regain her health. Had you been in her shoes, would you risk your life to get to the bottom of the mystery? Or would you have walked away?

7. Do you believe the length of your life is preordained? Why or why not?

8. Discuss how you trust God—or don't—day to day. Think of a concrete example or way you've trusted—or didn't—in the last week.

9. Why do you think this book is titled *Breathe?* Think beyond the physical aspect.

10. Which character are you most interested in hearing more about in books two and three in this series, and why?

Look for Book 2 in
THE HOMEWARD TRILOGY

SING

Four years have gone by and all three of the St. Clairs have furthered their dreams—Odessa is on the ranch with Bryce and has penned a best seller; Moira is in pursuit of her opera career in Paris; and Dominic is working his way along the fighting circuit in South America. But disaster is about to drastically alter the courses of all three. A bitter blizzard in Colorado, a thieving manager in Paris, and a ship captain out to collect a debt—all will have repercussions that will send the St. Clairs in search of what it means to sing God's praises, even in the storm.

Coming **summer 2010** from
LISA T. BERGREN

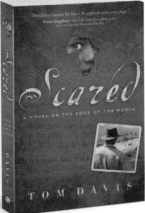

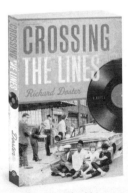